CARA GAYLE

Also by Geraldine O'Neill

Tara Flynn
Tara's Fortune
Tara's Destiny
The Grace Girls
The Flowers of Ballygrace

CARA GAYLE

Geraldine O'Neill

First published in Great Britain in 2008 by Orion Books,
an imprint of The Orion Publishing Group Ltd
Orion House, 5 Upper Saint Martin's Lane
London WC2H 9EA
An Hachette Livre UK Company

First published in Ireland in 2003 as
Aisling Gayle by Poolbeg Press Ltd

1 3 5 7 9 10 8 6 4 2

A CIP catalogue record for this book is
available from the British Library.

ISBN (Hardback) 978 0 7528 6012 1
ISBN (Trade Paperback) 978 0 7528 6102 9

Printed in Great Britain by
Clays Ltd, St Ives plc

The Orion Publishing Group's policy is to use papers
that are natural, renewable and recyclable products and
made from wood grown in sustainable forests. The logging
and manufacturing processes are expected to conform to the
environmental regulations of the country of origin.

www.orionbooks.co.uk

*This book is lovingly dedicated to
my old college boyfriend and my Anam Cara,
Mike Brosnahan*

Acknowledgements

I would like to give a big thanks to all the staff at Poolbeg, particularly Paula Campbell and Gaye Shortland, for their continued advice and support.

Thanks to my literary agent, Sugra Zaman, of Watson, Little Ltd., London, for pleasantly chasing up all my queries about the world of bookselling.

Thanks to Malcolm Ross McDonald for his personal appreciation of my work, and the Offaly Writers' Group for continued interest in my writing and poetry efforts.

Special thanks to our great Stockport friends Alison and Michael Murphy, for their constant encouragement in my literary career, and their willing help with organising events from birthday parties to trips to America.

Thanks to my lovely brother-in-law, Kevin Brosnahan, for his endless support and promotion of my work.

Thanks to Peter and Kitty Brady for their guidance with the Americanisms in *Cara Gayle*.

Thanks to my old Scottish teaching colleague and my dear friend Margaret Lafferty who encouraged me in the early days when publication seemed a long way off.

Thanks to all family members and Offaly and Stockport friends who were so supportive of *Tara Flynn*.

Thanks to my brother and fellow-writer, Eamonn O'Neill and his lovely, artistic wife, Sarah, without whose wedding in Upstate New York this book would never have been written.

A special thanks to my mother's old American penpal, Jean Harper, who in turn introduced Eamonn and Sarah as penpals – which led to the American wedding!

Thanks to Sarah's family and all the lovely Americans I met whilst staying at the place that became 'Lake Savannah'.

A little word of loving remembrance to Patricia, who would have raced through this book in a day. Also, Garda Evan Lillis who gave his parents, Marie and Michael, so much to be proud of during his young life.

A final thanks to my beloved Christopher and Clare, more supportive than I could ask for, and who are more precious to me with every passing year.

Come to the edge, he said.
They said: We are afraid.
Come to the edge, he said.
They came. He pushed them . . .
and they flew.

GUILLAUME APOLLINAIRE

Chapter 1

Tullamore, County Offaly

May 1963

The morning after her seventh wedding anniversary, Cara Gayle awoke to the early morning sun shining through the windows, and an empty space in the bed beside her.

She looked at the bedside clock. Quarter past seven. Quarter past seven on a Monday morning after a weekend away celebrating seven years of marriage. Neither of them needed to be up for another half an hour, and yet he was gone from their bed. He was downstairs and on the phone already.

Last week, they had sat with some of Oliver's drama group at a wedding, and a new member had made a funny comment about them approaching the 'seven-year itch'. Only no one had laughed. There had been a very awkward silence. The rest of the group knew – as Cara knew – that Oliver had always had the itch.

He had the itch even before they got married.

Cara threw the bedclothes back and padded across

the cold linoleum floor, her long blonde hair swinging like two curtains on either side of her face. She opened the door just a few inches. Just enough to hear who he was talking to. Just enough to be sure.

"Of course," she could hear Oliver say in a low voice. "You know I do. Why else would I be on the phone to you, at this hour of the morning?"

Cara leaned her head against the jamb of the door and closed her eyes. *Why else indeed?* she thought. *Why else indeed?*

Oliver gave a little cough to clear his throat. The sort of cough he gave when getting agitated. "It was a special occasion . . . what else could I do? It would have looked bad if I hadn't done something." Then there was a pause. "Listen," he said in his smooth Dublin accent, "I'll have to go. I promise I'll ring you later . . . same arrangements as usual."

Cara heard the click of the phone, and waited. But Oliver didn't come back upstairs. She listened and heard him first go into the bathroom, and then a few minutes later into the kitchen, and then she heard the rattle of the tap as he filled the kettle.

Cara closed the door and got back into bed. She shivered, even though she had woken several times during the night with the heat. The old familiar feelings of dread and hopelessness began to wash over her again. Though it was not half as bad as it used to be in the early stages of their marriage. She was twenty-nine years old now – no longer the naïve young girl who had fallen under Oliver's spell.

But still it hurt. It hurt very badly. Especially this morning. Especially after a romantic weekend in a nice hotel in Galway, which she had thought of as a fresh start in their marriage.

And now this. An early-morning phone call which heralded his latest infidelity. The latest in a long line of affairs. Cara reached over to her bedside table for her romantic novel – her escape from reality. Her sad escape from a faithless, loveless marriage.

* * *

"Good morning, good morning – I heard your alarm go off just as the toast was ready." Oliver was chirpy and cheerful as he elbowed the bedroom door open, to manoeuvre the breakfast-tray into the room. "Since you've become so accustomed to first-class hotel service this weekend, I thought I'd break you into the real world gently." He gave a little laugh. "But I'm sorry to say we only serve tea and toast in this establishment."

He placed the wooden tray with the varnished flowers on the bed beside her and, from the fleeting glance that she gave him, he knew that she was not fooled. Their eyes did not meet very often these days, because he couldn't bear the accusation that looked straight back at him. At one time those blue eyes had so captivated him that he had gone out and bought her the biggest sapphire engagement ring he could afford. Now, he could barely look into those same eyes.

"Are you not having anything?" Cara asked, for something to fill the silence.

"No, I've had a cup of tea. That'll hold me until I get time at the shop." He turned to the wardrobe to select a shirt. Although he left everything else in the house where he dropped it, Oliver's wardrobe was perfectly organised.

"I have a commercial traveller coming down from Dublin with a new range of fancy ties and hankies. I'm quite keen, but I'll have to knock his prices down a good bit. I'll have to make the poor mouth about business being slow and all that old shite. It's worse than being on the stage."

Cara took a sip of her tea. "Oh, I'm sure you'll perform well as always, Oliver," she said in an even tone. "Sure, aren't people always telling you that you're a born actor?"

"Thank you, m'dear," he said jovially, slipping the shirt from its hanger and throwing it on the bed. "I'll take that as a compliment."

Cara's eyes were cold and hard as she watched him take off his dressing-gown, revealing the firm, well-toned body that he was so proud of. As usual, he couldn't resist a glance at his reflection in the wardrobe mirror. An imaginary blemish on his shoulder, which he had to examine carefully, allowed him to draw out the process.

As she sipped her tea and bit into toast she didn't taste, Cara took in his curly black hair – still damp from his bath – and the rest of him down to the curly black hairs on his legs. Apart from being slightly below average height, he was – as the older women would put it – a fine figure of a man.

And didn't Oliver Gayle know it.

After the short pause to admire himself, Oliver checked his watch and then hurriedly threw on his clothes. Another quick look in the mirror as he did up his latest new tie, a dab of cologne – and he was ready.

"I'm not too sure what time I'll get in tonight," he said, rubbing the excess cologne into his hands, "so don't bother cooking me anything. I'll get something in town, and it'll keep me going 'til after rehearsals."

There was a pause.

"So you're rehearsing again tonight?"

Oliver made towards the bedroom door. "I don't know why you're surprised – didn't I tell you last week?" He blew a kiss in her direction from the bedroom door. "I've got my key, so don't feel you have to wait up."

And with that, he was gone.

* * *

Cara pushed the tray with the unfinished tea and toast over to Oliver's side of the bed. She swung her legs out of the other side, and then moved to the window. She drew back the curtains and leaned her forehead against the cool glass. She looked out into the large, flower-filled garden, the tending of which – like her romantic novels – gave her an escape from thoughts of her crumbling marriage.

What a waste, she told herself. *What a waste!* All those moments – of diverting her thoughts from the lie she was living – had grown into hours. And the hours into days. And the days into months. And it all added up to years of her life – wasted. Wasted on a shallow, hopeless charade of a marriage in which she was trapped.

For there was no future for her in her marriage with Oliver. And there was no future for her – out of her marriage – in Ireland.

To think of it hurt. It hurt badly, for she had loved Oliver once. She had loved him very deeply. That's why she had almost slept with him before they got married, why she had almost allowed herself to get carried away, risking the wrath of both her family and the Church. When she realised what she had done, she used all her powers to coax him into marriage. And a hard job that was.

In all fairness to him, Oliver had warned her. He had told her that he didn't know if he could live his life with one woman. And he told her that few women could live with his restlessness. But Cara didn't hear his warnings, because she was convinced that she could change him.

She wanted him, and she got him. But on Oliver's terms.

At the time it had all seemed worth it. Cara was positive that when they were married, and had started their family, he would settle down. But she was wrong on both counts. So far, there were no signs of a family, and there was no sign of Oliver settling down at all. She knew now that she would never have the life with him that she had dreamed of. But what else was there to do?

Of course she could leave him. Leave him and their sham of a marriage. How many times had she gone over the scene in her head, telling Oliver that she was leaving him, and then – the impossible part – telling her parents? How could she? *How could she?* It would kill her mother. Maggie Kearney couldn't take any more local gossip about the family.

There had always been the jokes and sneering remarks about Charles – Cara's older brother. Just because he didn't operate the same way as the other local fellows, and wasn't remotely on their wavelength – or at times, anyone else's – even in the family. But mainly because he preferred to keep company with the characters in his books than sit and have a pint with another man. And because he was thirty-one years old, and as yet had never been seen in the company of a woman.

And then there was the real cause for gossip. Cara's younger sister, Pauline, had been brought back home from

England three years ago. Unmarried and with a baby daughter. Maggie had never been the same since.

The whole family had never been the same since.

They had picked themselves up and dusted themselves down, but the fact was they were now marked in the eyes of the townspeople. They had joined the ranks of the fallen. Maggie's well-to-do farming background, and Declan's grocery shop on the outskirts of Tullamore town no longer gave them immunity from the gossips. Even the fact that Maggie had a brother who was a priest and Declan had two sisters who were nuns, cut them no sway with the Catholic moral majority. Nothing the Kearneys now did would lift them back into that comfortable, privileged little niche they had enjoyed.

Not even the fact that Mr and Mrs Kearney were planning a trip to America in the summer would impress their customers. They would forever be haunted by veiled – and not-so veiled – references to Pauline's situation on a regular basis.

Three years of getting their own back with little digs was nothing to customers who felt they had been overcharged by the Kearneys for the last twenty years – customers who didn't care or understand about overheads in running a business.

"And how is poor Pauline and the babby getting on?" Maggie would hear each and every day from women clutching loaves of bread and bags of cooking-apples. Their kindly smiles would never hide the dark reminder behind the words. *Poor Pauline and the babby.*

Maggie heard that question so often that she often woke up in the night saying it to herself.

And it wasn't just Maggie and Declan and Pauline who

suffered from the fallout of Pauline's indiscretion. Even if Cara was a teacher and living in a fine big farmhouse with modern furniture and a bathroom and running water, she still had a loose sister with an illegitimate child.

And though Cara could rise above it, being younger and more open to the modern ways of the world, and Declan – being a man – could shake his head and say, 'What's done is done, there's no good in looking back, you have to look forward,' Maggie was bowed over by the shame of it all. There was no consolation in any words about 'what's done is done' for her.

What Pauline allowed to be done to her should never have been done at all.

Cara knew this only too well. And knew what it all meant for her. One daughter who had brought shame on the family was enough. To have another daughter home with a failed marriage would be just too, too much.

So Cara plodded on. Her vague, 'if the worst comes to the worst' plan of one day just disappearing to England to live with Pauline had been well and truly smashed when her sister and baby returned home. Cara had no means of escape – and daily was becoming as good an actor as Oliver was in his local, amateur dramas.

A tide of sorrow rose up in her now, and she closed her eyes tightly to hold back the tears. There was no time for crying or feeling sorry for herself. She had to get dressed and get ready for school.

Eventually, when the tears had dried, Cara opened her eyes to stare out over the garden. Out over the trees, and out to the fields which surrounded their house. Then, her gaze shifted down into the garden again. A movement on the path caught her attention. She looked closer now, and recognised a small bird. It was a goldcrest – a tiny, yellowy-green thing. It was hopping aimlessly. First in one direction, and then another.

Without realising it, Cara smiled. It was a young bird, obviously learning to fly. She watched intently as it hopped a few inches into the air, wings flapping, only to descend again back to the ground.

For several minutes she watched, until she was rewarded with the sight of the bird taking itself several feet up into the air. It then disappeared into the depths of a small fir tree. Cara smiled and clasped her hands together in pleasure.

A few moments later she turned from the window, a thoughtful look on her face. She picked up her dressing-gown and made for the bathroom. A few minutes later she sighed out loud with annoyance when she realised that Oliver had used up most of the hot water. Thankfully, she had bathed and washed her hair yesterday morning in the hotel. Her long, thick hair took ages to dry, and she had to get up a good half-an-hour early on schooldays when she washed it. She filled the bath a third of the way up with the barely lukewarm water and got in. At least it was a warm, early summer morning. There had been many winter mornings when she'd shivered in the freezing cold, after Oliver had gone off early, leaving a grate full of ashes and a tank of cold water. It would rarely cross his mind to stack the fire up before he left. Cara did all that before setting off for school. There was no room in the house for two sets of vanity. Oliver's vanity took all that space up for him alone.

Later, as she towelled herself dry, a small seed of an idea started to grow in Cara's mind. A seed sown by her mother a few weeks ago – buried and forgotten but now brought to life again after Oliver's behaviour this morning, and further nurtured after watching the little bird's determined attempts to fly.

Cara Gayle was going to fly. She was going to rise up and leave her home. She was going to fly – far, far away. Even if it was just for a short time. She was going to leave Oliver – and everyone who pitied her for being his wife – a long, long way behind. She was going to join her parents on a trip to attend a wedding in a sunny, beautiful place. A place with a beautiful name: Lake Savannah.

She made up her mind as she rubbed the towel vigorously over her firm, attractive body.

She was going to fly away to America.

She was going to fly to Lake Savannah.

Chapter 2

"Surely you can do better than that?" Oliver said, an encouraging smile on his lips. "Surely you can do a better deal than that? An' me an oul' Dub like yerself." He put his wavy black head to the side, and a finger to his lips. He was putting on a good show, knowing that Fergal, the young salesman at the back of the shop, was listening to every word, and possibly the two women who were through the side door in the ladieswear department. "Now . . . what if I was to take three dozen of the ties and the hankies, would you do me a good deal on the scarves and the braces?"

"I would!" the salesman said, slapping a hand on the counter. "Begod, I would." He went back to his case, which lay open on the counter behind him. "Now, these new long-johns. I'd say they'd go down well with the farmers round here. They're a new make – just over from the States . . ."

Oliver shook his head, and tried to conceal his amusement. He had already knocked the fellow down half-price with the fancy ties and hankies, and anything further would be a bonus. "Oh, you're some man," he said, clapping him on the back. "You speak the same language as meself." While the commercial traveller checked some sheets on a clipboard, Oliver turned and winked over at the young sales assistant, delighted with his victory.

That was the great thing about Oliver Gayle. He could bend either way. Sideways, up or down. It didn't matter to him. He could speak the language of the farmers or the gentry, the young and the old. As long as he got what he wanted, and was paid a fair price. And people loved him for it. That was why Gayle's Drapery was the prosperous business that it was. Whether he was buying stock from salesmen or selling underwear to customers, Oliver Gayle enjoyed every minute of it. Oliver just enjoyed people generally. The more the merrier. And particularly the females.

It's just a pity that Tullamore town wasn't Dublin city. A town like Tullamore could never provide enough life or excitement for the likes of Oliver Gayle.

So Oliver had to provide the excitement for himself.

And he did. Almost every day at work. On his good days – which were often – he brought energy and enthusiasm in abundance to all who worked in his shop. He was good-natured and fair, jokey and flirtatious with staff and customers alike.

On his bad days, his dark mood was like a hurricane blowing through the shop. Wreaking havoc with everybody's nerves, and making them pray that he would disappear off for a lunch-break which would extend well into the afternoon. Which he often did.

"Now, Fergal," he said to the thin, younger man who was training as an under-manager in the shop, "did you pay close attention to that little bit of business? Did you see how I managed the fellow?" He smiled, and raised his eyebrows expectantly.

"Oh, I did, Mr Gayle," Fergal said, nodding his gingery-coloured head. His eyes were wide with admiration. "I was watching you and learning – just like you said."

"Good man," Oliver said, giving him a jovial punch on the shoulder. "Now, that's exactly what you should be doing." He motioned Fergal over into the corner of the shop, out of earshot of the women. "Now, Fergal," he said in a more serious manner, "I'm off out on a bit of business, which means you're in charge. I could be gone well into the afternoon . . . I'm not sure when I'll get back. Are you up to it?"

"Oh, I am, Mr Gayle," Fergal assured him quickly. "I'm up to it all right. I'll make sure that everything's just grand. There'll be no long dinner-breaks or anythin' like that. It'll be just the way it is when you're here."

"And if anybody phones or calls to the shop looking for me?"

"You're out on business, and can I take a message for you," said Fergal, proving he was no slouch at picking up his boss's commands.

"And young Dymphna?" Oliver raised his eyebrows, waiting to hear proof that Fergal had been paying good attention when he had last brought up the subject of time-keeping with the staff.

"Don't be worryin' about Dymphna," Fergal said, straightening his tie in an important manner. "I'll see she's back in good time – and on her own. I won't be slow in remindin' her to leave her friends outside the door."

"Good man!" Oliver said, going over to lift his car keys from the sales desk. "You'll make a great manager some day."

"Thanks, Mr Gayle," Fergal beamed, as his boss made his departure through the front door.

Chapter 3

"Isn't Oliver a great man that he doesn't mind Cara having a month away in America, without him?" Sister Concepta said, beaming around the group of teachers congregated in one of the classrooms for their tea and sandwiches.

Cara's face started to burn with embarrassment. She lowered her head so that her blonde hair draped in front of her face, and concentrated on taking the brown-paper wrapping off her sandwiches.

Then, thankfully, one of the other teachers chipped in. "Sure, Oliver Gayle has no worries. Cara will be well chaperoned. Isn't she being accompanied by her parents? You can't get safer than that."

Everyone laughed, and Cara was relieved and grateful when the conversation drifted away from Oliver to the travel details of her trip.

It made her angry and resentful, the way that her marriage had tainted other parts of her life. Her social life was often filled with awkward moments, with people

14

suddenly announcing that they had seen him here and there. Places she never knew he had been. It was worse when she was out with Pauline, or one of her close friends who knew all about his other women, for the evening would be completely spoiled. Harmless evenings at concerts in church halls and more exciting evenings at dances – all spoiled – just waiting on someone dropping a little nugget of information that they knew about her husband. Information she would never know about her husband if it weren't for strangers and friends telling her.

This was what she had become used to. This was married life with Oliver Gayle.

Cara had been through all the ups and downs of marriage to Oliver with her sister Pauline and her closest friend Carmel. She knew that at times they thought she was an awful fool for putting up with him, but after all their advice on the ultimatums she should give Oliver and the threats she should make, they always arrived back at where they started. Of course she should leave Oliver – but that was only in theory. Where would she go? And what about her family and the Church? And maybe the rumours were only rumours, and that it was just a kind of flirtation he had with women rather then anything *that* serious. And then it was back to the beginning again.

Because women like Cara Gayle never left their husbands.

Women like Cara Gayle didn't do lots of things. Admittedly, things were not as bad as a few years ago, when married women weren't even allowed to work in certain jobs. Cara watched her sister struggle in a country that was a long way off approving of single mothers. She watched the curvaceous, pretty Pauline having to explain to boyfriends and prospective boyfriends about little Bernadette. None of them lingered around long, for if they didn't mind the situation themselves, then their mothers certainly did. None of the older women were prepared to become mothers-in-law to a fallen girl. And her pretty face cut no sway with them either.

Cara's best friend Carmel was a teacher in the local secondary school. She was thirty next year and still single. She was a slim, vivacious, dark-haired girl who had missed her chance ten years ago. A local hotel-owner had set his cap at her, and Carmel had not been ready. After 'doing a line' with the steady, but predictable Seamus Donnelly for three years, she took fright at the thoughts of never having another boyfriend. Of never knowing any other man hold her, or kiss her – or do more exciting things to her.

She took to her heels to her uncle's in London, and stayed there for two breathtaking, exciting years. During which time she met several men – very attractive and very interesting – but none of whom were suitable, marriageable material. Well, not marriageable material for Carmel. In fact, she discovered almost too late, that one of them was already married. When she came back, Seamus Donnelly was engaged, and they were hanging up the bunting outside the hotel for his wedding to a more sensible, local girl.

A girl who knew a good thing when she saw it.

"The thing is," Carmel often told Cara, "I thought I would get better. I thought there was someone out there more suitable for me. Somebody exciting and really interesting . . . but I was wrong. Now all the half-decent local fellows are married." There was usually an ominous pause. "Be careful yourself, Cara . . . you could be left on your own, like me. The odds are stacked higher when you reach your thirties . . . and it's not as if you could get married again."

Weighing it up, Cara wondered at times if she was any better off than Pauline or Carmel.

She knew there were plenty of women who would envy her. They would say that at least she had him most of the time, and there was always the hope that he would settle down. That there weren't too many handsome, financially sound men around Tullamore town.

When they'd first got married, Oliver had started married life off in a promising fashion. He was new in town, and for the first year or two he had put all his energies into setting up the shop and organising the work that needed doing in the old farmhouse Cara had inherited from an old bachelor uncle.

Oliver had loved being the foreman on the job, advising the builders where he wanted walls knocking down, and walls putting up. Then he had taken a great interest in the furniture they chose – the most modern available from Dublin. From a fellow who knew a friend of Oliver's, and who could get him the latest styles at discount prices.

All the to-ings and fro-ings up to Dublin had kept him busy for months. All the visits to his family and friends while he was up there, and the overnight stays because it wasn't worth the trip back late at night. But eventually, the reasons for the trips had run out, and so had Oliver's interest.

The house was completed, and the builders gone, taking with them all the energy and buzz that Oliver needed constantly around him – the buzz that Oliver had since found in his amateur dramatic groups.

As Cara ate her cheese and tomato sandwiches, she looked around the group of six teachers – two nuns, two female teachers, the headmaster and another male teacher – and wondered if they knew about Oliver's philanderings. In all probability they would have heard rumours. Especially now that he had such a close relationship with the nuns on the staff. He was now producer of the drama group and they donated the bulk of their funds to local charities. The nuns were grateful for any help for their order's orphanages and the likes. They were so grateful that they worked hard at encouraging people in the town to support the group's plays.

Cara was sure that everyone – apart from her parents – knew of Oliver's weakness for the female members of his cast. The one he had been speaking to on the phone this morning was probably his latest leading lady.

"So when do you set off for New York, Cara?" Martin the youngest teacher asked. He was a shy young fellow, and Cara was sure that the headmaster had told him to make more of an effort chatting to his colleagues. Normally, she was happy to chat to him about difficult pupils and books and the like, but now she could have killed him for bringing attention to her business again.

She swallowed the last of her lukewarm tea. "Saturday morning . . . the day after we finish school." She managed a smile. "And it can't come quick enough!"

"You're going out for a wedding, aren't you?"

Cara nodded. "A cousin." She stood up now and walked over to the wastepaper bin. She threw the

18

greaseproof paper in the bin, and then held the brown paper over it and shook off the crumbs. Then, she came back to her chair, and started to fold the paper into small squares to use again the following day.

"Parts of Upstate New York are very green," Sister Concepta chipped in now. "Sister Monica has travelled all over the area, and I was looking at some of her letters the other evening, describing the places she'd been." The nun finished the last of her tea now, too. "I thought everywhere was like New York City, all tall buildings and shops. Still – you live and learn."

"My mother has photos of the place we'll be staying in," Cara said, much more comfortable with the general turn that the conversation had now taken. "It looks like a beautiful place, with trees of every colour and unusual wooden houses. It's by a lake too, so I hope to get some swimming practice in while I'm there." She rolled her eyes to the ceiling. "I could do with getting some exercise and toning up a bit."

Sister Concepta laughed. "Would you just listen to that! And not a pick on her! You're the last person who needs to worry about her figure, Cara." She grabbed a handful of the material in her black, voluminous habit. "Thank God for these garments we nuns have to wear – they hide a multitude of sins. 'Tis their only saving grace. I wouldn't want to be displaying what is hidden underneath in a bathing-suit!" She leaned towards the other, older nun. "What do you say, Sister Mary?"

"Indeed," said Sister Mary rather stiffly, not finding the conversation about matters of the flesh quite so entertaining as her colleague. "But Cara will have a wonderful time. It will be a lovely change altogether for you. Sitting by a lake, sunbathing and reading."

"It's sitting by a lake that we'd all like to be," said Mr Duffy, lifting the heavy copper bell from the window-ledge, "but it's back to class I'm afraid, until the summer is upon us."

Cara gathered her bag and copybooks and stood up, grateful for the routine of her schooldays that would get her through the next few weeks. Grateful for the nice people she worked with, and the innocent children she taught, who allowed her to escape from the reality of life with Oliver at home.

Chapter 4

Saturday morning came bright and cheerful, reflecting Oliver's humour as he drove Cara and her parents up to Dublin airport. He had been up at the crack of dawn, making Cara tea and toast and generally making sure that everything went like clockwork. There had been no early-morning phone calls recently, but Cara was in no way comforted by this. She knew that he would make good use of the time she was away.

In fairness to Oliver, he had been more than helpful with regards to the trip. He had insisted on her going shopping for several new outfits, and had even accompanied her to make sure that she bought all that she needed.

Then two days before her holiday, he turned up after work with a brand new suitcase for the journey. "A commercial traveller owed me a favour," Oliver said, lifting the leather case out of the boot of his car. "You won't see many like them around." He brought it in and set it down on the kitchen table. "Reinforced corners," he pointed out, "so it won't get banged around in the luggage departments, and pockets inside for all your bits and pieces." He laid the case wide open now, awaiting Cara's admiration and gratitude.

"It's beautiful," she said, giving him the warmest smile she could muster up. "It'll hold everything I need, with room to spare. It was very good of you."

Oliver waved away her thanks. "I thought you'd need room for any extras you buy in America," he said. "I believe they have shops over there that we could only dream of. And dreaming about America is the closest most people will get to it. You're very lucky getting the chance to go there." He gathered her into his arms now, rocking very slightly from side to side. Holding her the way that used to make her feel secure and loved and happy. "I'm proud of the fact you're going to America, Cara, and I hope with all my heart that you have a wonderful, wonderful time."

Cara had leaned her head against Oliver's chest, wishing with all her heart that he could change into the husband she had hoped she'd married.

* * *

"Give me a ring and let me know you've arrived safely!" Oliver called, as the three travellers passed through the departure gates, Maggie and Declan waving profusely. Cara nodded, and gave him a last wave and a smile. The thought struck her that she now humoured her husband – almost as she would one of the younger pupils in her school when they were upset. She smiled when he needed her to smile, and kept quiet when anything she might say would rock the boat.

Then, as the door on Oliver closed – Cara moved on. Looking out for her parents, and checking they had the right documents, and went to the right place at the right time – concentrating on all the details of the journey which would take her a long way from Ireland – and a long way from life with Oliver Gayle.

Like Cara, her father was looking forward to their first flight, whilst Maggie was definitely more apprehensive. Cara was doing her best to keep her mother soothed and occupied so that she didn't get too anxious.

"Oh, Cara, isn't that lovely?" Maggie held up yet another shamrock-embossed souvenir in the duty-free shop. "D'you think Jean and Bruce might like it for the house?"

Cara eyed the green-painted wooden shillelagh, complete with a picture of a leprechaun on the handle. She shook her head. "I'm not sure, Mammy," she said, trying not to smile. "You've brought loads of things with you already." Then, as Maggie turned back to scan the shelves again, she said, "What about a bottle of Irish whiskey . . . or something like that?"

"Drink?" Maggie said, her brow furrowing. She turned to her husband. "What do you think, Declan? Do you see anything in the way of a suitable gift?"

"I would agree with Cara," he said, lifting up a bottle of malt whiskey. "Bruce never turned down a drink when he was over in Ireland."

"Oh, well . . . drink it is," she conceded, as graciously as possible. Drink was not something she held with as a rule. But – in the interests of a good start to the holiday – she supposed the rules could be dispensed with on this occasion. A trip to America was not an everyday occurrence.

The flight was as pleasant as a long flight from Dublin to New York could be – and given Maggie's apprehension about flying, she coped fairly well. Their cabin was packed and there wasn't a lot of legroom. Maggie and Cara weren't too bad, since their lack of inches was an advantage in this case. Cara sat at the window with her mother in the middle. Declan, with his easy-going manner and longer legs, took the aisle seat where he could stretch out fully when it was quiet.

All in all, Cara was pleased to see her parents throwing themselves into the holiday spirit, oohing and ahhing over the meals, and wondering how they managed to prepare and store the food in such a small space. Declan sat back, alternately enjoying the complimentary drinks and dozing off, and Maggie even had a few tentative sips of a glass of wine with her meal, which the air-hostess told her would help her to relax.

Over the next few hours, while her parents' attention was taken up with chatting to an elderly Dublin couple who were sitting across the aisle, Cara sipped on wine and lost herself in her latest romantic novel.

The pleasant cool breeze they had enjoyed when they left Dublin airport that morning did not prepare the three Irish travellers for the wall of heat that hit them when they arrived in Idlewild airport.

Apart from the unexpectedly high temperatures – even high by New York standards – this was the bit of the journey they all felt rather apprehensive about. Their luggage had to be collected , and then they had to find another part of the terminal to take an internal flight up to Syracuse airport.

"Oh, God!" Maggie gasped when she saw the little

twelve-seater plane. "We'll never make it alive in that thing. It's no bigger than the Jimmy Martin's shooting-brake!" Then she immediately dropped the case she was carrying, to rummage in her handbag for her rosary beads.

Cara and her father made a good job of reassuring her that the small plane was perfectly safe, although later on they both admitted the trepidation they felt themselves as the noisy little aircraft took off.

"My fingers are paining me from clutching the beads!" Maggie complained as they made their descent into Syracuse airport, "but thank God the prayers worked, and we're all in one piece."

It was a grateful threesome indeed – in more ways than one – who threw their arms around Bruce and Jean after the plane touched down.

Chapter 5

Lake Savannah

Cara had never seen such luxury. She had no idea that her Aunt Jean was so wealthy. If the truth be told, all three had expected a nice, modern American house – but nothing of the grandeur they now found themselves in the midst of. The photographs Jean had sent over the years had not done justice to the house and beautifully cared-for grounds.

"I didn't realise that Bruce had such a big job," Maggie whispered in a shocked tone to Cara, as they followed her young-looking sister and tall, dark husband into the high, wooden house – the likes of which they had only ever seen in magazines or the films. "I could never have imagined my own sister – who I slept in the same bed with – owning a place like this."

"Make yourselves completely at home," Jean told them in an accent that was a mix of Irish and American. "I'll give you a quick guided tour, then you'll know where everything is." Then, she quickly bustled them from one beautifully furnished room to another, and then guided

26

them upstairs to view the bedrooms and second bathroom.

Maggie followed behind the nimble, neat-figured Jean and Cara, and in front of Declan. She could feel her face burning and her head whirling, and couldn't decide whether it was the unaccustomed heat or the exertion of rushing up two flights of stairs. On the other hand, she reflected, as she gratefully reached the top landing, it could have been the effects of the cocktail she had downed on arrival. Maggie wasn't at all used to drinking, and if she hadn't felt so flustered and overwhelmed by the house, she would have refused it. Instead, she had nervously downed the fancy sweet cocktail as though she were drinking lemonade – in two quick gulps.

When they arrived back downstairs, Jean called in to Bruce: "Honey? Is the kettle boiled yet?"

"It sure is," the fit-looking, tanned Bruce confirmed, with a clap of his hands. "Now, Maggie – how many spoonfuls of that special Irish tea do I put in the teapot?"

Maggie beamed at the mention of tea, and then suddenly rushed towards the kitchen. "I'll gladly make it, Bruce," she offered, "and if I know Jean, she'll be desperate waiting to have a cup herself. You can't beat a decent cup of Irish tea. Oh, the stuff they tried to pass for tea on that plane! How they get away with it is beyond me."

Cara looked over and caught Jean's eye. Then they both started laughing.

"I hate to tell her," Jean whispered guiltily, "but I much prefer coffee these days."

"I wouldn't worry about that," Declan laughed. "Maggie can drink enough tea for two easily."

A few minutes later, Maggie and Bruce appeared with cups of tea and plates of dainty sandwiches and cakes.

"After we've eaten," Bruce said, "we'll take you on a tour of the garden, and down towards the lake." He gestured to the big, picture window behind them, from where they could see countless tall pine trees towering over trees of every size and colour.

"If the garden is as big as the house," Maggie said, "you might never see me again if I go out on my own!" She shook her head and took another glorious sip of her tea.

"Oh, after you get your first day over, you'll find your way around just like you do back home," Jean told her, putting her arm around her sister and giving her stiff little body a hug.

"Don't be surprised if you wake up in the morning, and find me sleeping in the bath!" Maggie said with a roar of laughter, the effects of the cocktail still on her.

"After the long journey you've made to come visit me, honey," Jean quipped, "you can sleep between Bruce and me for all I care!"

"And would that be in or out of the bath?" Declan added for good measure.

Cara looked from her mother to her father, and wondered what had come over them. If this was the effect that being in America had on her normally staid parents, Cara wished they could have a holiday over here *every year*.

* * *

"Are you sure you won't change your mind and come with us?" Jean called, as the car prepared to pull off.

Cara shook her blonde, pony-tailed head and held up her novel. "I'm going to enjoy the peace and the beautiful scenery." Then she smiled. "I might even do a bit of swimming if I feel energetic enough!"

28

"Okay," Jean agreed, "but tomorrow I won't take no for an answer – we're going to a good shopping district, and I just know you're gonna love it."

"I'll definitely join you tomorrow," Cara promised. "So off you go, and enjoy your visit. I'll see you all later in the day."

"Don't get those legs burned like you did during that hot week at home last year," Maggie called now. "You'd be far better in a skirt or a light dress in this heat."

"I'll stay in the shade," Cara told her, knowing full well that Maggie was making a last attempt at getting her to cover up. Women showing off their legs didn't go down at all well in Maggie's little world – even if they were on holiday in America. Shorts were almost worse than women wearing trousers, which her mother couldn't come round to at all. And never would. And Cara knew that the fact her Aunt Jean almost lived in them must be a thorn in her mother's side.

"And don't forget to watch out for the bears!" Maggie suddenly remembered, sticking her sun-hatted head out of the back window of the car. Several of Jean's neighbours had related stories about bears in the locality. "Don't fall asleep down near the water or anything – keep your wits about you all the time."

"Don't worry, Cara," Bruce called from the front. "We haven't seen a bear in these parts for over five years."

"Help yourself to the fridge, honey," her aunt said, waving. "There's plenty of everything in it."

Cara heaved a sigh of relief when at long last the car moved off, taking Jean and Bruce and her parents to visit some elderly couple whose ancestors came from Mullingar. Since they had arrived in Upstate New York, they had spent the first few days in a whirlwind of visits and introductions, until Cara felt that she couldn't take in another face or another name. And while everyone had been so nice and friendly, if the truth be told they were all a bit on the elderly side for Cara. Definitely more suited to her mother and father's age group than hers.

Invitations had come from practically everyone they met for barbecues, lunches and brunches. If they had accepted every invitation, they would have had to stay for six months instead of one.

Cara turned back towards the house to pick up her sunglasses. Although it was only eleven o'clock in the morning, the thermometer on the garage wall was climbing well up towards the eighties. It was going to be another hot, sunny day, and Cara had all those hours stretching ahead in this beautiful place.

For the first time since arriving she could do whatever she wanted – when she wanted – without having to consider anyone else. She could eat when she wanted, read when she wanted, and swim when she wanted. And who knows – maybe even sleep if she wanted.

She went to the fridge to get a cool drink and some of the fresh fruit salad that Jean made by the bucketful.

She put her sunglasses on the top of her head and tucked a bottle of sun-lotion into the top pocket of her blue-checked blouse. Then, with her novel under her arm and the tray in her hand – Cara made her way down to Lake Savannah.

Every now and again, she came across the windchimes that Bruce had dangling from various trees, and she couldn't resist stretching up an arm to shake them. Like a child with Christmas-tree decorations, she found herself laughing as the metal and wood creations tinkled at the slightest touch.

The day after they had arrived at the Harpers' house, Bruce had spent time telling Cara where he had bought each windchime, and explaining the symbols and pictures that adorned them. There was a particularly striking one that hung from a weeping willow. It was positioned in the middle of the little ornamental bridge which stood at the bottom of the garden. It was made of bamboo canes and light metal, with flowers delicately painted on each part. It was her favourite one, and if she saw any like it in the shops while she was over, she planned on buying one to take back home.

When she reached the lake, Cara set her stuff down on the wooden picnic table and, slipping off her cream sling-back sandals, she walked down to the edge of the water. She stood still, drinking in the breathtaking view that surrounded her.

At first glance, it looked as though the lake was completely encircled with trees, but on closer inspection, Cara could see houses dotted every so often in between the gently swaying pines.

She had been down at this point several times in the last few days, but always with other people. Usually her mother – seeking Cara's advice in urgent whispers on whether they would like barbecues, and what sort of food would they be expected to eat at them. And how might all this unusual food affect Declan's very sensitive stomach.

On her own in the silence, Cara could take the time to really look around her, and appreciate the warmth of the sun and the balmy silence of the still, beautiful lake.

The morning passed into afternoon, and Cara ate and

drank, read and swam – exactly when she wanted. Moving in and out of the shade as she felt like it. It was bliss. Sheer bliss – with nothing to disturb it.

Every now and then, Oliver would creep into her thoughts. But she was actually surprised how little it bothered her. She discovered she did not miss him one little bit. Her only feelings were of relief. Relief at not having to pretend every day.

Nobody here in America knew Oliver, and they knew nothing of the life she led with him. Here – for this few weeks – she could be the Cara Gayle she wanted to be. Apart from a quick phone call to say she had arrived safely, he might never have existed. And, for the rest of the holiday, that's exactly how it would be.

She got up from the slatted, wooden deckchair now and stretched up as far her arms could reach. Then she took off her shirt and shorts, leaving only her swimsuit on. She climbed up on to the long, wooden pier, and – barefoot – walked along to the end. She paused for a few seconds, then dived deep into the clear, blue water. As she surfaced, she could feel the water was warmer than yesterday. It was like being in a huge, luxurious bathtub. A million miles away from the cool lakes back in Ireland, where she had learned to swim.

Cara swam first in one direction – about a quarter of the way around the lake's perimeter – then back to the pier and the same distance in the opposite direction. It was an easy, comfortable distance. As she continued to swim, and she stretched her path further by a few yards each time, she started to catch glimpses of the nearer houses through the trees. Six in all – spread out like the rays of the sun, each set back in more of the tall trees and multicoloured shrubs.

Occasionally, she could see some movement of people – but the houses were too far away to make out whether a person was male or female, young or old. She wasn't too bothered who was around the houses. Today, the only company she needed was her own.

She decided to go in search of lunch around three o'clock. She pulled her blouse and shorts back on and gathered up her bits and pieces. She smiled to herself as she headed back to the house, because her mother would not have approved at all. Back at home, dinner was at one o'clock every day – without fail. By one, Charles would have already sat down at the kitchen table along with Pauline and Bernadette, and probably Peenie Walshe as well, and Mrs Kelly would have served him potatoes, meat and vegetables.

The sun was at still at its height and its strongest, so Cara decided to eat indoors – some of the tasty, unusual cheeses from Jean's fridge, and more of the fresh fruit washed down with orange juice. She sat reading for a while, and then, having reached the last page of her novel she went in search of one of the many books Jean had suggested she might like to read.

She picked a few titles along with a couple of magazines and, armed with another cool drink, headed for the lake again.

Stopping by the little bridge, she stared around her. The view was almost like something from another planet. She smiled at the thought. That's precisely where she felt she was. All alone on another planet.

When she reached her little hideaway by the side of the lake, she moved one of the deckchairs and a small table out of the glare of the sun yet again. It was a constant game of

hide-and-seek in order to avoid the sun's strongest ray
s. Still, it was a good complaint after the cool, green climate
at home.

She got herself comfortable, and had just removed her
shirt again when she realised that she was not alone.

"Hi," a kind of flat American voice said from behind
one of the bushes.

"Jesus!" Cara said, completely startled. She grabbed
her shirt and whirled around – but she couldn't see anyone.
Her heart suddenly lurched as she realised that apart from
the owner of the voice, she was completely alone. Alone in
a strange garden in a strange country.

"Hello?" she said, in a voice she hoped didn't betray
her fears. She started towards the large flowering bush
from where the voice had come.

"Hi . . ." the flat voice said again, and Cara recognised
it this time as definitely a male voice. "Is – Jean in?"

Cara felt a wave of relief wash over her. It was
somebody who knew the Harpers, so that must be okay.
She hesitated before replying, and then suddenly the
owner of the voice appeared before her. As she looked at
the stocky teenage figure in shorts and a T-shirt standing
in front of her, Cara immediately knew that she had
nothing to fear.

She smiled now, and held out her hand. "I'm Cara –
Jean's niece, from Ireland."

The red-headed boy grabbed her hand, and worked it
up and down in an enthusiastic greeting.

"And what's *your* name?" she asked him gently.

He gave a broad smile. "My name – is Thomas," he
announced. "Thomas – Carroll."

"Thomas," Cara considered. "That's a nice name.

And where do you live, Thomas?"

"Over there." He pointed in the direction of the furthest house at the other side of the lake. "Me and Jean," he said brightly, "we're good buddies."

"Ah, I see," Cara now vaguely remembered a conversation with Jean when they had just arrived. Something about some neighbours with a slow child, but Cara was exhausted and fairly disorientated at the time, and a lot of the talk had gone over her head.

"You on vacation?" he said now, giving another big smile. "You staying at Jean and Bruce's place?"

Cara nodded. "Yes – that's right. I'm staying here for a few weeks. I've come over for Sandra's wedding."

Thomas clapped his hands together. "*I'm* going – " he started, but in his excitement, couldn't quite find the words.

Cara smiled and waited.

Thomas pointed a stubby thumb into his chest. "I –" he started again, more slowly this time, "I'm going to the wedding. Dad . . ." he paused to think, "Dad bought me – a swell new shirt!"

"That's great," Cara told him. "I've got a new dress to wear to the wedding, too."

Thomas beamed, then pointed in her direction. "You and me – we both look swell!"

Cara laughed out loud. "Yes, Thomas," she told him, "we'll both look really swell!"

Thomas then went on to regale Cara all about the wedding and fishing in the lake, his favourite milkshakes, and finally about all the medals he had won for swimming.

"Really? Medals for swimming?" Cara said, very impressed.

"Yeah! Yeah!" Thomas said, nodding enthusiastically.

"I'll show you – at my house." He tugged firmly at Cara's hand now. "Dad put them on the wall – so everyone can see them and say Thomas is a very good swimmer. Thomas is an – excellent swimmer." He was leaving no doubts in Cara's mind as to his capabilities. "Come on!" he pointed to the path that wound around the lake. "We can walk around . . . around to my house to see my medals."

"No, no, Thomas," Cara told him gently. "I've got to stay here to look after the house for Jean and Bruce. They'll be home soon." When she saw the smile slide from his face, she quickly added, "Maybe another time . . . maybe you could bring your medals back here to show me."

Thomas shook his head vigorously. "No – no! They're stuck on the wall. Dad says only he is allowed . . ." he gestured with his hands as though lifting a plaque from a wall, "to lift down."

Cara nodded. "Okay," she told him. "I'll talk to Jean, and maybe we can walk over to your house some time. Before I go home."

"OK," Thomas replied, smiling again. "But where is your house?"

"Oh, it's a long way away," she said, "in a place called Ireland."

"Ire-land," he repeated thoughtfully, mulling it over.

Their conversation was suddenly interrupted by a distant voice calling the boy's name.

Thomas's whole face lit up. "*That*," he said, thumbing in the direction of his house, "that's my dad!"

"I think he's looking for you," Cara said. "You'd better head back home."

"My hamburger," Thomas told her, rubbing his hands

together gleefully, "and my milkshake – probably on the table now!"

Cara looked across the lake to the boy's house. She could just make out a figure in the distance. "I think you'd better go across, Thomas," she advised him. "Your dad might be getting worried."

"No problem," he told her, shaking his head. "Me and Dad – we good buddies!" Then, he put four fingers in his mouth, and after a few attempts gave a piercing whistle.

A few seconds later another loud whistle came back.

"I gotta go," he told Cara with a shrug. "I'll see you again . . . tomorrow."

"OK, Thomas," Cara said, thinking it best not to argue with him. Maybe by tomorrow he would have forgotten all about her going to see his medals.

Thomas set off down the lake path in a purposeful manner. After a few yards he stopped dead. He turned to look back at Cara. "So long!" he called, holding up his thumb.

"So long!" Cara echoed, and held her thumb up too.

* * *

Maggie and Declan were full of all the wonderful places they had seen on the journey over to Jean's friends, all the lovely things they had eaten, and all the lovely people they had met.

"They ain't seen nothin' yet!" Bruce joked. "Wait until the wedding on Saturday – there'll be more invites to 'come over for drinks and barbecue' than they can handle."

"I think I'll be going back to Ireland an expert on burgers and steaks!" Maggie said.

"And we'll have to be building one of them barbecue-things too," Declan chipped in. "And we'll have all the neighbours peepin' around the place, trying to figure out what the hell it is."

They all roared with laughter, and once again Cara wished that her parents could be this open and carefree all the time, especially her uptight mother. She wished they could talk about religion so intelligently at home, the way they had talked late into the night here. She wished she had the guts to say that she had a lot of doubts about the Catholic religion, that she didn't believe in half of it, and felt you didn't have to attend church to be a good person. She could just imagine her mother's face if she dared even suggest it – especially with her being a teacher in a Catholic school.

Bruce was not a Catholic – and didn't subscribe to any particular religion – but it hadn't seemed to rattle Maggie too much at all. And Jean's divorced son was bringing a woman friend to his sister's wedding, and again Maggie had only commented on it in private to Declan and Cara.

But this was America where all cultures and creeds went, and Ireland was Ireland. Where Cara's sister was viewed as a fallen woman, and where Cara was tied for life to a man who did not give her the love and respect that a husband should.

Chapter 6

Feeling revived by her solitary day, Cara got up early and after a long, refreshing swim in the lake prepared to join the others for a day out shopping.

"Isn't Jean marvellous to take us around when she has the wedding coming up so soon?" she said to her mother over an American-style breakfast of crispy bacon strips, scrambled eggs and pancakes and maple syrup. Bruce was the cook this morning, and he was giving Declan a demonstration of how to make pancakes and scrambled eggs American-style, while Jean ferried plates of food back and forth from the kitchen. Maggie picked up the maple-syrup bottle and frowned suspiciously at it. "She's that type," she said, after a few seconds. "Always was – very confident in herself. She wouldn't be too worried what others would think – they can take her as they find her."

"But she's very good," Cara said, helping herself to more of the delicious bacon. "Nothing's too much trouble."

Maggie pursed her lips. "Oh, it's easy for Jean," she said in a low voice.

"What do you mean?" Cara asked.

"Well," Maggie said, "she has plenty of help . . . and they're certainly not short of money." She pointed her knife in the direction of the kitchen. "You just watch and you'll learn a lot. Jean won't be spoiling her fancy nail-varnish washing up the pots and pans. Oh, no – it'll be that poor Mrs Waters who'll cycle miles to come here, and do all the cleaning for a few oul' dollars."

"Mammy, that's terrible!" Cara hissed. "Jean is really nice to Mrs Waters, and she gives her food and things to take home."

"And Bruce," Maggie went on as if Cara had never spoken. "If she asked him to jump, he'd only ask how high. You wouldn't get an Irishman standing in the kitchen with a flowery pinny on."

Cara put her fork down. "Mammy, that's not fair – Bruce has taken a fortnight's holiday to take us around, and he's only making an issue of the cooking to keep us entertained. "

Maggie stood half-out of her chair to check that Jean was out of earshot. She leaned over and prodded the table in front of Cara. "Never mind *'Mammy that's not fair'* – just you listen and you might learn something!"

Cara's stomach tightened, and she suddenly felt she was fifteen years old again. How could she have been so silly as to think her mother could really change her deeply ingrained, narrow view of life? How could she have been so silly to think that a trip to America could make a leopard change its spots so quickly?

"Don't you be getting carried away with all the Yank-style talk over here," her mother warned now. "Jean's good-hearted and all that . . . but as far as hard work and religion go, she's lacking. She's made no excuses about the son bringing another woman to the wedding, and him still a married man."

"He's divorced, Mammy," Cara whispered. "He's not married any more."

"As far as I'm concerned he is," Maggie stated, "and in the eyes of the Church and God, he's still married." Her eyes narrowed. "I'm surprised at you standing up for divorce, Cara – and you a Catholic teacher. I hope all this heathen nonsense isn't giving you any notions . . . I would never have encouraged you to come with us if I thought for a minute you would be so easily impressed."

Before Cara had a chance to reply, Declan and Jean came back out from the kitchen, laughing and chatting.

"Maggie," Jean said, "I think your husband will be adding another string to his bow. He's now an expert on pancakes!"

"Well, that'll make a change," Maggie said, a smile now pinned on her face. "I've never known him to be an expert at anything before."

* * *

Entering the big, airy American shops with the soothing background music was like entering another world. The shops were like nothing Cara and her parents had ever seen before – not even in England. Thankfully, Maggie seemed to have forgotten her crusade against divorce and godless Americans, as they moved from one giant department store to another. She hadn't even passed comment on the fact that Jean was wearing bright red Capri pants with a matching scarf tied at the front of her blonde hair. Her favourite '*mutton dressed as lamb*' saying hadn't been whispered this morning so far.

41

Declan found more interest in the huge American supermarkets, and couldn't get over the ones that sold food, clothing and household items under the one roof. "I couldn't see them catching on in Ireland," he told Bruce, lifting up a fishing-rod. "You see, there just isn't the population or the money there. You've got to remember that we were only getting back on our feet from the Famine when the Civil War knocked us back to square one."

Bruce nodded vaguely, knowing little about Irish history, and having heard nothing but comparisons between America and Ireland since his wife's relations had arrived.

Cara wandered up and down the aisles in one of the big stores, unable to enjoy things as much as she would have liked. The heated, whispered conversation with her mother over breakfast had really disturbed her. When would her mother ever see her as a grown woman instead of a young girl?

"You all right, honey?" Jean asked her as they looked at a rack of brightly coloured summer coats. "You seem a little quiet this morning."

"I'm grand, thanks," Cara said quickly, lifting a duck-egg blue coat with a white collar and cuffs from the rail. She smiled at her aunt. "I'm just overwhelmed by the choice of things . . . I don't know where to start looking. I really love all your shops."

Jean touched her arm. "Don't mind your mom, Cara . . . it's just her way. Being brought up in Ireland back in the thirties and forties was tough. I still have problems with it . . ."

Cara turned and looked at her aunt. The heated argument between herself and her mother must have been overheard. Cara felt herself flush with embarrassment. It was just so rude of them to have been arguing in her aunt's house. Then, as Jean lightly squeezed her hand reassuringly, Cara suddenly felt as though she was going to burst out crying.

Thankfully they were both distracted for the moment as they caught sight of an ecstatic Maggie making her way towards them, holding up a pile of fancy towels.

"I – I think I might try on this coat," Cara murmured, turning towards the changing room.

They stopped off for lunch at a 'Western' restaurant with ranch-style doors, where they were served steaks, salad and French fries by waiters wearing cowboy hats and check shirts with neckerchiefs.

"This is more like the America we know from the films," said Declan, taking in all the decorative whips and spurs which adorned the walls. "I only hope there's no Red Indians ready to leap out on us!"

As they left the restaurant, Cara heard her mother say to her father, "I'm enjoying the change with the food and everything, but the only thing is, we haven't had a decent spud since we left Ireland. It's all chips, chips, chips and salad with everything."

Declan had nodded in agreement. "Only the Yanks would think to put a cold salad with steak. They don't seem so fond of the oul' cabbage and turnips, do they?"

Maggie nodded, her tightly-permed hair sitting as perfectly as the day it was done just before leaving for the holiday. "All I can say," she sighed, "is thank God I brought plenty of the tea over with me. The potatoes I can live without, but a decent cup of tea is the least any of us can ask for."

Declan clapped her on the shoulder, and winked over at Cara. "We'd have been shagged altogether, Maggie, if we had problems with both the spuds and the tea!"

The day was glorious, so Bruce suggested that they stop off at a country park to make sure that Declan got his daily walk in the shaded greenery, rather than just the concrete pavements of the towns. Refreshed, they moved on to the next town which was another hour's drive away.

Although she felt annoyed with her mother, Cara was pleased to see that, in spite of the niggles over potatoes and cabbage, her parents were actually getting great pleasure from the beautiful scenery and the lovely weather.

"Dublin won't hold the same attraction for me, after being in all these lovely big department stores," Maggie stated to no one in particular. "I never realised we were so behind the times in Ireland."

Cara smiled to herself, for her mother and father were lucky if they travelled up to Dublin once a year.

When they reached the town of Binghampton, Jean suggested that they all might like to have an hour or two on their own to look around. "Some of the shops are kinda small," she explained, "and it might be easier for you to get around in ones or twos than the five of us together."

Declan went off with Bruce to look at a shop that sold old-style saddles and cowboy boots, and Jean took Maggie off in search of a wool shop that might just have some stylish knitting patterns she wouldn't find in Tullamore.

"Are you sure you'll be okay on your own, honey?" Jean checked, as Cara went off with directions to the Town Bookstore that Bruce had been telling her all about. It was a fairly big shop, and one that might have some of the books Charles had asked her to find for him.

"Oh, that one could get lost in a book shop," Maggie told Jean as they walked along at a nice, easy amble, "and when she's reading, you might as well talk to the wall – she's in another world altogether. She's always been the same, since she was a child." She shook her head. "Strangely enough, they're all great readers. Pauline could sit all day with a book or magazine . . . and of course Charles spends half the time with his nose stuck in one. Weird kind of books he reads, about the oddest things."

"But you were fond of reading when you were a girl," Jean reminded her sister. "Those American books and comics our Auntie Philomena used to send over from Boston. You were mad about them."

Maggie raised her eyebrows. "True," she said thoughtfully. "Now that you say it . . . it's quare how we change over time without hardly noticing it. I suppose it was after I got married, that I got out of the way of reading. Now, I'd never think of starting a book – I'd be too guilty about doing nothing. It's never-ending, between the shop and the house."

"You have a full and busy life, Maggie," Jean said softly, "and as long as what you're doing makes you happy, that's all that counts."

"The only time I really sit down is when I'm knitting or sewing, and even then, there can be times when I'm up and down like a fiddler's elbow." Her voice dropped. "I think that's what made me decide to come over here for the wedding. It was a good excuse to make me have a break . . . to be honest, I think I really need it."

Jean took a chance, and put her arm around her older, frosty sister in the middle of the street – and was surprised when she didn't flinch. "I'm delighted you came, Maggie," she said, "and we'll make sure you have the best holiday ever."

* * *

On her way to the Town Bookstore, an unusual dress in a shop window caught Cara's eye. It was very different from the sort of dresses she would normally have bought at home. It had a fitted bodice with a deep rounded neckline, and had big, bold yellow and white flowers on a black background. She went inside and tried the dress on, and when she looked in the mirror she felt as though a stranger was looking back at her. A beautiful, blonde stranger who bought what she pleased, and wore what she pleased.

A blonde stranger who had never known Oliver Gayle.

Before she knew it, Cara was walking out of the shop with two of the dresses wrapped in tissue-paper in fancy paper bags with the shop's name on it. One for herself and a similar one in red for Pauline, who was much more adventurous with fashion than Cara. She smiled when she thought of the surprise on her sister's face when she opened the package back in Ireland.

The Town Bookstore was a wonderland. It seemed to go on for miles, with corners turning here and there, revealing yet more shelves stacked from floor to ceiling with every sort of book imaginable. Within minutes, Cara had picked out several titles by American authors that she had been looking for. She hugged them to herself, delighted with her finds. She found one of Charles's books on space exploration, and then she picked out a nice fashion book for her friend Carmel. After that, she headed into the children's section where she found two

Bobbsey Twins books and an illustrated copy of *Little Women* to take back to school.

On her way out, armed with her gift-wrapped parcels, she spotted a book on American fishing that her father might like. She was reaching on tiptoe for it, when she suddenly felt someone watching her.

"Can I do anything for you, ma'am?" a deep male voice said.

Startled, she turned to find a man standing close to her. Standing too close for comfort.

"No . . ." Cara said, stepping back to a more comfortable distance. "I'm grand . . . thank you."

He looked her up and down, then he flashed a smile of perfect white teeth, showing under a well-trimmed moustache. " I would agree with that statement, ma'am – you sure look grand." He spoke in a slow American drawl, which sounded to Cara as though he were mimicking a film star.

Instinctively, Cara found herself moving away from the shelf, and away from the man. He looked to be in his late thirties and almost six foot tall, dark-headed and quite good-looking in an obvious sort of way. He was dressed in a Hawaiian-style shirt and shorts, and Cara wondered at a shop-assistant being dressed so casually. He looked more suited to the beach than working in a bookshop.

Cara hurried off to the pay-desk with the American fishing book, feeling horribly self-conscious under the man's gaze. She wondered had she taken too long choosing her books, and was this the shop's polite way of hurrying people up. She paid for her book, and this time declined the saleslady's offer to gift-wrap it. She didn't want to loiter around in the shop with the weird salesman, and anyway – her father wouldn't care how the book came. He would just be grateful she had even thought of him.

Out in the sunshine of the main shopping area again, Cara drew a deep breath, and looked around, deciding which way to go next.

She turned down a quiet side-street and she wandered along it, coming to a standstill outside a ladies' lingerie shop. The window display drew Cara's gaze to it like a magnet.

Delicate lace and satin underwear peeped out of antique chests of drawers and pink and yellow and white-painted baskets. A row of tiny polka-dot knickers with matching bras hung on a piece of white rope as though on a washing-line. Cara had never seen anything so feminine and lovely. Not even in the bigger stores in Dublin did they have anything like this. Underwear was a most discreet, serious business there, and certainly not something to be flaunted in the front window of a shop, under the gaze of all the men passing.

In a few seconds she was standing inside the shop.

"Good day, ma'am," a middle-aged shop assistant greeted her, "would you like some help or would you like to browse?"

"Thank you," Cara said, blushing, "I'm just having a little look around."

"You just go straight ahead," the lady told her, smiling. She motioned to a space at the side of the counter. "You can leave your parcels here, and it will leave you free to have a good look at the merchandise."

And that's exactly what Cara felt – free. Free to wander

about on her own, and free to look at these, delicate, feminine things that she would love to own. She moved about the shop, gently fingering the silky garments.

There was a time when she would have loved Oliver to see her in skimpy little things like these, but not any more. Especially after finding another woman's brassierre under the seat of his car when she was cleaning it out last year. A much fancier sort of brassiere than the type she wore herself. Since then, Cara had constantly been aware of being in competition with someone else.

Even when they were staying in the hotel at their anniversary, she found herself covering up in pyjamas and long nightdresses – unwilling to have her body compared to another woman's.

Her hand lingered now over a beautiful, sleeveless, Victorian-style nightdress. It had thin blue ribbon threaded through broderie-anglaise cotton, and had rows of delicate lace stitched down the front and hem. This was something that she could happily wear in front of her mother and father, and it was perfect for the lovely, warm weather in America.

She picked a nice cotton brassiere and matching knickers, and one of the polka-dot sets. Then she left them, along with the nightdress and a matching dressing-gown she'd spotted, for the lady to wrap, while she wandered around picking up a heart-shaped nightdress case for Carmel and some small lace lavender-bags as gifts for the women teachers.

As she walked out of the shop, childishly examining the beautifully wrapped contents of yet another attractive American carrier bag, a familiar voice stopped her in her tracks.

"Buy anything nice?"

The hairs stood up on the back of her neck. It was the man from the bookstore. She turned around, and there he was – just standing looking at her. And just like before, he was moving too close for comfort. She backed off now – realising that he must have been watching her while she was inside the shop, watching her as she walked around looking at all the lovely underwear, watching her as she picked up brassieres and knickers and nightdresses, watching her as she held the nightdress to her body, and looked at herself in the mirror.

Watching her do things that she would never even want her husband to see her doing. Even at the best moment in their relationship, she would have felt embarrassed choosing underwear in front of Oliver.

But this wasn't Oliver. This man who had been watching her was a complete stranger. And he had been watching her and waiting for her outside the shop.

This time Cara did not make any pretence of being polite. Instinctively she knew she should not acknowledge him – that this was not a normal, friendly encounter. For all she knew he could be a rapist or even a murderer. The street was almost empty and he could easily grab her and drag her into one of the parked cars. He might even have a gun. You often heard in the news of people being shot in America.

Anything could happen – and no one would know where she was.

Cara turned on her heel, gripping her shopping tightly to her and headed for a gift shop further along the street. She walked straight into the shop, and then raced up one aisle and down another, without giving a glance to any of the merchandise. She was suddenly aware of feeling breathless and her heart was pounding. She slowed down, and after a few moments – safely near a pay-desk – she halted and looked towards the shop window.

Then, her hands gripped her bags so tightly that the knuckles turned white.

Just as she had dreaded – there – pressed up against the window – was the brightly coloured Hawaiian shirt.

Cara willed herself to stay calm, reassuring herself that he wouldn't dare approach her when she was beside two shop assistants.

He turned now – arms folded casually – to look in at her. Cara turned away and walked over to stand by an elderly woman who was stacking soft toys on a shelf. She put her shopping bags down, as the books were fairly heavy. Then, just as she was planning on what to say to the woman – something that wouldn't sound too paranoid or stupid – the shop phone rang. The woman hurriedly dropped the toys and rushed off to answer it.

Cara stifled a little sigh of dismay. Then, her heart suddenly froze as she felt a heavy hand gripping her shoulder.

Chapter 7

Cara took a deep breath and then whirled around to face the owner of the heavy hand.

"Hi!" a cheery young voice said. "I called for you – I called at Jean's house – this morning. To show you medals – my swimming medals!" Thomas Carroll was beaming with delight at meeting up again.

"Oh, Thomas!" Cara was more than delighted herself. In fact, she was almost faint with relief. She looked over his head, her eyes searching. "Who are you with?"

"Dad," he said brightly, "I'm with Dad. He's – he's over there." Thomas pointed towards the queue of people at the till.

Thank God! Cara said quietly to herself. Then, she stole a quick glance in the direction of the door, and all she saw was a wide expanse of glass. The weird man had gone!

She was still staring when she felt Thomas tug at her hand. "Da-ad! Da-ad! This my buddy, Cara. She's staying – at Jean's house."

Cara turned to her young companion, still half an eye on the window. "Sorry, Thomas . . . " she said distractedly, "what did you say?"

"This is my dad!" he said, beaming proudly at her.

Cara looked above his head to the tall, fairish-haired man he was referring to. He had a light growth of beard that was slightly darker than his longish hair. Their eyes met, and Cara suddenly found herself completely tongue-tied. She leaned forward to shake hands, forgetting about the bags of books and parcels she had sitting on the floor in front of her. "Oh, sorry!" she cried, stumbling forward..

A large, tanned hand came forward to steady her. "You, okay?" he said in a low, concerned voice.

Cara straightened up, completely mortified. "I'm really sorry," she said again. "I've just had a bit of a . . ."

His hand came out again now in a handshake before she could explain. "Hi . . . I'm Jameson Carroll – Thomas's father."

Cara nodded, and shook his hand. "Hi," she said, her face burning. "I'm Cara Gayle . . . Thomas told me about you yesterday – I met him down at the lake. I heard you calling across to him – something about a burger and a milkshake?" Then, she felt even more uncomfortable at saying such an inane thing.

Jameson Carroll looked back at her without saying anything.

How could she start telling him about the man in the Hawaiian shirt now? He would think she was completely mad. She gave a quick glance at the window, and thankfully, there was no one there. Hopefully he had gone away – so maybe there was no point in mentioning it now.

Thomas pulled a small package from his pocket. "New tie!" he told her loudly, and started to pull the bright red tie from its wrapping.

"Okay, Thomas, put it away now." His father's tone was patient but firm. "We don't want to hold everyone in the shop up."

Cara blushed again. "Sorry," she said blusteringly, "I shouldn't be holding you up like this."

Again, Jameson Carroll said nothing. Instantly, Cara decided that even if the weird man returned, she would definitely not ask this boorish man for help.

She bent now, and quickly sorted out her packages, and in her rush as she stood up again, she dropped one of the smaller bags which had been inside a larger one. She bent to pick it up at the same time as the tall American, and her self-consciousness was increased when their heads collided. Cara could not bear to look at his face this time. She muttered a 'thank you' as he handed her the small bag bearing the name of the ladies' lingerie shop.

Oh, the embarrassment! Could it possibly get worse? Cara thought. A strange man aware that she had bought underwear from a sexy lingerie shop. Thank God she was in America! If this had been one of the men from the village back home, she would have been the butt of suggestive remarks in the local pubs for the next month.

Thomas turned towards her, as they headed out of the shop. "Will you come and see . . . my medals?"

"Pardon?" Cara stuttered, her mind still cringing from the underwear incident.

"Swimming." He arms moved in breast-stroke fashion.

"Oh, yes . . . but I'll have to see Jean," she said, "when

54

I get back to Lake Savannah. I'll have to see what plans the others have made." She gripped her bags tightly. "I'm just not sure . . ."

"That's okay." Jameson Carroll's voice had an icy edge. "I'm sure you have a real busy schedule while you're over here. Thomas won't take up your time." He guided his son firmly through the door. Plainly, he thought that Cara was giving his son the brush-off.

"I'll know better tomorrow, Thomas," she called quickly, "when I've had time to check what's happening."

But the tall, long-haired American hadn't heard or wasn't in the least interested in her explanations. Thomas struggled from under his father's arm to give her his 'thumbs-up' sign, before being propelled down the street.

Cara wondered what on earth had she done that had made this man so defensive. Surely there was nothing that he could have misconstrued? They had hardly spoken at all. She shook her head now, vaguely deciding which direction to take. She took a few steps into the street when someone moved out from a doorway and stood directly in front of her. It was the man in the Hawaiian shirt.

"Hi," he said, with a dazzling smile. "Can I take some of the weight from your pretty little arms?" He reached his hands out towards her parcels.

"Don't touch me," Cara heard herself say in a threatening hiss. "Go away!"

She turned around, expecting a crowd to have gathered to see what was going on – but apart from the odd curious glance, nobody paid any attention. Cara pushed past him, expecting him to be shocked – but he actually laughed.

"OK, OK!" he said, holding his hands in the air. "I

guess I used the wrong tactics . . ."

Cara started to move away.

"I'm sorry," he called, coming after her. "Give me another chance . . . please! I just wanna get to know you."

Cara could hear him, but she kept going. Her heart thudding so hard it felt as though it were going to come up into her throat. She kept going, past all the shops and the other people, who were either oblivious as to what was going on – or just simply didn't care. They were moving down into a busier, more crowded area. Cara scanned the crowds, silently praying for the familiar faces of her parents or Jean and Bruce. But all the people were strangers, and she was still sure that the man was behind her.

If he didn't leave her alone soon, she knew that she would have no option but to hit him. She knew that it would be the only way to get rid of him. She was so afraid of him now that she didn't care what she did – as long as he left her alone. Even if it meant being hauled into an American police station. She could feel the muscles and tendons tighten in her fists as they clenched the handles of the carrier bags.

Yes, she decided, *if he comes near me again – I'll hit him with the bag of b*ooks.

Then, two familiar faces appeared. But Cara's heart sank rather than soared. It was not her father or Bruce as she had hoped and prayed for. It was the smiling Thomas and his dour-faced father.

In normal circumstances, she would have died rather than approach them. But these weren't normal circumstances – and the man who was following her was not normal either.

She had no alternative. She walked straight up to the

Carrolls – hoping that it looked to the weird man as though she had arranged to meet them.

"I know I'm being a nuisance," she said to Jameson Carroll, "but there's a strange man following me – and he's really frightening me. Can I please just stand here for a few minutes until he goes away?"

Jameson Carroll turned around, and looked down at Cara's smaller, trembling figure. The look of disdain slid from his face when he saw the tears welling up in her blue eyes.

His brow creased. "Where is he now?" he asked, his voice concerned.

She dropped her bags on the ground. "He was right behind me . . ." She couldn't bear to look round, for she suddenly felt weak at the thought of seeing the gaudy shirt again.

He put his hands on her shoulders. "Don't worry," he told her. "You're OK now – but you're going to have to point him out to me."

Cara nodded, wishing she could just collapse into his arms completely.

Then, he turned her back to face into the crowds. He bent his head towards her. "What does he look like?" he said in a quiet tone.

"Tallish and dark – with a moustache," she said in a breathless voice. "He was wearing a coloured – Hawaiian-type shirt."

"OK," Jameson Carroll told her, "there's no one like that around right now. He must be gone – or hiding."

Cara felt the tears come, and this time she could not stop them. "Oh God . . . I'm so sorry . . . I feel so stupid."

Jameson Carroll bent down and picked up Cara's bags.

He gave the lighter ones to Thomas, and the ones with the books he hooked on one finger. He put his free arm around Cara's shoulder. "Come on," he said softly, "I think you need a coffee. You'll feel better after sitting down for a bit." When Cara started to protest he smiled and said, "Look, I never get away with bringing this guy shopping and not having a Coke or a milkshake. We would be stopping anyway."

"I love Coke and milkshakes," Thomas gleefully confirmed, pointing to a restaurant further up the street.

"Thank you," she said, feeling overwhelmingly grateful.

Cara sank down into a deeply cushioned cane chair while Thomas and his father went up to give the order. Then, she took out her compact and a hanky to check what the damage to her face was.

Her reflection was every bit as bad as she expected. Red eyes and smudged mascara. She wiped away the traces of mascara, and ran a hand over her thick hair. She would have to do, for Jameson Carroll was making his way back to the table now with two tall mugs and saucers. Quickly, she stuffed the compact and hanky back into her handbag.

Jameson stood back to let Thomas put his tall glass of Coke on the table, and then the boy went hurrying back to the counter in a purposeful manner. Jameson set the mugs of coffee down, and slid one across to Cara.

She could feel his eyes on her now, and momentarily distracted herself by reaching for a spoonful of brown sugar.

Jameson Carroll pulled out two more chairs, and then waited for his son to join them. Thomas was back in a few seconds carrying a basket that held three buns, and a small bowl of whipped cream. Jameson stepped back to let Thomas sit at the table next to Cara, and then he sat down opposite them.

Thomas reached a pudgy hand out to cover Cara's with a comforting squeeze, just as a grown man might. "You – you okay now?" he checked, his innocent eyes staring worriedly into hers. "I guess – you got a scare."

"Yes, Thomas," she answered with a weak smile. "I'm okay now." She spooned some of the cream into her coffee, then held the mug between two hands, staring into the distance.

"Swell," said Thomas. Reassured, he reached for his Coke.

Jameson Carroll put his own mug down. He sat back in his chair, his eyes moving around the crowds.

Thomas now handed round the basket of buns, and although she didn't feel in the slightest bit hungry, she picked at one while Thomas regaled her with descriptions of his swimming medals.

Suddenly Jameson sat bolt upright in his chair. "Thomas," he said quickly, "go up and ask the lady for a clean fork, please."

"Yessir!" The smiling Thomas was up and on his feet, delighted to be of help.

Cara's throat tightened when she saw the serious look back on the American's face.

"OK," he said in a low voice, leaning across the table to Cara. "What did you say that guy was wearing, Ash . . .?" His voice tailed off as he struggled to recall her unusual name.

"Is he here?" Cara asked anxiously.

"Don't worry," he said, and his voice had an almost soothing tone to it. "I promise you I'll handle this."

And in that moment, Cara suddenly knew that she was safe with this tall, quiet American man.

"Did you say he was wearing a multicoloured shirt?" he asked.

"Yes, yellow and purple," she whispered. "Is he near?"

"I think so . . . I think he just sat down at a table behind us."

"Oh, God!" Suddenly realising he was so close, Cara forgot all determination about keeping calm.

"You're OK, you're OK," Jameson said, "but I need you to just turn round a little . . . and look at the table behind you."

Then Cara felt a large, warm, comforting hand on hers. And it wasn't Thomas's this time. It was Jameson Carroll's. And it felt so good and strong, and reassuring, holding hers.

"It's just that I don't want to make a mistake, and get the wrong poor guy," he said, his mouth in a sort of lopsided grin.

Then, with his hand growing tighter around hers, Cara dared to look back.

And there, sitting behind her was the loud, colourful shirt. And the guy wearing it, with the dark hair and moustache, was casually lighting a cigarette. He inhaled on it, and then he slowly turned his gaze to meet hers. Cara's stomach turned as he leaned forward and raised his eyebrows in a familiar manner.

"It's him – it's him!" she whispered urgently, panic rising now.

That was all Jameson needed to hear. In an instant, he was out of his chair and moving towards the other table, where the weird man was lounging in his chair in a deliberately casual manner.

Cara couldn't bear to look. Both hands were up now, shielding her face. Eventually, she got the courage up to turn around and look properly at them and she saw that the man in the gaudy shirt was now up on his feet, and matched Jameson Carroll inch for inch in height.

Jameson stepped forward now and, his jaw thrust forward, began to talk right in the man's face.

Oh God, Cara suddenly thought again, what if the man has a gun? If anything happened to Jameson Carroll it would be all her fault!

Cara Gayle's fault. And her, a complete stranger who had only known his handicapped son for a couple of days. Her heart turned over. What about Thomas? She looked now up towards the counter, and could see him laughing and joking with one of the women there who was making the milkshakes

What if something terrible happened to Jameson and Thomas saw it? A gun or even a knife? Her heart thumped so hard in her throat, that she felt as though she was going to choke. As she watched the weird guy squaring up to Jameson, she knew the possibility of some kind of violence was very real . . . and so near.

Her eyes darted over in Thomas's direction again. He was still chatting, making his diving gestures now, oblivious to the situation that was going on only yards away. Should she rush over to him and push him behind the counter, safely out of harm's way?

Then, when she looked back again, there was only one man standing there. And it was Jameson Carroll.

He headed back to the table.

"He's gone," he said simply, sitting down in Thomas's chair.

Cara looked along the street and she could see a flash of purple and yellow disappearing into the distance.

"Relax," he told her, his hand coming over to cover hers again. "He's gone, and I promise you he won't trouble you again."

"What was it all about?" Cara asked. "What did he want?"

Jameson's eyebrows lifted. "You, apparently," he said in a low voice. "He thought you might be interested in him."

"But I didn't – " Cara spluttered. "I did nothing to give him that impression. I was really rude and horrible to him . . ."

"Don't let it rattle you any more," Jameson said, shrugging. "He's obviously got some kind of communication problem – picks people up wrongly. I've warned him off real strongly, so you've nothing more to worry about."

Without thinking about it, Cara put her other hand on top of his and held it tightly. "I am so, so grateful," she told him, and he just nodded and smiled in response.

They were still sitting, hands entwined, when Thomas returned to the table with the fork that nobody wanted.

Later, Thomas reminded Cara once again of her promise to come and see his swimming medals.

Cara looked over at Jameson without any apprehension this time. "I would really love to see Thomas's swimming medals. Earlier on . . . when I met you in the shop, that awful man was outside. He'd been following me from shop to shop . . ." She halted, reliving the horrible incident. "That's the reason I was so distracted when Thomas was talking to me . . . I was absolutely terrified."

"It's OK." His face was much lighter now, and the brown eyes soft and understanding. "You don't have to explain. I get the picture . . . and it sounds as if I'm the one who should be apologising to you." He looked at Thomas, who was happily finishing off the remains of the buns that nobody else could eat. "I was rude and abrupt with you. I thought you were just being polite because . . ." he nodded over at his son, "you know . . . the way Thomas is."

Cara shook her head. "No . . . not at all. It's understandable – I can see how it looked." She smiled over in Thomas's direction and lowered her voice to a whisper.. "I would never treat him like that."

Jameson slowly nodded. "I guess I'm over-sensitive . . . but I'm used to it being the other way." He sighed now, and ran his hands through his hair. Then he leaned towards Cara. "Hell . . . I'm so damned rude! I didn't even catch your name properly . . ."

"It's Cara," she said, blushing. "Cara Gayle."

"Cara Gayle," he repeated. "That's a real nice name . . . unusual. And it's all the way from . . ." He raised his eyebrows in question. "Wales? No – don't tell me . . . Ireland?"

"Right, second time," she laughed. "I'm Irish. I've come over for the wedding. Jean's daughter."

"Jean – of course," he said, jokily slapping his forehead. "I should have thought of the Irish connection. A bit obtuse of me." His gaze moved to her wedding ring. "Did you travel alone? Or did you have company?"

Cara looked away, knowing that he meant a husband.

The last thing she wanted reminding of was Oliver. "I came with my parents," she said, turning the mug and saucer round in a circle. "Jean is my mother's sister."

"I see," he said, a broad smiling coming over his face. He reached out now, and took her hand in his. "Well, Cara Gayle – I sincerely hope you don't run into any more maniacs during the rest of your stay in America."

"I think I might stay put out at Lake Savannah for the rest of the holiday," she said, catching his eye and laughing now. "I'd rather take my chances with the bears than go through the experience I had today again."

It was funny, she suddenly thought, how she now felt comfortable and relaxed with this man – the man who earlier on had made her feel so clumsy and silly. As she looked at him now, she could see that all the hostility and distrust had vanished from his eyes. Just as the fear and embarrassment must have vanished from her own.

They ordered more coffee, and sat chatting for a little longer, Cara telling him all about the part of Ireland she came from and her work in the school, and Jameson telling her about Lake Savannah. He made no mention of a wife, alive or dead, and Cara avoided the subject.

When it was time to go, he asked her if she'd like to go back to the Town Bookstore with him and Thomas. "It's just that – I'm sure he's gone – but I wouldn't like you to bump into him again when you're alone."

"I'd be happy to go to the bookshop," Cara said. "And I'd be happier being with you two, than wandering about on my own."

"This –" Thomas said, motioning to the empty mugs and plates, "is my treat!" He reached into the back pocket of his jeans, and took out his wallet.

"No, no," Cara protested, lifting her bag.

"Let him," Jameson said, as Thomas made for the counter. "I've taught him to cope socially, and he needs to know how to do these things. Besides, he doesn't spend much on himself and he enjoys paying for little things like this."

"Okay," Cara agreed, "but really it should be me paying – to thank you for all you've done."

"After my initial rudeness, let's call it quits," he said, laughing. He got to his feet now, lifting Cara's bags. "Look, I'll just check Thomas is managing the money okay. Sometimes he mixes up the notes. We'll catch you at the door."

Cara walked outside into the warm sunshine, once again relaxed and happy to be having a holiday in America. Then, she heard a voice calling her name.

"So this is where you've got to," her mother called jovially from across the street. "We were getting worried – thinking that a strange man might have run off with you!"

Cara turned towards them with a big smile. "You don't know how close you are to the truth, Mother!" she said laughing.

"Why? Did something happen to you?" Maggie demanded, as the others gathered around.

Cara then related the story of the man in the purple and yellow shirt, and how Jean's neighbours had come to her rescue.

"Oh, my God!" Jean had exclaimed. "We're not going to let you out of our sight for the rest of the holiday."

"I only wish it was me who had met him," Maggie said, "I'd have soon sorted him out."

Declan came to put a protective arm around his daughter. "Are you all right, Cara – did he do you any harm?"

"No, Daddy," she reassured him, "I'm grand . . . honestly."

Jean suddenly let a whoop of delight out as Thomas and Jameson Carroll came out of the restaurant door now. "Here come the heroes!" she said, rushing over to put her arms around Thomas.

Declan stepped forward to shake Jameson's hand. "I thank you heartily for looking after my daughter. Both you and your son," he said. "In a strange country anything could have happened to her."

Jameson gave an embarrassed smile. "It was nothing, sir – and I can assure you that most of the guys over here are pretty harmless. Isn't that right, Bruce?"

"It sure is," Bruce agreed, nodding gravely, "but the bad guys can spoil it for the rest of us at times."

Jameson turned to Cara, holding out the bags of shopping. "You might miss these later," he said, handing them to her.

"Thank you," Cara said, colouring up as she thought of the contents of the lingerie bag, "and thanks again for the coffee and everything . . ." She looked up at him and his deep brown eyes met hers once again.

It was only for a few moments. But in that short time, Cara Gayle felt something stir inside her, that she had not felt for a long, long time.

Chapter 8

The following morning Cara woke up to the sound of her mother knocking on the bedroom door. "Come on, lazybones," she joked, coming into the room with a cup of tea for Cara. "We're eating outside this morning . . . you wouldn't believe the heat already. Jean said we might find it too hot later on, so we thought we might make the best of the morning while the heat is still comfortable."

Cara sat up in bed, delighted to see her mother in such good form. "Who's the chef this morning?" she joked.

"Me," Maggie said, sitting down on the bottom of the bed. "I'm trying my hand at the pancakes this morning – just to keep Jean happy. You know the Yanks. They like to make a big issue out of nothing. Anyway . . ." she absentmindedly ran a hand over the blanket, checking what material it was made out of, "there's no harm in learning how to cook different things."

"The change is good for us all," Cara said carefully. She took a sip of the hot tea.

"Are you okay, Cara?" Maggie suddenly asked, her

face creased in concern. "Did you get an awful fright yesterday?"

Cara shrugged, and tucked one wing of her blonde hair behind her ear. "I'm grand now," she said quietly, putting the cup of tea down on the little bedside locker, "but I was really frightened by the time I met up with Thomas . . . and his father." For some reason, Cara found herself self-conscious about calling Jameson Carroll by his name.

Maggie nodded. "Thanks be to God you did meet them," she said, her voice croaky.

Then, she suddenly moved up on the bed, and, in a most uncustomary gesture of affection, she gently put her arms around Cara's neck. "Thank God you're safe, Cara . . . I'd die if anything happened to you . . . and so would Oliver Gayle." Then, she lowered her head and kissed Cara on the cheek.

"Honestly, Mammy, I'm fine." Cara was almost breathless with shock.

Maggie sat back on the bed now, and took Cara by the hand. "I know he has his faults," she said, "but he's not the worst – he doesn't keep you short of anything. And though you might not think it," she rushed on now, "I'm sure underneath it all, that he worships the ground you walk on."

Cara picked her teacup up again and said nothing. What was there to say? What man – who supposedly worshipped the ground his wife walked on – would behave like an old tom-cat?

"This holiday," Maggie went on, her curled head nodding earnestly, "might be the making of ye both. Indeed . . . you'll see when we get back. He'll have missed you, and when he hears what happened to you yesterday, he'll realise that he doesn't want to let you out of his sight." She nodded away to herself. "A good-looking girl like yourself – and from a decent family."

Cara continued to drink her tea.

"Have you got anything to bring back to him yet?" Maggie continued.

Cara shook her head. "Not yet . . ."

Maggie brightened up. "Sure we've plenty of time left," she said, standing up now. "You'll find something nice for him the next day we're out, I'm sure." She patted the bed again now. "Be down in a couple of minutes, and the breakfast will be ready to take outside."

Shortly afterwards, dressed in a cool, pale-blue cotton dress and white sandals, Cara joined the others as they all picked their steps down the grassy bank to the lake. Each person was armed with plates of pancakes and bacon strips, fresh rolls and Danish pastries.

"What I'd give for a good plate of black pudding, some rashers and decent Irish sausages," Maggie commented to Cara, "and I know your father feels the same . . . it's just that he's not confident enough to say it out straight."

Cara shook her head, and concentrated on climbing down the wooden steps to the lower part of the garden. She knew that her father was perfectly happy trying out all the different foods, just as she was.

Half an hour later, everyone sat full and contented, chatting and looking out over the shimmering lake. Then, further down the lakeside path, a red-headed figure came running into view. He slowed down as he reached the group.

"Hello, buddy!" Bruce said. "Come and join us."

Thomas stopped and held up a hand of greeting. Then, hand on hips, made a great issue of getting his breath back.

"Don't tell me you've run all the way around that lake?" Jean said, trying to sound as though she were completely shocked.

"All the way around that lake!" Declan exclaimed, sitting up straight in the deckchair. "I don't believe it."

Thomas nodded vigorously, grinning from one to the other, delighted with the attention.

"And I – " he gasped, "can swim all the way – all the way – around the lake, too!" His arm swept in great wide circles to reinforce the point.

There were even more gasps of incredulity from the receptive audience.

Then, satisfied with his impact, Thomas sat down heavily in one of the empty deckchairs. He turned to Cara. "You!" he said, running a stubby hand though his damp red hair. "Come to my house to see my medals – now!"

"That's you told!" Maggie laughed. "You can't get out of that one!"

Cara smiled and nodded. "I promise you I'll come and see your medals later."

"I think," Jean said, standing up, "that what you need is a drink, young man – a nice cold drink." She winked over at Maggie. "And maybe some pancakes?"

Maggie jumped to her feet. "There's still some of the mixture left," she said, gathering up plates. "I'll make him some right now. A growing lad like that needs a good breakfast."

"Tell you what, buddy," Jean said to Thomas, "you

70

carry in some of those plates, and you can have some of Maggie's famous pancakes. Her first time making them, and they're the best I've ever eaten in America."

Thomas clapped his hands delightedly. "It's a deal!" he said, holding out his hand, palm upwards.

Jean gamely brought the palm of her hand down on his in a loud slap, then they went into a routine of slapping each other's hands in a variety of ways.

The men stayed outside in the sun, while Maggie, Cara and Jean went inside with Thomas. A little while later, while Maggie was serving up the pancakes, Cara gestured to Jean to come into the hallway out of Thomas's hearing.

"What do you think," she asked, "about me going over to see Thomas's medals?" She pulled a face. "I'm not too sure . . . you know . . . his father."

"You should go across to the house," Jean said without hesitation. "It means a lot to the boy. Don't be put off by Jameson's manner – when you get to know him, he's a real nice man. I think he's some kind of artist, and those creative types are often temperamental." She glanced towards the kitchen. "He's kind of wary of people – but I guess being on his own with a handicapped kid isn't easy. Even a nice kid like Thomas."

Cara nodded slowly. "I didn't realise they were on their own . . . what about Thomas's mother?"

"Honey," Jean said, raising her eyebrows, "your guess is as good as mine. When we moved here two years ago, there was only the two of them in the house on their own. Definitely no woman. And, as far as I know, there hadn't been one for some time before that. "

"Hasn't Thomas's father ever mentioned anything

71

about the mother?"

"Vaguely," Jean said. "Just odd comments about taking Thomas down to relatives in New York " She shrugged. "I guess he's not the kind of man who talks about personal things."

Maggie came into the hallway now. "What's all the whispering?" she asked, looking suspiciously at her sister and daughter.

Cara coloured up. She didn't want her mother to hear her asking about another man. Not after the things she had said about Oliver this morning.

Jean motioned with her hand for Maggie to keep her voice down. "I'm just filling Cara in on Thomas's details," she said in a low voice.

"What kind of details?" Maggie said, all interested now. "I've just set him down at the table with his pancakes and syrup."

"I'm just saying how Thomas and his father live on their own." Jean craned her neck to make sure that Thomas couldn't hear.

"On their own?" Maggie repeated. "What do you mean?"

"I mean there's no mother."

"Oh, the poor man!" Maggie said, shaking her head. "And that poor boy the way he is, and him with no mother. When did she die?" She looked back towards the kitchen. "Maybe we should have kept some of the pancakes for his father."

"She's not *dead*, Mammy!" Cara hissed. "She's just not living with them."

The compassion drained from Maggie's face, and it was replaced by a disapproving tightness. "Don't tell me

72

they're divorced too," she muttered, shaking her head.

"That's the last thing that poor lad needs."

"It's OK," Jean said. "Jameson Carroll is a very capable man. I should think he can cook his own pancakes, and a lot more besides. Thomas is very fond of his food, and he doesn't exactly look as though he's fading off the face of the earth, now does he?"

"True," Maggie agreed. "He's a fine lump of a lad, no doubt. And he's clean and tidy, well-turned out considering there's only a man looking after him."

Cara rolled her eyes over in Jean's direction, and her aunt smiled back knowingly.

"Weren't you a lucky girl yesterday, meeting Thomas and his dad?" Jean said, changing the subject.

Cara closed her eyes at the memory of the purple and yellow shirt. "Yes," she said nodding, "I certainly was lucky. It was awful. I was terrified – I don't know what I'd have done if I hadn't met them."

"What did Jameson actually say to the guy when he confronted him?" Jean asked curiously.

Cara shrugged. "I really don't know," she said. "I was just going to ask him that yesterday when you all arrived."

"I'd love to have seen the guy's face," Jean said, "when Jameson Carroll loomed over him. He's a good six-footer."

"Yes – but so was the weird fellow!" Cara said. "Thank God it came to nothing."

Maggie shook her head. "I can't imagine what Oliver would have had to say, if we had let anything happen to you . . ."

At the mention of Oliver's name, Cara felt herself flinch.

73

"And I wouldn't have liked to have seen the state of that fellow if Oliver had got his hands on him," Maggie told Jean now. "Oliver Gayle mightn't be the biggest man in the world, but he wouldn't let anyone touch a hair on Cara's head."

Then, they heard the scrape of Thomas's chair as he got up from the table, and the three women all rushed back into the kitchen – Cara grateful for the diversion.

"Those pancakes – swell!" he said. "Best in America!"

"You're very welcome, " Maggie beamed. "I'll save you some if I make them again before I go home."

Thomas stood in front of Cara, waiting.

"I get the feeling," Jean said, "that you're not going to get out of this. You might as well go now, honey – because we don't know what the rest of the day might bring." She ruffled Thomas's hair. "When this guy gets the bit between his teeth, there's no putting him off."

She leaned towards Cara. "Anyway, you'll just love the house. It's really something else."

"Go on now, like a good girl, Cara," Maggie said, "and make sure you thank that man again for saving you yesterday."

Cara turned to Thomas. "You go on down to the lake," she said, smiling, "and I'll catch up with you. I just need to pop upstairs for a few minutes."

Thomas nodded and after politely thanking the women again, he headed on out into the garden.

Cara ran upstairs and quickly freshened up. She piled her blonde hair in a casual knot at the top of her head and put on a touch of pale pink lipstick. She looked in the mirror and then blotted most of it off with a tissue, so that it didn't look too obvious.

Then, as she made for the bedroom door, she turned back to dab a little perfume behind her ears.

As Jean and Maggie stood on the deck watching Cara run down to meet Thomas, Jean turned to her sister. "She's a lovely, lovely girl. You must be very proud of her, Maggie."

"Oh, I am proud of her," Maggie said. "She's a good teacher, and a very good housewife. She manages to keep on top of everything well."

"She's such a beautiful-looking girl, too," Jean went on, "with her lovely long blonde hair and her slim figure."

"Oh, well . . . beauty is as beauty does," Maggie stated. "But fair dues to Cara, she's never let it go to her head. On the whole she has a nice, quiet nature." She looked at her sister. "A bit too quiet at times. I think it's all that reading she does. She's a bit of a dreamer. She's always been the same since she was a child."

"Well," Jean laughed, "she's only living up to her name."

"True," Maggie said, laughing now. "I often forget that. I didn't realise when we called her Cara that it meant "dream-vision"' in Irish. My Gaeilge was never the best. Maybe I should have checked it out beforehand, and indeed with Charles. God knows what his name means – but all I can say is that he's even worse than Cara for the books."

"Did you check what 'Pauline' meant before choosing her name?"

Maggie's face suddenly darkened. "No, indeed I didn't," she said. She moved closer to the large window, and watched as Cara and Thomas moved further and further into the greenery. "To me, all 'Pauline' stands for is a mother's broken heart . . ." Her voice tailed off, slightly cracking now.

"Oh, Maggie," Jean said, coming to put her arms around her sister. "Don't keep worrying about that – it's 1963 now and people don't mind so much."

Maggie stiffened in Jean's embrace, but didn't move away. "Maybe *here* they don't – but back in Ireland I'm never allowed to forget it."

"A child always brings love," Jean said. "I wrote that to you at the time, and I mean it more now."

Maggie managed a watery smile. "Oh, I know . . . and Bernadette's a grand little thing. A little dote – but God love her, she's going to have it hard with no father." She sniffed. "There's hardly a night goes past that I don't shed a tear over it . . ."

"Maggie, Maggie," Jean said, hugging her tighter, "you need to stop looking back, and start looking forward. Bernadette has as much right to be in the world as any other child."

Maggie nodded. "The thing is, it's easy to understand all that while I'm here. Everything seems simple and easy. Even all the religion thing with Bruce – it doesn't bother me. Listening to him, some of his views even seems sensible – but the minute I get back home it'll be a different story. You wouldn't survive over there to start questioning things too much, or going against the Church."

"It doesn't have to be," Jean told her. "The thoughts in your own head can be the same wherever you are – it's up to you."

"True . . ." Maggie said, but her voice was distant.

They walked out into the garden, Maggie stopping to examine the different plants and flowers. "I hope Cara's all right," she said now. "There's times it's hard to work out what's going on in somebody else's head."

"Cara sounds just fine," Jean reassured her, "and, aren't you always saying what a wonderful guy her husband is?"

"Oh, he is, he is. She's done well marrying him," Maggie said. "She has a lovely big farmhouse, and she goes short of nothing. Oliver's even talking of getting her a car in the near future."

"He sounds a real nice guy, and so full of life. Declan said he was a leading light in the local drama."

"Oh indeed," Maggie said, cheering up now. "And they give huge amounts to local charities." Then, she bent down to smell a rose bush. She picked one of the flowers and twiddled it around in her hands. "The only thing missing from Cara's life is a child."

Jean raised her eyebrows but said nothing. She found it hard to understand this sister of hers who could lie awake regretting the birth of the only grandchild she had – and yet say everything would be fine if only Cara gave her a grandchild.

"I don't know who's at fault," Maggie went on, "either him or her. And I don't know if they've ever found out . . . Cara's never said. But if they've not managed it in seven years of marriage . . ." Her voice tailed off.

"Oh, there's lots of couples who conceive babies just when they've given up," Jean said encouragingly, and rhymed off the names of girls they knew when growing up.

"I would doubt it now," Maggie said quietly. "Not after all this time."

"Cara seems fulfilled in her teaching career," Jean said,

"and I'm sure she's marvellous with children. You can just tell, even by the way she treats young Thomas."

"Oh, she has great patience," Maggie agreed, "there's no doubting that." She looked thoughtful again for a few moments. "If only she had one of her own. You see, it's Oliver I worry about. A man likes to prove himself . . . in that way. And you never know . . . he could be tempted in other quarters."

There was a silence.

"Have you any reason to feel that way about him?" Jean asked, realising she was treading on delicate ground.

"Good God, no," Maggie said defensively. "He's a good Catholic fellow – at Mass every Sunday. No . . . there's no reason whatsoever." She turned and started clearing the table. "It's just – it's just you would never know with men."

* * *

As Cara and Thomas turned the bend in the lakeside path, laughing and chatting, Cara caught a glimpse of Jameson Carroll's house for the first time. It was so tall – and yet delicate and almost regal – that it took her breath away. And the nearer they got, the bigger the house seemed and so full of details Cara had only ever seen in American films. But this wasn't a film – it was a house owned by real people. A house with balconies upstairs and a high white deck that ran all the way around it, full of rocking-chairs and tables and even a double wooden swing-seat.

A wave of anxiety washed over Cara as she mounted the white wooden steps that led up to the meticulous white house. Jean and Bruce's house was luxurious by anyone's standards, but this was in another league yet again.

What on earth am I going to say to this man? she thought, wishing now that she could just turn back. Then, a picture suddenly flooded into her mind, reminding her of the embarrassing incident that happened yesterday when she dropped the parcels. And then her face burned, when she remembered the way Jameson had deliberately avoided any eye-contact when he handed them back to her. And then she thought back to when they bumped heads and he seemed really irritated by her . . .

And then . . . Jameson Carroll was opening the door and just standing there – waiting for her.

He looked different from yesterday, although he was still casually dressed. He was wearing a pale blue denim shirt, loose and flowing, and close-fitting denim jeans. He looked like one of the American singers or film stars. Tall with long sandy hair and a trace of a fair beard and moustache.

"Hi," he said, his eyes warm and friendly. Then he laughed and shook his head as Thomas tore in past them, beckoning to Cara to follow.

Cara felt herself blush . "Hi," she said, smiling and trying to sound casual. Then, as she passed in by him, their eyes met . . . and Cara had that same feeling as yesterday. A feeling of self-consciousness. The intense awareness of an attractive man looking at her. A feeling she remembered from years back, when she was young and single.

"I hope this wasn't too early for you," he said apologetically, "I was trying to hang on to this guy for an hour . . . he was driving me nuts."

"It was grand," Cara said, stopping in the hallway. "We've been up for ages. Anyway . . . it's nice to visit another American house." She looked around the high, airy hallway, adorned with paintings of every shape and size. "This is absolutely gorgeous," she breathed. "I've never seen anything like it before."

She turned back to look at Thomas's father and he was smiling. A really warm, friendly smile. And Cara suddenly realised that when he smiled he was very attractive. Not in the usual way. Not attractive in the way Oliver was. Not smooth and handsome and meticulously dressed.

But Jameson Carroll was still very attractive – in a roughish, rangy kind of way.

"Down here," Thomas said, rushing down the hallway, and excitedly beckoning them to come behind.

"We'd better go see these damned medals first," the boy's father whispered. "I think he'll burst if we don't get that over with." He smiled again. "When you're all done, I'll fix us some coffee."

"He's a lovely boy," Cara said. "You must be really proud of him."

He nodded slowly. "Yeah, I am proud of him." Then his face clouded over. "Although there's lots of folks would think there's nothing to be proud of in a slow kid . . . but I know different. A lot different."

"Well," Cara said, picking her words carefully, "I can see why you're proud of him. He's got a lovely nature and that's the most important thing in any person. I really like him."

Jameson stopped and looked right at her. "Yeah," he said, smiling broadly, "I kinda like him too."

Then they both laughed in a nice, easy way.

As she followed him down the hallway she noticed

that his thick, unruly hair had three different shades running through it: the main sandy-blond colour, with an undertone of reddish – hence Thomas's gingery colour – and then there were odd threads of silver. The silver was hardly noticeable, but it was there.

Cara found herself wondering how old he was. People often went grey fairly young. He could be anything from mid-thirties to early forties. A bit older than her. And a bit older than Oliver.

Thomas indeed had all the medals and trophies he had talked so much about. He had them displayed in strict order – from the time he first started swimming and could swim only ten yards, through to twenty-five yards and fifty yards and so on.

For breaststroke and backstroke and butterfly strokes – and some strokes Cara had never heard of. Some of the awards – his father told her quietly – were for special kids like Thomas, and some were for swimming in classes of children of more than average ability.

"You are so clever, buddy," Jameson told Thomas when they put the last of the medals back in their boxes, and had put the last trophy back on the shelves. He then grabbed the boy in a bear hug and said, "What about the deal we made earlier?"

Thomas looked puzzled.

"Your bedroom," Jameson reminded him.

Thomas turned to the door of the sitting-room and started to kick the bottom part of it. "Don't want to!" he said in a low voice.

"No, no, Thomas," Jameson said in a patient but firm tone. "A deal's a deal."

Thomas now leaned his forehead on the door and then

moved backwards and forwards, lightly banging his head against the door.

Jameson shrugged and rolled his eyes in Cara's direction. "It's not gonna work, buddy," he said softly. "You're just gonna give yourself a headache, and you'll still have to tidy your room." He winked at Cara now. "I'll have a drink and something nice for you when you get finished fixing everything up."

There was a long pause, then Thomas slowly turned around and gave an exaggerated sigh. "OK, you win!" He gave Cara a weary thumbs-up sign and disappeared down the hallway. Then, a few seconds later, his heavy footsteps sounded as he went up the stairs to the next floor.

Jameson smiled and shook his head. "That guy would try anything. He promised me that he would fix his bedroom up first thing this morning, and then he wriggled out of it."

"It's good that he has the nerve to try to get out of it," Cara said. "It wouldn't be normal if he did everything you told him. He's just doing what any teenager will do."

"Sure," the tall American agreed. "We do have our fights – he's by no means perfect – but thankfully, there's more than enough ups to compensate for the downs."

They walked down the hallway towards the kitchen, and Cara's mouth nearly dropped open when she entered the huge, bright room. Like the outside of the house, it was almost completely white and filled with whitewashed, wooden furniture: old-style dressers, a huge, round table and high-backed chairs. A big rocking-chair with deep, checked cushions sat at the panoramic window that overlooked Lake Savannah.

The kitchen was of a style Cara had never seen before – in fact the whole house was like nothing she had ever seen before. And certainly not the type of thing she would have expected in a house with only a man and a boy.

As she looked around, something told her that there was definitely a woman's influence around this house.

"This is just so beautiful," Cara breathed, running her hand over the back of the rocking-chair.

"Thanks, it's real kind of you to say so," he said casually. He moved over to the large cooker now, and put the coffee-pot back on top to heat up. Then he lifted a basket with pastries and chocolate cookies and set it down on the table. He smiled. "I have to watch how much of this stuff Thomas eats – he'd eat rubbish all day long. He has it for treats, but I make sure that most of his food is good, wholesome stuff."

"He looks a really healthy boy," Cara said, "so you're obviously doing something right."

Jameson shrugged. "I wonder at times what the hell I am doing . . . but I try to give it my best shot." He reached in a cupboard and brought out two pottery mugs and a tall glass. "That's what pleases me most about Thomas's swimming. Apart from keeping him fit, it means he's on a par with the other kids his age . . . and better than a lot. He's a strong, healthy boy and although swimming isn't everything, at least I don't have to worry about him drowning if he's near water. It's one area he's completely independent in."

"I think you're really brave encouraging him to do all these things," she said. "It must be easier to just do things for him at times."

"Yup," Jameson said, "it sure is. Being a nagging dad

is no fun . . ."

The loud clumping of footsteps signalled Thomas's arrival back downstairs. "Finished," he said, panting. "Room – absolutely spot-on!"

Jameson nodded his head and laughed. "I'll be checking, buddy, so it had better be spot-on."

Thomas looked at Cara and winked at her. "He is very bossy," he said, nodding at this father. "It's not fair – he make me work too hard."

"Get the orange juice outa the fridge and stop grumbling," Jameson told him, "and there's some of Annie's chocolate brownies too – but go easy on them."

Cara's ears suddenly pricked up. *Annie.* So there obviously was a woman around.

Thomas clapped his hands in glee and headed for the fridge. He lifted a large jug of juice out on to the table. "You're a good guy – Jameson Carroll," he said, filling a tall glass with the drink. He reached across the table and lifted a chocolate cookie. He held it out towards his father in a 'cheers' type gesture. "You're my best buddy."

"Sure," Jameson laughed, pouring strong, dark coffee into mugs for himself and Cara. "I'm your buddy while the going's good!"

Then a phone ringing in the hall brought the banter to an abrupt stop as Jameson went off to answer it.

"You like brownies?" Thomas asked, holding the basket out to Cara.

"I've never tried them before," she confessed, "but they look lovely. I'll have a small one."

"Annie," he said, "makes best brownies – ever!"

Cara wondered again who Annie was. Maybe a girlfriend of Jameson's?

"Yup," Cara could hear Jameson say into the phone, "afraid so – I'm all tied up with a wedding that Saturday – so we'll have to make it the following week.." Then, there was a pause while he listened to his caller.

Cara moved to close the door, as she didn't want to eavesdrop on his call.

"Yeah," she could still hear him say, "I'm sorry, too – but I can't get out of it. I really would like to be with you – but it can't be helped." Another pause. "Okay, Melanie, we'll pick up where we left off – look forward to that. Bye." Then the phone clicked off.

First Annie and her brownies, and now Melanie on the phone. There were obviously women in Jameson Carroll's life. And why wouldn't there be? He was an attractive man in a rugged kind of way, although he had no obvious vanities about himself. Not like Oliver. She somehow couldn't imagine Jameson Carroll checking and double-checking his reflection in a mirror before going out. He looked like the kind of man who just pulled a T-shirt or sweater on in the morning without even glancing at himself.

Then, Cara shocked herself by wondering what he looked like without his T-shirt on.

He came back into the kitchen now. "Sorry about that," he said, and Cara felt herself blushing as if he could read her thoughts.

* * *

After thoroughly discussing Thomas's swimming awards again, Cara was taken on a guided tour of the house by the boy. "My room," Thomas told her, with a serious nod, "very, very special."

"As long," Jameson said wryly, "as it's very tidy."

As they moved from one room to another downstairs, Cara was completely taken by the paintings and objects displayed in all the rooms. Some of the things that were in frames she couldn't identify, as they were abstract shapes or pieces of material. Cara wished she had the nerve to have asked Jameson Carroll what they were, and where they had come from.

Maybe, she thought, if she came again she might eventually feel comfortable enough to ask.

She smiled when Thomas showed her into the bathroom, and she saw it had the same artistic treatment, with pieces of painted driftwood on the window-ledge and baskets with painted pebbles and stones.

When they moved upstairs to the bedrooms, the washed wood furniture was in evidence again. And the hallway had a display of some kind of needlework which looked like small, detailed crochet work. And yet it was not a kind of needlework she had ever seen in Ireland. The pieces were some sort of samples. Some looked like collars, or maybe the facing of a pocket – each piece in its own individul frame, painted or washed to complement the tone of the craftwork.

Each of the four bedrooms Thomas led her through had the wood washed in a different shade to co-ordinate with the curtains and bed covers. Everything took her breath away. It was all so different from the candlewick bedspreads which dominated all the bedrooms back home.

When Thomas threw open the door to reveal his own bedroom, Cara understood the look of pride on his face, for it was like entering his own private little world.

The room was a riot of primary colours from floor to ceiling – each wall adorned with a different, hand-painted mural. Cara stood open-mouthed as she took in the American baseball players on one side, every animal you could think of on another, and Disney characters on yet another.

But the scene painted above Thomas's high, wooden bed was the one that he was most proud of. It was a lake scene, complete with trees and clear blue water and there – poised and ready to dive into the water from the end of a small jetty – was an almost life-sized replica of the boy himself.

"Oh, Thomas," Cara whispered, "I have never seen anything like this in my life . . . you are such a lucky boy!"

Thomas nodded, his face suddenly earnest. "And Jameson Carroll – my dad – he's a very clever man. He painted . . ." His arms moved expansively around the colourful room, "he painted all of this – for me!"

"Your dad?" Cara said in a low voice "Your *dad* painted all this?"

Thomas's head bobbed up and down again. "Sure," he confirmed, his arms folded high over his proud chest.

Then, as she stared at all the intricate work on the walls, Cara had a sinking feeling in her stomach. A feeling that told her that she was out of her depth in this house. She suddenly dreaded the thought of going downstairs to try and make conversation with this talented man, who now seemed more of a stranger to her than ever.

The difficult moment was postponed as Thomas gestured Cara to follow him to the room next to his. Immediately she crossed the threshold, the dark, heavy furniture told her that she was in Jameson Carroll's bedroom. It could only be his room. The old, highly polished furniture spoke loudly of its owner. Cara stopped dead in her tracks – unwilling to move any further into the man's private retreat.

But just as she turned away, her eyes glimpsed the huge, Old-Colonial style bed that dominated the room. It had a headpost which almost reached the ceiling, and both that and the bed were draped in patchwork material in dark, masculine shades.

As she turned away from the bed, a small painting in a very old, gilt frame stopped her dead in her tracks. It was a picture of a naked woman. A woman with the classic, voluptuous figure adored by artists – worked in hazy greys and blacks, and discreetly captured in a sideways pose. Cara felt the blood rush to her cheeks. She wondered if Jameson Carroll had painted the nude. If he had – he must have spent hours working on this.

Hours in a room with a naked woman posing for the painting.

And he must have felt strongly enough about her to hang it in his room.

She shook her head in amazement, because there was no way she would have seen something like this in Ireland. Maybe in the art gallery in Dublin, but definitely not hanging in someone's house.

Then, she almost laughed, imagining their parish priest's face if he walked into a house and saw this painting hanging on a wall. Come to think of it – she could imagine her mother's face if she saw it. Maggie's artistic leanings were more towards holy statues and pictures of the Pope and John F Kennedy.

As she turned out of the bedroom, an identical small

frame by the doorway caught her eye, but the painting this time was merely the head and shoulders of a woman. The same woman in the nude painting. Cara inspected it closer this time, and noticed that both the frame and the painting were possibly quite old. Maybe Thomas's father wasn't the artist after all. But whoever had painted it, the fact remained that Jameson Carroll had no qualms about hanging a painting of a nude woman on his bedroom wall.

Whatever hesitations she had about going back downstairs when she'd seen the ordinary paintings, Cara now felt even more intimidated. This Jameson Carroll was definitely no run-of-the-mill character. He was probably a well-known artist – and everything about the house told her that he was obviously a very wealthy man.

Then, as she and Thomas started down the stairs, he was there standing at the bottom, staring up at her. "Tell me about Ireland," he said casually, turning back down to the kitchen. "My grandfolks came from there."

"Did they?" she said, surprised. She paused. "I suppose Carroll is a fairly well-known Irish name – but it never dawned on me. When I hear the American accents, I just imagine people are simply American."

He laughed now, showing even white teeth. Casual and very relaxed. Cara could see that he was a man who could be very easy with women. There was a confidence about him that made her think there was little that would shake him.

"There are very few Americans who are just American," he said. "We're all in a kind of melting-pot over here."

He poured them more coffee, and then sat opposite her, his elbows resting on the table. "So what's it like – this little country of yours?"

Cara thought for a moment, her hands cupping the mug. "It's nice," she said. "Very different from America . . . but it's nice in a plain and simple sort of way."

He leaned forward. *"Nice,"* he said, his eyes sparkling with laughter, "tells me precisely nothing. Is it possible to elaborate a little further in the interests of promoting your country?"

Cara dropped her head and started laughing, too. "I suppose I'm not a very good advert, am I?"

"Go on," he urged, his dark eyes watching her closely. "Ireland looks real good on television . . . I've always had a yearning to visit it some day. See where my folks came from." He took a sip of his coffee. "I should do it sometime."

As they chatted together, Cara became more and more relaxed and her self-consciousness gradually melted away. Jameson asked her lots of questions about Ireland, about the differences between living in the country and living in Dublin. And Cara found herself telling him all about her life growing up in Tullamore, all about her brother and sister and the shop, and things like how her father had taught them all to swim in the lakes in Mullingar.

Jameson Carroll sat back, watching her and listening to every word. "It sounds beautiful – simple and unspoiled," he told her. "You've made up my mind – I'm definitely going to visit Ireland sometime soon."

They moved on then to the subject of schools and education, but at the back of her mind, Cara knew that she really wanted to know more about Jameson Carroll. There were a hundred questions she would have liked to ask him, if only she had the nerve.

"The special education out here must be good, judging by Thomas," she said now. "What sort of school does he attend?"

Jameson explained that he attended a special school about twenty miles away. "It's expensive by regular school standards," he said shrugging, "but worth every cent. The school's very progressive in its methods – and really brings the best out in each individual kid."

Then, the subject crept back to the house and the lake. "It is so beautiful," Cara said. "It must be wonderful waking up every morning, and looking out at that view." Then, just as the words left her lips, an image of Jameson Carroll waking up in his huge, dark bed suddenly crept into her mind.

"Yeah," he said casually, "it's a real nice place. I fell in love with it the first time I saw it. In the last few years we've spent more and more time here. We bought it as a holiday place, but it's become more home now."

Cara wondered, if this mansion was his holiday place, what on earth his main home must look like.

Then, Thomas came rushing in. "Dad . . . Dad!" he said, out of breath. "Can we – can we go in – the boat?" He gestured to the window.

"Thomas," his father said, looking serious now, "you know I've set my stuff up downstairs – and I should be getting on with that . . ."

Thomas gave him a big smile, and joined his hands together. "Please, Mr Carroll –Dad – Jameson . . ."

"Good try, buddy," Jameson told him, "but rowing a boat doesn't get the work done."

Thomas had another try. He crossed the fingers of both

hands, then closed his eyes. "Please . . . please . . . please!"

Jameson shook his head, but there was a smile on his lips. He walked over to the window. Thomas, meanwhile, held the two crossed fingers up to Cara in a silent plea.

"Okay!" Jameson said, turning round. "You've got thirty minutes – not a second longer! Is that a deal?"

"A deal! A deal!" Thomas headed for the door. "I'll get the – oars!" His footsteps faded down the hall.

Cara stood up now. "Thanks for the coffee and everything," she said, "and thanks for showing me round your beautiful home."

He looked at her now, in the same way he had looked at her yesterday. The way that made her feel all funny and young. "I kinda thought you might come for a ride in the boat with us," he said now.

"I really should head off," she said, turning away from his gaze. "I've taken up enough of your time." She halted. "I really want to thank you again for sorting things out with that man yesterday . . . " Then, she glanced up and he was still looking at her in that same, intense way.

"I'd almost forgotten about that. It seems longer than yesterday." Then he gave a really broad smile. "OK then, since you owe me one after yesterday – you're gonna have to come with us." Cara had opened her mouth to refuse again, when he said, "I'd really like you to come with us. In fact . . . that's what made me give in to Thomas. I'd really like your company on the boat."

Cara held her breath for a second. "OK," she said, smiling. "I'd love to."

"Good," he said, guiding her out into the huge, airy hallway, "because Thomas would've got round you anyway."

The teenager had obviously been well-trained in

matters to do with the boat. In a few minutes he had it all set up. He pointed out where Cara and Jameson should sit at either end. Then, everything organised, Thomas sat in the middle and started to row in a very serious manner.

The lake was calm and empty of any swimmers or boats. As they moved out into the water, Cara saw yet another breathtaking view of the house. When she commented on this, Jameson told her that the house was the first one to be built on Lake Savannah, and the family who originally built it had also owned all the surrounding land. It had eventually been sold off and divided into lots, and now five more houses shared the beautiful lakeside hideaway.

"They were Southern folk," he told her, "and named the lake after the area they had lived in there."

"How long have you owned the house?" Cara asked, shielding her eyes from the sun.

Jameson looked back at the house now, calculating. "About ten years, I reckon. We bought it when Thomas was around five, when we realised he was good in water."

We, Cara thought . . . there was obviously a wife and a mother around at some point.

Curiosity made her bold. "And the other house you mentioned?"

"New York City. It's where my folks live."

"That must be a huge difference," she said. "So busy compared to here."

He nodded. "Yeah," he said solemnly, "it sure is a busy place."

After a while, Jameson noticed Thomas flagging and cajoled him into taking a break. Then he took over. Effortlessly he moved the oars and the boat glided over the glass-like blue lake. Thomas knelt up at the back of the boat, dragging a piece of rope in the ripples.

Cara sat back, letting her hand trail in the cool water. Her eyes followed the path of the boat, taking in all the tall trees and foliage as they went along. The layout and colours of each garden were completely different, and yet they all blended naturally where they met around the communal lakeside path.

As they sailed towards Jean's garden, Cara felt relieved that there was no one around to see her in the boat. She wasn't sure why she felt like that, because all they would probably do was wave and good-naturedly call out to them. But Cara was enjoying the peace and the scenery . . . and the different company of Thomas and his father. And she didn't want anything to disturb it.

As the boat gently turned back towards the house, she caught herself thinking of her own house back in Ireland. When she and Oliver had first got married she was so proud of it. She had worked alongside him, painting and decorating, sewing and hanging curtains, planting and then tending her garden.

She had repeated the process almost every year since. Every one of the seven long years.

She looked downwards now, into the deep, blue water and concentrated on the ever-widening circles made by the oars. So practised was she at blocking out thoughts of Oliver and home, that she was surprised when she looked up and they were on the last few lengths of the way back to Carroll's house.

"You, OK?" Jameson asked in a quiet voice.

Cara looked up and found his eyes gazing straight into hers. "I'm grand," she said quickly. "I was just day-dreaming . . ." She turned away, blushing to the roots of her hair, and when she stole a glance at him again, he was still staring.

She looked past him now, to the opposite end of the boat, where Thomas was still having fun with the piece of rope. Glad of the diversion, she reached her hand out to tip at Jameson Carroll's leg to make him look at his son. He turned for a few moments and then looked back at her, smiling. "Moments like this," he said, "are worth more than gold . . . I just wish they came along more often."

Cara nodded shyly and said nothing. There was so little she knew about this American artist – and so much she would like to know. Instead, she looked back into the depths of the water. Life was a lot less complicated down there.

When they reached the house, Thomas carefully stepped out of the boat, and in a gentlemanly fashion reached for Cara's hand to guide her to safety. He then made a joke of repeating the gesture to his father, and the three of them laughed.

"I'll put the boat away," he told his father. "You – show Cara paintings – downstairs."

"Woah, now fella," Jameson said, a frown crossing his features, "another time maybe – Cara has other things to do."

Having won most of the battles of the day, Thomas smiled and said, "Okay, Mr Carroll – you big boss!"

Cara laughed, enjoying the good-natured banter between father and son. "Thank you both for the lovely afternoon," she said warmly. "I think it's time for me to head back to Jean's and see what the plans are for the rest of the day – and let you get on with your work."

Without saying anything, Jameson Carroll walked

with her down the driveway of the white house until it met with the lake path. They halted for a few seconds.

"You'll come back again, won't you?" he asked, his eyes searching her face.

Cara looked back at him. "Yes," she said quietly. "I'd like that."

* * *

Later that afternoon when Maggie and Declan were off for a walk with Bruce, Cara gently probed Jean about Jameson Carroll while they were sitting on the deck together.

"I don't know too much about him, honey," she told Cara. "As you can probably tell already from your own experiences with him, he's very private. Apart from his art work – of which I know little – his whole life seems to revolve around Thomas."

"I find that wonderful," Cara said. "So many men would run away from the responsibility of a handicapped child. There has to be something special about a man who would dedicate his whole life to looking after his son."

"You're so right," Jean said, "and I think it's something that a woman appreciates even more than another man." She cocked her head sideways, looking thoughtful. "You definitely seem to have made an impression on Jameson. I don't know too many people who've been sailing around the lake with him." Then, a twinkle came in her eye. "I shouldn't be at all surprised if he asks you down to see his etchings soon."

"I don't think so," Cara said, her blonde hair swinging from side to side. "Thomas suggested he show me them this morning and –" Then she saw her aunt's shoulders shaking with laughter. "Oh – very funny! I get it now . . ."

She rolled her eyes in amusement. "Going to see his *etchings* . . ."

"Well, honey," Jean said, clapping a hand on her shoulder, "I'm over sixty years of age, and I would sure love to see his etchings!"

Cara laughed heartily. Then for the next few minutes, every time aunt and niece caught each other's eye, they went off in another fit of laughter.

Eventually Cara became serious enough to ask. "How old do you think he is?"

Jean shrugged. "I don't know, honey . . . maybe fortyish. Sometimes it's hard to tell with men . . ." She looked at Cara now. "Does he seem much older than Oliver?"

Cara turned her head away, looking off in the direction of the lake. *Oliver.* Her throat had suddenly tightened at the mention of him. "Yes," she said in a slightly hoarse voice. "I suppose he does seem a bit older than . . . Oliver."

Jean's eyes narrowed thoughtfully. Once again she noticed how silent and strained Cara became when her husband's name was mentioned.

* * *

The Harper household became a hive of activity that afternoon as preparations for the wedding gathered momentum. Bedrooms were aired and beds changed, and large dishes of salads and cold meats and fish prepared for the guests. The bride – Jean's daughter, Sandra – was arriving later in the evening with her husband-to-be Simon. They were travelling down from Boston where they lived and worked.

Most of the wedding arrangements had been sorted out months ago. The bridesmaid's outfits and the beautiful long, white wedding dress now hung in Sandra's old bedroom in her parents' house.

"I can't believe how casual they are about the whole affair," Maggie commented as she and Cara went outside to pick flowers for the table. "You'd think it was just an ordinary party the easy way they're all going on."

"I think that's nice," Cara said. "It means that people are more relaxed. It would be really uncomfortable for us if they were all worked up, and rushing about all over the place." She bent down to pick some lovely pink and white flowers, then held them to her nose, breathing in their spicy perfume. "We're so lucky being here for the wedding. The weather's beautiful, the house is lovely – and the garden and lake, just out of this world."

"True," Maggie said, her face lightening up a bit. "We're definitely having a nice break away." She paused. "D'you know, Cara – I can't remember the last time I picked flowers. I'm sure it must have been when I was a young girl, picking the poppies and primroses out in the ditches, and bringing them in jamjars in to my mother."

Cara smiled. "You don't have the time for things like that, Mammy, with the shop and everything."

Maggie looked thoughtful for a moment, then she gave a little sigh and moved on to an orange and creamy flowering rosebush. She carefully snipped a long-stemmed rose and adding it to the pile in the basket. "These roses are full of thorns. I'm sure ours haven't that many thorns at home."

"There's plenty of thorns on the rosebushes in our garden," Cara said, "especially the ones around the door."

Maggie snipped a few more flowers, then she suddenly turned to Cara. "Do you know that Jean's not wearing a hat to the wedding?" She took a large thorn off one of the roses. "Did you ever hear the like? Mother of the Bride and not wearing a hat!"

"It's up to her," Cara said, giving a little shrug. "I don't think things like that matter so much out here. Anyway, she said the hairdresser was going to put some flowers in her hair."

Maggie gave a deep sigh. "The thing is," she said looking agitated, "where does that leave me?"

Cara stared at her mother. "What do you mean?"

"What about my hat?" Maggie said urgently.

"What about your hat?"

"It cost me a fortune from Dublin," she stated, "and now I'm going to look over-dressed if nobody else bothers to wear one."

"Mammy," Cara said, putting her arm around her mother's shoulder, "wear your hat if it makes you happy. I bet everybody will tell you how lovely it looks."

"It's not always a case of being happy, Cara," Maggie told her now. "Sometimes it's a case of doing the right thing."

"Well," Cara said, looking towards the white house at the other side of the lake, "we spend all of our lives in Ireland worrying about doing the right thing. We're in America now – where nobody minds what we do. So, for the time being we can do what we really want to do."

There was a pause.

Maggie plucked yet another thorn from a perfectly formed rose. "I'll wear the hat so," she suddenly declared, "and if anyone doesn't like it – be damned to them!"

Chapter 9

Tullamore, County Offaly

"Right, Peenie," Charles Kearney said, shrugging off his brown shop overall, "you can take over while I have a bite to eat." He motioned to the front door of the shop. "It looks as though it could rain. Make sure you bring in the potato sacks and the boxes of carrots if it starts . . ." He suddenly halted, looking at the shocked look on Peenie's face. The shop assistant wasn't used to taking orders from Charles.

"My mother says we have to keep things ticking over just the same," Charles explained.

"Ah . . . yer *mother*. Sound as a pound, Charles," Peenie Walshe said, coming round from the back of the counter to have a look out at the weather for himself. He pushed his check cap high up on his head, and gave his thick mop of sandy-coloured hair a good scratch. "An' tell that oul' Kelly one to keep a bite of dinner for me when you're up there."

Charles looked at him. "You'll be lucky to get any dinner," he said, his eyes glinting behind his tortoiseshell spectacle frames. "Mrs Kelly ran you down the stairs the last day for complaining about her gravy."

100

"Never mind Mrs Kelly," Peenie grinned, folding his arms and leaning on the open shop door – a perfect vantage point to view anyone moving up or down the street. "Just run up them stairs and tell her to make sure the potatoes are nice and floury for me. Tell her you're the boss since yer mother went off – winging her way to Ameri-cay – an' what you say goes."

Charles shook his head and gave a lopsided smile. "You're some boyo, Peenie . . . I wouldn't like to be you if Mrs Kelly heard what you were saying."

Peenie laughed heartily, dragging in a sack of spuds now that the rain was starting. "Mrs Kelly's nothin' but an oul' crow," he said, "an' it gives me the greatest of pleasure to torment her."

"Don't think," Charles said, "that you're going to be taking advantage, just because my mother and father's away." He raised his eyebrows, and looked over the top of his specs at the skittish hired help. It was only for the fact that Peenie was as strong as an ox and could lift the heavy things that neither Charles or his father would attempt, that his mother put up with him.

"Now, Charlie-boy," said Peenie, winking, "would I do that?" He heaved the potato sack behind the door, then went to get the other one that was propped up, holding the door open.

"You," Charles said, "would chance anything." He turned towards the back of the shop in his slow, measured way, his shoulders stooped way beyond his years.

"Tell, me Charles," Peenie said, in a low voice, dropping the second sack "did you decide to pay Mrs Lynch another visit yet?"

Charles shook his head, and turned back. "You're a

mind-reader," he said, coming back to lean on the counter. He looked at his employee and erstwhile confidant. Not having any friends as such, Charles found himself seeking the advice of Peenie, who professed to be wise in the ways of women. "I was actually thinking of paying her a visit this evening . . ."

"Good man, yerself!" said Peenie. "I'm impressed with you now." The bit of sport with Charles livened up an otherwise dull afternoon. He gave a low whistle. "She's a fine bit of stuff . . ." Peenie thought nothing of the kind, but he knew that the line of chat would keep Charles's mind off the more boring and arduous tasks that were to be done around the shop. The seamstress was far too stodgy and heavy in the legs for Peenie's taste.

"Here! None of that coarse kind of talk." Charles pointed a warning finger, affecting the manner his father might take with the employee. "I'm only taking over a few things to be mended. I've only just got chatting to her . . . it's early days yet." He stood, waiting for the shop-assistant's next comment or word of advice.

Peenie sauntered outside and lifted the three boxes of carrots, one on top of the other, and carried them all inside. Then, he placed the boxes on one of the vegetable-racks. "If you want my opinion," he started off again, "you won't waste any time. For feck's sake, Charles – you're over thirty years of age."

"You're not far off it yourself," Charles retorted, shoving his specs high up on his nose.

Peenie shook his head. "Big difference, Charlie-boy," he grinned, taking a half-smoked Woodbine from behind his ear. "You see, I've been all over. I've worked in Dublin, Cork and London." He struck a match on the wooden counter and lit the cigarette. Something he wouldn't have dared to do, if the real bosses had been around. "*And*," he said raising his eyebrows, "I've had women every place I've been. Sure, those English women are mad for it. You should go over there yerself some time. You wouldn't be so slow over there, I can tell you."

Charles folded his arms. "Sure, I'm in no rush about anything."

"And *that*," Peenie said, "is precisely the problem." He shook his head. "Mark my words – if you don't make a move with Mrs Lynch, she won't be a widow much longer. You'll miss the boat, and some other lad will get in there."

Charles cupped his chin in his hands thoughtfully. "I'll be taking a run out later . . ." he said, "and I'll see how the land lies then."

"And remember," Peenie warned, "don't start talkin' a load of oul' shite about books or anythin' of that nature!" He shook his head solemnly. "There's no warm-blooded woman that wants to spend her time discussing dusty oul' library books – especially the kind that you're always carting around."

Charles stretched his rounded shoulders up to their proper height, and puffed his chest out. "Now, Peenie," he said, smiling in a mildly patronising way, "don't forget that I met up with Mrs Lynch in the library in Tullamore, and she had a pile of books in her shopping bag. That's *exactly* what made me feel that we might be kindred spirits."

"*Kindred spirits*?" said Peenie, looking baffled. "What's religion got to do with it? You either fancy her or you don't!"

Charles lifted his glasses up on to his forehead now, and rubbed at his eyes. "I don't mean to insult you, Peenie . . . but matters of an intellectual nature are something that *you* would know nothing about."

"And women, Charlie-boy," said Peenie, giving an equally patronising smile, "are something that a brainy fella like you would know nothing about!"

Heavy footsteps sounded towards the door. "Shockin' weather, isn't it?" Mrs Gilroy, a daily customer, said. "And isn't it well for yer mother, Charles – off out to the sun in America?"

"It's well for them indeed," he said vaguely, turning towards the back of the shop.

"It was just Cara that went along with them, wasn't it?" Mrs Gilroy checked, running a hand over her headscarf to see how wet it was. "Pauline and the little one didn't go – sure they didn't?"

"I'll leave you to it, Peenie," Charles said, not even hearing the woman's question. He fixed his glasses back on his nose, then wandered off out the back.

"Isn't that fella shockin'?" Mrs Gilroy said to Peenie, shaking her head and clucking her tongue. "The Kearneys are lucky they have you here. What would they be thinkin' of – leavin' that *amadán* in charge? Sure, he hardly knows what day of the week it is, never mind askin' him the price of anythin'." She lifted up a fair-sized cabbage and scrutinised it closely. Then she handed it across the counter to Peenie. "An' you wouldn't want to be dependin' on *him* weighin' anything out for you. The Lord help us and save us! You could be there all day while he cuts a bit off a piece of cheese, then has to add another bit on because it's too small."

"That's brains and education for yeh," Peenie said

philosophically, wrapping the cabbage in a piece of the *Irish Independent*. Then, he suddenly paused. "But havin' said that, poor oul' Charles is the finest. He's a decent fella, and fair to work for."

"True for you," Mrs Gilroy said. "He's about the best of the bunch in here, anyway." She lifted up a turnip now. "Although Pauline's nice enough." She inspected the turnip carefully. "And isn't that little Bernadette one only like an angel?"

"Oh, she's an angel right enough," Peenie said, ripping a page of the newspaper in half this time, for the turnip. "Although, she has her moments, the same girl." He winked knowingly now at Mrs Gilroy. "The minute she gets her eye on me, she's over like a shot, looking for a sweet or a bit of chocolate. But sure, yeh couldn't refuse her – she's the loveliest-natured little thing."

Mrs Gilroy handed over half-a-crown. "The cratur'," she said, smiling. "You'd wonder who she takes after now . . . wouldn't you?"

Peenie sorted out the change, then handed over the two newspaper parcels to his customer. "Oh, yeh needn't look far. She's the spit of her mother," he said lightly, "the very spit."

The older woman put the vegetables into her shopping bag, the handles of which were well-reinforced by thick twine. "She might as well be," she said, nodding her head gravely, "for we're never likely to see what her father looks like." She pulled the zip across the top of the bag. "An Englishman, no doubt . . . although there's some say she could have been that way when she was leavin' here."

"Now, Mrs Gilroy," Peenie said, "you know as well as me, that there's some that'll say anythin'." He came out towards the door, checking on the rain again. "As far as I'm concerned, that's all Pauline's business – and nobody else's." He held a hand out, checking how heavy the drops of rain were. "If people would mind their own business, they'd have no time to be talkin' about anybody else."

"An' you're right there, Peenie, so you are," Mrs Gilroy said, dropping her shopping bag to put her umbrella up again. "If they were half as good at cleanin' their houses, as they are at runnin' other folk down, they'd be far better off." She lifted the bag up now.

"You have it in one, Mrs Gilroy," he called, as she hurried off down the street, head and umbrella bent against the rain. "See yeh now!" He added to himself: "Yeh nosey oul' bitch!"

* * *

"I'll be ready for the dinner in five minutes, Mrs Kelly," Charles called, as he by-passed the kitchen and headed down the hallway to his bedroom. He closed the door carefully, then made straight for the highly-polished mahogany wardrobe on the back wall. He swung the door wide open, and then reached in for his good navy blazer. He lifted it onto the bed – hanger and all – and then reached in for his tweed jacket with the leather patches on the elbow. That joined the blazer on the bed.

He pushed the remaining hangers along, searching – until he spotted his dark suit trousers. He lifted them down, and inspected the length. *They would surely look all right with an inch off them*, he thought to himself. *Sure, what was an inch? Hardly anything.* He took them off the hanger, and measured them down the side of his right leg. *Would an inch make that awful difference*, he wondered again. He

106

would hate to ruin his good suit altogether.

Maybe, he thought, *the trousers will wait until the next visit. No point in taking everything over to her at one go . . . better to spread them out over a couple of weeks.* Charles hung the trousers back up in the wardrobe, and rubbed his hands together. *A couple of weeks? Sure, 'twould be the best part of a month before they were back!* All that time to do what he liked – go where he liked – without answering to anyone.

Then, he turned back to examine the blazer. There were a few stitches loose on the top of one of the pockets. He lifted it up, inspected the pocket closely. Then, with an unusually quick movement, he ripped the stitching halfway down the pocket. "That'll do fine," he whispered to himself. "She'll never know I didn't catch it on a door handle." Then, he went to the tallboy in the corner of the room, and lifted a pair of nail-scissors. It was the turn of the tweed jacket this time. Very carefully now, he cut the stitches holding one of the elbow-patches in place, then he did the same to the other.

He had a spare pair of patches – still in the cellophane – in his underwear drawer that he would take out to Mrs Lynch along with the jackets. That would keep her busy, and then he would have the excuse of going out to pick them up on yet another occasion.

All good, valid reasons to drive out to her house by the canal in Tullamore. Between that, and driving out some evenings when it was dark, to watch her house from his car – he would see plenty of her over the next few weeks.

Charles gleefully rubbed his hands together now at the thought of it all. Then, whistling, he headed down the hallway to the delights of Mrs Kelly's cooking.

Chapter 10

Charles gave a loud sigh, then he started the engine up, his eyes still glued to Mrs Lynch's house. It was getting dark now, and there was no point in hanging around. He had been out and about for the best part of two hours picking up vegetables and eggs from two farms, and delivering several boxes of groceries to customers who were housebound.

He had borrowed his father's car with the comfortable leather seats. His own little van with the two cramped front seats didn't compare with this two-year-old Morris Oxford, although it was obviously more suitable for throwing the vegetables and the like in the back. Charles would have to give the boot a good clean before his father came back, to remove any onion skins or other evidence that would give away the fact it had been used for the deliveries. But even if he found out, it was worth the row it would cause to have had the luxury of the car while his father was away.

En route back home, Charles had spun round past Mrs

Lynch's house on the off-chance that she might be out working in the garden or maybe out chatting to a neighbour. If he had seen her, he had planned to stop for a few words, explaining that he was just passing by after doing his deliveries. He could imagine her coming over to admire the shiny Morris Oxford, and maybe him even offering to take her a spin around the town in it.

But unfortunately, there had been no sign of the seamstress, and he was afraid to hang about too long in case she got the impression he was spying on her. Although he was keen to see and chat to her, he didn't want to frighten her in any way.

Thank goodness at least for the last time, when he'd driven out in the van to drop off the blazer and the tweed jacket with the missing elbow patches. A little smile came to his lips as he remembered the look on Mrs Lynch's face when he handed her the box of *Quality Street*. Absolute shock wasn't in it!

She had stepped back, clutching the parcel with the two jackets in it.

As he smiled down at her, Charles had noticed how lovely and shiny her hair was. He wondered if she rinsed it in beer the way Pauline occasionally did when washing her hair at home. How his sister's hair didn't smell like a brewery, he often wondered.

"No . . . no," Mrs Lynch said, blushing furiously. "I can't take chocolates off you."

"Just to say thanks for all your hard work," Charles had said – in something like the manner he imagined that Jay Gatsby might. He gave a low sweep of his hand towards the hallway. "I'm sure Dominic might like a few chocolates . . ."

Mrs Lynch suddenly stopped. "How did you know his name?"

"You mentioned it last time," Charles said with a grin. "I've got a great memory for names."

There was a silence during which Charles considered throwing Peenie's advice to the wind regarding the books. He was just on the point of asking her what sort of books she preferred, when, much to Charles's delight, her hand had come out and taken the box of chocolates – just as he was imagining himself placing them back on the shop shelf in the shop. Second row from the top – next to the fancy biscuits. Luckily, he hadn't entered them into the till – so no alterations would be necessary there.

"You shouldn't have," Mrs Lynch said, looking shyly down towards the linoleum. "Aren't you paying me for the sewing . . ."

Charles stepped back, and pushed his sliding glasses back up on the bridge of his nose. "Just a little gesture," he said. "It can't be easy bringing up a child on your own." His fist came up to his mouth now, and he cleared his throat in a loud, nervous fashion. "I have a sister at home in a similar position . . . bringing up a child on her own."

Mrs Lynch's face flushed. "I know about your sister," she said quietly, "but I think there's a difference . . ."

Charles sort of swung away to the side, his eyes no longer meeting hers. "Of course . . . of course," he said. "I just meant that . . . it can't be easy." This was not going the way that he had imagined. What on earth had made him mention her widowed situation? And his mother would absolutely kill him if she knew he had purposely brought up the subject of Pauline's plight as an unmarried mother.

He stepped backwards now, his trousers catching on

the thorns of a small rose bush. "Thanks, now . . ." he said, his voice trailing off as he unhooked himself from the bush.

Then, just as he was ready to go about his business, Mrs Lynch suddenly smiled. "Thanks for the chocolates, Mr Kearney," she said, "but really – there was no need. I'll have your jackets ready by tomorrow evening, if you'd like to call back around six o'clock."

"Charles," he reminded her, with another little cough. "You can call me Charles. No need for formalities. And I'll be seeing you around six tomorrow evening."

But Charles had found it very hard to wait until then. Some hours later, after his business was finished, he had swung the car around in the widowed seamstress's direction, and parked for a while further along the road where she lived.

There were about ten houses, all in a row, in a street just up from the Grand Canal. Mrs Lynch was the only widow in the street, the rest being all families or elderly couples. According to what he had heard his brother-in-law say to his mother one evening. And Oliver usually got his facts straight.

Oliver had recommended Mrs Lynch to the Kearneys when Maggie needed someone to alter the dress she had bought for the wedding in America. He had told her that this young, but mature, widow-woman had been doing alterations for customers of the shop for the last two years.

And it just so happened that Charles was sent out to Mrs Lynch's with the instructions that she had to take exactly an inch and a half off the bottom of the skirt. And an inch and a half was all she took off it. Unlike the lady in Ballygrace who had left a brand-new summer dress unwearable last year. Three inches she had cut off the expensive dress, completely ruining it and leaving Maggie without a new outfit for the Church summer dance. And leaving the Ballygrace seamstress without a name. For none of the customers in the shop would ever go near her again, by the time that Maggie Kearney had finished giving out about her ham-fisted sewing.

Mrs Lynch was now given any work that was needed doing by the Kearney family, and had also gained an admirer in Charles. Although Charles wasn't exactly sure what the attraction actually was. Up until he had met the widow, he had never had any great interest in women as such. They were an unknown quantity to him. Even his sisters. And especially his mother.

In fact, there were times when Charles found it hard to be interested in people in general. There were very few around who could hold an intelligent conversation. Apart from discussing the necessities of life – such as the business of the shop or what he would like to have for dinner – there was little else he found worth discussing with them. Charles found the facts or the characters in his books far more interesting – and far safer and more predictable than people in the flesh.

But there was something about Mrs Lynch that had struck a chord with him. Something he couldn't quite put his finger on. Something that had added a new dimension to his life. The possibility that he could perhaps sit on the opposite side of the fire with another person and discuss topics such as whether Atlantis really existed or maybe how the pyramids came to be, without the benefit of modern construction methods. Or maybe even divulge to the widow his dreams of writing his own book some day. Fact or fiction? He hadn't worked that one out yet. The possibilities were endless.

Charles would have time in the morning to discuss it all with Peenie Walshe. Bring him up to date, as it were, and seek his opinion on how he thought it was all going. He smiled now, thinking of Peenie's reaction when he told him how Mrs Lynch had accepted the Quality Street.

That had been one of the shop assistant's inspired ideas. Peenie had told him that women were easily got round where chocolates were concerned. It never failed to work. And in this case, Peenie had been spot-on.

Charles turned the key in the engine and smiled to himself. What with all this coming and going – his life was unusually hectic at the minute. Thank God his mother wasn't around. She would soon have put a stop to it.

Then – just as he turned his head to check there was nothing behind him – a great bang reverberated on the bonnet of the car! The bonnet of his *father's* car. The car he shouldn't be driving at this hour of the night.

Charles jerked his head forward, and found himself staring face to face with the wildest-looking man he had ever seen at close range. The man was leaning across the bonnet, banging and shouting in a deranged manner. He was so angry he could almost have been described as frothing at the mouth! Like the dogs in *The Hound of the Baskervilles.*

Instinctively, Charles hauled the gear-stick into reverse, and put his foot down hard on the accelerator. The car started to move backwards away from the madman.

But the madman clung on to either side of the bonnet.

Charles put the boot down further on the accelerator until the man eventually lost his grip on the slippery, shiny car bonnet and came to a half-running, half-staggering halt.

Wide-eyed with shock, Charles did a wide reverse swerve and then, shooting forward, took off up the little street with more speed than he knew the car was capable of.

"Jesus, Mary and Joseph!" he called out loud, having noticed the madman now running behind the car in his rear-view mirror.

This was like something out of an action film. A *James Bond* or something like that. What on earth was happening? And in Tullamore of all places!

Charles swerved around a corner, and in a few moments was heading out of the town. Out towards the blessed safety of the shop and home – and all the double-locks and bolts he could find to protect himself.

Chapter 11

"I'm still waiting for an answer, Charles," Pauline
Kearney said, her hands on her neat hips, clad in the new
green slacks that her mother would not approve of – even
for working in the shop. The tight slacks were actually a
bit too good for the shop, Pauline thought herself, but you
never knew who might call in unexpectedly.

Charles continued to scrub at the bonnet of his father's
car, counting the swishes of the cloth as it moved
backwards and forwards over the top.

"Where did you go last night?" Pauline repeated, her
voice on a higher note. "And why did you take Daddy's
car instead of the van?" Her older brother was infuriating.
Trying to get information out of him was like trying to get
blood out of a stone. She'd tackled him last night when he
came in looking white-faced and drained, but after a few
heated words, he'd stomped off to bed. Pauline was
determined that come what may she was going to get the
answer out of him this morning.

Charles, slightly out of breath now, came to a sudden

halt. He stood back, checking if the dull mark on the bonnet had diminished any. *Yes*, he thought, *it all looked the same now. Shiny all over. God knows what that fellow had on the knees of his trousers last night, that would have left such a streak on the bonnet.*

"Charles!" Pauline hissed, grabbing him by the shoulder of his brown overall. "Where the hell did you go last night?"

Charles pulled out of his sister's grip and stepped back to a safe distance, jiggling the cloth about between both hands. "I was doing the deliveries," he snapped, looking down at the ground.

"Why did you take Daddy's car instead of the van?" she demanded. "And what took you so long? You weren't doing deliveries for that length of time."

"I took the car for a bit of a run . . . to keep the engine ticking over."

"A bit of a run?" Pauline said, her eyes narrowed in disbelief. "Since when have you taken to going for runs in the evenings after work?"

Charles moved to the far side of the car – to a safer distance from his sister. "The engine's making a funny noise," he explained, "and my father says I have to give it a few good long runs to clear the petrol tank." Charles knew nothing about the workings of cars, but he was cute enough to know that his sister knew even less and couldn't argue with him.

"You *promised* that you would mind Bernadette for me," she said, her voice dropping now that she had noticed an elderly man – a regular customer – pushing a bike up the street towards them. "I was left sitting in all night like a feckin' eejit because of you."

116

"Less of the language," Charles admonished, folding the cloth into a smooth pad. "You wouldn't be so smart in coming out with stuff like that if my mother was around. And I know what she'd have to say about that get-up you're wearing as well."

"And it's just as well for you that she's not around," Pauline hissed. "Out for hours, and not saying where you've been."

"Grand day!" the old fellow called, leaning his bicycle on the wall of the shop.

They both turned to call a cheery greeting back, and remark on the reasonable day that it was.

He came forward to Charles. "Did you get any of them soft biscuits that the head-woman likes in yet?"

Charles lay the cloth down on the car bonnet, and held his glasses on the bridge of his nose while he thought. His eyes suddenly brightened. "Tell Peenie he'll find them on the middle shelf on the back wall."

"Grand, grand," the old man said, taking his flat cap off. "She has me tormented since she got the teeth out. All she can eat is oul' mushy stuff at the minute, and they're the only biscuits that don't break up in the tea."

Pauline turned away now, trying not to laugh obviously. She pretended she was looking in the car window for something.

"Peenie will sort you out," Charles said, lifting the cloth again and re-folding it into a more perfect square.

"He will that," the man said, folding his cap and putting it in his pocket. "Peenie's the boy to sort us all out."

When the customer was safely inside, Pauline followed her brother round the side of the car – all laughter about teeth and soft biscuits forgotten. "Well?" she demanded. "What's the story? Where did you go?"

Charles moved towards the bonnet, swiping out again with the cloth to where the muddy mark had been. "I told you," he said testily. "I went for a bit of a run."

Pauline sighed and folded her arms. "Rose Quinn called for me last night, and we waited and waited and eventually I had to tell her to go on ahead without me. I felt a right eejit, sitting there all dressed up and you nowhere to be seen." She moved closer to Charles, jostling his elbow. "Rose was in a fierce huff with me and it's all your fault. Apart from the fact she'd managed to get her father's car for us, she didn't know if she'd get anyone else to go out with her at such short notice."

"Where were you supposed to be going?" Charles asked, backing out of his sister's reach.

"To a dance in Tullamore," Pauline said. "I told you yesterday afternoon."

Charles shrugged. "I don't remember you saying you were going to any dance."

"Well, you wouldn't – would you?" Pauline retorted. "You had your nose stuck in a book as usual." She surveyed him now, arms still folded. "You need to waken yourself up, Charles Kearney," she told him. "You live in another world. Nobody can depend on you for anything. I've never met a fella like you in my life."

Charles rubbed a finger over the mark, checking for any scratches he might have missed. "My mother would go haywire if she heard you were going to a dance with Rose Quinn," he said. "You know she doesn't like that family."

"Mammy's not here though – is she?" Pauline said,

waving an arm around the front of the shop. "Not that you'd notice, for all the attention you pay to anybody. We could drop dead in front of you, and you'd walk straight over us."

Charles sighed and straightened up. "Listen," he said. "I'll look after Bernadette tonight, if it's any good." It would mean missing a visit to Mrs Lynch later on to pick up the items she had mended – but that might be no harm after his encounter with that lunatic last night. Give the man a chance to sober up – or sort out whatever was going on in his deranged mind, that made him go round attacking innocent drivers. And anyway, he thought, it would be worth it to get Pauline off his back. There were times she was nearly as bad as his mother. It was a pity that it had to be Cara who went off to America. She would have been far easier to work with in the shop.

Pauline paused. "There probably won't be anybody going out tonight," she said in a disgruntled tone. She knew perfectly well that there was a dance in Mullingar tonight, and if she phoned Rose and went to great rounds apologising, then maybe they would go there instead.

"Please yourself," Charles said, wondering what Mrs Kelly had on the menu today. He checked his watch. It would be dinner-time in twenty minutes. He'd finish off the car now in a few minutes, and then he'd go in and re-arrange that shelf with packets of Bisto and Bird's Custard Powder that Peenie had stacked this morning. That fellow had no eye for keeping things in a straight line, and threw things up on the shelf in any old way at all.

"OK," Pauline said, heading into the shop. "I'll ring round and see if anybody is going out – and don't you dare forget this time!"

Chapter 12

Pauline leaned her elbows on the deep window-ledge in her upstairs bedroom, and looked out at the showery Irish weather, imagining Cara and her parents basking in the hot American sunshine.

She gave a little sigh, thinking that if things had been different how she might have been out there along with them, enjoying her aunt's luxurious house and the wonderful weather. The wedding in America was just another of the occasions that she was now no longer considered suitable for.

Then, she turned her gaze towards the cot-bed in the corner of her bedroom, where her little curly-headed daughter lay sleeping – just six foot across from her own single bed. The bed she had slept in as a young schoolgirl, in the room she had shared with Cara. The bed she thought she had left forever five years ago, when she went to England.

Her chest tightened as she looked at the sleeping child. The sight of her, as always, provoked a mixture of emotions.

Without a doubt, Bernadette was the very centre of her life. She loved and adored her. And she would strangle – with her bare hands – anyone who would harm her. But – and it was a big but – the child had now taken her life in a completely different direction from the one she had planned.

Bernadette's arrival into the world had heralded the departure of every dream that Pauline had ever had. As one came in the door, the others went straight out the window. The big white wedding for one. Oh, her mother never let her forget that dream. How, if any man was prepared to take her on, the wedding would have to be a hole-in-the-corner, two-piece-suit wedding. No white dress – symbolising virginity – for her.

Then the dream of finishing her nursing course in England was smashed into little pieces. Along with her third dream of travelling around the world. Maybe working for a few years in America or Australia. Somewhere warm and exciting. Somewhere like the place Cara was now.

Still, there was no use in whining. Pauline knew perfectly well that she was only reaping what she had let a handsome man sow. She'd taken the good times, and now she had to pay the price for it. And there was no way she'd be allowed to forget it.

She turned back to the widow. Watching for Charles in the van, or Rose Quinn's car coming down the road.

Maybe, she thought, just maybe she would meet a nice lad at the dance in Mullingar tonight. Someone who would know nothing about Bernadette. A nice, decent fellow who would fall head over heels in love with her – and by the time she told him about her illegitimate daughter, he wouldn't care. He would be so besotted with her that he wouldn't let any obstacle stand in their way.

No interfering mothers, who didn't want a fallen woman for a daughter-in-law. No interfering priests to warn him against taking on another man's child. And no disloyal friends who would slyly hint at him marrying an easy woman, then try to make a move on Pauline herself when the decent fellow wasn't around.

Pauline sighed, and looked down at her newly painted, pink fingernails.

She had seen them all: the would-be mothers-in-law, the priests who would say anything that the families with money wanted them to say – and the sly, backstabbing friends.

The sound of a car engine made her move to the side of the sash windows to see further along the street. The vehicle that came into view was neither Rose Quinn's father's car or Charles's van – but it was a familiar vehicle none the less. And one that she had mixed feelings about seeing.

The car came to a halt outside the shop, and a youngish man got out – dressed in an immaculate suit and carrying a sober black hat. But there was a jaunty air about him that left you in no doubt as to his self-confidence. Just as there was no mistaking the quality of his clothes.

Pauline moved from the window, and pulled across the pink damask curtains – that went with the pink rose wallpaper. She left a bit of a gap in the curtains, allowing enough light in the room should Bernadette wake up. The child was afraid of the dark, and the curtains were never closed completely against the orangey streetlamp that was just outside the shop.

Then Pauline tiptoed across the room and went downstairs to open the front door of the house. Charles had closed the shop door at six o'clock this evening, and now visitors had to use the main entrance to the house.

"Good evening, Miss Kearney," the smooth, Dublin voice said. "And looking as gorgeous as ever!" His eyes took in the floaty, lilac chiffon dress with the low neck and the wide belt that emphasised her small waist.

"Get away with you," Pauline said in a light, breathy voice. "Sure, you say that to every woman you meet – young and old. You needn't think you're fooling me. I'm not one of your customers." She closed the door behind him, and then they both stood in the hallway. Pauline folded her arms over her bust, attempting to cover her cleavage.

"There's a big difference," he said quietly, his eyes moving downwards from her long, slim neck. "That's only ould business chat. Any compliments I ever gave you were genuine. From the first time I ever saw you." His eyes now flitted upwards to meet hers square on. "And well you know it."

There was a small silence. Then he moved forward to place his hands on her shoulders and draw her close enough to place a light kiss on her lips.

Pauline caught her breath, and her heart quickened at the touch of his lips on hers. She pulled away – laughing to cover her embarrassment.

"You don't fool me for one minute, Oliver Gayle," she said briskly. "Now head on into the kitchen, and I'll make you a cup of tea while I'm waiting for that Charles to come back."

Oliver did as he was told, but guided Pauline to walk on down the hallway ahead of him. As she walked, she could almost feel his eyes taking in every inch of her back view and legs.

"Charles sounds as if he's in the bad books," Oliver said lightly. "What's the poor oul' divil done this time?"

"Don't 'poor oul' divil' Charles Kearney to me," Pauline sighed as they reached the end of the hall. "He has me driven mad already, and my mother and father are hardly gone out of the place. You can't depend on him being in the right place at the right time."

"You shouldn't be giving out to him so much," Oliver said, following her in the kitchen door now. "In his own way, Charles is the finest."

"You wouldn't think so if he let you down the way he did with me last night," Pauline said crossly. She looked up at the clock. "And he's cutting it fine again tonight."

"You're off out then?" Oliver said, pulling one of the old pine chairs out from under the long, heavy table. "I thought you were looking even more ravishing than usual."

"Yes, I'm going out," Pauline replied, lifting her white cardigan from the back of a chair and quickly pulling it on. She did up all the buttons up to cover her cleavage. It felt more decent than walking around in front of a man in bare arms and low neck. Especially a man like her brother-in-law. Then, she moved about the kitchen, busying herself with the kettle and the tea-caddy.

"And who's the lucky man tonight?" he said lightly.

Pauline scooped two large spoons of Lyons tea into the smaller of the two teapots that sat beside the cooker. "You must be joking," she said, turning towards the large pine dresser now. "A man's the last thing I need at the minute. And anyway – who'd give me a second glance when they know about the little angel sleeping upstairs?" She lifted down two teacups and matching saucers and a small sideplate.

She put the china down in the middle of the table, conscious of his eyes following her every move. Then, she set one cup in a saucer, and slid it over in front of Oliver. As she went to move away he caught her by the wrist. Gently – but firmly enough to halt her in her tracks.

"You shouldn't put yourself down like that, Pauline," he said softly. "How many times have I told you? People will only have the opinion of you that you have of yourself. You're worth ten of the other girls around here – and you know I mean that."

Pauline nodded her head, but kept her eyes lowered. "It's okay you saying it, Oliver," she replied, "but not everyone around here would have that same outlook."

He released his grip now.

She went back to the cooker and busied herself with pouring boiling water into the teapot.

"Don't mind what anyone around here has to say," he told her. "What you do is your own business. Sure, they'll talk anyway. If you didn't have Bernadette, they'd find something else to say."

Pauline gave the tea a good stir with the long, thin silver spoon that her mother kept next to the caddy. Then, she moved around the kitchen cupboards locating the fresh cherry and sultana cake that Mrs Kelly had baked that morning, and the fancy gold tin of biscuits that only appeared when they had special visitors.

And Oliver Gayle was a special visitor as far as she

was concerned.

He was the one man that had spoken up for her – properly spoken up for her. When she had come home from England with Bernadette, both he and Cara had made sure that she never had to go to Mass on her own or into Tullamore on her own, until she felt ready to face everyone again.

Oliver and Cara had been the first ones to go out walking with her with the baby in the pram. One at either side. Daring anyone to look sideways at her.

God, if only Oliver wasn't married to Cara, she thought now as she came back to the table to pour the scalding tea. *Anybody else but Cara.*

* * *

"I told you I'd be back in plenty of time," Charles said piously to his sister, pouring himself a cup of lukewarm tea. Then, he wandered across to the window at the sink, where he stood drinking the tea and staring out over the herd of black and white cows that lived in the field behind the house.

"Well, Charles, how's business?" Oliver asked him. "I hope you're not losing any good customers while your mother and father are away."

Charles took another drink of his tea, and continued staring at the cows and thinking about the entry he would make in his diary when he got peace and quiet this evening.

"Would you look at him," Pauline sighed. "His mind's in another world as usual."

Oliver winked and patted her hand. "Sometimes our minds are happier places than the real world."

126

Pauline felt herself start to blush again, so she got up from her chair and put the lid back on the gold biscuit tin and started to tidy up. "Charles –" she said in a sharp tone, "be sure and listen for Bernadette upstairs. Don't have the radio on too loud – or get carried away reading or anything."

Charles drained the remains of his tea, and then walked over and put the cup into the sink. "I'll be fine," he said with an edge to his voice. "If she wakens then I'll just humour her until she falls asleep again." He shrugged his rounded shoulders. "It's not exactly brain surgery, Pauline . . . is it?"

Pauline's eyebrows shot up dangerously, then – before she got her answer out – the door knocker sounded.

"I'll get it!" Pauline snapped, looking daggers in her brother's direction. He could be so damned irritating at times, and she didn't need it this evening. Her high-heeled shoes tapped quickly out of the kitchen, and down the tiled hallway.

Rose Quinn came in behind Pauline, and halted to lean up against the jamb of the door, chewing furiously on a piece of spearmint gum. She was pretty in a slightly too obvious way – which did not endear Maggie Kearney to her – and was dressed up to the nines for her night out, sporting a tight-looking outfit and her bleached blonde hair carefully curled.

"Good evening to you, Rose," Oliver said, leaning forward in his chair. He gave her one of his charming smiles, taking in her tight blouse with the pearl buttons undone to her cleavage. Rose was a bit on the skinny side for his taste – and her manner not quite classy enough. "I believe you two ladies are out on the town tonight?"

Rose folded her arms and nodded, still chewing on the gum. She could be quiet when she liked, but she was known to have a watchful eye. Saying nothing – but taking everything in. She also had an eye for the men. Even married men like Oliver Gayle.

"Oh, sure it's only a church dance," Pauline said briskly, lifting her handbag and silk scarf from the back of a chair, "nothing to get too excited about."

"And what time," Charles said suddenly, "did you say you'd be back?" He took his spectacles off now, and proceeded to rub at the glass with the carefully ironed hanky he kept in his cardigan pocket exactly for that purpose.

"I didn't," Pauline said, checking that she had everything she needed in her handbag. Compact with mirror, lipstick, money, a comb and a small bottle of Coty Le' Maint cream perfume to re-apply later in the night. They were all there. "You head off to bed whenever you like, Charles," she said, clicking the bag shut. "You needn't bother waiting up. As long as Bernadette is settled, then you needn't worry yourself about anything."

Charles nodded vaguely, his thumb working hard on a smear on the glass, and his mind wondering where he'd left his good fountain pen. Hopefully, not in the shop. He'd be lucky to see it again, if it had come anywhere near the bold Peenie. It would have been straight into his overall pocket, and kept for writing out his bets at the bookie's shop in Tullamore.

"Have you heard a word I've said, Charles?" Pauline snapped.

Charles looked up from the glasses and grinned at his sister in a superior manner. "Yes," he said. "You've just been going on about me not having to worry about anything."

"And?" she said.

"And *I'm* not worrying," Charles said, still grinning. "As far as I can see – it's you that's doing any worrying . . ."

Pauline shook her head, not trusting herself to speak.

Oliver got to his feet now. There was no point in hanging about since there would only be Charles left here to entertain him. There wasn't even Peenie around in the shop for a bit of ould banter. "Sure, I suppose I'd better head back to my cold, empty house, and see if there's a bite in to eat."

"Oh, Oliver!" Pauline said. "You should have said you hadn't eaten . . ."

"I'm only codding you," he said, laughing. "Sure, I'm off home for a wash and change – and then I'm out for dinner with some of the drama crowd." He lifted his jacket and hat.

"Anywhere we'd know?" Rose Quinn suddenly piped up from her corner at the door.

"Now that," Oliver said, winking over at Pauline, "would be telling." He lifted his soft hat from the table. "See you, Charles, and don't be letting these women give you a hard time. We men have got to stick together."

"Oh, right . . ." Charles said absently, having suddenly remembered that he'd left his fountain pen on the sitting-room mantelpiece, well out of the reach of Bernadette's inquisitive little fingers. He suddenly made a dive for the door, head down – like a bull charging at a gate. Hopefully, Pauline hadn't moved the pen when she was tidying around today. She was worse than his mother for moving things – always closing books and newspapers when he'd deliberately left them open so that he wouldn't lose his place.

Rose Quinn shifted nimbly out of his way, hoping Pauline hadn't noticed the alarm on her face. Charles was an unknown quantity where women were concerned – and she wasn't going to give him the chance to collide headlong into her. You could never tell what was going on in the minds of over-brainy fellas like Charles Kearney. Probably nothing – but you never could tell where any man was concerned.

Rose's father's car was parked nose to nose with Oliver's.

"That's a fine-looking car you're driving," Oliver said to her, walking around it. "Will you turn on the engine for a few minutes, to let me hear how it sounds?"

Rose got into the car, still chewing on her gum, pulled the door shut and turned the key in the ignition.

Pauline followed Oliver to the bonnet of the car. "Any news from Cara?" she asked, feeling guilty that she hadn't even thought to ask about her sister and parents. That Charles had annoyed her so much, plus having Oliver sitting there at the table with Rose Quinn ogling him, had knocked her off her stride.

"No," said Oliver in a low enough voice for Rose not to hear. "Not a word since she phoned to say she'd arrived." He turned his hat around in his hands. "Hopefully, the holiday will do her good . . . she's not been in good form recently. Kind of strained and tight in herself."

Pauline's face clouded over. "Oh . . ." she said lamely. She didn't want to get into an awkward conversation now, especially within earshot of Rose Quinn.

"If you hear anything about how the holiday's going," she said quietly, "drop out and let me know."

"Oh, I will," Oliver said, giving a thumbs-up to Rose. "And you do the same . . . you could get Charles to drop you over at the shop around twelve any day next week, and we could go out for a bit of lunch."

Pauline nodded, not at all sure about his suggestion.

He touched her arm lightly. "I could do with having a bit of a chat about Cara . . . and you would be the very woman to understand."

Pauline glanced up towards her bedroom window. "I'll see how things go here," she told him. "Maybe a day that Peenie and Mrs Kelly are in to keep an eye on Bernadette."

"If not, bring her with you," he suggested. "Sure, wouldn't it just make my day to have *two* of my favourite girls out on a date with me."

"We'll see," Pauline said vaguely. "I'll let you know."

"Grand," Oliver said. He turned towards his own car. "And be sure to enjoy your night out, Pauline – you deserve it."

Chapter 13

Charles pulled out a carver chair from the end of the dining-room table at the large, bay window. He opened his page-a-day diary, dampened his finger on his tongue, then flicked through until he reached the correct month and day. Then, he rested the end of his fountain pen on his bottom teeth while he mused over the right words to use.

There was disappointingly little to report.

The visit out to Mrs Lynch's this evening had been fairly straightforward. It had been a simple matter of driving over, knocking on the door, getting the jackets from Mrs Lynch, and paying her the money.

There had been very little conversation between them – just the business of the jackets, with the seamstress showing him where she'd repaired the pocket on the blazer and then showing him how well she had sewed on the elbow patches. All fairly mundane stuff. She had seemed a little strange, Charles thought. Definitely not as friendly as she had been when he had given her the Quality Street on the previous occasion. He wondered now if he should take something else when he handed the suit trousers in. Maybe a box of fancy biscuits . . . or something along those lines.

Head bent low, Charles started writing in his tiny, sharp-angled script. He wrote for over half a page, then he came to an abrupt halt. The final part of the meeting with Mrs Lynch found him stumped for words – the bit when she had asked him if he had been in the area of her house the night before. Charles hadn't known what to say to that.

He hated the thought of telling a lie. He had taken a deep breath and said that he had indeed been in the Tullamore area doing deliveries, and he might have passed by her house – but he wasn't altogether sure.

Mrs Lynch had gone strangely silent at that point. Charles suddenly wondered now if she had heard the commotion with the madman that had jumped on his father's car. But he realised that mentioning that incident would only draw attention to the fact that he had definitely been in the area.

He was still pondering over this delicate part of his diary entry when he heard a door creaking open upstairs. He went out into the hallway to find his little niece making her way down the stairs in her pink teddy-bear pyjamas that her Auntie Jean had sent from America for her third birthday.

"Mammy . . ." she said, looking around. Then, "A drink?"

"Wait there!" Charles ordered, and moved as swiftly as he could to meet her, and carry her the rest of the way down. "I'll get you a nice drink now," he told her soothingly. "Uncle Charles will get you a nice drink."

"Where Mammy?" the child asked, as they headed into the warm kitchen.

"Oh, she'll be back shortly," Charles said, sitting her down gently on a chair. "Your Uncle Charles will be minding you until she gets back."

He opened the fridge and lifted out a jug of cold milk. Then, he went over to the old pine dresser and lifted a little two-handled mug from one of the hooks. He filled the mug three-quarters of the way up and then set it down on the table in front of the child. "Now . . ." he said, opening the cupboard that had Mrs Kelly's cakes in it, along with the plainer sort of biscuits that Pauline preferred for the child, "let's see what we have here . . ."

Bernadette selected a custard cream and a digestive biscuit from the tin, then sat up nice and straight at the table like her Uncle Charles had told her to.

Half an hour later, after having read two *Brer Rabbit* and one *Noddy* story, Charles carried Bernadette back out into the hallway, preparing to mount the stairs again.

"Say goodnight to the Lady!" Bernadette said, struggling in her uncle's arms. Charles gave a loud sigh, and then turned back towards the alcove at the bottom of the stairs, within which stood a fair-sized statue of the Blessed Virgin. It was a special statue – more church size than home – that Maggie had specially ordered through a convent in Dublin.

This was one of Maggie's little rituals, when she was taking the child up to bed. She would lift Bernadette up to kiss the statue, and the child would say: *Goodnight, Our Lady, and please help to make me a good girl tomorrow.*

Charles held Bernadette up now, gripping her tightly under the arms. Then he moved her towards the head of the statue. Bernadette made loud kissing noises and then said her little piece about being a good girl tomorrow. Then, just as Charles went to hoist her away, she suddenly lunged forward, and with one bite removed the holy statue's nose.

"Mother of God!" Charles spluttered, looking at the ragged plaster that had once been the Blessed Virgin's nose. "Oh, your granny will absolutely kill you!"

But Bernadette had suddenly discovered that the enticing-looking nose did not taste as good as it looked. She was now more concerned with spitting the horrible, sour, crumbly stuff out of her mouth, than worrying about what her granny would have to say.

As he set the child down on the second stair, a cold shiver suddenly went down Charles's spine. *What if the child was poisoned? What if there was lead or something dangerous in the statue?*

He whipped her up off the stairs and flew with her in his arms into the kitchen again. "Spit it out!" he ordered her. "Spit it out!"

The child spat out what remained of the plaster, and held her tongue out to her uncle to show him. "Horrible!" she told him, grimacing and shaking her head.

"And *horrible* is exactly your granny will be when she sees what's happened to her holy statue," Charles muttered to himself as he opened the fridge to pour Bernadette another half-glass of milk. He had read somewhere that milk neutralized acids and the like. Hopefully, the innocent-looking statue didn't contain anything more sinister than plain, ordinary plaster.

* * *

Pauline Kearney held her head high, walking in the door of the church-hall behind Rose Quinn. As she passed through the gauntlet of boys and men who were lurking around the door, she looked neither left nor right. Ignoring the comments and low wolf-whistles, she kept her arms folded over her chest and her gaze firmly concentrated on the back of Rose's blonde head, until they were safely inside the dimly lit hall.

"Did you see who I saw as we were coming in?" Rose giggled, as they headed for a table up near the band. The few lagers she had had in the hotel down the road had lifted her spirits admirably well.

"Who?" Pauline said, moving around the back of the small table, where she could see all that was going on in the hall.

"*Jack Byrne*," Rose mouthed, rooting in her bag for her cigarettes and lighter. "Didn't you see him? He was just inside the door."

"Don't tell me he was with that crowd that were leering at us as we came in?" Pauline said, her brow furrowed in disapproval.

"No, indeed he wasn't," her friend said. "He was sitting at a table at the side on his own." She put the cigarettes and lighter on the table. "And he was watching you when we walked in."

"Go away with you!" Pauline said, unbuttoning her white cardigan. "Anyway," she said, "I'm not in the least bit interested in Jack Byrne." She took the cardigan off, and hung it carefully on the back of her wooden chair. What she'd said wasn't entirely the truth, but she wasn't going to let Rose know that.

It had taken Pauline some time to catch on, but

gradually she had become aware that Rose had a habit of making a play for any fellow she expressed an interest in. And she was fairly sure that Rose let them know about Bernadette much earlier than she would have liked. She hadn't any concrete proof about it, and didn't want to get into a row with Rose over it – for the Quinns were renowned for their sharp tongues. But it had made Pauline wary of saying too much in front of her friend.

The fact was that Pauline couldn't afford to lose a friend like Rose. Even with her very obvious faults, Pauline knew she had some good points. Rose was someone who didn't judge her too harshly about having an illegitimate daughter, and she was fairly reliable for going out. Plus she had the advantage of being able to drive – with her father's car often at her disposal.

And they wouldn't be over in Mullingar tonight if it hadn't been for Rose and the car.

"Lemonade or tea?" Pauline asked now, lifting her handbag.

"Oh, lemonade," Rose said. "I always feel like an ould granny drinking tea in a dancehall." She leaned across the table. "By the looks of it," she said in a low voice, "there's plenty of grannies around tonight."

Pauline laughed. "Oh, you're terrible, Rose," she said. "Sure, they're not much older than us."

Rose lit her cigarette, holding the silver lighter aloft in an elegant manner, reminiscent of a forties film star. "I'd say there's a good few of them here tonight in their thirties," she said, "which is no harm – for it makes us look ravishingly young by comparison."

"I'm going for the lemonade," Pauline giggled, "before you say something worse." And as she walked across the hall in front of the band, towards the ante-room where the refreshments were sold, Pauline gave a quick glance at the tables nearby. She didn't find that any of the girls looked much older than herself. Then it struck her that Rose might be having one of her little 'digs', because she was nearly four years older than her friend. Nearer thirty than twenty. And still single. The thought made her chest tighten, and the feeling of self-consciousness quickened her high-heeled steps towards the ante-room.

An hour later as she twirled around the room to a hearty version of *The Wild Colonial Boy*, Pauline knew that there was no problem with her age or how she had looked.

Since the band had struck up, neither she nor Rose had missed even one dance. The fellows were making a bee-line for them. Sometimes they came in pairs, and sometimes one at a time. But if one of them was asked first, it was only a matter of time until the other one joined her on the floor.

If Pauline was vain or confident enough to register it, she would have noticed that they were easily the best-looking girls in the dance hall – regardless of the fact that she was nearer to thirty than twenty.

"Will we take to the floor?"

Pauline looked up to see Jack Byrne leaning over the table – once again. She had already had a spell on the floor with him earlier on, and she hadn't expected him back quite so quickly.

"Grand," she said, giving him a little smile. She didn't look to see what sort of expression was on Rose's face. She got up on her feet, and then took his outstretched hand and let him lead her onto the well-polished dance floor.

There was a faint smell of cologne off him. A very nice

smell. The sort of cologne that Oliver Gayle wore. And that was exactly what attracted Pauline to him. He was a similar type to her brother-in-law. On the few occasions that he had spoken to her, Jack Byrne had not minced his words.

"Well?" he said, as he guided her in a slow waltz. "What's the story? Am I driving you back home or not?"

"I already told you," Pauline said, smiling fliratiously, "that I came with my friend – and it's only right that I go home with her again."

"And what," he said, moving his mouth close to her ear, "if your friend was to find better company to travel home with herself?"

When he swung her round, Pauline had a clear view of the table, and she could see a fellow sitting down at the table beside Rose. And as she watched, his arm had came round to circle her shoulder – and Rose wasn't shrugging him away either.

"Well?" Jack Byrne whispered again, knowing what was going through his dancing partner's mind. His hand tightened on her waist.

"I'll have to see . . ." Pauline murmured. "I'll have to talk to Rose." She eased out of his hold a little. "Sure, I hardly know you," she said now. "I'm not the sort of girl that goes off with strangers."

"And I," he said, "wouldn't be asking you if you were. We danced together and chatted the last time you were here, didn't we?"

"But I know nothing about you," Pauline persisted. "You could be married with half a dozen kids for all I know."

"Well," Jack Byrne said, pulling her closer again, "we'll have to do something to sort that out then – won't we?"

Chapter 14

"Look, it suits us both," Rose Quinn said to Pauline, as they checked their hair, their clothes, and their make-up, in the full-length mirror in the ladies' lavatory.

"I'm not really sure . . ." Pauline said slowly, turning round to check that her petticoat wasn't hanging down below her dress.

Rose added another layer of orangey-lipstick, going heavier on her thin top lip to give it more of a pout. Then Pauline came to stand alongside her, adding another pink layer of lipstick to her fuller, more sculpted lips.

"All we have to do," Rose said, "is stick to the same story. Just make sure that my mother and father think I drove you home, dropped you off, and came home myself." She pressed her lips together, then checked that none of the lipstick had strayed on to her teeth. "It's as easy as that."

Pauline put her lipstick back in her little make-up purse. "I don't know . . ."

Rose sighed impatiently. "What's the problem?" she

said into the mirror, as she lifted a blonde curl back into place. "Jack Byrne's a good catch. He has his own car, hasn't he? He must be decent if he has his own car." She turned to face Pauline. "This could be your big chance, you know . . . he's a fine-looking fella."

Pauline bit her lip. "Do you like that McCarthy lad?"

Rose fluffed up the back of her hair. "He's not bad," she said, grinning, "and he's a great dancer . . . considering he has a fair few drinks on him. D'you know he had the cheek to come in with a half-bottle of whiskey in his inside pocket? He's been taking swigs from it all night."

Pauline rolled her eyes as though she found the drunken McCarthy fellow funny. She didn't want to upset Rose . . . but she wasn't interested in lads that got drunk and made fools of themselves. And she still wasn't sure about going off in the car with Jack Byrne. For one thing, she didn't know whether he was married or not. He was one of these fellows that people didn't know much about. Any of the girls they knew at the dance all said what a fine-looking fellow he was, and a more than passable dancer – but, when Pauline quizzed them further, that was about all they knew about him.

"What if we all just go for a walk?" Pauline suggested. "Or the four of us could sit in the car and chat for a while . . ."

Rose opened her mouth in shock. "For God's sake, Pauline," she hissed, "you're acting as though Jack Byrne's the feckin' *Boston Strangler*, or something! You're a right kill-joy tonight." Her voice lowered to a whisper. "What's wrong? I mean, it's not as if you're exactly shy with men, is it?"

Pauline shrugged, ignoring her friend's jibe. "Nothing's

wrong . . . I'm just not sure if I want to sit in the car all the way to Tullamore with somebody I hardly know."

"Grand!" said Rose, her eyebrows shooting up. "You can sit in the back of the car so, while I drive Jim McCarthy home to Kilbeggan." Her chin jutted out defensively. "He's let the other lads he came with go off in the van. If I don't take him now, he'll be left thumbing it home."

Pauline took a deep breath, and forced herself to say nothing. Surely Rose would see how unreasonably she was behaving, when she took a few minutes in the cool, night air to think about it?

Rose did exactly the same as Pauline. She took an audibly deep breath, and then she rummaged in her handbag for a pack of Wrigley's chewing-gum. She made a great performance of unwrapping a stick of gum without offering Pauline any.

Then, both girls buttoned up their cardigans, pulled their white wrist-length gloves on and walked back into the dance-hall in silence, arms folded defensively over their handbags.

Pauline was silently seething and vowing that she would never – ever – go for a night out with Rose Quinn again. How could she have been so stupid as to depend on somebody like Rose? She had thought she knew her well enough by now. She presumed that her friend had more pride in herself than to go off with some drunken, leering young fellow, that looked as though he had hardly left school!

Then, Pauline felt a light touch on her arm – and when she turned around, she was looking up into Jack Byrne's smiling face.

"Well?" he said softly. "Am I allowed to see you home?"

Pauline took a deep breath. Whatever reservations she had about him earlier had now diminished. Being driven home by this friendly, handsome fellow suddenly seemed a far better option than playing gooseberry in the back of the car to Rose and her jarred, schoolboy escort.

At least Jack Byrne was sober, and he was older and more reliable-looking than any of the other men in the place. What harm could it do to take a lift off him?

There were plenty of girls who went out dancing every week, and went off on the bars of bicycles with fellas they'd only met. And there were others who had no qualms about going around the back of buildings or into fields with fellas.

But Pauline Kearney wasn't like those other girls.

She might have a child without the benefit of a husband or a wedding ring, but she was not – *and never had been* – the type of girl that was easy with men.

She had only been with the one man in her life, and tragically, it had gone all wrong. A night when she was upset and drank too much, and let the wrong man comfort her. Although, in another time and in another place, he could have easily have been the right man.

But the fact was he was completely unavailable – and Pauline had paid the price for turning for comfort to the wrong man. She had been left literally carrying the baby. And she wasn't one of these naïve young girls who was going to wail and weep and say she'd been taken advantage of – because she hadn't. On the night that it all happened, she'd been as much to blame as the fellow. They had both gone into it with the excuse of having a few too many drinks – but the truth was both their eyes had been wide open to what they were doing.

It was one of those things that had just happened, one of those things that had been going to happen since the first time they had clapped eyes on each other.

And although now she was desperate to find a decent husband and a father for Bernadette, she wasn't about to make the same mistake twice.

She motioned Jack over into a quiet corner at the back of the almost-empty hall, while Rose stood sharing her chewing-gum with the McCarthy fellow.

Although she couldn't hear what they were saying, Pauline knew that they would be giving out about her – saying what a spoilsport she was.

"Okay," she said, looking Jack Byrne straight in the eye, "I'll let you take me home – but it's got to be *straight* home to Tullamore." She narrowed her eyes. "If you have any ideas about pulling off the road or anything like that – then you can forget them. I'd sooner walk than have any carry-on like *that*."

Jack Byrne held his hands up defensively – but his eyes were laughing. "What class of a fellow do you think I am?" he demanded. "I have a good reputation to think of – a businessman like myself."

He looked so like Oliver Gayle at that moment, that Pauline felt herself suddenly relax. Fun-loving – *great for the craic* – Oliver. Oliver – the man who always stood up for her. Oliver – her sister's husband.

Maybe, just maybe – Jack Byrne was cut from the same kind of classy material as her brother-in-law. Handsome, and with that devastating twinkle in his eye.

How the quiet, reserved, soft-natured Cara had ever landed him, Pauline would never understand. He needed a woman who was fit for him. Who would give as good as she got. Who would keep his interest both in and out of bed. As Pauline knew she could.

Never in a million years could Cara handle the likes of Oliver Gayle – and she should never have married him. But she had. And Pauline would have to make do with somebody who looked a little bit like him.

Jack Byrne moved closer towards her now, offering her his arm to link on to.

Pauline slipped her arm through his, and then she turned towards her friend. Rose was smiling and giving her a thumbs-up sign. She was delighted that things had worked out as she suggested.

Pauline smiled back – but it was a false, forced smile. Rose had well and truly burnt her boats. Rose was now on the way out as a friend – car or no car. From now on, Pauline would sit at home listening to the radio every night, rather than lower herself to Rose Quinn's standards. She'd even prefer to listen to Charles spouting his theories about life on other planets or have to join in with the family rosary – than put up with Rose's carry-on.

Pauline might have let the family down and let herself down having Bernadette – but she still had pride. And she would rather be alone and *without* a man – than risk having the wrong man.

Rose had no scruples. She'd made that plain tonight going off with a drunken young buck. She was laughing and hanging on to the young fellow, and calling to Pauline that she would see her tomorrow. According to Rose, it had turned into a grand night out.

According to Rose, they both had a lad now – and that made everything okay.

Chapter 15

It was very quiet in the car. Pauline wished it was like the American films, where you just leaned over and switched on a radio on the dashboard of the car – and then the silence was gone.

But this wasn't the American movies, and Jack Byrne no longer seemed like the confident, amusing fellow he had been in the dance-hall. After chatting for a few minutes as they walked along the main street of Mullingar to where the car was parked, he had suddenly run out of chat. He was still mannerly and pleasant – but he was definitely quiet.

Pauline could hear herself chattering on much more than normal. Filling the gaps. Trying to find something to say that wasn't about Bernadette – and avoiding anything that would locate her and the family easily. She didn't want to listen to him telling her that he knew this one or that in Tullamore. Or even that he knew the shop and the family. Or maybe even that he knew Oliver. Nearly everyone knew Oliver Gayle.

As soon as Jack Byrne could place her and the Kearney

family – he would know all about Bernadette. It was a foregone conclusion. It was too important a piece of gossip for people not too mention it immediately. It was human nature. And sadly – it was always the way.

Once they had pulled away from the streetlights, and the houses had started to become few and far between, Pauline suddenly wished that she hadn't agreed to go with Jack Byrne. She wished that she hadn't been so weak as to agree with Rose Quinn.

And the feeling of regret grew stronger as they drove further out of the town, and deeper into the country, where there was only the odd light dotted here and there in the pitch dark.

They drove along the winding road to Tyrrellspass, with little conversation as Jack Byrne concentrated on the driving and Pauline wondered how near home Rose was, or if she had even left Mullingar yet.

"So . . . what do you do, yourself?" Jack finally asked in a low, well-spoken voice.

Pauline swallowed hard, her mouth and throat suddenly very dry. This was the difficult part, when she knew that the men were weighing up whether or not they would ask her out again. Seeing how the land lay.

"I work," she said. "I work in the shop – my father's shop." She hadn't really meant to tell him anything that personal – but for some reason she wanted to let him know that she had a decent family that owned a shop. She didn't want him to think that she was like Rose Quinn – the type of girl that went off with young lads, who carried half-bottles of whiskey in their pockets.

There was a silence, as though he were considering her words carefully.

"Whereabouts did you say the shop was?" he asked, slowing down as they came to a bad bend in the road.

"Just outside Tullamore," Pauline replied, hardly aware of what she was saying. She hadn't noticed before how dark it was on this part of the road at night. She'd driven it with Rose a few times, and she'd often been on it with her parents and Cara and Oliver. But she'd never noticed just how dark it was.

She lowered her head to look out of the car window, but there was nothing to see. Not a house-light to be seen – and nothing in the sky but shifting, dark clouds. She couldn't even see the time on her watch it was so dark in the car.

Her mouth and throat were really dry now – and her hands clammy.

The lights of Tyrellspass came into view, and brought with them a great, silent wave of relief within Pauline. She found herself chatting again, asking whether he'd ever been inside the castle in Tyrellspass, or if he knew anyone from the village. They talked about a few of the well-known names, and before long they were back out in the dark again – heading towards Kilbeggan.

"What about yourself?" she said to fill the silence, and to steer the subject away from herself. "Do you work locally?"

"No – not locally," he said. "I spend a good bit of the week travelling. I'm only around at the weekends in the Midlands."

That still didn't tell Pauline an awful lot. But then, she hadn't exactly been forthcoming herself with information. She wondered again if Jack Byrne had something to hide. And if he had, no doubt it was the obvious thing. The thing men like that hid: a wife and family.

"I'm only back from England this last year," he said quietly, "and I go back and forward there every couple of months."

"You certainly get about a bit," Pauline said, trying to sound flippant and confident. "And I suppose you have a girlfriend in every town?"

"No," he said. "I don't go out that much – just the weekends." He turned his head towards her now, and she could just make out his profile in the dim light. "What about yourself?"

"Weekends," she said. "I'm too busy during the week, unless it's the odd play in town or something like that."

Pauline felt almost weak with relief when at long last they came in view of Tullamore town. She lifted her bag from the floor, and checked the buttons on her cardigan again.

Then, just as they neared the first house, the car started to slow down – and Pauline's heart jolted in her chest.

"I'm just going to pull over for a bit," Jack Byrne said in a flat, matter-of-fact tone. Then, before she could protest, he had turned off the road and was heading down a small, dark lane. A few moments later, the car came to a halt in the dark.

"I'd rather if we just went straight on," Pauline said, her heart now beating quickly. "My brother will be waiting up for me."

But Jack Byrne said nothing. He just sat there silently.

Pauline looked out of the window, her moistened palm gripping the door handle. Her mind was racing now, as she debated whether or not she could run in her high heels. She could always kick them off and run in her stocking feet. She could run fast – she had always come first or second in races in school.

"There's something I need to tell you," he said in a sudden burst.

Pauline took a gulp of air and forced herself to look at him. "What?" she said, her voice sounding strangled and hoarse – and her hand still on the handle of the door. She had slipped off one of her shoes, and if he made a move towards her – she'd brain him with it!

There was another pause. "I like you," he said quietly, "and I'd really like to see you again . . . but there's something you need to know about me."

"What?" Pauline repeated in a feverish tone.

"I was married . . ."

Pauline felt a huge wave of relief pass over her. He was married! So what? She hadn't expected any better from him. He would have been too good to be true otherwise.

"My wife . . ."

"Doesn't understand you?" Pauline said.

He shook his head. "No . . ." He gave a bitter sort of laugh. "She understood me all right . . ."

Pauline waited. But her hand had slid from the door handle.

"She died . . . two years ago. My wife died after having our little girl."

Pauline felt as though someone had thrown a bucket of icy water over her. "Oh, I'm sorry, Jack," she whispered. "I'm really sorry."

Chapter 16

"I'm not going to pretend that it's been easy," Pauline said in a slightly defensive tone, "because it certainly hasn't – but I've never once regretted having Bernadette."

"I admire you for that," Jack Byrne said gently. "A lot of girls over in England would just have had a child adopted or got rid of it – and no one back home would have been any the wiser."

Pauline took a deep breath, amazed at the easy way she had been talking to this fellow. They'd been sitting in the car talking for over an hour, and in that time they'd covered a lot of ground in each other's lives. First, Jack had told her all about his wife Peggy's heart condition which they hadn't realised was so serious until she was giving birth, and then he had filled her in on his life since Peggy had died. And all about how he had had to move back from England to have the baby near its grandparents and people who he could trust to help him out. Kind people who insisted that he needed the odd night out to have some sort of life for himself.

"Dancing is the one thing I love," Jack admitted, "and so did Peggy. We used to go to all the Irish dancehalls when we were over in England."

He had a natural and easy way of talking and listening, and before she knew it, Pauline had opened up and told him the story about Bernadette. "They asked me to consider both options in the hospital – but I could never, ever have gone through with an abortion." She fiddled with her hair. "And I spent a couple of nights lying awake thinking about having her adopted . . . but I couldn't go through with that either."

There was a little silence. "I don't mean to be nosey," Jack said quietly, "but what about the child's father? Did he offer to stand by you or what?"

Pauline's back stiffened. "It wasn't like that," she whispered heatedly. "He offered to help in any way he could, but I wouldn't let him. It was a mistake, a *terrible* mistake . . . and it was all my own fault. I knew he was married . . . *happily* married, and I should never have had anything to do with him." She paused to catch her breath. "I think if I'd asked him, he might have left his wife, but I *couldn't*."

"It must have been hard for you," he said in a low voice.

"It was hard for *both* of us," Pauline stressed. "I couldn't go breaking up a marriage, and it would always have been there between us . . . all those lives changed because of one stupid incident. That would have been a terrible situation." Then, to her horror, a huge sob suddenly came into her throat. "I'll regret what happened to my dying day. I let myself and other people down . . . but at least I didn't let Bernadette down. I've brought her up to the best of my ability so far. I've always put her first and I always will."

Jack's hand reached out and covered hers. "Well," he said quietly. "For what it's worth, I think you did the right thing, and I admire you for it. It's no easy job bringing up a child on your own."

"That's nice of you to say," Pauline whispered.

"I'm not just being nice – I mean it." He squeezed her hand lightly. "I'm glad we've had the chance to talk so honestly, and I think you and me have more in common than we might have thought."

Pauline nodded and squeezed his hand back.

* * *

As the car pulled up outside the shop, Pauline's eyes automatically moved up towards the bedroom window. "The light's on – Bernadette must have woken up."

Jack leaned across her and opened her car door. "You'd better go on in," he told her. "You'll only be worrying otherwise."

"I'm sorry," she said softly. "I really enjoyed chatting to you . . . I feel stupid for getting things so wrong about you. You've been so understanding about Bernadette and everything." She halted. "And all you've been through yourself . . ."

"Don't be worrying about anything," he said, smiling. "I'll phone you tomorrow."

Pauline glanced anxiously towards the downstairs part of the house now. "There's something going on . . ." she said, swinging her legs out of the car. "All the lights in the house are on!"

"Do you want me to come in with you?" Jack said, opening the driver's door.

Then suddenly, the front door of the house flew open.

"Where were you?" Charles demanded, his face bursting red. "Bernadette's not well – she keeps getting sick. I was just going to phone for an ambulance."

"An ambulance?" Pauline shrieked. She rushed towards the house, her high-heels clicking loudly on the flagged pavement. "Where is she – what happened?"

"I'm not sure . . ." Charles said to her disappearing back, "but it might have something to do with the statue . . ."

"The statue?" Pauline's almost hysterical voice echoed all the way down the hallway.

"Is there anything I can do?" Jack asked, coming to the front door. He was wary of intruding, and wary of what Pauline's brother might have to say to a man who had kept his sister out until two in the morning.

"Come in – come in," Charles said, a hand running agitatedly through his thick hair. "You might know what's wrong with her." He led the way down the hall to the kitchen. "I'm not convinced that it wasn't the statue."

The two men went down the long hallway and into the kitchen, where Pauline was nursing Bernadette on her knee.

"Been sick, Mammy," the child was saying, cuddling into her mother.

"How is she?" Jack asked.

Pauline shrugged her shoulders. "I'm not sure . . . she's a bit hot and clammy." She leaned forward to look at her brother. "How long has she been like this, Charles?"

Charles looked up towards the ceiling. "Well . . ." he started, "she first woke up around . . . nine or ten o'clock."

"And?" Pauline prompted. "What was she like then? Was she sick or anything?"

"As far as I know, she was fine," Charles said, trying to remember back.

The knocker on the front door sounded loudly.

"Jesus, Mary and Joseph!" Pauline said, alarmed. "You didn't actually phone for the ambulance, did you?"

Charles turned back into the hallway. "It'll be Oliver," he said. "I rang him just before you appeared – when I heard the car, I thought it was him."

"Why did you have to ring *Oliver*?" Pauline snapped. "What on earth can he do?"

"Well," Charles said, "he's very good with her . . . and I couldn't think of anyone else."

"Oliver's my brother-in-law," Pauline explained to Jack. "My sister, Cara, is in America with my mother and father."

Jack nodded.

A few moments later, Oliver came rushing into the kitchen followed by Charles. He was in his shirtsleeves – the missing jacket a sign of a crisis.

"What's happened the child?" he asked, going down on one knee at the sofa beside Pauline and Bernadette. He gave a sidelong glance at Pauline's companion, but said nothing to him.

"We don't know," Pauline said. "She's been getting sick . . ."

Oliver put a hand out to feel her forehead. "I'd say she's running a small bit of a temperature."

"Have you any aspirin or anything?" Jack Byrne asked quietly. "That might just bring the temperature down."

Pauline looked at Oliver. "This is a friend of mine – Jack Byrne. He brought me home tonight."

Oliver looked at Jack for a few moments – as though weighing him up – and then gave him the barest of nods. "I saw the car at the door and wondered who it was at this hour of the night," was all he said.

Charles cleared his throat. "Before you give her anything," he said – then cleared his throat again, "I think I'd better explain about the statue in the hall – the statue of Our Lady."

"What about the statue?" Pauline asked. Then, her eyes suddenly grew wide in horror. "It didn't fall on her?"

"No, no," Charles said, fiddling with the leg of his glasses. "It was when I was lifting her up to kiss it . . ."

"What?" Pauline prompted, rocking the child in her arms.

"You know the little ritual my mother has?" he said. "About kissing the statue goodnight and asking it to make her a good girl –"

"Get to the point!" Pauline demanded. "What happened with the damned statue?"

"She bit –" Charles stuttered, "she bit the nose off – and it's possible she might have swallowed some of the stuff – the marble or the plaster or whatever the material is."

"Jesus Christ! Where is it?" Oliver said, jumping to his feet. "We'd better have a look at it – see what kind of stuff is in it –"

Pauline lifted the half-asleep child in her arms, and followed the men out into the hall.

There was a silence, while everyone surveyed the nose-less statue.

Oliver put his hand up and rubbed his finger over the bare, rough surface under Our Lady's eyes. He put the chalky substance up to his nose, and then tentatively put his tongue out to lick it. "I think it's only harmless plaster," he deduced. He turned to Charles. "And was she sick straight after she got it in her mouth?"

"Well . . ." Charles scrunched up his forehead in thought, "I think she spat it all out . . . she wasn't really sick until later."

"And was she very sick?" Jack Byrne asked.

"No . . . just a little bit," Charles said. "You see, she woke up looking for Pauline . . ."

His eyes swivelled to the child's mother, who now flushed red with guilt and worry.

"And what happened then?" Oliver said.

"Well, she just didn't want to settle," Charles recounted. "I gave her drinks of milk – just in case there was any acid in the plaster – and then drinks of water and orange juice. And some biscuits . . . and then I thought some custard might be good for her." He gestured with his hands. "With it being made with mainly milk. So I made a pot of custard and she had two bowls of it."

"Two bowls of custard?" Pauline said incredulously.

"She didn't really want to finish the second," Charles said lamely, "but I encouraged her to finish it. I thought it would help her stomach – just in case any of the plaster had been digested. You see, I thought the alkaline in the milk would help counteract any acidity in the plaster . . ."

Pauline looked from Oliver to Jack Byrne. "Is it any wonder she was fecking sick? Eating two bowls of custard at this hour of the night. Sure, that would nearly make a grown man sick!" Then, she suddenly thought. "Have you ever made custard before, Charles?"

Charles shrugged his shoulders. "I've watched my mother and Mrs Kelly often enough." He pushed his glasses high on his nose. "It's simple enough to follow a recipe. Sure, it's only the same as following a scientific formula."

Pauline shook her head and muttered, "I should have known better . . . two bowls of custard." She cuddled the sleeping child high up her arms.

Jack Byrne leaned over and touched Bernadette's forehead lightly with the side of his hand. "I don't think her temperature is too high," he said, "and it's a warm enough night."

"Do you think we should take her to the hospital – just to be sure?" Pauline asked, looking directly at Jack, then around the others.

"I don't think there's any need for that," Oliver said in a low voice. "I think the statue was harmless enough." He caught Pauline's eye. "I think it's just a mixture of everything that's upset her."

"I would agree with that myself," Jack Byrne said, but Oliver never looked at him, just barely nodded his head.

Pauline heaved an audible sigh of relief. "Thank God . . ." she said. She was silent for a moment, then she looked up at her brother's miserable face. "You did your best, Charles," she said quietly. "And you were right to think of the hospital if there was no one else here to advise you."

Charles dug his hands deep into his trouser pockets. "I was trying not to panic . . ." he said, brightening slightly.

"I think I'll leave her down here with us for the time being," Pauline said. "If you'd bring me down a pillow and a blanket, Charles, then I can keep an eye on her."

Charles went rushing off to do as he was bid.

Half-an-hour later everyone was sitting around the table drinking tea, and casting watchful eyes over the sleeping child.

"I think I'll head off to bed now," Charles said, looking exhausted from the whole ordeal. He went over to give a last look at the child, and check her forehead. "She's cooled down a good bit," he said, giving everyone a relieved smile.

"She'll be grand now," Pauline whispered. "You go off and have a long lie in the morning, Charles. Last Mass will do us all."

Then, when he'd finished his cup of tea, Jack Byrne stood up. "I think I'll be heading off home now, Pauline," he said quietly. He put a hand out to Oliver. "It was nice to meet you even if the circumstances weren't the best."

Oliver stood up and shook his hand. "Yes. It's a pity about the circumstances."

"Maybe we might all meet up again for a drink sometime?" Jack asked.

Oliver did not reply, and instead reached out to fill himself another cup of tea.

"That would be lovely," Pauline said quickly, getting up to see Jack to the door, "and maybe when Cara gets home from America, the four of us could go out together."

"I'll look forward to that," Jack Byrne said.

And as they walked out to the car together, Pauline noticed that Oliver had still said nothing.

Chapter 17

Lake Savannah

The morning of the wedding dawned, and with it the house broke into the chaos that Maggie associated with such occasions. People, flowers and gifts started to arrive at regular intervals and in various numbers, while the bride and groom and the family all took turns bathing and showering. The wedding ceremony wasn't until three o'clock in the afternoon, but there was still plenty to be done around the house.

Cara helped Sandra and the bridesmaids with all the little last-minute things like painting all four sets of nails with a shimmery mother-of-pearl varnish, and then helping them with their make-up and jewellery.

Maggie and Jean bustled about making tea and coffee and piling trays with bagels and toast.

Later, as Cara welcomed another group of people at the door and then brought them cool drinks to have on the deck outside, she thought how different it all was to the morning of her own wedding. Maggie had fuffed and faffed, making sure that everything was done in the proper, customary way. Her parents had started saving in a special account when Cara's engagement was announced, in order to pay for a lavish wedding reception in the biggest hotel in the area.

This was Maggie's reward to her daughter for proving she had been brought up properly. That she didn't have to have a 'hole-in-the-corner do' like some of the local girls did. Or the rushed weddings over in England, that often heralded the arrival of a baby some six months later. No, Cara had not let her parents down, and the memory of that white wedding had been a balm to her mother's nerves when her sister returned home in shame.

Around eleven o'clock, the arrival of the hairdresser moved things into a different gear in the Harper household. The sitting-room became a salon, as the bride and three bridesmaids fluttered around watching each other have tiny fresh flowers woven into their carefully piled-up hair.

Maggie became slightly alarmed, when she saw her sister displaying uncharacteristic panic as it neared lunch-time and she still hadn't had her own hair attended to.

"This is starting to get like bedlam," Maggie said, feeling harrassed on her sister's behalf. She checked her watch for the third time in as many minutes. "I only hope to God that we're all ready and in the church for three o'clock."

The hairdresser kept calm, and shortly afterwards Jean – her blonde hair teased into a straight sophisticated style – was back to her relaxed self. Then, she and Cara and Maggie went off upstairs to help the bride and bridesmaids into their outfits.

"We'd better get ready ourselves," Cara said some

time later, guiding Maggie into her bedroom. "The men are all dressed and having a walk down at the lake, and the bridal party are more or less ready – so that leaves only us and Jean."

Maggie donned a flowery creation which was the staple design back home for women of her age, while Cara had gone for a plain, edge-to-edge suit.

Maggie stood back to admire her daughter. "You look like Jackie Kennedy," she stated proudly. "Apart from her having the dark hair, of course."

Cara wasn't sure if she wanted to look like an older President's wife, but she knew her mother meant it as a compliment. She looked at her reflection in the mirror, and was happy with what she saw. Pink, box-style jacket with a wine-coloured trim, and a matching sleeveless dress underneath, just on the knee. The suit was decorated with black and gold buttons. Pink, kitten-heeled, sling-back shoes and a matching envelope-style handbag completed her outfit.

She brushed her long blonde hair out, already lightly streaked by the American sun. She could have had it curled or waved by the hairdresser, but decided to leave it more casual, since she was probably going to feel dressed-up enough in the suit.

Then, she carefully applied her make-up. Not too heavy, but enough to cover the sun-kissed parts of her face that hadn't quite turned into a tan, and enough to make her good skin look perfect. She smoothed a pale blue powder shadow on her eyelids, then she carefully wet her brown block mascara, and brushed it on her lashes with careful strokes. Finally, a slick of pearly pink lipstick and a touch of Evening in Paris perfume – and she was ready.

"All I can say," Maggie stated as she looked at herself in the mirror, "is thank God I had a perm before coming over." She lifted her flowery concoction of a hat, and balanced it on her curly, silvery-grey head. She smiled now, delighted with her reflection. "All this nonsense downstairs with the hairdresser – and Jean as bad as the young ones. If she'd had a decent perm last week, then she wouldn't have got into that state earlier."

Cara stifled the large smile which threatened to spread on her face, and stuck a hatpin in Maggie's hat. It never failed to amuse her that her mother was so self-congratulatory at her own ordinariness.

The next hour flew by and soon it was a flurry of cars and taxis as the different groups all left for the church, leaving the bride and her father behind awaiting their pony and trap.

* * *

"Does my hat still look okay?" Maggie whispered to Cara for the hundredth time as they sat in the second front pew in the beautiful, small church. It was surprisingly old-fashioned with lovely old statues and floral displays everywhere.

"Your hat's fine," Cara hissed back. "Now try to forget that you're wearing it."

Then her father leaned across to her mother and commented, "They're all very casual here. Would you believe that I've seen a few men with *no* ties – and d'you know that you're the only woman in the church with a hat on so far?"

"I knew it!" Maggie whispered back, throwing an

accusing eye at her daughter. "Didn't I tell Cara that? But she insisted that I should wear it."

"Don't let it be bothering you," said Declan, oblivious to the agitation he'd now caused. "Sure, it looks fine on you anyway."

Cara closed her eyes and offered up a silent prayer.

* * *

The ceremony was beautiful, and Cara was relieved to notice several hats in evidence when they got out into the sunny churchyard. People were gathered in clusters – watching as the photographer organised the bridal party for the wedding portraits.

"If I didn't know different, I would have sworn we were in an Irish church," Declan was saying to one of the guests. "It has the very same feel as our churches back home –" Then he was distracted when another man came up and tapped him on the shoulder.

"I've got something that might interest you and your wife," the man said.

Cara recognised him as a neighbour of her aunt and uncle's.

The man gestured to a small cemetery across the road. "If you have a couple of minutes to spare while the wedding party are busy, you might like to have a look at the headstones. I've just been looking myself, and I noticed that most of them are Irish immigrant. Some of them even give dates and details of when they arrived in Ireland."

"Oh, God bless their souls," Maggie said, a pained expression on her face, "and them buried out here in a foreign country."

"You never know," the man said, guiding them towards the cemetery, "you just might come across someone who hails from your homeplace."

"Stranger things have happened," Declan said, raising his eyebrows at Cara.

Cara moved away to join a younger group of people, friends of the bride and groom whom she'd been introduced to earlier in the day. Everyone stood around, chatting lightly in the afternoon sunshine as the photographer took shots of group after group. Then, Cara heard her name being called and she whirled round to be confronted by a very smart, beaming Thomas. She glanced around, but he seemed to be on his own.

"You – look very beautiful today," he said, looking her over from head to toe. "You look very – different."

'That," Cara laughed, "is what we call in Ireland a back-handed compliment."

Thomas beamed at her. "Very beautiful," he repeated giving a reassuring wink and a nod, as an older man might do.

"Well, thank you," Cara said, "you're very kind."

"He's not being kind . . ." came a familiar, deep voice from behind. "He's being truthful."

Cara turned now – she hadn't noticed Jameson Carroll come up behind her.

"You look lovely," he said, his eyes sweeping over her.

And again, as their eyes met, Cara suddenly felt self-conscious and shy, because the tall, rangy American looked very different himself. Gone were the casual shirts and jeans – replaced by a well-cut, navy suit with a pristine white shirt and a subtle navy and white-spotted tie.

"I suppose we all look very smart and very different," Cara said, smiling. For some reason, she felt embarrassed at the thought of directing a compliment to him alone.

"Well," he said, grinning, running his finger inside the shirt collar, "I reckon this won't last too long. As soon as the speeches and formalities are over, the tie's coming off."

Then, Thomas moved forward and touched Cara's hand. "You – Cara – look like my mom! She's a very beautiful lady – too."

Cara saw Jameson Carroll stiffen up as though he had just been punched. But he said nothing.

"My mom," Thomas went on, getting quite animated, "she wears beautiful clothes – and she smells *be-a-utiful* . . ."

Cara could almost feel the tension coming from his father.

"Thomas," Jameson said in a quiet tone, "that's enough now. Cara doesn't know your mom." Then, seeing the confused look on the boy's face, he put his arm around Thomas's neck and pulled him towards him playfully.

Cara stepped back now, her hand shielding her eyes against the sun. "I think they're getting ready for a whole-wedding-group photograph . . . they'll probably want us to join in."

And then Cara spotted her mother and father coming out of the cemetery – with perfect timing. They were laughing and chatting animatedly to their companion.

When the photographs were finished, everyone dispersed into cars and small coaches to head off for the reception, which was being held in a local hotel. Cara and her parents went along with the man from the cemetery, all three discussing the old headstones in great depth.

When they arrived at the hotel, Maggie steered Cara along in the direction of the ladies' room. "The hat was near-torture in that church," she told Cara, as she removed the hatpins first, and then the hat. She shook her head from side to side. "The biggest pin was sticking into my head all through the Mass . . . and then I didn't want to show myself up taking it off when we were with the nice man." She moved to the mirror now, checking that her hair had stayed in place.

"You're hair's fine, Mammy," Cara said, touching up her lipstick. "It's sitting perfect."

Maggie turned the hat round in her hands. "Ah, well . . . that's it till the next wedding," she sighed. "I wonder whose turn it will be next?" Her eyes dimmed for a moment. "Please God, it might be Pauline . . ."

Cara turned to her mother, smiling reassuringly. "Come on, Mammy," she said quickly. "Everyone else will have arrived now and will be taking their seats."

Waitresses greeted them at the wedding function room with trays laden with glasses of chilled champagne. Cara gratefully accepted two, handing one to her mother.

Maggie held the glass up to the light, her brow wrinkled suspiciously.

"Just hold it," Cara told her. "You don't need to drink it if you don't want to."

They moved to the far side of the room, where they stood admiring the fashionwear as the groups of women came through to join them.

Then, Cara spotted Thomas and his father coming into the room. Quickly, she lifted her glass and took a deep gulp of the bubbly drink.

"There's that neighbour of Jean's, " Maggie hissed to

Cara. "The fellow with the handicapped son. Wasn't it good of her inviting them?" She craned her neck to get a better look. "And they're both well got up in their shirts and ties and everything." She leaned closer to Cara, whispering. "The poor lad. And their kind don't get any better – only worse. What kind of life can his father have?" She dug Aising with her elbow. "I'm surprised now – he's quite passable-looking when you see him in a decent suit and with his hair tidy."

Cara took a deep breath.

Maggie pursed her lips. "I feel sorry for the man. There's no woman will look at him with a handicapped son . . . not even out here, where anything seems to go."

"Mammy," Cara whispered, "that's a shocking thing to say. Thomas is a lovely boy. Any parent would be proud of him."

Maggie gave a little smile and shook her head. "Oh, you've a big heart, Cara, and you're very good with children – but actually having one of your own like that would be a whole different matter." She put her head to the side. "If the truth be told now, would you honestly feel happy having one of those children yourself? You and Oliver growing old, and them always remaining a child?"

Cara bit her lip, and swallowed back the words that would only cause a row on this lovely day. "Look," she said, motioning over to the doorway, where a woman was standing in a floaty, pinky-coloured ensemble, "isn't that the most beautiful dress and matching coat?"

"It certainly is," Maggie agreed, Thomas and his father forgotten for the moment, "but isn't she a bit long in the tooth to be wearing that long hairstyle? They say women over thirty should always keep their hair short and tidy . . ."

Cara pinned a smile on her face and took a deep gulp of the champagne.

* * *

The wedding buffet was completely different to anything the Kearneys had experienced in Ireland. Maggie and Declan were very vigilant as they approached the line-up of servers willing to heap their plates up with the most suspicious-looking dishes going by the name of spicy meatballs and hash-brown potatoes. A very far cry from their local wedding fare of turkey and ham or sliced beef – and not a boiled spud in sight.

"Actually," Declan said, dabbing a napkin to his mouth, "that was very nice. It's surprising how you take to things. I think after a while I would come to like this kind of food."

"Yes," Maggie said, still carefully picking around her plate, "but would your stomach like it? How would your stomach take to all those spicy things after a while?"

The puddings were a different matter entirely. Cara smiled as she watched her mother pile up her plate with a meringue smothered in an exotic fruit salad and cream, and accept the offer of a spoonful of a chocolaty creation to the side of it.

"It's grand to try something different," Maggie said, as she carefully sorted out her strawberries and peaches from the suspicious green and blue fruits.

The meal over, the guests moved into another festooned room to finish the evening off with a dance band.

"Are you enjoying yourself, Cara?" her father asked, as he guided her in a waltz. "You're looking very thoughtful today . . ."

Cara looked up at him, and saw concern on his face. "I'm really enjoying myself, Daddy. In fact, it's a long time since I've enjoyed a holiday so much."

"Good, good," he said, squeezing her hand. "I would hate you to feel that you were trailing after us or anything . . ." Then, as they swirled around the floor he said, "You're looking very well, my girl. The sun and the swimming suits you. Wouldn't it be grand to have this weather and everything at home?"

"It would," Cara laughed, "but there's no chance of that happening. Anyway, Ireland has its own appeal. But aren't we lucky to have come all the way out here? It was good of you both to bring me . . . and I'm really glad I came."

"And I'm glad you came," Declan told her, "for your mother, no harm to her, would wear you down at times."

Cara looked up at her father, and suddenly felt a rush of affection for him. "She doesn't know she's saying half of it," she said, trying to push a picture of Thomas out of her mind.

"Of course, it's all this with Pauline and the little one," he said resignedly. "She wasn't near as bad before that happened. And yet, she loves the child . . . in a way it's brought her happiness if only she could see that."

"She will eventually," Cara told him. Then, to lighten things up, she smiled and squeezed her father's arm. "Oh, listen! That's one of your old tunes now."

"Glen Miller," Declan said, grinning. He guided Cara into a quickstep now, delighted that she remembered the steps he had taught her years ago. "We still have nearly three weeks to go," he said, "and a lot more to see. We'll be big Yanks by the time we go home." His hand tightened on hers again. "Forget about everything back home, Cara, and enjoy yourself."

Cara drew back slightly and caught the look in her father's eyes. Did he know, she wondered, about how things were with her and Oliver?

After the dance, Maggie and Declan took to the floor, and Cara sat watching them as they glided easily round the floor. Her parents loved dancing, and they were both very good at it.

Then, catching Cara's eye, Jean waved over from another table, and a few minutes later came to sit beside her. "Well," her aunt said with shining eyes, "how are you enjoying your first American wedding?"

"I love it," Cara said. "In fact, I love nearly everything about America." She laughed. "I might never go back to Ireland."

"Oh, honey," Jean said, throwing her arms around her niece, "I'm so pleased you all came – it has made the wedding even more special for me."

"But we've taken up so much of your time," Cara said, "and you're so good. You never get worked up about anything."

"You are so welcome, Cara," Jean said, patting her hand. Then she gave a girlish giggle, and reached for the champagne bottle. "Your mother's nowhere in sight at the moment, is she?"

Cara glanced around the floor, and saw her parents heading out of the door with the cemetery enthusiast. "Nope," she said to Jean, with a quizzical look on her face.

"Good," said her aunt, filling Cara's empty glass, and filling a fresh glass for herself. "Drink this down quickly, and we might steal another one before she comes back! Here's to fun and lots of it!"

"I'll definitely drink to that!" Cara said. "We need all the fun we can get!"

Jean clinked glasses with Cara, and then she suddenly bent her head and whispered, "Don't look round, but speaking of fun – I think there's some heading right your way."

Cara wondered if the champagne had gone straight to her aunt's head, when suddenly she saw Jameson Carroll weaving his way through the dancers towards their table.

Cara felt the colour rise in her cheeks. "He's probably looking for you," she said to her aunt. "I'll go outside and see if my parents are – "

"Honey," Jean whispered, "you stay right where you are."

He came to a halt by the table. "Would you care to dance, Cara?" he asked, stretching his hand out towards her.

"I'd love to," Cara said brightly and, as she stood up, she noticed that his tie was still in place. It was looser and the top button of the shirt was undone – but the tie was still there.

She stole a glance at her aunt, who was discreetly moving to the table behind, then she took his hand and let him guide her onto the floor.

Thankfully the band were playing a lively jazzy number, and they wouldn't have to get too embarassingly close. But, by the time they reached the floor, the band had finished playing the quick number, and had slid into a slow waltz.

Then, as easily as if he had done it a hundred times,

Jameson Carroll moved towards her. One hand came to encircle her waist while the other hand tightened around hers. Cara suddenly felt as though she had just received an electric shock. Every nerve in her body had became alive and alert, and she found that she couldn't look up at him.

Silently, they moved around the floor together – Cara more aware of his closeness with every beat of the music.

Eventually, she lifted her head to make some lighthearted remark about the wedding, but the look on his face stilled her tongue. His eyes were piercing into hers and they were very dark and serious. He held her gaze for a few long seconds, then, when she started to feel too uncomfortable, she turned her head away.

Maybe, she told herself, it was the effects of the champagne. Then – when his arm tightened around her – Cara knew it was not the alcohol. The closeness of this man to her and the feel of his muscular arms were the cause of her discomfort. He was holding her in a way that only Oliver had ever held her. But the feelings Jameson Carroll was stirring up were much stronger and more intense than any Oliver had ever aroused.

Cara felt lightheaded and was struggling to catch her breath. Then she looked up and caught the serious expression on his face again – the expression that had been there the first time they met.

She wondered now what kind of man he was. This dark demeanour one minute and the friendly, almost intimate demeanour the next. Why did she react to him like this? Why did he make her feel so tongue-tied and awkward? Almost like a silly schoolgirl

Suddenly, the blushing, self-conscious feeling started

to drain away. And it was replaced by a very different feeling – a feeling of heat which rushed to her head. A feeling she had no trouble recognising. A feeling of intense anger.

Anger at the games he was playing with her – anger at him for making her feel gawky and silly.

It was anger – because anger was much easier to deal with than the other things he made her feel.

Then, the dance came to an end, and when Cara made to step back, his arm was still there preventing her from moving. She stepped back sharply, almost pulling out of his arms. Then she heard the intake of his breath and realised she had shocked him.

When she looked up and saw the look on his face, she knew she had provoked some sort of reaction, and she might have to explain herself.

"Have I done something wrong, Cara?" he said, his voice low and concerned. "I'm real sorry . . . I didn't mean . . ."

And before he could say any more, Cara felt tears rush into her eyes and she knew she was just about to make the biggest fool of herself. Blindly, she turned away from him and pushed her way through the dancing couples. She had to get out. Out, anywhere. Anywhere that was far away from Jameson Carroll.

Chapter 18

Cara rushed out the doors at the far side of the large patio, out through the groups of wedding guests – avoiding the area where she'd last seen her parents. Then she headed down the steps and out into the beautiful sprawling garden.

Mercifully, she met no one she knew or even vaguely recognised. She slowed up for a moment to let the thudding in her chest die down, and then she spotted a white wrought-iron bench at the far end of the garden almost hidden by shrubbery. Relief flooded through her when she saw the bench was empty – and that there didn't appear to be anyone else around this part of the garden.

She made herself walk now at a reasonably normal speed until she reached it.

By the time she had sat down and given herself time for her breathing to return to normal, Cara was asking herself, *What on earth have I done*? And what on earth had Jameson Carroll done that had made her react in such a ridiculous, teenage way?

And the answer was – nothing.

Even now she was beginning to think she had imagined him holding her too tightly.

And even if he had – as boys had often done in the dance-halls in Ireland – had she any reason to react so violently?

And on the face of it, she knew she had no reason at all.

Oh, God, she thought, her hands coming up to cover her face. How could she have been so stupid – so childish – running away from him like that?

She wondered now if anyone had seen her – and she wondered what Jameson Carroll must have thought of her. Probably he thought she was a complete lunatic. A hysterical, paranoid woman.

Then Cara wondered if he'd noticed the tears suddenly spilling down her cheeks.

And then she didn't need to wonder any more – for he was coming across the grass towards her right now.

Cara didn't know whether to run or stay put. Her mind raced, panicking as to whether she should tell him why she had run out – or whether to pretend she had felt ill. Or too hot . . .

He sat down beside her and she found the easiest thing was to say nothing at all.

"Cara," he said, and when she didn't respond, he said it again, "Cara . . . have I done something to upset you? Are you okay?"

Cara just sat there, wishing she was a million miles away.

Wishing that she was anywhere – even back in Ireland – anywhere at this moment but here. And she wished she was doing anything else but having to sit here and face him. For she had no explanation for her silly, juvenile behaviour.

She turned towards him, willing the right words to come. And then their eyes met – and she didn't need any words. He reached towards her and gathered her into his arms. He crushed her to him – holding her so closely that she could feel his heart beating, almost in time with her own.

Then, he paused for a brief moment, giving her the chance to pull away, and when she didn't move, he bent to kiss her. Gently first and then hard – and full of an almost angry passion.

The burning feeling coursed like an arrow through her body again, and Cara recognised it this time for what it was. The same sensation she had felt when she first met him. The feelings she had in the boat on Lake Savannah. She now knew without a doubt, that the feeling was that of intense desire. Pure desire for this strange, complicated, American man – a man with his own sensitivities, a man who had put his son before everything else.

Deep down, Cara had known it all along – and that very knowledge was what she had run away from.

After what seemed like an age they parted – both breathless. They moved away a little, looking questioningly into each other's eyes. Looking for recognition of what was happening to them.

Then Jameson bent his head towards her again. "You're beautiful," he whispered, and his words made Cara's heart soar. "And you're special . . . very special. I knew that from the first moment I set eyes on you."

"I was sure you thought I was stupid," Cara whispered back.

He moved to hold her at arm's length now. Then a little smile came his lips. "I've thought a lot of things about you," he said, "but never once have I thought you were stupid."

Cara looked at him now – really looked at him. Then she felt the tears threatening again. "But we're very different," she said, her voice cracking a little. "Even though I don't know much about you, I know that we're completely different in loads of ways."

"We can learn about each other," he said, his hand moving to stroke her blonde hair. "I'm kinda looking forward to that. I like everything I've learned about you up to now."

But we haven't talked about the fact that I'm married, thought Cara. She leaned towards him, drawn by the strength and the warmth of his body. "I'm only here for a couple of weeks," she said weakly.

He nodded, still smiling. "That'll do for now . . . it just means that we have to go faster at getting to know each other." He bent and kissed her lips again. "I want to know everything about you. I'm not real good at talking – I've kinda lost the habit. Apart from Thomas, it's a long time since I've wanted to talk like this to anyone." His voice dropped a little. "It's a long time since I've needed to talk."

Cara nodded – warmed by his rich deep voice, his lovely American drawl, and the wonderful words he was saying. Then, a movement in the bushes behind them made her suddenly aware that they were not on their own. She rose up from the bench, alarmed that someone might have seen them.

Jameson stretched back over the bench, and parted some of the greenery. Then he turned and looked back at her. "Relax," he said quietly. "It's only a cat stalking a bird."

Cara gave a deep sigh, then came to sit back down.

He stretched a hand out towards her and pulled her close towards him, and although she knew she was taking a risk, she could not help herself. She was in his arms again, and he was kissing her and holding her so close it almost hurt.

And she found herself clinging to him in a way she had never clung to Oliver Gayle.

Eventually, when she felt she was almost drowning in this wonderful feeling, a little voice at the back of her head told her that it needed to stop. She knew from the way their bodies were meeting so naturally and easily together, that she would have to pull away from him. Breathlessly now, she eased out of his grip and somehow managed to stand up. She straightened her pink suit skirt, and smoothed down her hair.

He looked up at her, with a smiling but shy sort of look on his face. "You okay?" he asked her gently, vaguely straightening the tie he had loosened earlier.

"I've got to go back in," she told him, her voice halting. "I don't want to – but I've got to. My parents and Jean – they might be looking for me."

"Sure," he said, nodding slowly. "I guess I'd better check on Thomas." The smile appeared again. "He was dancing when I left. He loves it – but sometimes he gets carried away, and doesn't know when to take a rest."

He stood up, and then reached to take her hand. He held on to it, taking it in both of his. Then he lifted it to his lips and kissed each finger very gently.

Cara caught her breath, a wave of desire rushing over her at his touch.

"Look," he said now, "I don't know what's happening

here between us . . . and I can sense that it might be full of problems. But for now, it feels real good to me." His voice dropped a little. "Later . . . whenever you can find the time . . . we can talk and see what we can sort out . . ."

Cara looked up into the deep brown eyes again, and she felt as though her whole insides were turning upside down. "I'm not sure," she whispered, then had to close her eyes tight to stop the tears from spilling down again.

"What's so bad?" he said, cupping her face in his hands.

"The fact that I'm married," she told him in a flat voice.

He nodded slowly. "Yup," he said, reaching for her left hand. "I noticed your wedding band the first time I met you . . . within a couple minutes I looked to see if you were wearing one." He touched her hair. "Things in life are not always black and white . . . I've been married myself."

A tear slid down her cheek.

"Hell, Cara," he said, drawing her close again, "don't take on so . . . we haven't done anything too terrible . . . a kiss isn't such a bad thing."

Cara managed a watery smile. "I've never, ever done anything like this before," she said. "I've never even *contemplated* it. I've never kissed another man since I got married."

"Okay," he said soothingly. "I can tell this is real difficult for you, and I sure don't want to upset you." He drew a carefully ironed hanky from his inside pocket, and dabbed it to her eyes. "We'll leave things for now – we'll go back inside and join the party."

They walked across the grass very slowly, without speaking, touching or looking at each other. But both reluctant to start the separation. They paused at the bottom of the steps and when Jameson looked into Cara's eyes again, the intensity of his gaze started the hot burning feeling inside her again.

"I think," she said, "we'd better – you know, go back to our own tables." She lowered her head, feeling like an awkward schoolgirl. "It's just that my parents and Jean might notice something . . . if we're together."

He nodded his head slowly, not taking his eyes off her. "If that's what you want, then that's okay by me. But . . ." a little unsure note had crept into his tone, "I will see you later tonight . . . won't I? You won't just leave it this way?"

Cara couldn't stop herself from touching his arm – the arm that had held her close to him just a few minutes ago. "I promise I'll see you later, but I have to go back inside now."

Then, she turned and made her way into the foyer of the hotel and straight to the ladies' room. She rushed to the mirror, checking for any obvious signs of what had just happened to her. But she was surprised that there were none. Apart from most of her lipstick having been kissed away, she looked more or less the same as she had earlier in the day. She scolded herself for rushing out without her handbag and make-up, and after cooling her wrists under the cold tap, she pursed her lips together to make the traces of lipstick more even, and combed her fingers through her hair. Then, she took a deep breath and headed back out to the main function room.

As she neared the table, she was relieved to find only Declan and Bruce sitting there chatting, and it was obvious from the way they greeted her that they hadn't missed her at all. While they chatted on about American baseball, Cara discreetly retrieved her handbag, took out her compact and dotted a bit of powder over her nose and cheeks, and then reapplied her lipstick.

Maggie and Jean appeared some ten minutes later. "Where on earth did you disappear to, Cara?" Maggie queried. "I had a look around the hall and outside in the corridor, but I couldn't find you anywhere."

"Did you go for a breath of fresh air, honey?" Jean cut in, wafting her own face with a paper napkin. "You mentioned feeling very hot earlier."

Cara gave a vague nod, grateful for her aunt's intervention. "I had a bit of a walk in the garden . . ."

"Don't mention hot," Maggie said, rolling her eyes. "We're just not used to this heat in Ireland. I don't know how you stick it all the year round."

"Oh, we get cold winters here, too," Jean told her, "and it can get very cold at night, even in summer." She turned to Cara now, still fanning the napkin. "Talking of night – the plan for the evening is food and drinks back at the house, and fireworks down at the lake."

"I'm really looking forward to that," Cara said. "I've never seen a proper firework display before – only in the films."

"Well, it's a custom round these parts to celebrate important occasions with fireworks," Jean said, "and my daughter's wedding sure is an important occasion to us." She patted Maggie's hand now. "Your mom and I are going to head back home to check that Mrs Waters and the other women have everything in order, and to help out with the last-minute things. Bruce and your dad and Michael will be sorting the fireworks out."

She craned her neck to look across the room to her son and girlfriend's table. "I think Ali prefers to stay on here for a bit – she's already made friends with the bridesmaids and some of Sandra's friends. She's a wonderful girl, a great mixer, and she just loves dancing."

Cara noticed her mother's face stiffen at the mention of Michael's girlfriend – but although her face gave her feelings away, at least she didn't say anything. No matter how nice everyone else thought Ali was, or how happy she was supposed to make Jean's son – she would never be anything else but another man's wife as far as Maggie was concerned.

Cara's stomach did somersaults at the thought of how her mother would react if she knew what had gone on between her and Jameson Carroll out in the garden.

"Would you like me to come back to the house with you?" Cara offered.

"No, honey," Jean said, "I'm sure there's nothing much left to do. Your mom and I plan to put our feet up for an hour before all the others come back to the house."

"And have a nice cup of tea," Maggie said, smiling at the thought. It had been hours since she'd had a decent cup, but she hadn't passed any remarks about it to anyone – not even Declan or Cara. All credit to herself now. Today above all days, she wouldn't have dreamt of making anybody feel awkward about the watery American tea. She had gritted her teeth and drank it, but her system was getting a bit rattled now for want of a decent, strong cup of Irish tea.

Jean winked at her niece. "Oh, we won't forget the tea. And if you run out of energy for dancing, Cara, you can keep all my friends entertained with your stories of Ireland and your little school." She waved her napkin towards the back of the hall. "Oh, I should have told you, Cara.

Thomas came across to ask you for a dance, so I think you might have to go look for him before the dancing finishes." She paused. "And, honey . . . if you need a lift back to the house later, Jameson said he'd be happy to bring any guests along with him."

Cara nodded and reached for her glass of now lukewarm orange juice. *How have I got away with this*? she asked herself. *I've done something really shocking. Something that only me and Jameson Carroll know about.*

"So we'll see you later," Maggie said, struggling to her feet. She wasn't used to dancing in this sort of heat. Hopefully, a cup of tea and putting her poor, swollen feet up for half-an-hour would sort her out.

Then, a tall shadow came across the table. "If it suits you all – I've organised a trip for us out to Cooperstown tomorrow. I hope you folks can get away."

Cara turned around in her chair to come face-to-face with the man who had eagerly escorted her parents around the graveyard back at the church.

"Some folks I was talking to about the interesting headstones we'd been looking at this afternoon told me all about this cemetery in Cooperstown," he said, pulling a chair out beside Maggie. "From their descriptions, I reckon this is a much bigger place, and the headstones are from *all parts* of Ireland. I think you and your husband will find it fascinating."

Maggie sat up, and with elbows resting earnestly on the table, proceeded to interrogate her tour guide about the details of the journey and the type of area the cemetery was in.

"I think," Jean said, nudging Cara, "that you might just have another relaxing day by the lake."

Cara nodded and smiled, her thoughts drifting back to the stolen minutes in the garden with Jameson Carroll, and the touch of his lips on hers.

Tea and rests were forgotten for the next hour, and when Declan came back to the table, they all sat chatting, and made plans to hit several cemeteries the following afternoon.

Then, when Maggie made another move to head back to the house, all the guests gathered in a massive circle, with the bride and groom in the centre. The happy couple danced round the circle a number of times, then the guests formed a long archway, through which they both had to pass, giving each one on their side a kiss. Amidst cheers and laughter, everyone waved them off as they left in a limousine to prepare for their honeymoon.

Shortly afterwards, Cara's parents and Bruce and Jean set off for Lake Savannah. "I've told Thomas and his father that you'll ride back with them later," Jean reminded her as she left. "They're across the other side of the room, near the band . . . Thomas loves the music."

And because she had no other option – and because it was exactly what she had been waiting to do – Cara made her way across the floor, to the table where he was sitting. Thomas was once again on the dance floor, this time with the bubbly Ali, and Jameson was sitting alone at the table, watching him.

As she approached him, Cara was torn between anticipation and dread. Knowing deep in her heart that she should have gone home with the older group, and not given this situation the chance to grow any deeper. But she couldn't help herself. And worse still – she didn't want to. The feelings that were running through her now were too new and exciting to walk or run away from.

The truth was Cara Gayle wanted more and more of these feelings.

Jameson turned his head now, and caught sight of Cara coming towards the table. His deep brown eyes lit up. As he rose to greet her, his whole body seemed to shift into a different gear. Easily and very, very comfortably, he reached his hands towards her and guided her into a chair beside him.

Cara sat down, leaving her hands in his warm grasp. Her parents had gone, and suddenly she didn't really care if anybody else saw them.

"At last," he said smiling, his eyes taking in every inch of her face and his hands growing a little tighter around hers. "It seems like an awful long time since I last saw you."

Cara nodded her head and laughed. "That's funny – it feels exactly the same for me." Then, as he released his hold of her to pour her a glass of wine, Cara looked at him, and she knew that it was not going to be easy to walk away from this. Whatever *this* turned out to be.

Thomas came back to the table, hot and sweaty after dancing.

"You – me!" he said to Cara, motioning to the dance floor as the band struck up a rock-and-roll number.

"No, buddy," his father told him firmly. "Into the washroom and splash some cold water on your face, then go and ask the lady at the bar for a cold drink with ice."

Thomas wiped his brow with the back of his sleeve, and gave Cara a big grin. "I am – boiling!" he told her.

"That," his father said, shaking his head, "is the biggest understatement I've heard all evening." He beckoned his son to sit beside him. "Let me roll up the sleeves of your shirt, and get rid of this darn tie for you."

As she watched Jameson Carroll gently and discreetly organise the boy's clothing, Cara felt a lump forming in her throat. It was obvious from his easy, but careful handling, that this man deeply loved his endearing son. And it was also obvious that there was nothing he couldn't or wouldn't do for him.

Thomas poked Jameson on the arm. "I look just like Dad now!" He beamed, pointing out his father's loosened tie and casually rolled-back shirtsleeves.

Jameson ruffled Thomas's hair. "Go get freshened up and then get the cold drink, otherwise the dancing will be all over by the time you get back."

"Yessir, Mr Carroll!" Thomas said gleefully, giving his father a military-style salute, before disappearing into the dancing crowds.

"You're so good with him," Cara said quietly. "You've made sure he's achieving everything he can achieve. His full potential." She paused, picking her words carefully. "I know a few children who have a similar condition to Thomas's. I'm not sure what words you use over here, and I don't want to put my foot in it . . ."

Jameson Carroll sat back in his chair, his fingers laced together thoughtfully. "The only acceptable term I find is Down's syndrome but not too many people use it or even know it."

"I've never heard it called Down's syndrome," Cara admitted. "But it sounds much better than the words people use back home."

He gave a little shrug. "You won't offend me whatever name you call his condition. I know you like Thomas, and that's all that matters."

Cara felt relieved that he was happy about her attitude to Thomas. She now realised that it was the yardstick he used to measure people with. "Well," she said, tucking a wing of hair behind her ear, "it's just that I'm used to people back home expecting very little from kids like Thomas."

Jameson shrugged. "It's not just in Ireland. I've seen it happen with kids I grew up with. Some of the schools just leave them sitting in a corner – or have them doing stuff that pre-school kids could do."

Cara raised her eyes to the ceiling. "We don't even have special schools where we live – the children are just kept at home. And the thing is, so many of these kids are like Thomas – friendly and lively."

"You think so?" Jameson's tone had an almost angry note in it. "You wouldn't believe how rare your attitude is. Most people treat him like a cute little pet rather than a human being."

"No . . ." Cara said, frowning, "maybe you're just being a bit sensitive . . . it's just that some people aren't used to children like Thomas. If they spent more time with them, got to know them properly, then they would be totally different."

"And what," said Jameson, "if that person happens to be the *mother* of a Down's syndrome child?"

Cara stared at him in shock. "I'm not sure what you mean," she stuttered, thrown completely off the thread of conversation. She could feel she was now treading on thin ice. She was afraid she might not get the words right. She was afraid she might provoke the same cool reaction she got when they first met.

"I'm talking about *Thomas's mother*," he said, a bitter smile on his lips. "I'm talking about a mother who had all the time in the world to get to know her son real well. I'm talking about a mother who had all the money she needed, and all the help she wanted to cushion her from the worst of his problems." His head lowered. "No matter what I did – she still couldn't accept him."

"I'm sorry," Cara whispered. "I'm really sorry . . ."

"It's okay," he said abruptly, sitting back in the chair and casually crossing one long leg over the other. Except he wasn't casual and he wasn't relaxed. He ran a hand through his thick, mane-like hair. "It's me who should be saying sorry. I shouldn't be bringing all this stuff up at a wedding – this is supposed to be a happy time." He tilted his head slightly, his jaw tense. "You must be regretting ever meeting me . . . most women would. I'm not the easiest person . . ."

Cara reached over and took his hand. "I'm not regretting a thing – not one single thing. The longer I spend with you, the more I want to know about you. Besides," she said, "I've a few problems of my own . . . if I start telling you about them, I might end up frightening you away first."

His shoulders suddenly relaxed. A few seconds later, a smile came to his lips. "If this wasn't such serious stuff, it would be funny. First we meet, and we're almost fighting – and then we're sitting here trading lonely-heart stories."

Cara shrugged and smiled back at him, a wonderful, warm feeling spreading all through her. God, she wanted to move right over beside him, and put her arms around his neck, and tangle her fingers in that lovely, thick, rough hair. And she wanted to press her lips hard against his, and even more to feel his body pressing hard against hers. The way it had when they were together in the garden earlier on. And yet she knew it was totally wrong. He was a married man and she was a married woman. With two anxious parents chaperoning her – who would have a fit if they thought she had the remotest interest in anyone else but Oliver.

He looked at her now, as though he were reading her thoughts. "I could listen to your lovely Irish accent all day," he suddenly said. "I want to know everything about you, even if it means having to hear about a husband and another life back in Ireland."

"I think there's a lot more to know about you," Cara said, "and I'm half-afraid of that . . . because the bits that I know already make me feel that it's totally ridiculous that we should become more friendly or whatever . . . " She halted now, embarrassed.

But Jameson didn't seem at all perturbed. He was still smiling, and looking more relaxed than before.

"Whatever happens," he told her, "nothing about our relationship is ridiculous. It's already making me happier than I've been in a long, long time." He looked at her now, his eyes soft and shining. "We're both grown-up people, and it sounds as though neither of our stories is the stuff that fairytales are made of – but that doesn't matter. It's what we feel when we're together that matters. Now – right now. What's gone before and what's coming ahead doesn't matter at this time." His voice lowered. "*This*," he said, "is what's real. What's happening at this very minute."

Cara looked at him and, in that moment, she believed every word he said. In a matter of days, her whole life had been transformed.

She suddenly felt alive again – and in a way she'd never felt before.

Chapter 19

As they pulled into the driveway, they saw the first of the fireworks shoot up into the darkening sky.

"Wow!" Thomas clapped his hands in delight. As soon as they ground to a halt, he was out of the car and heading down to the lake as quickly as his legs would carry him.

"Watch out in case you hit something in the dark!" Jameson called after him, but Thomas was gone in his single-minded pursuit of the soaring, sparkling colours that were lighting up the sky.

"You go on down to the lake," Cara told Jameson. "I want to get changed into something more casual, and get out of these heels." She looked down at the delicate, pink, high-heeled shoes. "I'm a bit like Cinderella – I can't stand heels when it gets late in the evening."

"I hope," Jameson said, "that you're not going to disappear like Cinderella. Are you?"

She laughed and shook her blonde hair. "I'm not disappearing anywhere." She paused, biting her lip. "Just as long as we don't make things too obvious to anyone . . .

I've already explained how things are with my mother and father."

"Sure," he said, "I understand. I'll just have to be content watching you from a distance."

"I'll see you in a bit," she whispered. "I'll get over to you just as soon as it's OK."

He smiled and inclined his head. "I'll be waiting."

As she passed through the kitchen, Jean and Maggie were bustling about organising trays of sandwiches and crackers with cheese, and a selection of unusual-looking American savouries that Maggie would no doubt comment over later.

"Did the wedding party finish off okay, honey?" Jean asked Cara. "Did everyone have a good time?"

"Wonderful!" Cara said, running a hand through her lightly tossed hair, her eyes shining. "Just wonderful . . . the best wedding I've ever been to!"

Maggie gave her a curious look. It wasn't like Cara to be so gushing, especially when the wedding was *nothing really* compared to the weddings back in Ireland. Hardly anyone had bothered to really dress up or wear a hat. All in all it was quite casual.

She wondered now – taking in her daughter's sparkling eyes – if Cara might have had a glass of wine too many. She gave a little shrug, and moved some strange-looking things (that Jean had referred to as 'cheese straws') from a baking tray to a decorative plate. She had to remind herself that Cara was a grown woman – not all that far off thirty – and a married woman. And, after all, she was on holidays and supposed to be enjoying herself. What harm would a little bit of excitement do?

In the next couple of weeks the novelty of it all would

have worn off – the fine weather, the fancy shops and the nice views down at the lake. Cara would have had enough of the strange American ways, and would be glad to head back to the familiarity of home and to Oliver.

And she was sure that Oliver would have had a shock to discover just how much he had missed his wife. Everyone knew that absence made the heart grow fonder. And that was exactly the reason she had suggested to Declan that Cara accompany them to America in the first place. To give her and Oliver a bit of a break from each other. A break that would make them appreciate just what they had.

She watched, smiling to herself as Cara ran upstairs, carrying a pink shoe in each hand. This trip over to America had already brought the colour back to Cara's cheeks, and the light back in her eye. The bit of a tan made her look bright and attractive, like a young girl again. And that would all be to the good when she got back home. Seeing her look so well would make Oliver smarten up his ideas.

The holiday would definitely give them a chance to start afresh.

* * *

Cara rushed into the room, unbuttoning her suit jacket and wondering what top would look best with her cream trousers and flat loafers. Before she met Jameson Carroll she would have just pulled on a blouse or short-sleeved jumper without thinking. Now every item had to be carefully examined, because she wanted to look attractive for him. Jameson was different to any of the men back home – particularly Oliver.

The main outward difference was his casual dress. Even his suit and shirt had ended up looking casual but attractive. Oliver never looked anything other than pristine. And that's how he liked Cara to look. Feminine and pretty. But she knew that the American would probably prefer her looking casual too.

Stripped down to her brassiere and panties now, she paused to looked at herself in the dressing-table mirror. The underwear was one of the sets she had bought in the lingerie shop the day she met Jameson. She wondered what he would think if he saw how she looked now. Would he still find her attractive? Would he find her slim . . . or would he think she was a bit heavy around the hips and thighs as she often thought herself?

Then, as she buttoned up a pink gingham shirt and threw a cream cardigan over her shoulders, Cara suddenly wondered what Thomas's mother had looked like – and what sort of clothes she wore. She pondered over it for a few moments, coming to the conclusion that she would probably be very casual like Jameson. An arty, beatnik type, with jeans and sweaters and probably loads of beads. And she would probably wear exotic, frilly underwear. The sort of underwear that Cara would never dare to walk into a shop and buy.

Cara shrugged to herself. It was silly to let her imagination run away. It didn't matter how Thomas's mother looked, because there was little likelihood of them ever meeting. She turned to the little box that contained the few bits of jewellery that she had brought with her. She hurriedly tipped the contents out on the dressing-table, and sorted through the necklaces and chains. She lifted the two-strand pearl necklace that she often wore to school, and immediately rejected it. Pearls were definitely too formal. Then she picked up a fine gold chain with a small crystal pendant. It was one Pauline had bought her for her twenty-first birthday. She loved the way the light changed the colour of the crystal from blue to green or purple. She quickly fastened it around her neck, and changed her elaborate wedding earrings for a smaller gold pair.

As she slipped her suit onto a hanger, she paused to glance at herself in the mirror. A familiar, maybe above-average-looking face, with sun-streaked blonde hair looked back at her – but her eyes looked different. A dewy, gleam that she'd never noticed before looked back. A gleam that she knew had been put there by Jameson Carroll.

Next, she tackled her hair. She rummaged in the small bag that held her clasps and ribbons. After trying a few on, she settled on a broad piece of cream-coloured lace.

She brushed her hair through, then tied it back in a pony-tail with the lace. She gave her make-up and lipstick a quick touch-up, and she was ready. Ready and tingling with excitement at the thought of the party at the beautiful lakeside. Ready and tingling at the thought of being close to the handsome American again.

As she crossed the little bridge at the bottom of the garden, a rocket suddenly soared up over the tall trees. She stopped in her tracks to watch as it left its silvery trail along the black night sky. Then – just as it seemed to have disappeared – a burst of colour exploded in the darkness and thousands of tiny rainbow stars scattered amongst the real ones. Cara caught her breath and smiled broadly at the beauty of it.

As she neared the lake, she could make out clusters of figures amongst the trees. The long, wide branches were lit up by strings of coloured lanterns, and more light came from flickering candles on the tables and in the nooks and crannies in the trees.

"Cara, honey!" Jean called. She was presiding over a long trestle table of food and drinks. "Are you going to have a sandwich or something to eat? There's food down here and more back at the house, if you prefer to eat indoors."

"It's the flies," Maggie whispered, passing her by with a tray of hot drinks. "You couldn't touch anything out here with all the bloomin' flies. There's some huge ones – I've never seen anything like them before in my life."

"You get used to them, Mammy," Cara laughed. "They're not that bad."

Maggie tipped Cara's elbow with her own. "I'll be taking my own bite to eat inside, when I've finished helping out here – and I'd advise you to do the same."

"I'll see how it goes," Cara said. "I wonder if Jean needs any help now."

Maggie gave a smile. "The fireworks are lovely – and if the flies don't bother you then you may as well sit back and enjoy yourself." Then she headed off purposefully with the drinks.

Cara made her way over to the Mother of the Bride. "Oh, Jean, this is lovely," she said, picking up half a bagel spread with cream cheese. "The whole celebration is lovely." She gestured to the lanterns and candles. "It all looks like something from a fairytale."

They stood chatting for a while, then a frown crossed Jean's face. "I'm real happy you're enjoying everything so much, Cara," she said, "but I'm a little concerned about your mom . . . I think she's getting tired. I've tried to persuade her to have a lie-down, but you know what she's like – soldiering on and that kind of thing. It's just that they have another busy day planned tomorrow . . ."

Cara patted her aunt's arm. "Don't worry. I'll have a word with her later. But you need to slow down a bit too – we don't want our holiday wearing you out." She lifted a tray of sausages on sticks. "I'll take these round the groups and keep an eye out for my mother."

Maggie was talking to a group of women at the small pier and when there was a lull in the conversation, Cara said quietly, "Why don't you go and have a sit-down beside Daddy? He's over on the bench with the Irish musician," she smiled mischievously, "and the graveyard expert."

Maggie's eyes lit up at the mention of the graveyards, Cara's humour lost on her. "Indeed! I'll have a few minutes' chat with them so," she decided, "then I'll go back up to the house for a last cup of tea." She glanced around her, checking nobody was listening. "I know eating outside sounds a great idea with the fine weather and everything – but you could have anything floating in your drinks and taking bites out of your food."

"Well, after you've seen Daddy and the man, you should go on inside," Cara urged.

Maggie raised her eyebrows ominously. "I don't mean to be moaning – especially with the night that's in it. But they're not the kind of insects we get back home. Your father found one the size of his thumb inside his shoe only this morning."

Cara bit her lip, trying not to laugh.

"He was lucky that he checked first before putting his foot in," Maggie went on, "for God knows what kind of bite he might have got." She pursed her lips and shook her head. "Of course we didn't say anything to anybody. We wouldn't like to be complaining."

Cara stifled a grin as her mother went off to join the men. As her father often said, she was never happier than when she was moaning. Then, as she turned to head back towards her aunt, she caught sight of Jameson Carroll.

"How is the beautiful Irish colleen?" he said quietly, coming over towards her.

At the sound of his voice, Cara felt a tingle rush over her body like a little electric shock. "Grand," she whispered, looking up at his smiling face, "and now that I've seen you – very grand."

Without saying anything, they moved further down the grassy bank to an empty spot, where they could watch the fireworks. There they stood chatting companionably, enjoying the colourful scenes around them. And enjoying each other's company. To anyone watching them, they looked like two people who had just been introduced, rather than a man and a woman now linked by some secret tie.

"I think I've enjoyed your enjoyment of the fireworks more than anything." Jameson said when another spectacular display of rockets had finished.

"We don't see fireworks much in Ireland," Cara told him, "and certainly not at weddings. This has been so fantastic – I feel nearly overwhelmed by it all."

"I'm sure there's lots of things about Ireland that I would feel overwhelmed about," he said. "That's the thing about people – we always like things that are different to what we're used to."

"Some people," Cara said with a smile, thinking of her mother. Then, just at that moment she caught sight of her parents further down the path, weaving their way through the trees and back towards the house. "If you don't mind," she said, "I'm going to run back to the house for a few minutes – I just want to check my mother and father are okay – I promise I'll be back as quick as I can."

"I'm not moving anywhere," he told her, leaning up against a tree. "I'll be right here when you get back."

When she caught up with them, Cara linked arms with both her parents as they made the last few steps back up the path.

"I hate to look like a kill-joy," Maggie said, slightly breathless at the uphill incline, "but I'll be no good tomorrow if I don't get a decent sleep – and I want to be at my best with that poor man driving all the way over here for us."

"A night's sleep will do you the world of good, Maggie," Declan said. "You've done grand today with all the dancing and running up and down to the water this evening."

"Ah, well," Maggie sighed, "it's been a good day all round – a very good day."

"You go on. I'll help with clearing up later," Cara reassured her mother, knowing that Maggie would find it hard to pass a cluttered kitchen.

"Good girl," Maggie said, squeezing Cara's hand.

Cara helped sorting out the tea and toast that her parents took upstairs to bed with them, and then she ran off to her bedroom. She abandoned the light cardigan and pulled on a thick Aran sweater instead and headed back down to the lake.

Jameson came out of the shadows of the trees to meet her at the bottom end of the garden. He had obviously been watching and waiting for her.

"I'm really enjoying this party tonight," he told her, as they walked down the steps side by side. "I usually do things like this just for Thomas . . . but tonight I'm having a real good time because I'm with you."

As they started moving into the groups of guests, Thomas suddenly appeared with an almost dazed grin on his face. They stood listening to him, while he described his favourite rockets, and how high they had gone over the trees. After a while, Jameson leaned over and whispered to Cara, "I'm gonna take this guy home now. I reckon he's dead on his feet although he'd never admit it."

Cara looked up at him, not sure whether he was saying goodbye.

"I'll be right back," he said reassuringly. "Or – if you could get away, you could come back with us . . ."

"I'd love to," Cara said, looking up at him wistfully. Apart from the desire to be alone with Jameson, she would have loved time to have seen his beautiful house in a more relaxed way than before. "But I'd better not . . . I need to spend a bit more time with Jean and Bruce and my cousins. I've hardly had time to talk to Michael and his girlfriend since we got back and I want to have a bit of a chat to them."

Thomas gave Cara a weary grin and a handshake, and then he and his father set off into the darkness, heading towards the white house at the opposite side of the moonlit water.

Cara went back and joined her aunt and the others

who were now drinking hot fruit punch and watching the last of the firework display.

An hour or so later, the crowd started to disperse from the lake, the fireworks all spent and the breeze now chilly. Groups wandered up towards cars to head off home, and the remaining family and friends moved inside to the warmth of the house.

The sound of Jean's son, Michael, playing very competently on the guitar drew everyone into the large sitting-room, and his girlfriend Ali surprised everyone by accompanying his playing in a beautiful, clear voice. A neighbour then joined in with his flute, and suddenly there was another party going full swing in the house with people singing and clapping. Drinks and food were once again brought out, and Cara circulated amongst the guests, chatting and handing out glasses and plates.

Sometime later, Jameson Carroll appeared at the door of the sitting-room and stood listening to the music and talking quietly to Jean and Bruce. Cara approached him with a tray of drinks, but apart from the odd word and look, there was nothing that she felt gave any clue to their relationship.

Then, as she squeezed past him with a pile of empty glasses and plates, he moved towards her. "Let me do that," he said, taking them from her.

Cara pointed him in the direction of the kitchen, and then followed behind. She started washing up the crockery in the sink, while Jameson went off outside to pick up glasses that had been left on the deck.

"What *have* you done to that man?" Jean whispered as she filled a bucket with ice. "I would not have put him down as being the slightest bit domesticated. I can only assume that it's your good influence!"

Cara flushed and tried to think of something light and funny to say back. But by the time her brain had got into gear, her aunt had gone.

The party finally came to an end around two o'clock. Bruce had managed to coax his slightly 'merry' wife off to bed, tactfully using the excuse that they had another busy day coming up tomorrow. Then the last of the guests set off for home and those in the house headed for bed.

Then, there were only Jameson and Cara left in the downstairs part of the house. As the last pair of footsteps disappeared out of earshot, they both gave a sigh of relief. Grateful that at long last they could relax and be natural with each other, without looking over their shoulders.

Jameson reached out and took her in his arms. He lowered his lips to her ear. "Come back to my house for a little while . . . I don't feel good leaving the little guy on his own for too long."

Cara hesitated, then she looked up into his eyes. "I should really say 'no' but . . ."

"But?" he said, waiting.

"*But,*" Cara said, "I'm going to say 'yes' instead. I've spent all my life always saying and doing the right thing for everyone else."

"And now?" he prompted.

"*And now,*" Cara said, smiling, "I'm going to do the right thing for *me.*"

He moved his forehead downwards so that it rested on hers. They stood like that for a few minutes, and then they both moved silently through the house, hand-in-hand.

They stayed silent, as they walked all down through the garden, round the lake with the yellow moon reflected across its surface until they reached the brightly lit fairytale house.

As they opened the front door, Jameson put his fingers to his lips, and then he went upstairs two at a time to check on Thomas.

"He's completely zonked out," he whispered when he came back down. They stood for a second in the large hallway, just looking at each other. Then, Jameson moved to wrap his arms around her, and Cara felt all the reservations deep within herself fall away. They kissed and swayed against each other – then eventually Jameson held her gently at arms' length. "I can think of lots of other things I'd like to do . . . but I guess we need to talk."

"You're right," Cara agreed in a low voice, but there was a reluctance within her to spoil all this. To spoil it with unknown things that might emerge from serious talking.

They went into the kitchen and Jameson made coffee in a large pot. Then he brought out two white pottery mugs, a small, poppy-decorated jug of thick cream and some kind of gingery-oaty home-made biscuits.

Cara watched him as he worked about, marvelling at how mundane objects like mugs and biscuits seemed so different and almost artistic compared to those at home. She wondered if she were influenced by the unique feel of this particular house, or whether it was just that being American, things were naturally different.

Jameson carried the things across the room and then came to sit beside her at the old pine table. "I'll start the confessions off first," he said, pouring steaming dark coffee into the white mugs. "Because we need to get a lot of stuff out of the way . . . things that might make a big difference to what's going on with us." He passed a mug and the cream jug across to her. "I'm thirty-nine years old, divorced, and I've been on my own with Thomas for a long time. I guess I've had relationships with other women during that time – but nothing that lasted."

Cara felt a stab of jealousy at the mention of 'other women' – but she immediately fought it back. How could she possibly allow herself to feel jealous – when she had a living, breathing husband back home?

"There's absolutely no one in my life at the moment," Jameson continued, "and there hasn't been for some time . . ." He lifted his dark eyes towards Cara's face now – waiting.

"Okay," she said, her throat suddenly feeling dry and tight, "I'm twenty-nine years old, and I've been married for seven years. I have no children . . ." She halted for a moment. It felt really strange – laying her life out like this. "My husband . . . Oliver," she said, "has been unfaithful to me more or less since the beginning of our marriage." She gave a little shrug. "It sounds strange, but in his own way I think he does actually love me, but I know that I'll never be enough for him."

She saw the American's eyebrows rise in disbelief.

"Oliver seems to need the variety, the excitement and, I suppose – the constant newness of it all. After seven years, I'm not a novelty any more." She stopped there. What else was there to say?

And yet, as they sat drinking the coffee and ignoring the biscuits – they found plenty to say. Cara heard herself telling this quiet American stranger things that she had not voiced to another living soul. Not even to Pauline or Carmel. She told him about all the nights she had waited up for Oliver, and about all the blind eyes she had turned.

And then finally, she told him about their anniversary weekend and the early-morning phone call.

"That was a few months ago," she recalled, "and it was a shock to realise that I didn't even feel hurt any more. I didn't actually feel anything. I decided then, that I would never depend on him . . . never believe in him again . . . and that's what I intend to do."

"Are you going to divorce him?" Jameson asked quietly.

Cara gave a wry smile. "You obviously don't know – but divorce is not an option in Ireland." She dropped her head. "I wish it was . . . but then there's my parents. Especially my mother. She's very religious, a strict Catholic, and I think it would nearly kill her." She gave a quick glance at his face – knowing that however he looked, he would be shocked at what she was saying. "It probably sounds really stupid to you, and it must be hard to imagine what it's like living in a little village, where everybody knows everybody else's business."

He listened, a slight nod confirming that he did understand.

"It's very, very difficult for me," Cara said, suddenly conscious of sounding like a real moan. "But I know I can't carry on living a lie forever. And I know that Oliver won't change. And even if he did, I don't think I could ever forget what he's done."

There was a small pause. "Do you still love him?" Jameson said quietly.

Cara lifted her eyes to meet his gaze. "No," she said in a very definite tone. "No, I don't love Oliver any more. I don't hate him . . . but I don't love him. I'm not sure that I ever really did." She hesitated, looking for the right words to explain the awful mistake she had made in her life. "I was young when we met and I fell for his good looks – I felt he was the best I was going to get. And even when I realized we weren't entirely suited, I would have stuck it out, if he had been different."

"What d'you plan to do when you go back home?" Jameson asked.

She lifted her shoulders slightly. There was so much she didn't know, hadn't thought out. So much she had been trying to ignore. "I'll wait and see. The holiday here was to get away from the situation, so that I could think clearly."

"And has it helped?" he said.

"Well," she said, raising her eyebrows, "I think I knew the answer before I came – I either learn to live with things or I leave. It's as simple as that." She lifted her coffee, but before she could drink it, Jameson's hand came to cover the mug.

"I'll get you a fresh one," he said, smiling. "That's gone cold."

Cara watched him as he got two more clean mugs and poured the coffee into them, and she wondered how she could be this comfortable with someone she hardly knew.

But as he walked towards her now, she knew the answer. Deep down there was something achingly familiar about him. And it had been there from the start. Something inside him that echoed something deep inside her.

"Thanks," she said, taking the fresh coffee from him. "Now you've heard all the bad news about me – I think it's your turn again."

A shadow crossed his face, and Cara could tell that

however long ago it all was, it was still very painful for him.

"The reason I divorced her is plain and simple: Thomas. And," he gave a bitter little laugh, "that's precisely what she thought he was – only I think her description was *ugly and simple.*"

Cara gasped. "Oh, God . . ." was all she could say.

"Verity was a model," Jameson said in a flat tone.

Verity was a model, Cara thought ruefully. It just had to be something glamorous and unusual to make her feel plain by comparison.

"Her looks were everything to her," Jameson said. "They still are."

Cara dropped her gaze to the floor. Verity's exotic name obviously went with her exotic looks.

Jameson got up from the table now and walked over to the window. "She just couldn't believe that she'd produced a less than perfect child. She blamed me – said she hadn't wanted kids anyway. She only had Thomas to keep me happy and to keep my money." His voice had a strained note in it now. "She couldn't even pick him up when he was born, and when they came home she was so depressed that I had to get a woman in to look after him. That was her ticket to freedom. She was out then – pretending that she'd never given birth to him."

"What did you do?" Cara asked.

"I just took it . . . thinking that it would eventually change. That she would get it out of her system. That things would eventually get better . . ."

"I know that feeling . . ." Cara said quietly.

"I carried on, took all the shit – for three goddamn years." He leaned on the window-ledge now, staring out into the floodlit garden. "Then, one day I woke up to it all, and I just took Thomas and left. Verity got what she wanted. The house in New York, and freedom from me and Thomas."

"And you've coped all this time on your own?" Cara said.

"Yup," he nodded. "Just him and me. Any help we need, I pay for. I reckon it's the best way. I owe nobody a thing."

"What about your family?" she said. "Have you parents, or brothers and sisters?"

"I'm the only one. My folks are in New York City. I have another place near them, and up until last year Thomas went to school there."

"And now?"

"And now," he said, turning back towards her, "Thomas and me are here on our own. And that's exactly how I like it." He came back to the table now, looking a little more relaxed. He sat down in the chair, close by Cara. "This place brought me peace and escape from the rat-race in New York. First I used it for weekends and holidays, and then eventually I moved out here full-time. I've found a good school for Thomas, and he's real happy here."

"What about you?"

He raised his eyebrows and smiled. "You mean am I happy? I don't know. I don't know if such a thing as happy exists. But, I've definitely settled for an easier, less stressful existence." Then suddenly, he reached out and caught her hand. "If happy does exist . . . I've a feeling I might find it with someone like you."

Cara looked up at him, and their eyes held for a long time.

He lifted her hand and kissed her fingers. "I know it's a ridiculously short time . . . but I feel something with you, that I've never felt with anyone else before. What do you say to that, Cara Gayle?"

But Cara said nothing. Instead, she threw her arms around him, and buried her face in his beard and neck, and held on tightly.

As they sat together, watching the sun come up over Lake Savannah, Jameson asked the question he had been dreading since he met her. "How long do we have, before you go back home?"

Cara looked up at him. "I don't want to think about it," she said.

"How long?" he repeated, almost whispering.

"Nearly three more weeks," she said.

"Do you think," he said, "that three weeks is long enough?"

"Long enough for what?"

"To get to know each other real well . . . to see if this might develop. Long enough to see if we might even have some kind of a future together . . ."

There was a long, long pause. "Oh, Jameson," she whispered, "I'm scared . . . I'm so, so scared. Scared of lots of things. Scared that this is just a holiday romance. And even more scared that when you get to know me properly, you'll be disappointed."

"Disappointed?" Amusement crept into his eyes. "In what way? What dark, forbidden secrets have you still to tell me?"

Cara lowered her head. "You might find me more exciting if I had more secrets. The fact is I'm just dead ordinary . . . nothing like a model." Her shoulders drooped now. "There's nothing special about me, I'm just a plain, ordinary old-fashioned teacher from a plain ordinary town in Ireland. I'm not the kind of woman you've been used to."

He gripped both her hands. "You've got me figured out all wrong . . . but go on, I want to hear everything that's on your mind."

"It's not just about me," she said, feeling really embarrassed at what she felt compelled to say next. "I'm not used to all this luxury." Her arm swept around the huge kitchen. "All these lovely things . . . and all the money it takes to buy them. My life is so much more simple. There's nothing big and exciting about my life . . . or about me." Her voice wavered a little. "With me, what you see in front of you now – is all there is."

"Oh, Cara, Cara," he pulled her closer, "you do not know what a rare thing you are. You are a breath of fresh air in my life." And then he kissed her again – her hair, her eyes, her lips – longer and harder than ever before.

His tongue explored her mouth, his hands moved over her shoulders and down her back. And then gently . . . very gently, she felt them brush against her breasts.

A feeling of both shock and pleasure shot through her. Automatically, she moved her body against his, feeling his strength and warmth engulfing her. At the same time feeling the newness of him and yet – that familiarity again. A feeling of knowing the very essence of him. As though they had known each other a long time ago.

"Oh, Cara," he breathed into her hair and neck, "I want you so, so much – I want to be with you all the time. To lie beside you, to talk to you, to touch you . . . and I really, really want to make love to you." His sensitive, artistic fingers moved up to trace her face. Every part of it. Her forehead, her closed eyelids, her nose, her cheeks and then her mouth. "I want to do all those things . . . while you are here beside me. I don't want to regret it long after you've left me and gone far away back to Ireland."

Cara eased herself out of his embrace, and moved back to look at him. "I want to do all those things, too," she said, her eyes brimming with tears, "but I'm so frightened . . ." A large, heavy tear dropped. "I'm afraid of breaking my marriage vows . . . of my parents finding out . . . and everything I've been brought up to believe is wrong in the Catholic Church. But . . ." she paused, gulping back more tears, "right now, I want to be with you more than anything else."

Jameson took a deep breath. "Don't worry about a thing," he told her in a quiet voice, drawing her into his arms again. "Look, it's five-thirty in the morning – we've had a long day. We'll talk some more later."

"I don't think I'll be able to sleep . . . I'm wide awake," she whispered.

He gave a slow, lazy kind of smile. "Me too . . . but it'll all keep." He stood up now, and reached out a hand. "C'mon, young lady – time to go back before the others are up and moving across at Harpers'."

"They won't be up for hours yet," Cara protested.

"I'm actually being selfish," he confessed. "If your folks don't notice what's happening here, then they won't complain. But," he said, kissing the tip of her nose, "if they discover that you've been missing from the house, there could be more fireworks than we saw last night!"

Cara held her hands up in defeat. "OK, OK – I've got the message, Mr Carroll. I'm going." Then, an impish smile spread on her face. "I know you older folk need your sleep."

Jameson raised his eyebrows. "Hell . . . does it bother you? I never really thought of the age difference."

"Not a bit," she said laughing. "If you want to get out your wheelchair, I'll push you round the lake."

Hushing their laughter as they left the house for fear of waking Thomas, they walked hand in hand along the lakeside path until they reached the entrance to Jean's garden.

"I wish I had brought my camera," Cara said, as they stood at the edge of the water. "I don't think I've ever really seen a dawn break before." She kicked at a little stone. "Living with Oliver . . . I never took the time to notice things like this."

"I never took the time myself," Jameson said, squeezing her hand. "Not until I came out here at the beginning, when I couldn't sleep and I took the time to watch what was happening around me." He drew her towards him. "From now on, I'm not going to miss any of the beauty around me . . . I'm determined not to take my eyes off you."

Cara blushed and laughed. "I'm beginning to worry about your eyesight, Mr Carroll. I don't know whether it's a sign of lack of sleep . . . or maybe it's another sign of getting older?"

"Neither," he said in a whisper. "It's quite simply the truth." Then, he bent his head and placed his lips hard on hers, and they clung together as the new day dawned.

Chapter 20

There was not a sound as Cara tiptoed through the house, then made her way upstairs carrying her sandals. She quickly undressed and washed, then slid between the cool sheets. Then, she folded her arms behind her head, closed her eyes – and replayed every single moment of the time she had spent with Jameson Carroll.

From the dance at the wedding, to their first kiss when they were sitting on the garden bench. Then, she went over the hours they had spent in his beautiful white house tonight – as though she were sitting watching it on a film. She reached out for the spare pillow and hugged it tightly to herself, until her mind eventually relaxed, and sleep finally came.

Several hours later, a panicky Jean awoke to discover that the cemetery guide was due to arrive within the next half an hour. She ran downstairs and her first task was to light the gas on the cooker and put the kettle on, knowing that Maggie couldn't function without her morning cup of tea. Then, she ran back upstairs to waken everyone else, vaguely wondering why on earth they had agreed to go on this outing the morning after the wedding. Especially after such a late night, and maybe one too many drinks.

"What d'you think, Declan?" Maggie asked, as she paced up and down the kitchen floor. Waiting for people to arrive always made her anxious, and she felt doubly so having got the vague feeling that Declan and the others were only going on this tour to humour her.

"What do I think about what?" Declan said patiently.

"Should we waken Cara? I'm bothered that she might think we're leaving her on her own too much. And what about Mass? She has no transport to get to Mass if we go without her."

"Look, Maggie," Declan said in a distinctly fed-up tone, for he had been having this conversation all through their hurried breakfast. "You can't expect a young girl like her to be enamoured of the same things as us. As Jean says, by the time she gets up she'll be just as happy swimming and sunbathing."

"And what about Mass?" Maggie demanded.

"What about it?" Declan countered. "Weren't we all there yesterday for the wedding? Surely, for once, that'll hold us for the week?"

"Well," Maggie said briskly, turning to rinse her cup under the tap, "it might hold you, Declan Kearney, but I fully intend to find a church somewhere this holy day when we're out. I've never missed a Sunday Mass unless I'd just given birth or wasn't fit to get out of the bed. And just because we're in America, I'm not going to start now!"

"Fine, fine," Declan said in a defeated tone, "we'll find a church when we're out, but leave Cara in bed for now."

"Don't be worrying about Cara," Jean said, coming into

the kitchen. She'd already been through the conversation twice with her sister, and was tiptoeing around her sensitivities regarding the church. "If Cara wants to go anywhere, there are plenty of people who will take her. Michael and Ali have offered to take her out."

Maggie's mouth tightened. "Oh, she won't want to be bothering them – they'll probably have their own plans." And *Mass*, Maggie thought, most certainly won't be high up on their list of priorities.

"Thomas's father said if we need any drivers he'd be happy to help out," Jean said now. "If you like, you could leave a note for Cara with his phone number, and say that he'll drive her anywhere she would like to go."

"Oh, isn't it good of the poor man!" Maggie said, her face crumpling in something between gratitude and sympathy. "He's probably glad to have someone like Cara who can chat to the young lad, and give him a bit of a break. I suppose it's with her being a teacher, and used to all kinds of children." She turned to her husband. "She's the very same with a young spastic lad that comes into the shop. She just treats them the very same as if they were normal. Isn't that that right, Declan?"

"It is indeed," Declan confirmed dutifully.

Maggie shook her head, smiling. "She's all heart, our Cara. There's times I think she needs to harden herself up a bit."

Bruce caught Jean's eye and shrugged, unable to make head or tail of what Maggie was going on about.

Then, the crunching of gravel alerted everyone to the arrival of their tour guide and the companions he had mustered up for the trip. There was a quick rush around, a grabbing of cameras and handbags, and cardigans in case it got cold, and then they all started to move out of the house, Maggie more relaxed now she had left a note to let Cara know about the offer of lifts should she be up in time for Holy Mass.

* * *

When Cara woke around midday, there wasn't a sound in the house apart from the wooden ceiling fan whirring downstairs. She lay for a few seconds, working out where she was, and what time of the day it might be. Then, her mind was flooded with the scenes from the previous night. Pictures of herself dancing with Jameson Carroll, talking to him, and then lying in his arms in the house across the lake. Again, she found herself leaning across the bed to hug the spare pillow tightly to her.

She pulled on her dressing-gown and padded barefoot downstairs to see if there was anyone around. Her mother's note was on the kitchen table, and Cara smiled as she read it. She went to the fridge and poured herself a glass of orange juice, wondering what Jameson was doing. Whether he was still sleeping or up and about.

Then, unable to face breakfast, she showered and shampooed her hair. Later, wrapped in a dressing-gown and her wet hair in a towel, she went outside to check the temperature on the gauge on the garage wall. Just as it had for the previous week, the figures showed signs of another hot day.

Cara stood for a while, looking at the summery dresses hanging in the wardrobe, and then decided upon a deep blue sleeveless dress scattered with brilliant red poppies. It had a cross-over neckline, and a full skirt with two casual pockets in the front. It was a favourite outfit she had bought last year, and worn only a couple of times due to the wet Irish summers. She was surprised how well it looked on her now that she had a bit of a tan, from the days spent down at the lake.

After letting her hair dry hanging loose over her shoulders, Cara then tried tying it high up on her head in a pony-tail. Not too sure how she felt about it, she brushed it out again and then fiddled about with it in various styles. After a few tries, she caught sight of herself in the dressing-table mirror and started to laugh. *What on earth are you doing?* she asked herself.

Then suddenly, the smile froze on her face and the laughter caught in her throat and turned to tears.

Just what am I doing? she asked herself again. *I'm a married woman with a husband and home in Ireland. And I've got to go back there.*

Then the tears started to fall, and continued to fall until she had to throw herself on the bed, and weep harder than she ever remembered doing before. She wept for the love she had lost with Oliver, and for all the time she had wasted in trying to keep her marriage alive. Then she wept for the children she had desperately wanted – but never managed to have.

And then last of all she cried because she had found something beautiful and worthwhile in her life – the happiness she had found these last few days with Jameson – and the mountain of guilt that had come with it. She had found a man she desperately wanted and she could find no reasonable way of keeping him. And she shed more tears for the fear she felt about changing things in her life – and the fear of her parents' disapproval, anger and hurt.

After all the crying, she turned in towards the pillow,

and fell into a deep, exhausted sleep.

Sometime later, she woke with a start to the sound of the porch-bell ringing. She shook her head to clear her thinking, and was rewarded by a dull throbbing at the back of her eyes. Then she remembered about the silly hairstyles and the crying.

Quickly, almost stumbling, she moved from the bed to the mirror. Unlike earlier on, she saw nothing to laugh or smile about. A swollen, red face looked back at her. The sight of it nearly made the tears start again, but instead she forced herself to go into the bathroom and splash cold water all over her face. It made little difference. Too many tears had caused the damage, and a little drop of water was not going to make it suddenly disappear.

The bell rang again, and Cara froze at the thought of answering it with her face such a mess. What if it were her parents and Jean and Bruce back already? No, she argued with herself, they wouldn't ring the bell. She would have to answer it now. There was obviously no one else in the house. Michael and Ali and their friends must have gone off when she was asleep.

She forced herself down the stairs, hoping whoever it was would be gone by the time she reached the ground floor. As she neared the bottom of the stairs, she could see a tall, shadowy figure through the mosquito netting on the front door.

When she heard her name called in a low tone she knew it was Jameson Carroll. Her heart lurched and a part of her wanted to fly back up to the bedroom and hide – but she didn't. The sensible part made her stop for a few moments, gather herself together and walk towards the door.

Very slowly, she opened it. Before he had a chance to see

her face, she turned away and walked back towards the kitchen.

"Cara?" he said quietly, and when she didn't answer he followed her inside. It was obvious by the hunch of her shoulders that something was wrong. Very wrong. She went over to stand by the window, her back to him.

"What is it?" he asked in a low voice. "What's wrong?" Then, in a few long strides he was across the room and pulling her into his arms.

"I can't . . ." she said, pulling away. "I've been so stupid . . . I shouldn't have got involved in this . . . it's not fair to you."

"It's OK," he said soothingly. He moved one hand to gently stroke her hair. "We've done nothing wrong, Cara . . . we're just two people who have got to know and like each other. It's natural and it's good." Gradually, he released his hold on her and, as she moved to a chair to sit down, he noticed her swollen face. "Hell," he said in a broken whisper, "have I done that to you? Have I made you that unhappy in the little time we've known each other?"

"You haven't caused me any unhappiness, Jameson," Cara said. "It's just the opposite. I've never felt so happy in all my life." She stopped. How could she explain this to him? How could she make him understand what all this meant to her? How their lives were so different. He was so totally and completely in control of his life . . . made all his own decisions. While she lived her life pleasing everyone else. "Could we . . ." she said in a halting voice, "could we just be friends for the rest of the time I've left?"

Jameson closed his eyes.

Cara watched him, and waited.

And then he finally nodded. "Okay," he said, with a

catch in his voice. "If we're going to be friends, then let's start right now." He gave a little cough to clear his throat. "We'll go get Thomas, and we'll go for a friendly trip out this afternoon."

"Thanks," Cara said hesitantly, unable to look him in the face. Although her heart was sinking, one part of her was greatly relieved that he had agreed to what she'd asked. While she was hugely flattered that a man like Jameson Carroll could experience such strong feelings for her – his acceptance of the situation left her free from the guilt she would carry if she went too far with him physically. And it left her free to pick up her life back home just as she'd left it – without the burden of knowing she'd broken her sacred marriage vows. It would mean she could face Oliver and her family with a more or less clean conscience. It meant she could go back home the good, selfless wife and daughter she had always been – if that was what she wanted.

But another part of her felt suddenly bereft at losing the closeness she'd found with Jameson. Losing the person she had become with him. And losing an important bit of herself in the process.

* * *

Thomas was delighted to see Cara, and even more delighted when he was told that he could pick where they would go for their trip. Any tension that was evident between herself and Jameson had dissolved when they reached the house, and Thomas's enthusiasm swept over everything else.

"You wait," he told Cara excitedly, "you just wait – wait until you see this place!"

"Okay, buddy," Jameson said, throwing him the car keys, "just keep it calm now, because it's a good little ride out there."

Cara rode in the front of the car with Jameson while Thomas sat in the back, chatting and pointing out things as they went along. Sometimes they lapsed into an easy silence, and Cara caught herself looking across at Jameson as he concentrated on driving. At one point her gaze took in his hands and arms and then moved down to his jean-clad thighs and she was amazed at the sudden physical effect it had on her. She felt a rush of damp heat in her face and low down in the depths of her stomach – a strong, sexual heat that left her feeling terrified that Jameson might somehow sense what she was thinking.

More than a few times he caught her eye, and she could not stop herself from looking back longingly into his – but they both said nothing. Then, as they were coasting along a seemingly endless, straight road, his hand came across to rest on Cara's upper leg and she instantly felt her lower body burning up again. When she looked up at him, she could see by the intensity in his eyes that touching her had had the same effect on him.

They stopped off to buy cold drinks and ice creams at a kiosk along the way, at the entrance to a waterfall. Then, with Thomas taking the lead, they had a walk along the narrow hilly path that took them in view of the gushing water. Thomas rushed further on ahead to a spot where he could safely throw in pebbles. After a spell of shouting words of praise for all his great shots, Cara and Jameson went on a picnic bench, where they could sit in the sun and watch both Thomas and the thundering waterfall.

Cara sat down first on the bench, and she was half-relieved and disappointed when Jameson went to sit at the opposite side of the table. Then, after a few minutes she felt his long legs collide with hers under the table. She stiffened for a second, wondering if she should move, but the feel of him against her drew her like little pieces of metal to a strong magnet – and her legs stayed still locked against his.

"I'll have lots of lovely memories of America to take back," Cara said, for something to distract them from the physical tension. "The trees and flowers, and the lovely blue water at Lake Savannah and amazing places like here."

"Yeah," Jameson said. "I guess it has a good effect on you. I decided to move here full-time because I reckoned that I was less tense and angry up around Lake Savannah than I was in New York City." He raised his eyebrows. "I suppose it suits my temperament better."

"Is that when you started painting?" Cara asked.

He thought for a moment. "Yeah," he said, "I suppose it was. I'd always dabbled about at painting since I was a kid, but I hadn't done anything serious for years. I had more time on my hands when Thomas was little – he's always slept a lot, and it kinda filled the time."

"I'd love to have a proper look at your work."

"Sure, I'll show you round the studio tomorrow if you have the time.

Then Thomas suddenly came rushing back towards them.

"Dad! Da-ad! I'd like to dive – in there!" he said, pointing in the direction of the waterfall.

A dark frown crossed Jameson's face, and he got up from the picnic table. "No, Thomas," he said, shaking his head. "People don't dive or swim in there – it's real dangerous. You could be drowned."

Thomas shook his head vigorously. "Not me! I'm a very good swimmer." He grinned up at Cara. "I've got lots of medals . . ."

Jameson put a hand on either side of Thomas's face, determined to have his full concentration. "Listen, buddy," he said very seriously, "you must never, ever, swim anywhere without checking with me. D'you understand?"

Thomas's shoulders slumped, and his eyes looked back dolefully at his father. "Yes, sir," he replied obediently.

"Good boy," Jameson whispered, then he reached forward gave the boy a great bearhug, almost lifting him up off his feet. "OK," he said, letting him go, "we'll catch you at the car in two minutes. You have a headstart –" And before he could say another word, Thomas was off and running down the path.

Jameson sank back down onto the bench. "Je-sus!" he said, running his hands through his hair. "That's the one thing that really gets to me. I get real scared when Thomas talks like that. It suddenly hits me smack in the face that there are things he really doesn't understand." He gestured to the thundering waterfall, then shook his head. "Answer me honestly, Cara – do you think he'll ever get to be more sensible and mature? D'you think he'll ever be able to work things like this out for himself?"

Cara took a deep breath. "It's hard to tell," she said carefully. "Like everyone else, boys like Thomas are individual, and they learn in a different way. Some will be more capable in one area than in others. He's still young and I'm sure he'll become more conscious of safety as time goes on."

"Yeah . . ." Jameson said, looking back at the waterfall, "I reckon you're right."

They headed back towards the car now, and as they walked along, Cara found herself slipping her hand into his. She had done it almost before she realised, and was grateful when Jameson squeezed her hand, but said nothing. She knew she was contradicting what she'd said earlier, and hoped that he wouldn't feel she was playing around with his feelings.

* * *

When they drove into the town Thomas had picked, Cara was relieved to get out of the car because every minute spent in close proximity to Jameson was a sweet torture that was difficult to endure.

Thomas babbled on about how it was an old-western cowboy-style town, and kept pointing out the traditional craft shops selling patchwork quilts and old-style cross-stitch cushions and wooden toys and suchlike things – delighted to have a new audience in Cara.

As they walked down the wide streets, Cara found she was starting to match the boy's enthusiasm, as she was fascinated by all the details of the wooden buildings – from the ranch-style doors to the galloping horse murals on the walls.

"There's not too many shops open on a Sunday," Jameson said apologetically, "but it's nice for a walk out anyway."

"I don't mind at all," Cara said. "I'm enjoying just looking around. It's absolutely amazing." She stopped to look at a shop window filled with traditional rag-dolls. "I think my sister's little girl would love one of these – I won't be a minute."

"Let's go – to my *favourite* place!" Thomas said, tugging on his father's sleeve.

"We'll be there soon, Thomas," Cara could hear Jameson say as she made for the shop door. "Just be patient for a little while longer. Cara wants to get some stuff for her folks back in Ireland. She has to buy them today in case she doesn't come back here again . . ."

Cara's heart dropped at his words. At the awful thought of never seeing this gorgeous man again. She turned on the doorstep of the shop and found him looking at her. For a few seconds their eyes held, and Cara felt like rushing over and burying her head in his chest, and then dragging him off somewhere secret where she could lie in his arms.

Instead, she went into the shop and bought a rag-doll for Bernadette.

Five minutes later, they crossed to the other side of the road and Cara immediately understood why Thomas had been so animated about this 'special shop'. As she stepped inside, she knew that there couldn't be a child from America or Ireland who wouldn't share his feelings.

It was a Christmas shop, a huge colourful, twinkling place – full of every decoration and toy imaginable – and it was open all the year round.

Thomas caught Cara by the hand, dragging her from one display to another. Cara could hardly contain her own delight as she took in imitation Christmas trees in every size, shape and colour, and all the different tree decorations and baubles.

"Oh, the children at school would love to just come and look at this," Cara whispered to Jameson. "It wouldn't matter about buying things – just looking at this place would be enough to keep them talking about it for weeks."

She wandered about, lifting round glass balls with snow-scenes that produced storms of snow if you shook them, and countless coloured ornaments with Christmas scenes that when wound up played familiar festive music.

Feeling a tug on her sleeve, Cara turned around to find Thomas holding up a Father Christmas doll about eighteen inches in height, dressed in red velvet down to the last detail. He even carried a matching velvet sack, full of miniature teddy-bears and toys and, wound up, played a Christmas tune.

"This is just perfect," she said, taking the doll from him. "Completely perfect."

Jameson laughed as Thomas shot off towards a corner of the shop. "He's found the female figure – they make a pair."

Cara picked her way through the baskets of glittery things towards Thomas, where he stood holding a green-hooded figure, with the same sack and tiny toys as the Father Christmas she held.

"It's a Mother Christmas," the saleslady told her, "and they're cheaper if you buy the pair together."

"In that case," Jameson said, taking the figures from Thomas and Cara, "then we must have the pair." Waving away all protests from Cara at the cost, he had the assistant wrap them up separately, first in sturdy boxes, then draped in gold paper with silver stars. He handed one to Cara and the other to Thomas. "The green for Ireland and the red for America," he said, smiling. "And hopefully, they might meet up again some Christmas."

"Thank you," Cara whispered, giving him a light kiss on the cheek. She looked down at the beautifully wrapped parcel, wishing with all her heart that his words would come true.

When they finally dragged Thomas out of the shop, they strolled down the streets again, and then stopped off at a ranch-style steakhouse for a traditional cowboy meal of fried potatoes, beans and steak.

The journey back home passed quicker than the journey in since they didn't have a stop-off. Thomas – fortified by the hefty meal – soon fell asleep, and Cara and Jameson chatted quietly or listened to the radio.

Then a particular song came on the radio that caught Cara's attention. It was a male American singer, different to anything she'd heard before. She leaned forward and turned the volume up a little.

"You like that song?" Jameson asked, smiling.

"I love it," she said, closing her eyes to concentrate on the words. "He has a fantastic voice."

"Good – it's one of my favourites and I have it back at the house," he told her, delighted.

"Who is he?" Cara asked. "His voice and style is really different to any of the singers we have back home or in England."

"It's Bob Dylan – I have a couple of his albums. The song you're listening to is from his latest album, and it's called *Girl of the North Country*."

"If the other songs are as good as this, I'd love to hear them," Cara said.

"You can listen to it next time you're over," he said casually. Then, when she didn't say anything, he took his eyes from the road for a moment. "Cara," he said quietly, "you are going to come back to the house again . . . aren't you?"

Cara turned her face towards the window. "I want to," she said, "but I'm afraid of what might happen . . ."

"Nothing will happen," Jameson stressed, "if you don't want it to. I promised you that earlier."

Cara moved around to face the front. She watched as he manoeuvred the car past a huge truck, her eyes drawn towards the strong, brown forearms with the sleeves rolled up. Then her eyes flickered upwards to his chest and then his hair which curled well past the back of his neck. She noticed a strip of dark, tanned skin where his hair ended and the collar of his blue denim shirt started. And as she looked, the betraying flush of desire crept over her again, and it was all she could do to stop herself reaching over to touch him.

Jameson glanced at her and catching her eye suddenly said, "You know there's something real special between us . . . don't you?"

There was a long silence. Then, holding the gold and silver parcel tightly to her chest, she said, "Yes, I know that."

They drove the rest of the way back in silence, apart from the low music and the odd little snore from Thomas as he lay fast asleep in the back.

As they pulled into Harpers' drive, Jameson reached over and grasped Cara's hand. "When will I see you again?"

Cara slid her hand from his, and started gathering her parcels and bags together. "I honestly don't know," she said. "I don't know what plans will have been made while we've been out today."

"OK," he said, "I'll definitely be around for the next few days."

Cara stopped what she was doing to look at him. "Are you going away?"

"I have some business in New York . . . sorting out an exhibition." He touched his hand to her cheek. "Just let me know when you can come over, and I'll sort my plans around your schedule."

"Oh, God!" Cara said, her voice full of frustration. "This is totally pathetic! I'm like a stupid schoolgirl – all this worrying about my parents and what they'll say!"

"It's OK," he said quietly. "Really, it's OK. I understand what's going on, and how hard it is for you. Truly . . . I do." He leaned across her and opened the car door, his arm resting on her body for a few moments. "Just come round to the house any time. Day or night. It doesn't matter . . ." He gave a little laugh. "For some reason, I'm not sleeping too good at the moment."

Cara looked up at him. "I'm not sleeping too good either." Then, she stretched to look into the back seat. "Thomas seems to making up for us both . . ."

"Listen . . ." he said, giving a slow smile, "if you fancy sharing an early breakfast with me any morning, just call across. It doesn't matter how early."

Before she could reply, the porch door creaked open. Jean stuck her head out. She gave a wave and disappeared back in.

"I've got to go," Cara said, clutching the parcels. "I'm really sorry."

He looked back at her without saying anything.

"Thanks," she whispered, "and thanks for another wonderful day."

She closed the car door, and walked down the path and into the house.

Chapter 21

The next two days flew past with a final family get-together, as Michael and Ali had to head back to New York, and then visits to more towns and more wool shops looking for knitting patterns for Maggie to take back home. Cara also checked out several more bookstores, and was delighted when she found the last book on Charles's list. She smiled as the saleslady wrapped up the grave-looking tome entitled *Nostradamus*, and wondered, as she often did, where on earth Charles got his odd ideas from.

Declan had discovered American vintage clothes stores that sold outfits he thought only existed in 1920's gangster films. He had a great time looking through the mobster-style suits and hats, while Maggie trawled through the rails of well-preserved fur capes, coats and dresses.

There was never any chance of Declan actually buying anything, as he wouldn't have dared appear in Tullamore in the dandified outfits, but he told Bruce and Jean that just seeing them and trying some of the hats on had given him more than enough pleasure.

Cara found the shops a distraction from her constant thoughts of Jameson, and was grateful to arrive back home like the others – tired and ready for an early bed.

In between shopping trips and visits to the Harpers' friends and neighbours, Cara spent any spare time sitting out on the deck with her book. It lay open on her lap, unread, as her eyes wandered in the distance to the white house across the lake.

Several times she was tempted to walk down to the path leading to the house, but cowardice prevented her, and she never went any further than the little jetty at the Harpers' side of the lake.

Thomas appeared on the Tuesday afternoon asking Cara to come out in the boat with him, but she had to decline as they were heading out for a barbecue at Bruce's brother's house.

"Oh, the poor cratur'," Maggie said, shaking her head as the boy ran back down the path. "He's taken a real shine to you, Cara. You'll have to make a bit of time for the lad before you go back, you know. God knows when he'll get anyone else to pay him attention."

Cara turned away. "I'm just going upstairs to get my bag," she said, not trusting herself to get into a conversation about Thomas. Her mother's patronising attitude about handicapped people really annoyed her. If Jameson had to put up with this sort of stuff regularly from ignorant people, it was little wonder he was so reserved at times.

* * *

On the way back from the barbecue that evening, Jean swung round from the front seat to Declan. "Did you

231

decide whether you're going to get in touch with your cousin or not?"

"Oh, sure I'm sick of telling him," Maggie butted in. "He was all talk travelling over about contacting Martin, and, now we're here, he's put it off."

"Now, Maggie," Declan said, "it's not just as simple as that. You see," he explained to everyone, "I'd no idea how big America actually was until I came over here and saw it for myself. I knew it was big, but I somehow had the impression that it was like England – that you could travel from place to place in a few hours!" He laughed. "Wouldn't you think that I'd know right well the size of it – and all the maps and globes of the world we studied in school!"

"Well," Maggie said, ignoring his geographical comments, "you know that your brothers and sisters back home will be disappointed if you go back and haven't even been in touch with him. And," she said, wagging a warning finger at him, "don't be looking at me like that! I know you too well. We won't be home a week and you'll be kicking yourself for not making the effort to even pick up the phone to talk to your cousin."

"OK, OK," Declan said wearily. He'd had a pleasant afternoon and evening out, and had more than a touch of indigestion after the big, overdone steak he had consumed at the barbecue. "But I haven't seen him for over ten years – and I've never even met his wife."

"Maybe," Bruce intervened, "a phone call would do no harm. At least you can say you *spoke* to him, and it would keep everyone happy."

"There you are!" Maggie was delighted now, having Bruce take her side. "A phone call certainly can't do any harm."

Later that evening, fortified by several bourbons, Declan found himself chatting to his cousin, and came off the phone to relay the whole conversation to his wife.

"You said we'd do *what*?" Maggie said in a high voice, almost choking on her tea. "That we'd visit them *this* Thursday!" she repeated. "What in the name of God made you say that?"

Cara held her breath. Was there a chance that her parents might go away for a few days?

Declan held his hands up in despair. "Now, do you all see what I'm up against?" he said, brave with alcohol. "I can't do right for doing wrong."

Maggie was on her feet. "I can't leave you to organise anything by yourself."

"Didn't I ask you to come on the phone?" he argued.

"How long," Maggie interrupted him, "did you say we would stay for?"

"Just a few days – no more," he assured her, "and it had to be this week, for they're off on a fortnight's holiday to Florida next week."

"*Florida?*" Maggie said, her voice higher still as though Florida meant something to her. She sank back down in her chair.

"Oh, Maggie," Jean put in now, "you'll just love it. It will give you a chance to see a bit more of America while you're here. You'll be close by New York, and you'll be able to visit the Statue of Liberty and go shopping in the city."

"Jean's right," Cara said, leaning on the back of her mother's chair. "It's a brilliant idea – and you'll be able to pass on all the news about Martin when we get back home. And I bet you'll have no trouble finding the lacey knitting patterns in New York."

"You'll come with us," Maggie said quickly. "Won't you, Cara?"

Cara suddenly saw any chance of seeing Jameson Carroll flying out of the window.

"No, no, Maggie," Cara's father said. "I said we would go on our own – they only have the two bedrooms."

Maggie's mouth opened and closed like a fish in water.

"Cara will be just fine with us," her aunt said. "She was just saying that she hasn't got as much swimming in as she would like. We'll be delighted to spoil her here, won't we, Bruce?"

Cara tried desperately to avoid the smile on her face turning into a huge grin. At last, she was going to be able to spend some time doing what she wanted, and with whom she wanted.

The day or so leading up to the visit was spent in a flurry of activity as Maggie got herself sorted out and packed for the Connecticut visit. There were clothes to wash and iron and now more presents to buy to take to the cousin and his wife.

Declan was grateful to escape from the accusing eye of his wife, and sloped off with Bruce for a peaceful afternoon's fishing.

"We're going into town for a few things, Cara," Maggie called from the kitchen. "Are you coming with us? If you don't, you'll be on your own."

"I'm going to go for a swim," Cara said casually, "so I'll see you when I get back."

As soon as the cars had pulled out of the drive, Cara found herself heading down the garden and towards the lake – and swimming was the last thing on her mind.

It had been three days since she had last seen him. Three whole days. Three days during which she had hardly slept, hardly ate and hardly been able to think of anything else.

She stood at the bottom of the Harpers' garden now and looked across towards Jameson's house. But there was no sign of life about it.

Maybe, she thought, *he's gone away to New York after all. Maybe he got sick of waiting.* Cara felt a stab of disappointment under her ribs. *Surely, she thought, he would have let me know?* But another little voice inside her said, *Why should he?*

He had made his feelings plain, and she had given him no reason to hope that she would make the effort to see him.

She sat down on one of the slatted wooden chairs at the edge of the water, gazing vacantly into the distance. But minutes later, she was back on her feet again, craning her neck for any signs of life at the white house.

But still there was nothing.

Eventually she gave up and made her way back up the little hill to the house for a drink and to find something to read to distract her mind. She poured an ice-cold orange juice, and then wandered into the sitting-room to check out the bookcases. She needed something – anything at all, that would take her mind off Jameson Carroll.

She knelt down on the floor in front of the bookcase in the silent, cool room. Absentmindedly, she flicked through the pages, pausing to read a verse here and there, or scan summaries on the back of the novels.

One small, beautifully bound book held her interest

more successfully than the others – a collection of inspirational poetry and quotes. Cara found herself smiling at the witty pieces and taking her time to ponder over some of the more serious ones. Then, one of the pages seemed to jump out at her. It read: *If you do what you've always done you'll get what you've always gotten.*

Cara read it – then read it again. Then read it several more times.

Then she dropped the book in her lap and closed her eyes.

Suddenly – for the first time in days – a picture of Oliver Gayle crept into her mind. A picture of the man she had almost forgotten. A picture of the man she was married to – but did not love.

And in that moment, Cara Gayle knew that if she went back to him and the life they were living, nothing would ever change.

She would get more of what she'd always gotten.

Oliver would never really change And she would never change. Not dramatically anyway. She couldn't be one of these wives who pretended to be blind forever. She would just slowly wither away, or drown in a sea of bitterness and regret.

And it would all be her own choice.

She opened her eyes and looked down at the quote in the little pocket book. Slowly, she read the dozen or so words again that had mirrored such a strong reflection of her own life. Then she flicked over the pages, reading more of the quotes. The more she read, the more of them seemed to be written especially for her – and the stronger the feeling grew in her, that she could not go back to the life she had been living in Ireland.

She stood up, and hugged the little book close to her heart. And as she did so, she thought back to the morning she had watched the dawn come up over the lake from Jameson Carroll's window.

She wrapped her arms around herself, the hardness of the book's edge digging into her ribs, wishing that it were the tall, rangy artist's arms that were hugging her.

And then an ache of emptiness and loneliness shot through her, and she rocked back and forth in an attempt to ease it. It was so strong she found her breathing short and almost painful.

She lifted her orange-juice from the shelf and drank it down quickly, then ran across the room and out into the hall and porch and back out into the garden. Within minutes, she was on the path leading down towards the lake. She stopped at the water's edge, and looked over towards Jameson's house. This time she saw the unmistakable figure – and the red hair – of Thomas kicking a football in the garden, and her heart soared.

A short time later, she had run around the path dotted with grass and wild flowers and was calling out to the boy.

"Cara!" he yelled back, giving a whoop of delight. Then, his face suddenly became serious. "Come on," he said, tugging at her hand. "Dad – he's down – in room."

Cara followed him into the house, all the doors thrown wide open, and along a corridor. At the end of it, a door opened on to a spiral staircase which took them down to the basement.

"Dad! Jameson Carroll!" Thomas called. "It's Cara from – Ireland." He pointed down the stairs. "You go first – surprise Dad!"

By the time she had reached the middle of the stairs, Jameson had moved from his easel and was coming up to meet her. Then his hands were reaching out and encircling her neat waist, and he lifted her down the rest of the steps. His strong touch made Cara's heart race, and she buried her face into his warm neck.

"God, Cara . . . I've missed you so much," he whispered into her hair. "I didn't know whether I would ever see you again . . ."

Cara swallowed against the huge lump that had suddenly come into her throat. "I've missed you, too," she said in a hoarse voice. "I really tried to stay away . . . but I couldn't do it."

"Dad?" came the voice from the top of the stairs. "My paintings – can I show them to Cara?"

Jameson loosened his embrace. "Come on down," he called, his face beaming.

Thomas's footsteps thundered down the wooden staircase. He came over to take Cara's hand, then he brought her over to a bench beside one of the French windows. He lifted up a pile of paintings. One after the other, he handed them to Cara for inspection. As she looked at each one in turn, her smile grew broader. They were all versions of the same thing. Paintings of Thomas's boat. Basic drawings in larger-than-life colours, but perfect in proportion and detail.

"I did them – yesterday!" he informed her proudly.

"They are excellent, Thomas," Cara said, nodding across at Jameson. "Much, much better than I could ever attempt to do."

Thomas beamed with pride. "Him –" he said, thumbing in his father's direction. "Him – very good artist!"

"I was hoping I might see some of your dad's work, too," she said smiling.

Jameson shrugged his shoulders, kind of embarrassed. "It's all here," he said quietly. "Feel free to look around."

Cara turned around, her gaze taking in the huge collection of framed and unframed pieces that hung on walls, and more stacked on the floor in all shapes and sizes. A few of the pieces were instantly recognisable as scenes from around the house and lake, although worked in a very individual, stark kind of style, using earthy tones rather than definite colours.

Others were brighter and more detailed, but still showing the unmistakable hand of the same artist. Then there was a mixture of subjects and styles, some veering more toward the abstract but again stamped with Jameson Carroll's unique style.

Already Cara knew that she would pick his work out anywhere. Just as she had felt the individuality within the artist himself, she could now see that difference reflected in his work.

"They are just beautiful," she whispered.

"Good," he said, coming over to rest his hands on her shoulders. "I'm glad you like them. I was kinda worried about showing them to you."

Cara picked up one of the lake paintings. Not too big, not too abstract – and not too bleak. The lake looked just as it did in real life, and it captured the colours that were in the shrubs and trees just now. "I like this," she told him. "It really captures the atmosphere of the lake."

"Keep it," he told her.

"No," Cara said, suddenly embarrassed, "I couldn't . . ." She put the painting back down by the window.

"I want you to have it," he insisted. "It's yours."

Then Thomas appeared, asking if he could go back out on the boat.

"Okay," Jameson said, "but be real careful. We'll be out in a couple of minutes when Cara's finished looking round.

When the boy had disappeared through the French windows, Jameson bent down and lifted the painting up again. "Take it, Cara," he said. "Please. I really want you to have it."

She hesitated for a moment. "Thank you," she whispered, feeling tears coming into her eyes. "It's beautiful."

"I'm not too sure about that," he grinned, "but since you think it's beautiful – it's only fair that it should go to a beautiful owner."

Cara lowered her head, then, when she lifted her eyes again she met his, and she knew that he meant every word. And with him she did feel beautiful. Much more beautiful than she had ever felt with Oliver Gayle.

She put the painting down on a table, and this time it was she who moved towards him.

Her arms reached up and slid around his neck – the neck that she had imagined touching and stroking these last few lonely nights.

"I missed you," she told him now, "and I thought about you all the time."

Jameson looked back at her without saying a word. He didn't need to. It was all there in his face.

"I'm sorry for being so scared . . . so mixed-up about everything," she whispered. "I've never been in this situation before. I never imagined how this sort of thing could feel." Then she suddenly felt herself being lifted from the ground. He looked deep into her eyes without saying a word, and then his lips came down on hers. His body pressed so hard against her that she could feel his pounding heart.

For a moment she felt overwhelmed, then, she clung to him as though she would never let him go. As little ripples of pleasure rushed through her body, Cara knew that she couldn't walk away from what she'd found with this man.

Regardless of their short time together, she knew that there was something deep down in both of them that connected in all the right ways. In the way that the two Christmas figures had echoed each other. Like two halves of the same thing. There was that kind of sameness with her and Jameson. Underneath all the differences of culture, nationality and religion, there was a kind of old familiarity that could not be ignored.

And Cara knew that she would never want another man the way she wanted him at this very moment.

He moved his lips away from hers now, and she felt his mouth first on her eyelids and then moving down her neck. His hands came to caress her shoulders through the light material of her blouse, and then he started to undo the little covered buttons, one by one.

His lips followed the soft trail of her newly tanned skin, as it was exposed inch by inch. Cara closed her eyes tighter as his lips moved on to the top part of her breasts. The part her lacy bra did not quite cover. Then Jameson led her by the hand over to a big heavy sofa draped with a tartan shawl, and they lay down together. They spoke in low whispers of their feelings, and kissed and caressed each other – inching nearer and nearer to the complete intimacy they both now wanted so badly.

Then, Thomas's voice sounding in the distance brought them back down to earth.

"I'm real sorry, Cara," Jameson said, kissing the little hollow at the base of her throat, but I've got to go see that he's OK. With the water and all."

"I know," she said softly. "I know."

Hand in hand, they walked towards the French windows and out into the garden. When they came to the end of the building, they could see Thomas down at the water beside the rowing boat. He waved when he saw them, and came running back up the path.

"The boat?" he panted. "In the boat – now?"

Jameson glanced at Cara. "Do you have time?"

She nodded. "I'd love to go out in the boat. There's no one back at Jean's – they've all gone off for the afternoon."

"In that case," Jameson said, "we've no real excuse not to."

They all got into the small vessel, Thomas taking the oars in the middle, while his father and Cara sat at either end of the boat, aware of very little except each other.

As they circled around the lake in the hot, hazy sun Cara constantly caught herself looking at Jameson and wondering what it would be like to make love with him.

It would be unlike anything she had ever experienced with Oliver. She knew that instinctively, from the feelings that ran through her when they kissed and when she felt his hard body on top of hers . . . when she felt his fingers touching her through her thin summer clothes.

After an hour or so on the lake, the hot sun eventually drove them back into the shade of the garden. Jameson disappeared into the kitchen and emerged minutes later with a bottle of Coke for Thomas, and glasses and a bottle of champagne for himself and Cara.

"Good God!" Cara gasped. "Pink champagne!"

"And why not?" Jameson smiled. "It's a lovely drink for a lovely lady – and anyway, I'm celebrating." He poured the drinks quickly, the bubbles trailing down the side of the crystal flutes. "A contract I've landed for a couple of businesses," he explained. "They like the bigger lake scenes."

How casual he was about something so exciting, Cara thought. And how different her life had become in the short time she'd known him. Here she was, sitting by a blue lake in the sun with a handsome stranger and about to drink champagne – pink champagne! Back at home she would be either out working in the garden or helping out at the shop.

She reached across to touch her glass to his. "Congratulations," she said, suddenly feeling sort of shy – then she took a sip of the sweet, fizzy drink.

"I'm also celebrating the fact that we're spending another lovely afternoon together. That's definitely worth a bottle of pink champagne!" he laughed.

Then they sat and talked – drank more champagne – and talked again.

Thomas went off into the house to change into his swimming clothes, and Cara and Jameson sat watching him as he dived under the water time and time again. By the time they were on to their third glass, Thomas had headed into the house to dry off, and Cara was explaining to Jameson in more detail about the religious problems of divorce, and how serious that was to a devout Catholic like her mother. She also admitted that her own religious convictions were certainly not as strong, but she had to keep that quiet for her parents' sake and the fact she was a teacher in a Catholic school who was expected to uphold the Church's views on these matters. Then she went on to tell him all about her sister Pauline and her illegitimate daughter, and how that situation was viewed in a small parochial village.

Jameson listened quietly, taking every word in. Apart from an understanding nod or an encouraging comment, he said very little. He seemed neither shocked nor willing to pass judgement. The few questions he did eventually ask were more practical and related to Oliver.

"I've no feelings left for him," Cara said. "None of it hurts any more."

Then Jameson talked.

He told her about the fairly solitary, but happy life he had led as an only child. Then he told her more details about his marriage and the life he had led before he moved up to Lake Savannah. Cara was surprised to learn that up until recently he had worked in the property business.

"It was a family business," he explained with a shrug. "My father and uncle were involved in it all their working lives." He gave a wry smile. "It wasn't my bag at all, although I gave it a good shot for a long time. Too long. My father's retired now, and we've sold up most of the business. We still rent out a few apartments, but that's about it. We all have enough to live on comfortably for the future – and it means that I can spend most of my time with Thomas and my painting. So I'm mighty grateful to the property business for that."

Cara shook her head. "My life is just so small

compared to all these things you're talking about . . . and I dread to think of how my parents' little shop would compare to your big business deals."

He reached a hand to touch her gently on the cheek. "I don't give a damn about the money, Cara – and I don't want you feeling it's some kind of issue, or difference between us. The only good thing about it is that it's bought me this place and some freedom." He smiled now. "And if I hadn't come to live up here, I wouldn't have met you."

"And if it hadn't been for Thomas," Cara said, smiling, "we probably would never have met."

"That's a bit of a miracle. Thomas has never been happy seeing me around women. Usually, he's pretty wary." He lifted Cara's hand now, and held it between his own for a moment. "It's not just me," he said, lifting her fingers to his lips. "We both saw how special you are."

"I'm not special at all," Cara said, drawing back a little from him. "If I were here much longer you would both find that out fairly quickly."

"For one thing," Jameson went on, ignoring her protestations, "the fact that you saw something good in Thomas tells me a whole lot about you. Then there's your lovely Irish voice that I could listen to all day long." His hands came to rest gently on her shoulders, and he looked into her eyes. "And then there's all this – your beautiful face and your lovely blonde hair . . . and then all the other bits." He gave a low chuckle. "I'm sure the very best bits are all hidden." Then, he drew her into his arms. "But one day . . ." He kissed her long and hard, then said, "Have I convinced you now just how unique you are?"

Cara smiled and blushed – but somehow felt more

relaxed again. And then they sat for a while longer enjoying the afternoon sun – talking about nothing in particular and finishing off the pink champagne.

"I'll have to go," Cara said, checking her watch. "My mother and Jean will be back from their shopping trip soon, and they'll wonder where I've got to."

Jameson reached out and caught her hand. "Don't go just yet . . ."

"I have to," she said. "My parents are leaving in the morning for Connecticut – they're going away for a few days."

"Does that mean that you'll be free?" he said hopefully.

Cara looked at him. "What do you think?" she asked in a low voice. "Will it just make things harder for us?"

He touched a finger to her lips. "I'll settle for anything just now, Cara . . . anything."

She nodded slowly.

"I've sat out here, in the garden or on the deck, every morning," he told her, "just looking over towards the house, wondering what you were doing. Wondering whether you were lying awake or still asleep. Wondering all sorts of things about you. And I know I'll do that every single morning until you go back to Ireland." His voice dropped. "And when that happens . . . I don't know what I'll do."

"I wish I never had to go back," she whispered. "If I were here on my own, I think I would be brave enough to stay for a while longer with Jean and Bruce . . . but I'm not on my own. I came with my parents, and I have to go back with them."

"Don't make any decisions yet," he said quickly. "I reckon we should wait and see what happens in the next two weeks. I'll put off my trip to New York for the time being . . . I'm not going to waste a minute of the time we can spend together."

Jameson called in to the house to check on Thomas, and then he and Cara walked around the lake together – hardly talking and hardly touching – both so relaxed and easy with each other that it wasn't necessary.

As they neared Harpers' house, Cara heard the sound of a car engine. She turned towards him. "I'll be back to you, as soon as I get the chance."

"And I'll be waiting," he told her. "Any time of the day or night."

Chapter 22

Tullamore, County Offaly

"Weighing everything up," Charles told Peenie, "I reckon that things have improved all round." He lifted a large meat knife to attack the well-sealed packaging on a box of Dinky toy cars. It was nearly half-past eleven o'clock in the morning, and his father usually had any deliveries opened and on the shelves by ten at the latest. Still, they were quiet at the minute – considering the dry, sunny morning – and they should be finished the last few boxes shortly.

"Improved in what way, exactly, Charles?" Peenie asked. He leaned one elbow on the wooden counter, and dug into his overall pocket for Woodbines and matches.

"Well," Charles said, thrusting the knife in deep, ripping through a particularly large mound of sticky tape. "Pauline's humour has certainly improved . . . and that in itself makes life an awful lot better for me, personally."

"Indeed?" Peenie said, striking a match. "And is it the Byrne lad you were tellin' me about from Mullingar? The lad that brought her home in the car the other night?" He watched now, amused as Charles tried to wrestle the knife

248

back out from the depths of the box. "An' would you say that he's the cause of her good humour?"

"Undoubtedly," Charles said, his jaw clenched with the effort of retrieving the knife. He gave a huge sigh as it eventually came loose. "She's never been off the phone since. Although in all fairness, he's the one who's been doing most of the phoning up. He even phoned her from Dublin last night."

Peenie took a long drag on his cigarette, the blue smoke curling its way up into his hair and greasy cap. "An' tell me, Charles – is it all love talk on the phone? Have you heard what's been said?"

Charles clattered the meat knife down on the counter, then, with both hands, wrenched the box open. Dinky cars and lorries came flying out in all directions. "Aw, feck it!" he exclaimed as the bottom of the box gave way, scattering the remainder of the miniature vehicles on the floor.

"Well?" Peenie prompted, as he scooped up some of the cars. "Do you think they'll be at it soon? Pauline and the Byrne lad?"

"At *what*?" Charles asked, examining a small blue and yellow caravan. He was surprised to note that they had even put a tiny towbar on the caravan. Amazing, what they could do with even toys these days. He wondered if the towbar had been attached by hand or by machine. Probably machine. These big factories in England could handle anything.

"At *it*," said Peenie. "You know . . . a bit of what you'd like to be getting' up to with Mrs Lynch." He made a suggestive thrusting gesture now with his hips. "Up, ya boyo! That's what I mean!"

Charles set the toy caravan down on the counter. He pushed his tortoiseshell working-glasses up to the bridge of his nose. "Now, Peenie," he said, wagging a finger at the assistant. "What have I told you before about that coarse kind of talk? I won't have you talking like that in the shop – or have any of that crude behaviour you just displayed." Charles was in his stride now, an excellent take-off of his father. "And furthermore – I won't have you talking about my sister or Mrs Lynch in that fashion. Two decent women who deserve a bit of respect . . ."

Peenie lifted one of the little vehicles from the counter – a red Brooke Bond Tea van – and inspected it for any dents or cracks it might have sustained in the fall from the parcel.

"*And*," Charles went on, "you know well that you wouldn't be coming out with that foul kind of language if my father was around – you're trying to take advantage of me, and it won't work." He put his hands on his hips for emphasis. "Come to think of it," he said now, "you wouldn't have a job in this establishment, if my father was to hear about this kind of carry-on. We have our good name to think of in the town."

Peenie sniggered, the Woodbine dangling from the corner of his mouth. He parked the Brooke Bond Tea van down on the counter beside the other vehicles. "Aw, get away with you, Charles. Where's yer sense of humour? Sure, isn't it only a bit of oul' male banter? A bit of coddology. Sure, if two oul' pals can't have a laugh and bit of coddin' together – life wouldn't be worth the livin'."

Charles was silent for a few moment – musing over Peenie's last statement. You had to be careful with Peeenie Walshe. In the midst of his nonsense, he sometimes came out with the odd gem of wisdom. Especially where women were concerned. And in any case – it was nice to be referred to as a *pal*.

"Right," Charles said, clearing his throat. He would say no more on the matter. The point had been made and Peenie put firmly in his place. He motioned to the Dinky cars. "Let's get these up on the shelf where they can easily be seen, and then you can stack the Lucozade bottles and the bleach and disinfectant on the back wall."

"Righto, Charles," Peenie said, stifling a grin. "You're the boss-man, and no mistake about it!"

* * *

Peenie perched a packet of porridge oats on the top of Mrs Flannigan's shopping bag. "I've put the eggs on the top," he told the deaf old woman in a loud voice, gesturing towards the bag for greater emphasis, "so they should be safe enough."

Mrs Flannigan nodded vigorously and smiled at Peenie and then at Charles and Pauline – not having understood a word of what Peenie had said.

"The porridge oats," he told her, "are the lightest, and they won't harm the eggs, as long as you're careful."

Mrs Flannigan nodded and smiled all around her again, and went to lift the bag from the counter.

"Mind yerself, now," Peenie said, taking the bag up in his hand. "I'll carry it to the door for you." He chatted to the old woman, taking her arm as they headed out to the door.

"Now that," Pauline said, turning to Charles, "is why my father keeps Peenie Walshe on here. He's great with the customers – and he has a good heart."

Charles's hand came up to his chin. "True," he said thoughtfully. "I suppose he has his good points, like everyone else." He decided that he would elicit Peenie's opinion on another visit out to Mrs Lynch's this evening.

Peenie came back, rubbing his hands together. "Ah, God be good to her – but isn't the poor oul' divil very bothered? She'd put years on ye, when ye're tryin' to serve her, and her not understandin' a word of it." He gave a shrug in Pauline's direction. "I've spent nearly a half a blidey-well hour trailin' round the shelves with her, tryin' to make out what she's pointin' out – and then tryin' to ask her how much I need to weigh out of cheese and rashers and so on. No harm to her now – for she's a nice oul' soul, but it'd feckin' wear ye out – no word of a lie." He shoved the cap back and scratched his head. "Wouldn't you think the family would take her, and sort her out with some class of a hearin' aid or some feckin' thing like that?"

Pauline laughed, turning towards the back of the shop. "Oh, you'd have everything sorted out if it was left up to you, Peenie," she told him.

"You have me in one," Peenie said, taking the compliment as serious and sincere. "And I'd sort a lot of others out an' all, if I had the chance," he said. *And I'd well and truly sort you out, Miss Pauline Kearney*, Peenie thought, as he watched her trim little figure disappearing through the door into the house part of the building, *if God was only good enough to give me the chance.*

* * *

Later, Peenie came back through to the shop having enjoyed a 'good feed' of Mrs Kelly's bacon and cabbage and new potatoes, along with home-made rice pudding adorned with a generous tablespoonful of strawberry jam. He brought his mug of tea to finish in the shop along with a couple of digestives that he had stowed in the top pocket of his overall.

"So what do you say, Peenie?" Charles asked. "If you were me, would you take the risk of another visit out to Mrs Lynch?"

Peenie dipped a digestive into his steaming mug. "It all depends," he said, taking a bite of the softened biscuit, "on whether that madman's been put behind bars or not. I wouldn't go near the place if there was any chance of him being in the vicinity, like. Who's to know what he might do next?"

Charles looked startled. "Do you think," he said fearfully, "that he might be around Mrs Lynch's locality, on a regular basis?"

Peenie shrugged, taking a slurp of the tea. He hadn't a clue what Charles was going on about – he'd been rambling on for the past week about the madman that had leapt on his father's car outside Mrs Lynch's house. Who knows what it was all about? For all Peenie knew, it might all be in Charles's head. He might finally have gone completely mad altogether, and was now imagining things. You just never knew with over-brainy lads like Charles Kearney. They didn't see things the way other people saw them. Always going on about weird things like planets and *Nostradamus*, and carrying library books around the place. Mind you – there wasn't an ounce of harm in Charles. All in all, as Peenie often told customers and the other fellas in the pub at the weekend – Charles Kearney was the finest.

Pauline and little Bernadette came into the shop through the front door now, Pauline humming happily to herself.

"Uncle Charles!" Bernadette said, rushing over to him with a brown package. "Look at the jigsaw that my Uncle Oliver bought me."

Peenie's eyebrows shot up. So that's where Pauline and the little one had been – dining with the bold Oliver Gayle. Peenie had missed them at the table at dinner-time today. He'd had to dine with Mrs Kelly and Charles on his own, and it wasn't the same at all. Peenie enjoyed the female company and the childish nonsense that Bernadette came out with. Things had been grand these last few weeks – much more lighthearted altogether than when the real bossman and the missus were at home. Things would soon change back to normal, when they got back home from their trip to America.

Charles examined the jigsaw – a picture of some cartoon or other. "I'll help you with that this evening," he said, looking at the back of the box to see which company had manufactured it. It had the look of an American design about it. And he was right. He could just make out the blurred stamp of *Seattle, USA.*

"Any calls while I was out?" Pauline asked, as she passed through the shop to the house.

"Not to my knowledge," Charles said, his mind now floating back to Mrs Lynch.

"What about the phone call earlier?" Peenie said, lowering his brows in thought. "You wrote something down on a bit of a notepad inside there." He motioned to the back shelf at the door to the house.

"Oh, right . . ." Charles said vaguely, adjusting the leg of his glasses. "Now that Peenie mentions it – I believe there might have indeed been a call . . ."

"Charles!" Pauline snapped. "Would you ever pay attention to what's going on around you?" She rolled her eyes in Peenie's direction. Then she went over to look at the note. Her face softened as she read the message – the call was from Jack Byrne.

"So your advice is that I should steer clear of Mrs Lynch's house?" Charles said, when Pauline and Bernadette had gone through to the house and were well out of earshot.

Peenie drained his tea with a last noisy slurp. "I wouldn't go that far," he said, wiping his mouth with the end of his overall sleeve. He banged the empty mug on the counter, and reached into his top pocket for the Woodbines and matches. A cigarette might just help him to come up with a suitable answer, plus – it would prolong the nice, easy dinner-break that had gone on for well over the appointed hour. As long as he was dealing with Charles's romantic problems or *imagined* romantic problems – Peenie was able to dodge getting down to actual work for a little while longer.

"Well . . ." said Charles, looking perplexed. "Do you advise me to go to see her – or to stay away?"

"I reckon," Peenie considered, "that that particular fella is probably in the Portlaoise asylum by now. I reckon that he'll have been picked up by now, and they'll be sorting him out."

"Do you think so?" Charles said, suddenly feeling a weight lifting off him.

"Oh, definitely," Peenie said in an authoritative tone. "If there had been any more shenanigans, I would have heard about it by now. Sure, I know all the lads in Tullamore, and that kind of lunacy would have been reported back here in no time." He took a drag on the Woodbine. "Even the Gardai would have mentioned it, and I heard nothing from that quarter either." He clapped a hand on Charles's shoulder. "Ah, I'd say ye're safe enough, Charlie boy! The madman has gone!"

Chapter 23

Lake Savannah

"What an awful waste of time," Maggie said to Cara and Jean in the railway station. "All this time travelling down to New York, and then back again at the weekend. And then travelling all the way back down to New York again to fly back home the week after. It's an awful lot of travelling when we hardly know the people."

"Don't look at it that way," Jean told her. "Since they're going away you have no choice but to go this week. And anyway, remember what you told Declan – when you all get home, you'll be glad that you got to see his cousin."

"Oh, I'm sure," Maggie said, not looking sure at all. She turned to Cara. "What will you do to fill the time while we're away?"

"Oh, we'll look after her well," Jean said, putting a protective arm around her niece.

Maggie cast an anxious glance at Jean, and then back to Cara. "Don't be going into any shops on your own or anything like that. After what happened the last time we all separated."

"I'll be fine, Mammy," Cara reassured her.

"It's just that anybody seeing you out here on your own might get the wrong impression," Maggie went on. "You know . . . they might think that you're a single girl."

"Mammy!" Cara hissed. "I've already said that I'll be fine."

"I know you think I'm only an ould fuddy-duddy," Maggie persisted, "but don't forget that half-cracked lad that followed you round the shops . . . and you've not been in touch with Oliver since you came over. I thought you'd be writing him letters every day."

"For goodness sake, Mammy," Cara sighed, "I've sent him a postcard, and I'll be phoning him next week to sort out times for us arriving home.

"Oh, well," Maggie sniffed, "I suppose you know your own business best."

"I do," Cara said firmly, but with a smile. "Now, away you go, and enjoy your few days with Martin and his wife."

At the mention of the relatives, Maggie pulled a face. "I hope she's not as odd as she sounds."

A few moments later Declan returned with the tickets, and they hurried to join the queue to get on the train. As they reached the ticket barrier, Maggie turned to look back at her daughter and sister with a panic-stricken face. "I hope that Martin and the wife are waiting for us at the other end," she said woefully. "It would be just like the thing, for us to be left wandering about New York on our own! We could be robbed or even murdered and no one would be any the wiser, for they wouldn't know where we were!"

"Don't worry," Jean reassured her. "If anything goes

wrong, just give us a ring and we'll come and get you – or we'll tell you what train to catch back up here." They had been over this scenario numerous times already.

"Declan," Maggie said, pulling at her husband's sleeve, "have we got Jean's phone number?"

"In the little notebook in your handbag," he sighed, losing his patience. "You wrote it down yourself. Now, come on – or we'll miss the damned train, and then it will be Martin and the wife who are wandering about looking for us!"

"No need to lose the rag," Maggie told him. "It's better to be safe than sorry." She looked back at Cara and Jean. "Please God we'll all be together this time next week."

With a final wave and painful smile pinned on her face, Maggie went through the ticket barrier like a condemned woman heading for the gallows.

"Thank God!" Cara said with a loud sigh and a weary smile as they got into the car. "I nearly thought Mammy was going to change her mind at the last minute."

Jean gave a grin. "When she was younger, that's just the thing she would have done. She was quite capable of changing her mind if it suited her. Let's just hope that there are no emergency phone calls waiting for us when we get back home!"

When Jean had negotiated the traffic out of town, they relaxed into the journey home. Jean was in a talkative mood, and she launched into an energetic discussion about how things had changed in Ireland since she had left. Then she mused out loud about all the things she still missed about Ireland, and the things she preferred about America. After a while, the conversation quietened down, and they listened to the radio in companionable silence. Following a string of Country numbers on came one of Bob Dylan's songs from the album Jameson had – and Cara hummed lightly to the music while she listened to the words.

Inevitably, her mind drifted to the endlessly difficult situation they were in. She wondered for the hundredth time whether it was madness to keep this holiday romance going. Were they merely torturing themselves with something they could never have?

The soulful words dug deep into her heart.

As the song came to a close, Jean slowed up the car to point out an unusual building. When she got no response, she turned her head and caught sight of the tears trickling down Cara's cheek. "Are you feeling homesick, honey?" she asked worriedly. "Are you missing Oliver? You know you're welcome to ring home any time – ring as soon as we get back. It won't be too late Irish-time."

Cara shook her head. "Thanks," she said, gulping back the tears. "I honesty don't want to phone home. There's no reason to get in touch – Oliver will manage perfectly well on his own. He doesn't really depend on me for anything."

"OK," Jean said, wary of saying the wrong thing. "Is anything else wrong?" she ventured. "Has anyone upset you . . . is there something you're not happy about?"

"No, no," Cara reassured her. "I'm grand – honestly."

"If you want to talk about anything, honey," her aunt said carefully, "I'm a real good listener. Anything you tell me will be entirely confidential. You needn't worry about me telling your mom, or that sort of thing." She slowed the car down again, taking her eyes from the road to have a good look at Cara. "I promise you that I'm not easily shocked."

Cara looked out of the car window, wondering if she had the courage to tell her. A few moments passed, and then she found herself searching for the words to start. "I don't know where to begin," she heard herself say feebly.

"Wherever you feel like to begin, honey," Jean said. "We have all the time in the world."

"Well . . ." Cara started, her voice a little hoarse, "things at home with Oliver aren't as perfect as my mother makes them sound."

"She has kind of contradicted herself a few times," Jean admitted, "and I did wonder about things. But I think I get more a feeling about it from you . . .when Oliver's name is mentioned."

"Is it that obvious?" Cara whispered.

"No," Jean said, "not really. I'm sure no one else would have picked it up. It's just that you sometimes have a kind of startled look when he's mentioned – as though you've forgotten all about him."

"I wish I could *forget* all about him," Cara said. "I wish I had been brave enough to forget about him years ago."

"Is it that bad?" Jean asked.

Cara turned her face towards the window, looking out at the vividly coloured trees flanking either side of the highway. "It depends on how you look at it. For years I put up with being left on my own, while he carried on with his life – and carried on with other women." She joined her hands together tightly, the way she did in the confession box. "Oh, he was good to me in other ways. And when we were first married, I thought he would change. But of course he didn't." She paused. "And now, the thing is, I've *suddenly changed*. I don't want to put up with him any more – and I really, really don't want Oliver any more."

"And you've just realised this?" Jean said, her voice high with surprise. "Has being over here made you feel differently about him?"

Cara shrugged. "In some ways . . . but my feelings had changed earlier on this year. I decided to come on this trip to get away from it all for a while." She ran a hand through her hair now. "I think being away has made me see the situation more clearly. I realise now that even if he's glad to see me when I get back, that it will soon go. He'll soon be seeing some other woman, when the novelty of having me home wears off on him."

There was a long pause.

"So what do you plan to do when you get back home?"

"I really don't know . . . it all depends on a number of things. And whether I've got the guts to go through with it."

"And would Jameson Carroll have anything to do with your decision?"

Cara felt her heart start to pound and the blood rush to her face. And for a moment she considered denying it all. But she knew there was no point. And she knew that she needed to talk this out with someone. "Oh, my God," she whispered, "how did you know?"

"Just a guess," Jean said, "just an older woman's guess."

Cara took a long, deep breath. "Yes," she admitted. "There is something between us . . . but exactly what it is, and where it will lead . . . I just don't know."

Jean gave a low whistle. "Boy . . . that sure complicates things for you, Cara."

They drove along for a bit in silence, then Cara realised that they had pulled off the highway, and were now coming to a halt in front of a small diner.

"Come on," Jean said cheerily, getting out of the car. "I think a nice, long coffee-break is called for. I know we're only a short drive from home – but we can chat here without having to explain anything to Bruce."

Over several cups of coffee, Cara poured the whole story of her marriage out, while Jean just listened.

"Okay, honey," Jean said, patting Cara's hand when she had finished recounting the anniversary scenario. "Don't upset yourself going over any more of it. You've been through hell with that rat, and how you've hidden it for so long from your mom and dad, I'll never know."

"I think it would nearly kill my mother if she knew," Cara said tearfully. "She still hasn't accepted Pauline's situation."

"Oh, pity about your mother!" Jean said angrily. She leaned across the table. "Listen, honey," she said, prodding the table for emphasis, "you must live your life for yourself. You can't live it for your mom or anybody else. It seems to me that you've wasted enough of your youth on that no-good husband of yours. Don't waste any more of it."

Cara nodded slowly. Then she said, "What about Jameson . . . are you shocked? Do you think I'm terrible?"

"Shocked?" Jean repeated, a smile coming to her lips. "No, sir . . . I'm not shocked. It takes a whole lot more to shock me than that. People feuding and being hateful to each other shocks me – but not two people having loving feelings towards each other. Whatever people like your mom have to say – love affairs have gone on throughout all the ages. They even went on when we were young back in Ireland." She shrugged, her eyes glinting mischievously. "It really ain't all that new, honey. Besides, you're a very attractive young woman, and he's a very charismatic, attractive man." She rolled her eyes. "A little bohemian for an old dame like me – but I can certainly see his charms." She leaned her elbows on the table. "Go on – tell me all about it. When did this thing start?"

Cara blushed and covered her face with her hands, like an awkward teenager. "I'm not even sure . . . probably at the wedding." She moved her hands a little, and when she looked at her aunt, suddenly they were both smiling. "Actually, it was before that – shortly after we met." She gave a shy giggle. "When we first met, it was the opposite – we were very hostile to one another."

Jean nodded. "That didn't last long, though? I could tell there was something at the firework display. I wasn't sure what, and I kind of forgot it with everything going on at the house."

Cara's face suddenly reddened. "I haven't done anything wrong – we haven't – I haven't been unfaithful to Oliver."

Jean held her hands up. "That's your business, honey – you're a grown woman."

"Oh, God," Cara said, her voice barely a whisper, "I'm so scared. I'm scared of committing myself . . . and I'm more scared of what will happen if I don't. I could regret this for the rest of my life."

Jean's hand came across the table to cover Cara's. "You still have time to find out. You have a couple of weeks left. Just spend as much time with him as you can, and find out as much as you can about each other. It's the only way." Her grip tightened on her niece's hand. "Do you have any idea of the extent of Jameson's feelings for you? How serious do you think it is?"

Cara bit her lip. "I know he likes me a lot," she admitted. "An awful lot considering the short time we've known each other."

"He's a real decent man," Jean said, "and I would have complete trust in anything he said. Any man who would take on the responsibility of Thomas the way Jameson Carroll has is a real special guy." She paused. "I don't want you to think I'm encouraging you into some kind of cheap holiday affair – but I don't want you to miss something that could change your life in a wonderful way. Like meeting Bruce changed mine."

"What about my parents?"

Jean gave a toss of her head. "Forget them just now. They're safely in Connecticut for the next few days." She gave a devilish grin. "At least we hope they are, and not wandering round some train station in New York!"

Cara managed to raise a little smile at the thought herself.

* * *

It was evening when they arrived back at the house, and Bruce met them at the door with news that some neighbours had dropped by to invite them over for supper and drinks. The Ashtons were a nice, friendly couple who had talked to Cara at the wedding. They had four young boys, and they were very interested on Cara's views on the best way to teach children to read. They had also told Bruce that they had some good photographs of the wedding reception that the family might like to see.

"You don't have to come," Jean whispered to Cara. "If you have something else you want to do, then you just go right ahead."

"I think," Cara said cagily, "that I'll have a quick shower and change, and then see how things are . . ."

"That's fine by me, honey," Jean said, "but I'm real happy to have supper at the Ashtons' tonight. Lesley always does fabulous food, and it'll save me cooking for Bruce." She rolled her eyes mischievously. "I'll go get him to fix us some nice cocktails, since I don't have your mom here, worrying about us all ending up gin-soaked in the gutter!"

Cara laughed and headed upstairs. She showered, dried the worst of the dampness off her hair with the hair dryer and then combed it out to finish off drying naturally.

She picked a yellow floral dress that Jameson hadn't seen. It was a simple shift-style dress that came just below the knee. She quickly zipped it up and slipped on her cream sandals. She took a few moments to touch some light perfume between her breasts and behind each ear, then she went downstairs to join her aunt and uncle who were watching the *I Love Lucy Show* on television.

"This is an experiment," Bruce warned Cara, handing around the V-shaped Martini glasses. "So blame my darling wife if it tastes damned awful."

"Oh, shush, Bruce!" Jean laughed. She turned to Cara. "It's a new recipe I got from a magazine," she explained enthusiastically. "It's called Magic Lady. It has brandy, coffee liqueur and Dubonnet shaken up and poured over crushed ice." She tossed her head in her husband's direction. "That's if the goddamned bartender got all the measurements correctly!"

Everyone roared with laughter and tipped their glasses together in a toast.

"I'll give it a go, anyway," Cara said gamely. She had never heard of half the drinks, far less tasted them. She took a little sip of the cocktail. It had a lovely, syrupy-sweet taste.

"Well?" Jean said, her eyebrows raised expectantly. "What's the verdict?"

"Delicious!" Cara pronounced. "Really, really nice."

"Oh, good!" Jean said. "I can add that to my list when we have friends over next. It's really supposed to be drunk after a meal – but what the heck!"

When she'd finished the sweet drink, Cara turned to her aunt. "I'm just going to call over to . . ." she nodded in the direction of the Carroll's house. "Then I'll phone or come back over to let you know what I'm doing."

Jean patted her hand in answer – her eyes discreetly fixed on the comedy show.

Cara pushed the lightweight mosquito-door open and headed towards the now-familiar lakeside path.

Twenty minutes or so later, she was back – sorely disappointed.

There was no sign of any life around the big white, wooden house. The car had gone and the house was all locked up. Cara wondered if something had happened – if Jameson had had to go off to New York. Or maybe someone had called him up and invited him and Thomas out. Maybe another woman. Maybe one of the women who had phoned him up the first day she was in the house. And maybe he'd gone – because he'd given up waiting for her.

* * *

The evening passed pleasantly. The Ashton family were like most of the other Americans she had met – extremely hospitable and welcoming – and the kids had kept Cara very well occupied. They ranged in age from two up to seven – and she quickly discovered that Lesley and Alan needed no advice on how to help the boys read. The eldest three were already fairly adept at it, and their love of books and the pictures in them was more than obvious. There were children's books in every room in the house, and the boys all sat in a perfect row – with Cara in the middle – as she read them several stories before they went off to bed.

The adults then sat down to eat at a friendly round table set with large wine glasses and sharp steak knives, and some easy music playing in the background. The meal was casual and relaxed with roast vegetables and beef in a spicy sauce, mopped up with large chunks of crusty bread. A home-made pudding of apple strudel and cream followed.

Cara was surprised that she felt hungry, and she polished off most of the meal with a couple of glasses of wine that helped to relax her into the whole thing.

Since meeting Jameson Carroll, Cara's appetite had suddenly vanished, and food now no longer seemed either important or comforting. But tonight, she didn't want to think of him, because he could be off out anywhere. Maybe even off out with another woman.

She didn't really think that was the case. In fact she knew that he wasn't with another woman. But there was a childish, jealous little bit in her that entertained the idea every so often over the evening.

He was off out somewhere, and Cara didn't have a clue where that somewhere might be.

The night passed fairly quickly, and if Cara's thoughts

hadn't been dictated by her feelings for Jameson then it would have been a perfect night out. She enjoyed the food, the company and the conversation. And later she enjoyed looking at the photographs that the Ashtons had taken at the wedding and back at the lake later that night.

Cara's heart had almost stopped several times when she caught sight of Jameson or Thomas in one of the frames. Thomas figured prominently in several of the photos, but his father was always in the background – where she knew he preferred to be.

Cara glanced over at Jean as they passed the photographs to each other, but apart from Jean commenting on how nice Thomas looked in one of the photos, she made no issue of Jameson in front of Bruce or their neighbours.

* * *

It was close to midnight when they got back to the house, and Cara fought back the urge to walk down to the lake and look across at the white house. Just to check whether a light was on – a sign that Jameson was back home, a reassuring sign that he wasn't too far away from her, that she could lie in bed and know that he was a lakeside path away from her. She could have made some excuse to Bruce and Jean about wanting to look at the stars, or feeling like a last walk out in the fresh air before bed.

But she didn't.

Instead, she sat and had a hot cocoa with her aunt and uncle, and then headed upstairs to bed around half-past twelve. She lay for a while, staring at the same page in a magazine, and eventually dropped it on the floor unread. Then she turned out the light and closed her eyes, and finally drifted off into sleep.

At some early hour in the morning she awoke with a start, her heart pounding, her mouth dry and the palms of her hands damp with perspiration. She sat bolt upright in bed, wondering what on earth had brought this awful bout of anxiety on. And then a picture flashed in her mind – and she knew exactly what had caused it.

It was the thought of losing the American artist from across the lake. The thought of never seeing him again.

Whilst she had successfully managed to block him out of her mind for some of the time earlier on, at night her mind had refused to ignore it. She now knew, beyond all shadow of a doubt, that nothing was going to stop her from seeing Jameson Carroll.

The decision made, the panicky feelings immediately started to subside, and were replaced with a feeling of energy. She threw back the bedcovers and quietly made her way downstairs and into the kitchen. She gulped down a glass of cold water, and then went over to the window to look out into the darkness.

It would be several hours until it was daylight, and there was no point in staring out at the shadowy trees until then.

She forced herself to go back upstairs to bed, and to close her eyes. To convince herself – like a child who is waiting for Christmas to come – that sleep is the quickest way to pass the time.

Chapter 24

Tullamore, County Offaly

The shop doorbell tinkled and Pauline looked up from the bacon slicer which she had just washed and was now putting back together. Her face stiffened as she saw the blonde head of Rose Quinn appear through the door. She put the last piece of the machine back in its place, then she turned to her co-worker.

"Are you all right there, until it's time to close the shop up, Peenie?" she asked, her arms folded over defensively. She glanced back at Rose then gestured for her to go on through to the house. "You can make a start on lifting in the potato sacks," she told the assistant, "and the vegetable boxes from the front door. And Peenie – would you keep an eye on Bernadette? Two of the Murphy girls are playing with her outside."

"Sound as a pound, Pauline!" Peenie said, straightening himself up and holding an illicit cigarette behind his back. "Sound as a pound!" Pauline was nearly as easy-going as Charles in the shop, but she was still a Kearney none the less. He tipped his cap now and gave the sullen Rose an ingratiating smile as she passed him by without a glance. He only vaguely knew her as one of the uppity Quinns from somewhere off out beyond Ballycommon – but he knew by the well-dyed head on her that she wouldn't be too uppity when it came to a bit of sport with the men. Although by the look of her – only certain kinds of men.

As soon as both girls had their backs to him, Peenie moved forward, craning his neck over the counter to get a look at their legs. It was almost a wasted exercise as both girls were clad in trousers – but at least he had the pleasure of watching their neat, firm backsides disappear through to the back.

He clapped his hands and then rubbed them together, thinking how the sight of a good-looking girl fairly lifted a man's heart. Then, he took a last few drags on the cigarette, and crushed it under his heel on the wooden shop floor. That, and any other signs of laxity would be well swept out of the shop by the time Declan and Maggie Kearney returned. Then, Peenie headed out to lift in the sacks and boxes he had put out there at ten o'clock that morning.

* * *

"I wasn't expecting to see you around here in a hurry," Pauline said, going over to lift the steaming kettle from the top of the cooker.

Rose's head and shoulders drooped. "I meant to come over earlier in the week," she said, fiddling with her double strand of pearls, "but I haven't been too grand."

"Well," Pauline said, now busying herself with the tea-making paraphernalia, "things weren't too grand here when I got back home that Sunday night." She came over to the table and landed a small plate of digestives on it

271

with a bit of a thud – just to leave Rose in no doubt as to her mood.

"Oh?" Rose said, not sure which way to go. She folded her arms and crossed her legs now. "What happened?"

There was a painful, protracted silence.

"I thought we had nearly lost Bernadette," Pauline stated, highly exaggerating the situation.

Rose's hand came to her mouth, and Pauline noticed that her nail-polish was very chipped and neglected-looking altogether. Most unusual and careless for the up-to-date Rose who liked to have everything just right.

"There was nearly an ambulance on its way out from the General Hospital," Pauline continued, "and poor Charles was practically gone out of his mind with worry. He had to get poor Oliver Gayle out of his bed to come over and see what he thought. If I hadn't landed home when I did – God alone knows what might have happened."

"What happened to her?" said Rose, her voice low with dread.

"She was almost poisoned," Pauline said, pouring out two cups of tea. She was enjoying Rose's discomfiture greatly, and wasn't going to ease off until she had made her pay.

"*Poisoned?*" Rose said in a high, nervous voice, twisting the pearls around her fingers.

"Yes," Pauline said, nodding her head and raising her eyebrows dramatically, "poisoned." She poured milk into the two cups, and then pushed the sugar bowl across to Rose. "She got hold of some kind of plaster – the kind that a statue or an ornament would be made of."

Pauline had no intentions of telling Rose the story of

the Virgin Mary's nose – it was much too light-hearted and comical for the serious point she was trying to hammer home. And she certainly wasn't going to mention the two plates of lumpy custard that Charles had concocted – and that surely was the real cause of Bernadette's sickness. To start laughing about it would only be letting Rose off the hook, and it was far too early for that.

"And what did it do to her?" Rose asked, putting two large spoonfuls of sugar into her cup.

"It made her violently sick," Pauline said, "and gave her a raging temperature." She took a sip of her tea, surprised that Rose didn't quiz her further as to where Bernadette would have got hold of plaster in the first place. She was usually quicker off the mark about things, wanting to know all the details. "We were up the whole night with her," Pauline elaborated, "damping her down with wet cloths and everything. And then I had to take her into Doctor Morrell first thing the next morning, just to be sure." Then for a finish-up, she added. "She was on this horrible medicine for the rest of the week – the poor little thing."

Rose looked dolefully into her cup of tea. "And has she been all right since?" she asked in a low voice.

"Grand," Pauline said in a kind of snappy tone. "Thanks be to God and his Blessed Mother." A fleeting picture of the nose-less statue came into her mind, which she immediately banished lest she should give an inappropriate grin.

There was another silence.

"I had a bit of an awkward predicament myself," Rose suddenly said.

Pauline looked over the rim of her teacup and waited. She wasn't going to coax it out of her fair-weather friend.

"That fella," Rose said, "the McCarthy lad . . . he turned real strange on me."

"How do you mean *strange?*" Pauline asked, interested in spite of herself.

"The drink must have got the better of him," Rose said, trying to sound flippant and failing due a watery quiver in her voice, "because he came from a decent enough family. He turned very nasty altogether . . ."

"In what way?" Pauline asked, her tone less icy. "Did he do something?"

Rose shrugged and lifted a digestive that she didn't really want. "He had a fair go," she said, breaking the biscuit in two, "but he didn't get as far as he would've liked."

Pauline looked closer at Rose now, suddenly realising that this was not just an ordinary social call. "What exactly did he do, Rose?" Her voice was softer, all anger about last Sunday now being pushed to the side.

Rose's head drooped again.

"You'll have to tell me," Pauline said. "I can't just guess . . ."

Rose put the cup and the biscuit on the table, and without any preamble lifted up her pink jumper to reveal several bluish-red bruises around her waist, and one very nasty weal.

"Oh, my God!" Pauline said, putting her own cup down now.

"Those bruises are from his hands gripping me," Rose said dully, "and the scratch from the buckle of his belt when he got up on top of me. He had his mickey out and everything – he was determined to have a good go at me."

"The filthy pig! Oh, I'm so sorry, Rose!" Pauline came over to put her hand on her friend's shoulder.

Rose then proceeded to pull one trouser-leg up – which again had bruises – and there was also a large sticking-plaster on her shin bone. "That was when I tried to get out of the car," she explained. "I hit my legs on the car door when he was trying to drag me back in." Then she rolled her trouser leg back down. "I had a close call – if he hadn't been so drunk, I wouldn't have been able to fight him off . . ."

"What did your mother and father say when you got home?" Pauline whispered, aghast at her friend's news.

"Nothing," Rose said, "because they don't know about it. They were in bed, and they only called out from their bedroom." She shrugged. "I've been wearing trousers since, so they haven't seen the state of my legs."

Pauline's eyes were wide with shock. "I can't believe it," she said. "He looked so young and harmless. He looked a bit of a drunken eejit all right – but I would definitely have said he was real harmless."

"Ah, well," Rose said, taking a drink from the tea, "I've learned a hard lesson – no mistake about it."

"I'm so sorry you did," Pauline said, rubbing her friend's arm. "Are you going to take it any further? Go to the Gardai or anything? You should, you know. What he did was against the law."

Rose shook her head. "No . . . I just want to forget all about it. Apart from the few bruises I'm none the worse." She pursed her mouth tightly now, and looked down at the table. "Thanks for being so nice, Pauline," she whispered. "I wasn't so nice to you last Sunday night."

"Forget it," Pauline said. "It's all behind us."

Rose gave a weak smile that didn't reach her watery eyes. "As I say – I've learned a fierce hard lesson. If I'd travelled home the same way I'd gone in – none of this would have happened."

Pauline squeezed Rose's hand and decided to say nothing else about the matter. It was all water under the bridge. And anyway – who was she to throw stones where making mistakes with men was concerned?

* * *

"So you never looked in on Mrs Lynch this afternoon at all?" Peenie said in surprise, as he handed the keys over to Charles outside the shop.

Charles slid one sleeve of his loose jumper up to the elbow, and then did the same with the other. "Well," he said, folding his arms and leaning up against the side of his father's car, "it wasn't just as straightforward as that."

Peenie – looking unfamiliar out of his brown shop overalls – came to lean on the car beside him and light the butt of a cigarette he'd saved from earlier. "So, what's the story?"

"I passed her in the town," Charles explained. "Her and the son were heading up the High Street. So I said to myself that I might as well head on in to the library, and then take a wander around to the house later on." He took his glasses off now, rubbed his eyes, and then chewed thoughtfully on the end of one of the legs of the glasses.

"And what happened then?" Peenie prompted, suddenly thinking of the sausages and eggs his mother would be frying up for him at any minute.

"Well, *nothing* really . . ." Charles said. "As it turned

out, she wasn't at home later on either." He put his glasses
on. "I might take another run out there later on this
evening – maybe around eight or so."

Peenie's eyebrows shot up. "Ye'd want to be careful
calling out to womens's houses late in the evening.
Especially when they're on their own."

Charles shrugged. "What harm? Hasn't she got a good
blazer of mine out there?" He straightened up his
shoulders, as his mother was always reminding him to do.
"I'm only calling on a business matter. Surely, there's
nobody could find anything strange about that?"

Peenie shook his head. "Ye'd want to be fierce careful
goin' around a widow wumman late in the evening . . ."
He clenched the inch-long butt in his teeth, and hoisted
up the waistband of his brown corduroy trousers. "I had a
bit of trouble meself, when I was over the water in
England – I nearly had a woman go high-sterical on me
for calling out to the house late at night. And I wasn't
even terrible jarred or anything – only a few oul' pints on
me."

Charles nodded his head knowingly. "English women
are a different kettle of fish now, Peenie. Indeed they are.
England has a terrible effect on their nerves. Even the Irish
women who go over there for a while seem to be affected.
You can tell that from my own sister." He shook his head
sadly. "Poor Pauline's never been the same since she came
back. She wasn't half as cross and suspicious as she is now
before she went." His face brightened. "Now, Mrs Lynch
wouldn't be a bit like that."

"Well, you sound like a man that knows his own
business," Peenie said, lifting his eyes to heaven. He could
almost hear the rashers of bacon crackling in the pan.

"Now – I'd better be on me way. The head-woman will have the oul' bite nearly ready by now."

"Mrs Lynch is a down-to-earth woman," Charles continued, "and wouldn't take a person up the wrong way." He gave Peenie a knowing smile. "Believe you me, Peenie – I know what I'm talking about."

Peenie flicked the cigarette-butt high in the air over the car. "A thought just crossed my mind, Charles," he said, "a *mighty* thought. You don't think that mad fella could have been doin' a line with Mrs Lynch or anythin'?"

"A line?" Charles said, his brow creasing.

"Courtin' . . . *you know*, walkin' out with her," Peenie said. "Because that would explain everythin' – now that would paint a whole different picture entirely."

"You mean Mrs Lynch could be romantically entangled with somebody else?" Charles asked, sounding incredulous. "I would hardly think so. And certainly not somebody of that fellow's calibre – certainly not somebody that would throw himself on top of a moving vehicle. A complete lunatic."

"Well . . ." Peenie said, buttoning up his old navy suit jacket, "I wouldn't be too sure about it, Charlie boy. I'd give it a bit of thought if I were you." He gave Charles a friendly punch on the arm. "Good luck to ye now, Charles – an' I'll be seeing you in the morning."

And on that parting word of advice – Peenie took his leave, his step hastened by the thought of the grand fry-up that lay waiting in the pan for him.

Chapter 25

Lake Savannah

Jameson was the first thought on Cara's mind when she woke with the early morning sun glinting through the window as he had been the last thought in her head when she closed her eyes only hours earlier.

It was Jameson again as she slipped out of bed and into a warm bath, and he was there again she did up the buttons on her pale pink blouse and zipped up her ankle-length white trousers.

And her mind was full of him as she padded barefoot across the polished oak floors carrying her leather loafers in her hand, and as she silently left the house.

The light inside door creaked slightly as she closed it behind her, and she waited for a few moments to see if she had disturbed her aunt and uncle. But there was not a sound to be heard in or out of the house. Not even a moan or a creak from the tall pine trees outside. Not even a tinkle from the windchimes hanging from the beam on the deck. Not a sound from the birds or the noisy crickets.

Cara paused for a few moments looking up at the sky, wondering whether the light was coming from the leftover moon or a very early sun – or maybe a combination of them both. But it didn't matter, it was light of some kind.

She looked across the lake and wondered if Jameson would be awake and up as he told her he would. If he would be across the lake, sitting in his rocking-chair – waiting for her.

Then, before she had time to wonder any more, she felt her feet start to move and she was running. Off down the garden path, through the trees and flowers, over the little bridge and down to the side of the lake. She slowed down then, and her eyes scanned the front of the house looking for him. But she could see nothing. Nothing to convince her that he found the possibility of her company more desirable than sleep.

Then, her heart suddenly soared as she heard her name called out.

She looked again, and then he appeared – beside the garden swing. A figure in shorts and a brown sweatshirt. And she knew even from this distance that it was the same shade of brown as his eyes.

He waved to her, beckoning her to hurry over.

She felt her feet desperate to break into a run again, but restrained herself. It was bad enough appearing at a man's house at this hour of the morning, without running hysterically towards him.

She moved into something between a light jog and a quick walk.

But Jameson wasn't concerned about showing any kind of restraint or control. He was running towards her, and leaping over the white picket fence. And now he was moving at a fair speed around the lakeside path.

As soon as they met, their arms were wrapped around each other, and he was lifting her up and off the ground. "You've come!" he said into her hair and neck. "You've actually come."

"I have come," she told him, laughing with excitement. "And this time, I am sure."

He halted for a moment, and then held her at arm's length to look into her eyes.

She nodded – giving her answer to the question he hadn't yet asked.

Then, he reached down and took her hand in his and they walked silently back to the house, smiling at each other. As they climbed the steps to the open front door, Cara glanced back to the Harpers' house. Her mind gave a fleeting thought to her mother and father in Connecticut – oblivious to the fact that their daughter was about to commit adultery. About to jump into bed with a man she had known for a very short time. And about to die with desire if he didn't ask her.

But there was no asking to be done. Without a word, he led her through the large, airy hallway filled with his paintings. Past the sitting-room that smelled of wild and garden flowers. And past the kitchen that smelt of cinnamon and freshly ground coffee.

He led her straight to the room filled with the dark, beautifully carved, masculine furniture. He led her to the room that held his bed.

When the door had clicked shut after them, he turned towards her. "Are you sure about this?" he said in a low voice. "I don't want you to regret anything . . ."

There was a bare pause.

"I'm sure," Cara whispered. Then she stood up on tiptoes to wrap her arms around his neck. His beautiful soft, tanned neck. And she kissed him long and deeply, letting him know that she was really sure of what she wanted. When that kiss ended there was a little pause. Then his lips came down hard on hers, and their bodies automatically locked together, each knowing what was to come.

Everything that his fine artistic hands had promised – and everything that Cara had imagined – was now about to become reality. And she suddenly felt herself tremble as he slowly undid her pink blouse buttons – one by one – and then slipped it from her shoulders.

Her breath came in short gasps as his head bent and he placed the lightest of kisses between her breasts. Then, in an easy, natural way, he reached his hands to undo the clasp on the back of her bra. Then, very gently, he slipped that off too.

He stood back now to look at her. Not far enough back to embarrass her, but far enough to look upon her lightly tanned body.

The body that had completely possessed his mind for the last week.

"You are so – so beautiful," he told her.

And something in his voice touched somewhere deep in Cara, and she found herself brimming with confidence – the kind of confidence she had never felt with her husband.

Now she moved towards Jameson. Her trembling hands lifted the sweatshirt up over his tanned, hard chest and then she laughed as she dragged it over his unruly, thick hair.

Then, he drew her close to him, and she could feel the heat from his skin against the cool softness of her naked breasts.

Then it was Cara who took his hand and led him towards the big, carved wooden bed, where they finished undressing each other between slow and ever-deepening kisses.

Jameson stopped at one point, and his eyes looked deep into hers.

"I want you so much, Cara – much more than I ever knew a man could want a woman. I've wanted you so much, it hurts." His voice was low "But I need to know you are okay about this . . ."

Cara put a hand on either side of his handsome, worried-looking face. "Listen, Mr Jameson Carroll," she told him as though he were one of her pupils, "the only regret I will have – is if this thing doesn't happen between us." Her tone was suddenly more serious. "I came over here this morning, because I'm afraid of throwing this wonderful thing away. I'm afraid of never knowing you properly. You're the best thing that's ever happened in my life – and I am not going to spend the rest of my life wishing I'd been braver."

"Oh, Cara – Cara Gayle," he whispered now. "I can't believe that something this good has happened to me. I never expected to feel this strongly about a woman . . . I've never, *ever* felt it this way before."

And when he lay her back on the patchwork quilt to move his hands over her body, she felt a hot rush of wanting that she had never experienced before. She marvelled that he had such smooth, fine hands for a man – and not only sensitive hands but a deep and sensitive nature, too. So different from the cold, defensive exterior he had shown when they first met.

He now moved his lips along the same route that his hands had taken, until she felt every single nerve in her body jump to alertness. When his mouth finally found hers again, it was hotter and rougher this time and his tongue was searching. And then she suddenly felt his hardness lower down, moving heavily against her stomach and thighs. And when he finally positioned himself to move within her, Cara Gayle did not feel or show the slightest resistance.

Her body arched high to meet his until he was deep inside her. And then they moved together in a rhythm so natural and easy that they could have been lovers from a long way back. She felt herself respond with an eagerness she had never thought she was capable of. But then, she had never imagined wanting someone desperately the way her body now wanted him.

And the deep pleasure she had never imagined continued until suddenly her whole body started to soar like one of the rockets in the sky – and Jameson held her there, at a peak she had never known before, for one ecstatic moment after another.

And then – when he could hold back no longer – he joined her at that pinnacle, pouring every last drop of himself inside her.

For what seemed like an age, there was not a sound in the large white house, apart from their breathing as it eventually slowed down and returned to normal.

Jameson reached a hand to smooth Cara's hair and then he gently touched her face. "You realise that I love you? Really, *really* love you?"

His question demanded no answer, no commitment – nothing. It was simply a statement, a fact.

And when Cara's eyes met his, there was no need for words to give an answer, for he could see the love shining from them. Instead, she lifted her head from the pillow to once again seek his lips. And then they clung together as though nothing in the world would ever come between them.

* * *

By the time that Thomas had come down for breakfast, his father was teaching Cara how to make pancakes, American-style – although teaching her in a very light-hearted, messing-about sort of way. Thomas was delighted to see her, and in his innocence, never questioned the fact of having such an early morning visitor. He immediately joined in the spirit of the morning, searching out a selection of syrups and spreads to accompany the pancakes. Then together the three of them sat at the table as though they were used to having breakfast in this way every morning.

"I'll clear up," Thomas said, thumbing towards the sink. "You two cooked, so it's only fair."

"Okay, buddy," Jameson said, throwing an arm around his son. "I won't argue with that! We'll take our coffee out onto the deck, and leave you solely in charge."

The boy immediately draped a clean tea-towel over one shoulder, in the fashion of a busy kitchen hand, and set about collecting up the used crockery

When they had settled themselves outside, Jameson turned to Cara "What about the rest of the day?" he asked anxiously. "Do you have to go back?"

"No problem," Cara said with a smile. "I've already sorted things out with Jean. She won't mind what I do for the next few days."

"Really?" he said, his eyebrows raised in surprise. "Does she know about . . ."

Cara nodded, blushing slightly. "Yes . . . I didn't really have to tell her. She'd worked it all out by herself."

"What did she reckon to it?" he said quietly.

Cara shrugged. "She was very understanding. We talked a lot yesterday about my situation back home and everything . . . and she understands."

Jameson looked over his shoulder, checking that Thomas was still occupied in the kitchen and then he moved behind Cara's wooden deckchair and wrapped his arms around her and nuzzled his face in her neck. "I'm glad we have some real time together. Since meeting you, everything else just seems a waste of time."

Cara rested her head on his arms, and they both sat looking over the lake.

"I know I'm a bore saying this again and again," Jameson whispered, "but I really do love you, Cara Gayle – with all my heart."

"And I, Jameson Carroll," Cara whispered back, "love you, too. And whatever happens now – happens."

Chapter 26

Cara called back over to Harpers' house later in the morning. Jean was busy pottering around with her indoor plants and Bruce was outside in shorts and a hat, working with the hose in the garden. Each greeted her with smiling faces, telling her that her mother and father had rung to let them know that they were safely in the hands of Declan's cousin. Then, they offered to drive her to the shops or to sightsee, but she thanked them both and declined. Over another cup of coffee, she told Jean that she had gone across early in the morning to see Jameson.

The older woman smiled and patted Cara's hand. "As I said yesterday, honey, we only have one life. We're here if you want us, but Bruce and I won't interfere with any plans you have for the next few days. As far as we're concerned, you're down by the lake reading and swimming, or taking a walk." She shrugged. "The less we actually know, the easier it is all round. I can't tell your folks anything I don't know."

"Oh, Jean," Cara said, her eyes shining with emotion, "I don't know how to thank you –"

"Just be happy, Cara," Jean said. "That's all the thanks I want. The older you get, the more unhappiness you see around you, and I reckon a lot of it is people regretting missed opportunities." She took a sip of her coffee. "At least I won't feel that, and neither will you." She tilted her head, a thoughtful look on her face. "You know I had it real difficult when I wrote home and told them I was seeing Bruce? According to everyone, he was too old, had been married before, wasn't a Catholic, and worst of all – he was American!" She gave a roar of laughter. "How absolutely dreadful – having someone in the family who was married to an American." Then she looked serious again. "My parents who objected are long dead, Cara, and after all this time nobody else really gives a damn."

"What about my mother?" Cara asked curiously.

"Oh, your mother didn't approve, that's for sure," Jean said, a resigned look in her eyes, "but it was the way we were brought up, and she always took her religion very, very seriously. She's always been afraid of the Church."

"And what about your own religious views?" Cara asked.

Jean shrugged. "Oh, I have strong enough beliefs in God and all that kind of thing, but I always believed that it was people's behaviour towards others that counted more. It's no good kneeling in church counting rosary beads night after night, or wearing sackcloth and ashes if you're real mean to people. I think Jesus would have wanted us to follow his example by not judging other folks."

"You must have had real courage to go against everyone," Cara said.

"I'm not real sure what made me brave enough to break the mould, honey – but I think it was love." She rolled her eyes, laughing. "I bet you're shocked at the thought of an older woman like me talking about love."

"No," Cara said, "I think it's lovely . . . I really do."

"Well," Jean shrugged, "that's the way it is, honey. Having said all that, your mom and Bruce get on real well now . . . so, what the heck. I don't hold any grudges. As I said, time changes everything."

"You're right," Cara said, smiling. "What the heck!"

After freshening up and changing, Cara made her way back over to Jameson's house, and they spent the rest of the day there, swimming, talking and enjoying doing just ordinary things together. Thomas was with them for most of the time, and several times Cara caught herself shaking her head in wonder at the easy way she had slipped into their lives.

"Da-ad?" Thomas said, as they headed back into the house for a chicken salad Jameson had organised. "Shall I put out – paints for the Saturday group later?"

Jameson stopped in his tracks. "Saturday?" he repeated, his brow creasing in confusion. "Holy shit!" he said, slapping his palm to his forehead. "I'd completely forgotten . . ." Then, he turned to Thomas, smiling. "Yeah – okay. Thanks for reminding me. You can put the stuff out after we've eaten."

"I'd better wash – hands first," Thomas said, racing on ahead.

"I'm really sorry," Jameson said to Cara. "I have a painting session tomorrow with some of the kids from

Thomas's school. The last one for the summer should have been last week, but I cancelled it because of the wedding, and swapped it for this week. Do you mind having a bunch of teenagers around in the morning?"

"No," Cara said, an amused grin spreading on her face. "In fact I'd be delighted."

"What's so funny?" Jameson said, putting his arm around her.

Cara leaned her head on his shoulder. "You got a phone call about that last week when I was here, didn't you? From someone called Melanie?"

Jameson thought for a moment. "Yeah," he nodded vaguely, "I did – but I'd completely forgotten about it with everything . . ."

Cara rolled her eyes in amusement. "I thought . . ." she giggled like a schoolgirl, "I actually thought you were arranging a date with a woman . . . and I felt . . ."

"What?" he said, looking curious. "What did you feel?"

Cara's cheeks turned pink with embarrassment. "Oh . . . it was stupid. I suppose I felt . . . sort of . . . jealous. I felt you were this stranger with a mysterious life I knew nothing about."

"I hope I'm not a big disappointment," Jameson laughed, "because instead of illicit dates, all I'm doing is splashing a bit of paint around the studio with some kids."

"I can assure you that I'm not a bit disappointed," Cara said, squeezing his arm. "You're much more interesting than I could ever have imagined . . ." Then her voice dropped. "I suppose my natural instinct is to expect other women to be in the picture . . . living with Oliver for so long."

Jameson pulled her towards him, and tenderly took her

face between his hands. "Never," he said, "as long as there is a chance for us to be together, will there ever be another woman." He kissed her lips. "There will never be another woman who will make me feel the way I feel when I'm with you, Cara."

"It's really weird how things have turned out," Cara whispered. "I was nearly afraid of you when we first met – when I dropped all those parcels."

His eyebrows raised in a question. "You mean the little lingerie parcels?"

Cara looked at him, her face colouring up again. "So you *did* know what was in the parcels?"

He grinned. "It didn't take a genius to work it out," he said. "It had the name of the shop on the wrapping paper, and anyway – everyone round here knows that shop."

"Oh, God!" Cara said, laughing again. "I was so embarrassed when I met you that day – what with that lunatic following me around and everything – and then I went and dropped my parcels. I nearly died, but I just hoped you hadn't spotted the name of the lingerie shop!"

"Well," he whispered now, "if the little lacy things you wore this morning happened to come from one of those packages, then I have to be glad you paid the shop a visit that day!"

Cara prodded his chest in her best schoolteacher manner. "You weren't so funny that day, Mr Carroll – you were anything but funny. In fact, you had an extremely high-handed manner."

"Oh, Cara," he said, looking contrite, "if you knew the number of people that speak to me when I'm with Thomas – the number of do-gooder types who approach me, just to let me know that they don't really think he's some kind of freak . . ." His voice cracked a little. "I'm really sorry that I treated you like them . . ." Then, he gathered her into his arms. "I nearly made the biggest mistake of my life – I could have easily missed getting to know you. It frightens me when I think of it – all these lovely days we might never have had."

"I'm only codding you," Cara said gently. "I don't care how we met – in fact we owe it to that weird fellow who was following me – otherwise we'd probably have never met."

"No, " Jameson said, ruffling her hair, "I reckon we'll let Thomas have the credit for that."

The day passed into evening, and after another brief visit over to Harper's, Cara came back to spend her first full night at Jameson's house.

Thomas headed up to bed around nine o'clock in preparation for the art class in the morning, and Cara and Jameson were left on their own. Since the evening was still warm, they sat out on the floodlit deck drinking cold beer and eating salted pretzels and crackers and cheese.

"I love this," Cara told him with a lazy, contented smile. "I've never had any man prepare lunch and supper for me before. I could quite easily take to this way of life."

"I'd happily fix us lunch and supper every day for the rest of my life," Jameson told her in a low voice. Then he looked at her for a few moments, his eyes narrowed. "Tell me you're not going back to Ireland, Cara."

Cara ran a hand through her hair, turning her gaze away from him. "I have to, Jameson. I don't want to – but I have to go back."

"Why?" he asked, his voice rising. "*Why* do you have to go back to Ireland? It just doesn't make any sense. You told me earlier you didn't love your husband."

"This isn't just about Oliver," she said. "It's all so complicated . . . I have commitments – school and family and friends. I can't just not go back." She bit her lip. "I don't want to go back to Ireland – and I don't want to go back to Oliver, but – "

"Jesus, Cara!" he said now, his voice cracking. "I can't even bear you mentioning his fucking name! I feel so jealous and angry that you're married to that guy – especially when he's someone who doesn't deserve you."

"Please leave it," Cara said, putting a finger to his lips to silence his words. "Not *tonight*. We can talk about things like that later . . . but not tonight." She put her glass on the wooden table, and then reached to take the glass from his hand. Then, she moved closer to him and wrapped her arms around his neck. "I have a much better idea for tonight."

Chapter 27

Cara woke early in the morning, hardly able to believe that she had spent the whole night with this American man in his high, dark wooden bed – this American man who was a stranger only a short time ago. She turned towards him and gently ran her fingers over the back of his neck, and then traced a path down the outline of his spine. When she reached the lower part of his back, he suddenly turned around and playfully pulled her into his arms.

"I thought you were still asleep – you cheat!" she giggled, pretending to struggle.

But Jameson merely laughed and pulled her closer, burying her protests in his warm chest. Then, just before the new day dawned – they made slow, glorious love once again.

Later, as they lay in each other's arms, Jameson turned towards her. "Surely, there's some excuse we could find, for you not going back just yet?" His eyes raised to the ceiling, as though searching for an answer. "What about if you were to say you were sick or something? You could stay on for another month – I'll buy you another ticket.

Cara was silent for a few moments. "It wouldn't work," she said quietly. "If I said I was ill, my parents would stay on with me. They would never go back home to Ireland without me. And anyway, there's school. I have to go back for work."

He propped himself up on one elbow, determination written all over his tanned face. "Look, what if you just tell them *everything*? Explain it all to your parents – tell them you've decided to stay on here. Phone your . . ." he halted, choking on the word, "your *husband* . . . and phone the school. Just tell them you're not coming back."

"I couldn't!" Cara gasped. "I just couldn't. It would practically kill my mother . . . and even if I didn't have all these problems – I couldn't just stay on here. What would I do for a living? Where would I stay?"

"Why would you have to work?" he said in amazement. "Money's not a problem . . . I've more than enough for all three of us. Money will never be a problem for us, Cara. You can take that little issue out of the equation." He touched her arm gently. "You would live with Thomas and me – it would make me the happiest guy in the world to look after you."

Cara looked at him, her eyes growing moist. Then, with a catch in her throat, she said, "I've only known you for just over a week . . . and yet, you're offering to have me live out here and keep me financially." She shook her head. "This kind of thing doesn't happen to me."

"It does," he said quietly, "if you'll only give me the chance to make it happen. But I don't want you to feel that I'm trying to force you into anything . . . I'm just trying to be realistic. Some things in life are real problems, and some things aren't. We gotta get the things that aren't problems out of the way – and money is one of them. I just wish," he said quietly, "that I could deal with all the other problems like your family so simply."

She pondered over his suggestion for a few moments. "Look, Jameson," she said in a small, weary voice, "I really cannot make such monumental decisions in such a short time. When the holiday is over, I need to go home and think about everything –" She shrugged. "I need time to decide how to go about things – then maybe I could come back for a holiday at Christmas or something –"

He interrupted her. "Tell me honestly, Cara . . . are you saying there is a chance you may decide against coming back? That I may not see you again?"

"No, no – I'm not saying that . . ." But there was the slightest hesitation in her voice. She lowered her eyes. "I want to be with you more than anything in the world – you know that. But there are so many things to sort out . . . we just have to give it a bit of time."

He nodded slowly, but the look on his face told her that he was not convinced.

* * *

Later that morning over breakfast, Jameson turned to Cara. "There's something I want to ask you – something real personal."

"Ask me anything you like."

"I don't mean to pry . . . but how come you haven't had children? It's just that you're obviously so good with them . . ."

"It's OK," Cara said. "People ask me that all the time.

Back at home, everyone's supposed to have half a dozen children at least – so I'm a bit of a curiosity with none."

"And?" he prompted.

"And," Cara shrugged, "nothing ever happened. I don't know whose fault it is, because we've never really got around to doing anything about it." She looked down at her hands. "I've a feeling the problem might be mine . . . I've always had difficulties with . . ." She stopped, embarrassed at talking this way with a man. "It's just that . . . my monthly cycle has always been a bit wonky. Either too often, or disappearing for months."

"What about your husband?"

"Oh," Cara said, "he went through a phase of talking about babies a few years ago . . . but when it came to the stage of seeing a specialist, he backed out." She sighed. "He said he'd rather leave it and see what happened . . . but I'm sure he just couldn't face finding out that he might have a problem."

"And you?" Jameson asked.

"When I first got married," Cara said, with a little quiver in her voice, "I used to pray for a baby first thing in the morning and last thing before going to sleep. I thought it was the one thing that might make things better between me and Oliver." She swept one wing of her hair back behind her ear. "It's all water under the bridge . . . I can see it was all for the best. And anyway," she said, giving a little smile, "if I'd had children, I'd never have been able to come to America."

"And," Jameson said, "we would never have met."

* * *

The painting class revealed another side of Jameson.

Having met Thomas first, Cara supposed now that she had taken for granted the relationship father and son had. Jameson was just the way that any good father should be, although Cara knew that it was an unusual arrangement. Even by American standards, it was not usual for a father to have sole responsibility of a child. Especially a child like Thomas.

Even taking all that into account, she was not prepared for the way he connected with the other kids in his class. From the moment the small coach had pulled into the drive – and the kids all poured out – Cara saw a depth to the man she had never seen in any other.

There were three boys and three girls, ranging from around twelve to sixteen. Each one came up to Thomas in turn and demanded that he 'gimme five' – a high hand-slap – by way of greeting. Then they repeated the performance with Jameson.

"He sure is marvellous with them," the stout, middle-aged lady driver said, getting out of the coach. She held her hand out to Cara. "I'm Melanie, by the way." She pointed to a dark-haired boy in the group. "David's mom."

"I'm pleased to meet you," Cara said, shaking her hand warmly. She smiled to herself – this was the woman who she'd thought was Jameson's girlfriend.

"I'm real pleased to meet you," Melanie said. "It's nice to meet a friend of Jameson's. He doesn't have other folks up here too often."

Jameson clapped his hands. "OK, kids," he said in an easy drawl. "Before we start, I want to introduce a very special lady this morning." Thomas stood up to attention for the important announcement, holding a finger to his lips to warn the others to be quiet.

"This is Cara," Jameson said, bowing in her direction, "and she's a teacher who's come all the way from Ireland."

"Cara!" Thomas emphasised loudly in his slow, deliberate way.

Cara felt herself blushing.

"And," Jameson said, "she's going to join in with the session this morning."

When they'd all finished cheering, Cara turned to Melanie and said, "I'm not too sure if this is a good idea – painting is one of the talents I definitely do not have."

The bus driver raised her eyebrows and smiled. "Mr Jameson Carroll will tell you painting is a talent you just haven't discovered yet. That's what he tells all the kids anyway." She climbed back into the coach and started up the engine. Then, as she pulled out of the driveway, she called back to Cara. "I look forward to seeing your masterpiece when I collect the kids!"

The group all trooped around to the back of the house, led by an important-looking Thomas. As Cara turned to speak to Jameson, she saw him scoop up a tiny girl who had difficulty walking. He carried her high up until they caught up with the others, and made her laugh out loud when he made several joking attempts to fit in through the door in the studio without touching her head on the frame.

The other kids all gave a noisy applause when he and the girl eventually came through the door, and were delighted when Jameson carefully dropped to his knees to allow her to climb down.

Then it was down to business. Jameson ushered them to their various tables and easels, and then did a quick check on the paintbrushes that Thomas had selected for them, and the session went into action.

"Since it's our last meeting for the summer," Jameson said, "I thought we'd make a little present to take home to your folks." A delighted cheer rose from the group. "Hold on," he laughed, "you don't know what it is yet. I'll show you how to do it first." He held up a piece of card with the outline of a swan on one half of it. He folded the card in two and then cut around the swan shape, which resulted in a double image of the swan joined at the bottom. "We'll glue this into a basket shape," he said, deftly showing them, "and after you've all painted and decorated it nicely, we'll fill them with some nice things." He held up a bowl of bath-oil pearls that looked like small eggs, and a box of round, foil-covered chocolates. Again, claps of appreciation resounded around the room.

By the time the coach arrived back to collect them, each of the group had a recognisable present to take back home, mainly thanks to the deft touches of a paintbrush or glue from Jameson, just where it was needed.

After clearing up all the paints and glue and sparkly bits, Jameson, Cara and Thomas had a sandwich lunch outside in the sun.

Then Cara prepared to head back across to her aunt's.

"I'll be back sometime later," she promised, brushing her lips on Jameson's forehead. "This'll be our last night together," she reminded him quietly. "My parents are due back tomorrow."

His face creased in a mixture of defeat and anger. "Goddamnit, Cara!" he said. "We shouldn't be parted – it's so wrong. We're adults, and shouldn't have to answer to anyone."

Cara looked back at him, her eyes full of embarrassment and hurt. "You're right," she said slowly. "In an ideal world we shouldn't have to answer to anyone else." She paused. "But the world I'm used to back in Ireland is far from ideal – and it doesn't operate in such a simple way."

Chapter 28

Cara's last night before her parents' return was spent playing games with Thomas and having a final trip around the lake and then, when the boy was in bed, she and Jameson settled down in the large sitting-room. In the last hour or so, the temperature had suddenly dropped, and a bit of a drizzly wind had whipped up, so Jameson set about organising a log fire in the huge grate. Then they had pottered around in the kitchen fixing a supper of cheese and cold meats and fruit.

Jameson carried a huge wooden tray into the room, laden with the food and a chilled bottle of wine. Cara sorted out glasses and napkins as Jameson moved around drawing curtains to keep out the growing wind and rain, which Cara had not yet experienced since coming to America.

Her eyes followed Jameson as he moved around – the denim jeans and casual checked shirt, and the tan suede waistcoat, and the chunky suede boots in the exact same shade. By the time she had worked her way up to his unruly hair and face, she felt a lump forming in her throat. *God*, she thought, *he is so attractive . . . and yet so different.* What on earth would the people back home make of someone like him? An *American beatnik*, would be the first impression. With his clothing and odd American ways, they would see him almost as a creature from another planet. And suddenly she, Cara Gayle, schoolteacher and conventional to the last – would be seen in the same way.

"A dime for your thoughts," Jameson said, leaning across the table to pour the wine.

Cara stared into the flames for a few moments before answering. "I feel as though I'm one of the characters from a romantic novel . . . I can't believe that something this beautiful could happen to me."

"It's your choice, Cara," he said. "You could live like this every day of your life."

She looked up into his dark brown eyes.

"You know that I – that Thomas and me – want you here," he said. "You just have to make that decision when you're ready."

She nodded very slowly.

He reached out and crushed her tightly against him. Then he kissed her long and deeply.

"I have never," Cara whispered, "felt as happy or safe as I feel when I'm in your arms."

He held her at arm's length, and looked at her. Really looked at her. "The fact I'm happy goes without saying . . . but you make me feel very safe, in a different kind of way." He paused, searching for the right words. "I know I can trust you, like I've never been able to trust anyone else in my whole life."

And the evening passed into night. Talking and eating

and drinking. And later, when the fire had dimmed into a pale grey and orange glow – they once again made beautiful, passionate love on the rug in front of it. Oblivious to the wind and the rain – and the rest of the world outside.

* * *

The following morning the telephone rang early. Jameson answered and then passed it across to Cara's side of the bed. It was Jean.

"Hi, honey," she said brightly. "Sorry to spoil your fun, but I've had a call from your mom to say that they're arriving in town this afternoon." She paused. "Do you want to join me for the ride . . . or do you want me to give your excuses?"

At the mention of her parents, Cara's throat and stomach tightened. There was a short pause. "I'll come with you," she said in a low, flat voice. "I'll be across in a few hours."

"There's no rush," Jean said. "I just wanted to warn you. I thought if we left around twelve, then we could stop for lunch on the way there. Does that sound okay to you?"

"Grand," Cara said, " and Jean . . . I'll never be able to thank you for being so understanding."

"Oh, hush now," Jean said, "what's there to thank for? I'll see you when you're ready, okay?"

"Okay," Cara replied softly. After she hung up the phone, she lay back in the bed, staring out towards the window.

"Anything wrong?" Jameson asked.

She closed her eyes against the tears that had suddenly

welled up. "The time's come," she managed to struggle out. "The time to go back to reality and my parents . . . and I just don't want to go back to it all. I want to stay here."

He looked at her, words tumbling through his brain, the words of a man who saw things fairly simply, in black and white. Just telling people how it was. But he held the words back. They would only make her feel worse. "Have you time for breakfast?" he asked instead.

"I have a couple of hours," she said, feeling grateful that he hadn't made her feel like the stupid teenage schoolgirl he must undoubtedly think she was.

"It'll have to do," he said, reaching for her.

"Did you have something in mind?" she asked, curiously.

He hugged her tightly. "Just the same old thing I have in mind all the time you're near to me." Then, he moved until he was on top of her, his hard, toned body pressing against the warm, pliable softness of hers. He covered her mouth with his, and once again they moved into that special world that Cara had only discovered in the last few days.

* * *

Later, as they sat chatting over what was probably to be their last breakfast together, for the foreseeable future, Jameson said, "You know I have to go up to New York later this week?"

Cara nodded. "Your exhibition."

"And Thomas," he said. "I have to drop him up to my parents for a few weeks. He goes every summer."

"Will you be gone long?" she said quietly.

305

"I'll be back as quick as I can." Then he looked at her for a moment without speaking. "Why don't you come with us? It would let you see a bit more of the country, and it would give us a bit more time together." He leaned across the table and touched her hair, still damp from the shower. "You could meet my folks, too . . . I'd really like that. I just know they'll love you."

"Oh, Jameson," she whispered, "I couldn't . . ."

He shrugged. "Why not? You could make some excuse."

"Because," she said in an unsteady voice, "there's no way I could explain my going to New York to my mother and father. And how could I meet your parents? Have you forgotten that I'm actually a married woman?"

He sat back in his chair, his spine pressed tight up against it. "I wish we could both forget about that." His eyes darkened. "But it doesn't have to get in the way of everything . . . let's enjoy the bits we can. My folks don't pry into my life. Hell, I'm a grown man with my own life."

"Well," Cara said, swallowing hard, "that's where the difference lies. In Ireland – well, the part I live in anyway . . . parents are still very involved in their families long after they've left home." She fiddled with her hair. "I feel really stupid at my age worrying about what my parents think – but it's just the way things are. I can't change it all over a few weeks."

Jameson covered her hands with his. "I'm sorry for making you feel bad . . . forget New York . . . it was selfish of me."

"I would really love to come," she said softly. "I would love to come and see New York with you and Thomas.

306

And . . . if things were different, I would love to meet your parents."

"Let's forget I mentioned it," he said, kissing the top of her head. "C'mon, the coffee's getting cold."

They walked around the lake, shielded from the rain by a large umbrella, Cara's heart heavy because there was a tension between them that had not been there before. When Harpers' garden came into view, Cara gripped Jameson's arm to bring him to a halt.

"What day are you going to New York?" she asked.

He shrugged. "Probably tomorrow or the day after. My folks don't mind, and I can go across the city to the place that's exhibiting my stuff when I want."

"I would just love to see your exhibition," she said, a catch in her voice.

"Please, Cara," he said, " I really do understand." He moved the umbrella slightly, checking if the rain was still heavy enough to need it. It was light but still fairly penetrating. "There might be other times."

"I'll spend every waking minute with my parents," she said, "and then when you come back . . . I'll find a way to come across and see you."

"Day or night," he said simply. "I'll be waiting."

* * *

Maggie and Declan were full of stories about their visit to his cousin. "Oh, they gave us a real Irish welcome," Maggie gushed as they drove back to the house. "And they were delighted with the tea I brought over to them. More delighted with that than the presents."

"It was a pity about the change in the weather though," Declan commented. "I was beginning to feel we

307

were back home in Ireland."

"Oh, it didn't hold us back," Maggie pointed out. "Martin drove us all around, and his wife is a grand baker. We had home-baked soda bread – imagine! Soda bread in America. They've some kind of shop that has a lot of the Irish things in it. I got a good few recipes off Catherine, so I'll try my hand at them when I get home."

"You needn't wait until you go back home," Jean told her. "You have my oven at your disposal, and we're all willing to be guinea pigs, especially if there's chocolate in any of the recipes."

"Begod," Maggie said, "I just might have a go at one tomorrow. Mind you, we may have to go to the shops for some of the ingredients. I'd like to go back to that wool shop in town anyway." She gave a little sniff. "Catherine's not a knitter, unfortunately, so we didn't find any decent shops for wool. I think I'll go back to the one in Binghampton. It was about the best I've seen so far."

Any time the conversation veered towards what Cara had been doing while they were away, she carefully switched it back by quizzing them all about their trip.

"It sounds as though Martin's wife is very nice," she said. "Are they planning a visit over to Ireland some time?"

There was a silence. "Well," Maggie said, "I don't know what kind of reception she would get if she came over."

"Or Martin for that matter," Declan said with a sigh.

"What do you mean?" Cara asked.

"Well," Maggie said again, "it's the religion part for one thing and then . . ." She hesitated for a few moments. "Well, she's not just American . . . she's got what you'd describe as a well-tanned skin. Too well-tanned, if you know what I mean."

"Do you mean she's foreign?" Jean asked. "Mixed race?"

"Something like that," Maggie said. "Not that I would be against coloured people myself . . . we had a very nice black missionary priest at the church last year. It's more the religion bit that's the problem – she doesn't seem to have any." She dug Declan in the ribs. "What did she call herself?"

Declan looked vague. "A humanist . . . or a humanitarian or some such thing."

"Anyway," Maggie rattled on, "she's a very nice woman, and her colour and religion are not my business."

Cara could feel her face starting to burn. "Other people's religions have nothing to do with us," she said pointedly.

Maggie looked at Declan and raised her eyebrows. "I'm not disagreeing with you, Cara. Sure, that's exactly what I've just been saying." She gave a little sniff. "It'd be different if it was my *own* family, but thanks be to God, for once it's not."

Cara's heart dropped like a stone. Nothing had changed. The holiday in America and staying with Bruce and meeting Martin's wife had made not an iota of difference to her mother's outlook. It was still firmly rooted in the small-minded ways of back home.

"We went to see the Statue of Liberty," Declan said, changing the subject.

"And New York City," Maggie gasped. "You wouldn't know where to begin describing it, but your father bought a nice book with pictures of all the places we went to." She leaned forward and tapped Cara's shoulder. "It's a great pity you missed it. You would have loved seeing New York."

"Maybe I'll get to see it another time," Cara said, in as bright a voice as she could muster.

But inside she wondered what her mother would have to say if she announced that she was planning a trip to New York with Jameson Carroll. That, she knew only too well, would be quite a different matter.

The next few days passed fairly quickly with visits to more places and more people. The temperature had continued to fluctuate, hot in the day and then plunging down to fairly cool in the evenings accompanied by showery weather.

Jean kept apologising for the change in the weather, as though she were responsible for it, and explaining that it was most unusual for the time of year.

Cara spent the time when she was in the house either reading or watching the American television channels – anything to keep her mind off the big white house at the other side of the lake.

"Is everything all right, Cara?" her mother asked, when she came upon her staring out at the rain-splattered window. "You're not homesick, are you?"

"I'm fine," Cara said, turning back to her book, "and I'm definitely not homesick."

A while later Maggie came bustling back into the sitting-room. "Jean says you have to phone Oliver. She says you'll feel better after that." Her voice dropped. "To tell you the truth I'm getting a bit homesick myself. I'd like to hear how they're doing up at the house and the shop."

Cara stifled a sigh of annoyance, but she got to her feet and went into the hall to the phone. It rang out. She tried several times later that afternoon, checking the time difference for Ireland, but there was still no reply.

The following evening, with Maggie almost glued to her elbow, she tried again. Just as Maggie had stuck her ear to the phone to check for herself, it was finally picked up.

"Yes?" Oliver's self-assured tones echoed over the line.

By the time Cara had the phone back, she found herself flustered and not quite knowing what to say to this husband of hers, whom she had neither spoken to or thought about for what seemed an awful long time.

"Hello, Oliver . . . I'm sorry for not . . ."

But before she could say another word, his voice cut through.

"Cara, I'm sorry I didn't get a chance to ring – but I've been caught up with the play. Have you been trying to get through to me?"

"Just a few times," she said, trying to put some feeling into her voice. "It doesn't matter . . . as long as there's nothing wrong."

"No, no," Oliver said, "Indeed no. There's nothing wrong at all." There was silence for a few seconds. Then, he said quickly. "Are you having a good time? What's the weather like out there?"

"Fine," Cara said automatically, despite the rain. "Is everything OK back home? Pauline and Charles and Bernadette?"

"Grand. I've called in regularly. Charles is making a grand job of running things with Pauline and Peenie keeping an eye on him. And little Bernadette is the finest,

311

running around the place and wrapping everyone around her little finger." He said nothing about the holy statue episode. That could wait until they got back home. "And the weather's not too bad. The odd drop of rain as usual, like."

"And your play?" she checked, still aware of her mother hovering around.

"Oh, that went off well," he said. "We got a great crowd, and a very fair write-up in the local papers."

"Oh, I'm delighted for you," Cara said, her voice pitched unnaturally high to sound enthusiastic for her mother's sake. She was rewarded by a smile appearing on Maggie's worried face, before she disappeared back into the kitchen.

"Sure, it's not too long until you're due back home now, is it?"

"No . . . around . . ." A picture of Jameson Carroll crept into her mind, and she could hardly get the words out, "around another week or so."

"A week?" Oliver's tone was high with surprise. "I thought it was nearer a fortnight . . ."

"Sorry," Cara corrected herself. "It is actually around a fortnight . . . counting the travelling and everything."

"Oh, right . . . a fortnight then." Oliver repeated. "Well," he said in a brighter tone, "you've nothing to worry about – I'll be at there at the airport, waiting for ye all."

"That's good of you," Cara said quietly.

"I've got the times all written down and everything," he said, as though he was talking to one of his commercial salesman. "So you've nothing to worry about at all."

There was silence for a few seconds. "So . . ." he said,

sort of awkwardly. "I won't waste your phone bill . . . chatting on. Tell your mother and father that I'm asking for them . . . and that I hope ye all enjoy the rest of your holiday."

"I will," Cara said.

"Goodbye to you all now." The line clicked and he was gone.

"There you are now!" Maggie's face was beaming when Cara went back into the kitchen. "You'll feel the better for speaking to Oliver." She smiled triumphantly at her sister. "Did he say how things were going at the shop, and what the weather was like? And if there was any news? Nobody dead or anything since we left?"

Cara took a deep breath. "Everybody's fine back at the shop. The weather's not too bad, Oliver's play went well and got a great write-up, and he'll be there to pick us up from the airport."

"So, nobody died at all?" Maggie said, sounding almost disappointed. "Oh, well . . . as long as he doesn't forget to pick us up the day we land home."

"Oh, Maggie!" Jean said, catching Cara's eye and winking. "Don't be talking about going home just yet. We've lots of things we still haven't done."

Later on, when Declan and Maggie had gone into the sitting-room to write some postcards, Cara poured her heart out to her aunt in the kitchen.

"Oh, Jean," she whispered, "I don't know what I'm going to do. The time's flying so fast . . . and before I know it, I'm going to be saying goodbye to Jameson."

"You still have some time left together," Jean said, touching her arm.

"No," Cara shook her head, and Jean could see the

313

tears forming. "He's in New York now, and even when he comes back . . . I don't know how we're going to see each other again . . ."

"How does he feel about you now, Cara? How serious has it got?"

"Very serious," Cara said softly. "I've no doubts at all about his feelings. He loves me . . . and I love him, Jean." Her hands came up to cover her face, and she struggled against the flood of tears that were threatening.

"Oh, honey," Jean commiserated, stroking her hair. "I feel so awful about all this – if you hadn't come out to the wedding, you wouldn't be suffering so much now."

Cara shook her head. "No, you're wrong. Coming to America has made me waken up to what was happening in my life . . . I couldn't keep closing my eyes to Oliver and what he was getting up to. That's why I came away for the summer in the first place. I think I was hoping he'd make the decision and walk away. I was leaving it to him, because I was afraid of what people would say if I took the decision to destroy our marriage."

"When you say 'people', Cara . . . you really mean your mother, don't you?"

Cara nodded. "Well . . . she's the main one. I could probably face my father and Pauline and Charles . . . but it would kill Mammy."

"Look at me, Cara," Jean said in a firm tone, and she waited until Cara's watery eyes met hers. "You're wrong – I don't think it would kill your mother at all."

Cara moved across the kitchen floor to close the door tightly.

"Your mother," Jean stated, "is flesh and blood – same as the rest of us! Whether she likes it or not, other people have to make their own decisions in life." Her face softened a little. "Now, she's my sister, and I grew up with her . . . but she's no saint. If she was, her first thoughts would be for other people – not for herself."

"It's just the way she is," Cara heard herself say weakly "It's the way things are with everyone back home. Sometimes, I think I'm a bit inclined that way myself."

"Oh, tosh!" Jean snapped. "Maggie's just the way she is because people let her be that way! I'd actually forgotten how selfish she really is. Haven't you noticed that she wants to dictate to us all what time we eat, *when* we eat and *what* we eat! She really would like to be a dictator if she got the chance. I can tell the way she talks about your brother and sister that she is trying to dictate their lives as well."

"She doesn't mean any harm," Cara said.

"Harm bedamned!" Jean stated. "If I hadn't stood up to my own mother and people like Maggie, I would have missed out on a lovely man like Bruce. And I'm not fooled, Cara . . . she's only happy to see me because we live so far away, and there's nobody that really knows us both. It would be a very different story if Bruce and I started coming to Ireland every summer. A very different story."

Cara's head and shoulders drooped. "I know what you're saying," she admitted, "but it's not all about Mammy. How would I face the people at school, the people who come into the shop?"

"Oh, Cara," Jean said with a weary smile, "that's what you call taking responsibility for your own life. Having the courage to make decisions for yourself." She covered Cara's hand with her own. "Now, although I don't share your mother's fervent religious views, I do believe that

God gave us all free will. There would be no point in us having a mind and a brain if we didn't use it. Look at the Bible stories – Mary having an illegitimate child and Joseph marrying her even though everyone knew it wasn't his child. He went against all the rules and regulations of his culture, didn't he?"

Cara nodded, not entirely understanding what her aunt was getting at.

"To find out what's right for you," Jean said, "you have to follow your own heart and conscience."

"I know exactly what's right for me," Cara whispered. "It's finding the right thing for everyone else that's the big problem."

"You'll never please everyone," Jean said, "so if you really want something – go for it. Just wait for the right time. Like most mothers, your mother is a lot stronger than you think." She suddenly gave a wry grin. "D'you know . . . it's just dawned on me that this household has now changed into a replica of hers in just a couple of weeks. We're all doing things exactly the way she likes, because it's easier than arguing with her."

The conversation came to a sudden halt as Maggie's feet came tapping along the hallway. She stuck her head in the door. "That film you were on about earlier is on the television in five minutes, Jean." She looked suspiciously from her sister to her daughter, and then headed over to the kettle. "Would either of you like a cup of tea before it starts?"

"Thanks, Maggie – but no," Jean said in a decisive manner, "but you have whatever you fancy yourselves. There's some nice cookies in a box there, too." She went to the drinks cupboard and lifted out a bottle of Martini and another of gin. "Bruce and I often have cocktails at this time of the evening, and we seem to have got out of the habit since you heavy tea-drinkers arrived."

"Cocktails?" Maggie said in a high, disapproving voice. "I wouldn't thank you for alcohol. Tea suits me just fine. I'm not hard to please." She rummaged in the cupboard for mugs.

"As I said, Maggie," Jean said in a sharper tone, "you're welcome to have what pleases you. I often have a cocktail when I'm preparing dinner, but with us eating much earlier since you've come, I've kinda got out of the habit. Still, I suppose we can have them *after* dinner just as easily as before."

Ignoring Maggie's disapproval, Jean started sorting out all the different ingredients and checking that the cocktail mixer was put together properly. "Cara, honey," she said now, "would you mind getting me a bag of ice, and some slices of lemon and limes from the fridge, please? They're in a little round container with a lid. Now that I've started, I want to do this right."

Maggie opened the box of cookies, and peered inside. *Thank God*, she thought lifting out some vanilla buns, *cakes and biscuits were one thing you could rely on in America. At least they got that right.* She put two big spoonfuls of tea into the teapot. The giddy way Jean was carrying on, she would need good, strong tea.

Cara handed over the bag of crushed ice and the container with the sliced fruit. "Thanks, honey," said Jean, adding ice to the mixture, then giving the container a few good vigorous shakes, "and that little jar of olives in the fridge door, please. Bruce likes his Martinis with those." She handed the container to Cara. "Give it a good,

317

youthful shake, while I sort out glasses." She looked over her shoulder. "Sure you won't change your mind, Maggie?"

Maggie's brows came down and her lips set in a hard line. "No . . . no. You and Bruce do whatever ye're used to, but tea's fine for the rest of us."

"I'm going to have a cocktail," Cara suddenly said. "I really fancy something different for a change." She gave the container a last shake, then set it down beside her aunt. "I'll just check if Daddy wants a cold drink or tea —"

"No need!" Maggie said, but Cara was already out in the hall. She came back a few moments later to say that both men would love cocktails while watching the film.

Shortly afterwards, ignoring a stony-faced Maggie, Jean and Cara loaded up trays with drinks and salted pretzels and biscuits.

"For once," Jean said, with a twinkle in her eye, "we're going to watch a movie, American-style." She put her arms around Cara. "I know it's not as nice as spending an evening with Jameson Carroll . . . but a weepy movie and a couple of cocktails is a nice ending to any day. Who knows what tomorrow might bring?"

The effects of the slow-moving film coupled with the unaccustomed drinks made Cara feel sleepy. She headed off to bed around midnight, and after a short while she fell into a deep sleep. When she awoke some hours later, it was to the sound of heavy rain battering against her slightly open window and the low howl of wind. For a few moments she felt disorientated and thought she was back in Ireland. Then, as awareness dawned, she threw back the quilt and padded over to the window to close it.

As she stood stretching on tiptoes, she could just see

the tops of the trees in the garden in the bright moonlight. She looked out at the swaying, dripping branches and wondered if Jameson was back home yet. In his white house . . . just five minutes' walk away.

She came back across the room, her feet cold now on the wooden floor, and climbed back into the bed. She sat upright, the covers draped around her, and her gaze fixed on the closed window. It was unusually cold, the first time Cara had felt properly cold in America. It reminded her of the nights that she had sat up in Ireland, waiting on Oliver to come home. The nights when she had dozed over, curled up in front of the turf fire, only to waken hours later, the fire dead and her limbs stiff and aching from the cold. The difference now was that she had a choice.

She now had somewhere to go – and someone who wanted her.

Even after wrapping extra blankets around her, Cara could not warm up. She toyed with going downstairs to the kitchen for one of the hot-water bottles that Jean had hung behind the door for them. Jean had warned them that the temperatures sometimes plummeted at night like this.

She threw the bedcovers off, but instead of grabbing her dressing-gown, she found herself pulling on jeans and a blouse, and then she went to the wardrobe and found a heavy cable-knit sweater that she'd brought for this type of weather.

She went downstairs quietly, lifted her hooded jacket from the coatstand, then silently headed out of the front door.

The garden was eerily quiet, with just the background noise of the rain and the odd chirrupy cricket sound. She half-walked and half-ran down the moonlit garden and then she reached the lakeside path – that she now felt she knew every step of – and she kept moving until at last the familiar white house came into view. But even before she reached it, she knew that Jameson was not there.

She walked up the garden path and knocked hard on the door, but – just as she had dreaded – there was no reply. She gave it a few seconds, then walked around the side of the house to the garage. The door gaped open, the way it had been left a few days ago when they departed.

Disappointed – and suddenly aware that she was out alone in the middle of the night – Cara drew the hood of her jacket tightly around her damp hair, and ran all the way back to the safety of the Harpers' house.

A steaming cup of coffee put some warmth back into her, and then she headed upstairs very quietly and had a hot shower. She felt the tension leave her muscles as she lathered soap over her body and then turned around and around, rinsing it off under the hot jets of water. She stood there under the water, her mind running over the situation with Jameson again and again. What if he didn't come back? Maybe he had decided that the relationship was going nowhere – because of her cowardice, and fear of taking control of her own life. Maybe he thought it was easier if they didn't see each other again.

How long she stood in the shower she didn't know. It was only when she became aware of the water having suddenly turned cold that she reached to turn it off. And then, when she stepped out of the shower, she realised the water still pouring down her face was in fact tears.

Chapter 29

The early part of the following day passed with a visit to an art gallery in a nearby town, lunch at a favourite steakhouse of Bruce's, and shopping in another small town they had not yet visited. As she walked around the art gallery, Cara's thoughts were drawn to Jameson's work, and the exhibition she wished she had been able to see in New York.

Later the time passed more quickly as she busied herself buying more presents to take home. She was delighted to find a really nice blue swing-jacket for Pauline at a good price. She knew her sister would be delighted, because she had very little money to spend on herself, and she would never get these sorts of styles locally. Then, a few shops further down, she bought a pair of red-check Capri pants for herself, and when she reached the pay-desk, she ran back and got another pair in a blue check to match Pauline's jacket.

Later that evening, more friends of Bruce and Jean called around with photographs they'd taken at the wedding, and to see the ones that Bruce and Jean had picked up in town that afternoon. It passed another drizzly evening, chatting and sorting food and drinks.

Cara looked at the pictures of the smiling bride and groom and thought how optimistic and happy they looked. Just like her and Oliver. Then she looked at the photographs taken at the wedding – of her in her pink suit and pink shoes – and wondered in amazement at how long ago it seemed. And yet it had only been little more than two weeks ago. So much had happened in so short a time, and she knew she would never be the same again.

It was only a matter of time until she would be walking off the plane to be greeted by Oliver. Only a matter of time until she would be back in the life she led before she met Jameson Carroll.

The visitors stayed until quite late, and Cara forced herself to remain downstairs laughing and chatting, and being generally sociable for her aunt and uncle's sake. When they left, around midnight, Cara went outside with her mother and Jean to wave them off.

"Thanks be to God that the rain has eased off," Maggie commented as they walked back in the drive, being careful to dodge the heavy drops of rain from the dripping branches.

"The forecast is for the hotter weather to return," Jean said, "so you'll be able to get back to your swimming again, Cara."

The kettle was put on for a final hot drink of the night, and everything tidied up.

"I'm going to head on upstairs," Cara said, unable to contain a fairly large yawn.

Then as she was bidding everyone goodnight, a loud

knock sounded on the door.

"I wonder if it's our guests . . . maybe they left something behind?" Jean said, rushing to check.

Maggie looked in alarm at Cara. "Who else could it be, at this hour of the night?"

Cara shrugged in answer, but her heart lurched a moment later when she saw the tall figure of Jameson Carroll walking in behind Jean – and one glance at his serious face told her that something was wrong.

"Hi . . ." he said, looking round at everyone. "I'm real sorry for disturbing you folks at such a late hour, but I've just got back from New York, and I've . . ." His hand came up to his forehead. "Well . . . I reckon I've just got some very bad news."

Cara felt her legs suddenly go weak. "What is it?" she whispered.

"Sit down, Jameson – sit down," Jean said, rushing over to pull a chair out at the kitchen table for him.

"Thank you, Jean." He sat. "You see, I just walked in the door and the phone was ringing, and it was a hospital in New York to say that Thomas had been brought in after a car accident." He lowered his eyes. "It seems he's pretty bad."

Cara stood rooted to the spot. Then, her legs eventually moved and she went over and put her hand somewhere between his shoulder and his tanned neck. "What happened?" she whispered.

"It seems," he said hoarsely, "that he was in a parking lot with my parents . . . and he was carrying some boxes. He had them piled up, and a car came tearing round . . . and he didn't see it."

Cara's eyes were wide with horror. "Oh, Jameson!

How – how bad is he?"

He turned to look up at her, and she could see the pain written all over his face. "He's in theatre right now. Apparently there's internal bleeding . . . they reckon it might be from his spleen, and broken ribs . . . and whatever else they find."

"Oh, dear God above!" Maggie said, blessing herself.

Jean now moved across to Jameson, and wrapped her arms around him. "Oh, Jameson – I'm so, so sorry . . . poor little Thomas!"

"I'm going to have to do a return journey to New York, right away. My parents have had to give consent for the operation since I wasn't there . . . and I want to be right by his side when he comes round."

"Of course, of course . . . the poor boy," Maggie said, dabbing a hanky to her eyes. "It's his daddy he'll be looking for when he wakes up."

"Are you sure you're going to be up to the drive?" Jean said quietly. "It's a lot after the drive you've just made back here."

Jameson's head moved up and down slowly. "If I have to drive for the next twenty-four hours solid – I'll be there for him."

"I'll come with you," Cara suddenly blurted out. "I'll help to keep you awake."

"No, Cara," her mother said, giving her a strange look, "we'll ask one of the men. It would be far better if a man went with him."

"I actually came over to ask Cara to come along," Jameson said, standing up. "Thomas would love to see her more than anybody else."

That was all Cara needed to hear. She touched his

hand. "I'll only be a minute – I'll just go and pack a few things." Then she bounded off upstairs.

"There's some hot coffee in this pot," Maggie said, her manner distracted. "Or maybe you should have something to eat?"

"I'd appreciate the coffee, ma'am," Jameson said quietly, "but I couldn't eat anything just now." He looked from Maggie to Jean now. "I'm real sorry about all this . . . I hope I haven't spoiled any plans you all had. You know . . . with Cara and everything."

"This is far more important," Jean said. "Cara would only be fretting about Thomas in any case. She's become extremely fond of him – hasn't she, Maggie?"

Maggie nodded her head. "Oh, she has indeed." She came over and placed a mug of coffee on the table in front of Jameson. "I'll just go and see if I can help Cara . . . and maybe talk her into letting one of the men go . . ."

Jean followed her out into the hall. "I wouldn't do that, Maggie," she told her sister quietly. "Cara's a grown woman – and a very kind and good woman. She's got to do what she feels is the right thing for herself."

Maggie's face tightened. "We've all got to do what we feel is the right thing," she said, turning on her heel and marching up the stairs.

She met Cara coming out of the bedroom as she reached the final step.

"I'm going, Mammy," Cara said, not meeting her eyes. "Please don't say anything . . ."

Maggie shrugged. "What's there to say? You've obviously made up your mind."

"Jameson needs me . . . and so will Thomas when he comes out of the operation."

"It's his *mother* the child needs," Maggie said, her eyes full of anger, "not someone he's just met – a black stranger."

Cara took a deep breath. "If the world was perfect, then that's the way it would be – but it's not. The fact is, Thomas is in a strange hospital with his elderly grandparents, and he needs as many people who care for him around as possible."

"I'm not a fool, Cara," her mother said slowly. "If it was only helping out that you were doing – I wouldn't say a word. But it's just dawned on me – God help my foolishness – that there's more between you and the boy's father than you just being helpful. It was written all over both your faces."

Cara flushed a deep red. "Look, Mammy – if this accident hadn't happened, it's likely that I wouldn't have seen him again before we go back. He was in New York, and he could have stayed there for weeks . . . he often does."

Maggie shook her head, her eyes pained. "You know perfectly well what I'm saying, Cara." Then, after a long, awkward pause she said in a strangled little voice, "You're a married woman, and if you do anything you shouldn't with that man – you'll be breaking your marriage vows. The vows you took in front of God." Her voice dropped. "Make no mistake about it, Cara. You'll be committing a mortal sin."

* * *

As they pulled out of the drive, Jameson stretched a hand across to Cara. "I'm sorry that I put you in an awkward position – but I really needed you to come with me."

"Don't worry," Cara said quietly. "Thomas is all that

matters . . . I still can't believe what's happened."

"I can't either," Jameson said, looking out into the damp, dark road that stretched way ahead of them. "It's like I'm in the middle of some kind of nightmare . . ."

She stroked his arm gently. "We'll just concentrate on getting there. Who knows, by the time we arrive, things might be much better."

Jameson moved the car into a higher gear. "Yeah," he said, disconsolately, "but on the other hand, they might just be a whole lot worse."

Chapter 30

New York

Apart from a quick stop for coffee to help keep them awake, they made the journey in good time considering the wet conditions. Any conversation between them was overshadowed by the thoughts of Thomas lying on an operating table fighting for his life.

As they pulled up in the deserted hospital carpark, Cara was grateful to be able to move her cramped limbs and climb out of the car. She closed her door and went round to the driver's side – but there was no attempt from Jameson to get out of the vehicle.

She bent down to the window, and then she saw him – his head on the steering-wheel, cradled in his arms – and his whole body heaving with racking sobs.

Cara hauled the heavy car door open and pulled him into her arms.

"I don't think I can face it, Cara. I can't go in." He shook his head. "What if. . .?"

Cara took a deep breath. "We have to go in, Jameson." She ran her fingers gently through his thick, wiry hair.

"And if he has come round from the operation, then he'll be looking for you, and wondering why you're not there."

Then, slowly, he moved – and together they walked into the hospital building, Cara holding on to his hand very tightly.

When they checked in at reception, they were informed that Thomas had come through his operation, and was in a special care unit on the fourth floor. Jameson was relieved that he was safely over the first hurdle, but as they rode upstairs in the lift, Cara saw the colour suddenly drain from his face.

"Are you all right?" she asked anxiously.

"Yeah," he replied. "It's just that the thought of seeing him sick . . . he's always been so healthy." He paused. "Considering he's a Down's syndrome kid, he's had very few problems apart from the expected chest infections and stuff like that."

"And he'll be healthy again," Cara told him confidently. "You'll soon see."

When they reached the unit, Jameson had to spend a frustrating few minutes convincing the staff that he was indeed Thomas's father before being allowed in to see him. They then started checking on Cara's relationship to Thomas – and Jameson's temper broke.

"For Chrisssake!" he snapped at the officious receptionist. "We've just travelled hundreds of miles to be with my son! If you don't show me where he is – I'm going to barge right through and find out for myself!"

The lady's hands came up in defeat. "Okay," she said, "but we have to obey regulations. He's a pretty sick boy – and he hasn't come round fully from the anaesthetic." Her face softened a little. "It's nothing personal, Mr Carroll –

we have to check out all our visitors."

They followed a nurse down the corridor, and then they had to wait outside the room while the nurse checked on Thomas. She stuck her head out of the door a few moments later, beckoning them to come in. "Just for a few moments," she whispered.

Jameson went in first, with Cara following close behind. She felt herself stiffen up when she heard the gulp of air that Jameson took when he saw Thomas lying on the bed.

He stood like a statue just staring down at the prone figure.

Then, mechanically, he turned to the side to allow Cara to move in closer. As she looked at the almost unrecognisable shape on the bed, her earlier confidence plummeted. He was fast asleep . . . or still unconscious. Cara couldn't tell which. And he seemed to have an endless number of tubes and drips attached to his arms, face and chest.

His chest was also heavily bandaged and swollen to twice its normal size.

All in all – he looked barely alive.

"Thomas?" Cara said softly.

But there was no reaction. Nothing to tell that he was there, apart from a slight rise and fall in his bandaged chest.

Cara kept watching – frightened to take her eyes off him in case she missed something. And frightened that if she did move her gaze – she might have to look into Jameson's eyes.

She couldn't bear that. Not just yet.

They stood in silence, close together, without saying a

word. Just watching and waiting. Then, the nurse came back in, and indicated that the doctor was now available to speak to them. Cara looked up at Jameson – and his dark eyes were every bit as hollow and empty as she had feared.

The doctor was in the ward office waiting to see him. "Technically speaking," he said, "the operation to remove your son's spleen has been a success. " He halted for a moment. "But – there are unfortunately some complications."

Jameson's eyes glazed over.

"He has a number of fractured ribs – and his arm is badly broken."

"They'll heal," Jameson said, "won't they?"

The doctor hesitated. "Normally they do . . . but at the moment we're more concerned about any recurrence of internal bleeding. When Thomas comes round from the anaesthetic fully – we'll have to keep him very still for a while to give him every possible chance of recovery."

Cara glanced at Jameson. He had a finger poised on his lips, preventing any questions from slipping out. Questions that just might provoke answers he didn't want to hear.

He gave a jerky kind of nod, indicating that he'd taken in the information.

They walked along the corridor, and went back down in the lift to the ground floor where the restaurant and restrooms were.

"If you want to freshen up," Jameson said, "I'll order us some breakfast and coffee."

Cara stretched up and gave him a kiss in answer, and headed off in the direction of the ladies'.

She looked in the mirror and sighed at her washed-out appearance and flattened, lifeless hair. She rummaged in her handbag and found a hair-elastic to tie her hair back in a pony-tail, and then she washed her face thoroughly. She patted it dry and looked in the mirror again – wishing that her make-up bag was not in the car along with her fresh clothes and perfume.

Then, she felt an enormous surge of guilt for thinking of such trivial things when poor Thomas was so ill – and possibly even dying.

As tears started welling up in her eyes, Cara took a tissue from her bag, and pressed it tightly to her eyelids. Things were bad enough without Jameson having to comfort her as well as worry about his stricken son.

Looking as reasonable as she could, she headed for the door in the restroom. As her hand reached for the handle, it was suddenly pushed inwards – almost knocking her off her balance. Then a very polished-looking, dark-haired woman in a red suit wafted past her, without a glance or word of apology. She headed straight for the mirror, checking her perfectly styled shiny black bob, and reaching for her blood-red lipstick.

The hospital restaurant was almost empty, with only a few people dotted here and there. Jameson was sitting at a corner table waiting for Cara. "I called my parents," he said, pulling out a chair for her. "They're both in a bad way . . . blaming themselves for what happened to Thomas. They sounded completely exhausted."

Cara stretched out a comforting hand. "These awful things happen . . . but it's not anybody's fault."

"I guess these things do happen . . ."

Cara lifted her bag. "Shall I get us some breakfast?" she asked, trying to sound brighter. "You might feel better after eating."

Jameson stood up. "I'll get it," he said quickly.

"No," Cara said firmly. "You buy everything for us – and this is only breakfast. Let me do it for you this time."

At the counter, Cara looked at the display of rolls and pastries, searching for something that just might coax his appetite a little. She eventually settled for some croissants and coffee, plus a couple of portions of fruit salad. She paid for them and then turned to lift the tray, when she noticed a figure in red standing by their table.

It was the glamorous, black-haired woman who had so rudely bumped into her in the ladies' room.

Something made Cara halt in her tracks – and she stood for a few moments just watching them. Watching the way the elegant woman was now stretching a hand out to pat Jameson's shoulder in a familiar manner. A too-familiar manner. Watching the way her dark head was now bent low – with her face almost touching his.

Very slowly, Cara made her way back to the table, hoping all the while that the woman would move. But instead, she actually sat down in the chair next to Jameson. Then she dragged the chair in closer to him – until their knees must have been almost touching.

Cara felt her throat tighten as she moved nearer the table, and neither Jameson or the woman seemed to notice her until she actually placed the tray down on in front of them.

"Oh, hi," Jameson said. He first looked up at her, and then quickly glanced at the woman. "Cara . . ." he said, kind of awkwardly, "this is Verity. Thomas's mother."

Cara's legs suddenly felt wobbly, and she sat down hurriedly in the metal chair, her heart sinking. Her intuition had been right. Now she knew why the woman had made her feel uneasy.

She forced herself to stretch out a hand towards the Jackie Kennedy-type woman. After just the tiniest pause, Verity offered a well-manicured hand.

Cara noticed her nails were painted scarlet to match the suit.

"And *you* are?" Verity asked, arching her meticulously shaped eyebrows.

Cara's eyes darted in Jameson's direction, wondering who or what she should describe herself as. His girlfriend? His travelling companion?

Jameson reached over to take her hand. "Cara is my friend," he said quietly. He lifted her hand up, making sure that there was no mistake about their close relationship. "My very special friend."

Verity sat back in her chair, her arms folded. "I see," was all she said – but her tone was not warm.

"I'm also Thomas's friend," Cara said. "That's why I travelled down here to be with him."

"That was real nice of you," Verity said, her eyebrows lifting high again. She leaned forward now. "And just how long have you all been such good friends?"

"Since Cara came over from Ireland . . . some time ago." Jameson was deliberately vague, and Cara noticed that his voice had now taken on the cool tone she'd heard him use when they first met. "Cara's staying in one of the houses up at Lake Savannah. She met Thomas out swimming in the lake . . . and they got along instantly. She's a teacher, and I'm sure she has a wonderful instinct for all kind of kids." He paused, obviously making a point. "Anyway, Thomas introduced us."

"How touching," Verity said, smiling. She looked from one to the other, her brow slightly furrowed. "So," she said a few moments later, "what do you think after seeing him . . . do you think he'll pull through?"

"Sure," Jameson said, his eyes steely. "Sure he'll make it."

Verity nodded. "Good," she said, her smile showing off a row of perfect, white teeth.

"I think he'll make it, too."

Cara passed the coffee pot and breakfast plates across the table to Jameson, then she turned to Verity. "There's enough coffee for three in the pot – shall I get another cup for you?"

Verity stooped to the floor to pick up her black patent handbag. "No, no," she said. "I don't want to interrupt you guys."

Jameson pushed his chair back. "You're not interrupting us, Verity," he said in a flat voice. "I'll get the cup."

She looked up at him, her head tilted slightly, and her eyes were bright this time. "Thank you, Jameson," she said, "I guess I will have some coffee – it might help keep me awake." She ran a hand through her sleek, bobbed hair, and when he moved away from the table she reached in her handbag for her compact to check her make-up and re-apply her lipstick.

"I look an absolute fright," she told Cara, surveying herself in the mirror. "Jameson is not at all used to seeing me like this." She gave a little shrug and snapped the compact shut. "But, I suppose it is a crisis."

"It certainly is," Cara replied curtly.

Verity put her compact away. Then, she leaned her elbows on the table with her hands tucked daintily under her chin and said: "You sure do surprise me."

"In what way?" Cara asked, not sure she wanted to hear the answer.

"Because," said the elegant Verity, "you're not at all Jameson's usual type." She paused for a moment, waiting for Cara to respond. When there was no response forthcoming, she said: "Well – you could hardly say that we two are alike. Could you?" Her eyebrows quivered.

"No . . ." Cara said, wondering where this was going.

"You see, men are funny creatures . . . they usually go for similar types. And given the fact that we were man and wife for a number of years, you would imagine he would pick someone similar to me in some way. But then . . ." She broke off with a little smile, and lowered her head.

"But then?" Cara prompted, curious to hear what was coming next.

"Well . . . Jameson did say you were particularly good with kids . . . I presume he meant handicapped or retarded kids like Thomas."

"I like most children," Cara said, lifting a croissant she didn't really want onto her plate. "Being handicapped or otherwise makes no difference."

"Well," Verity said, admiring her nails, "that probably explains the attraction. I would imagine that Jameson finds it difficult at times – you know – having complete responsibility for him . . . Thomas." She threw back her hair. "Not that I haven't offered to help out myself, God knows. But I refuse to bury myself in that glorified cabin in the wilds. And if Jameson is still too stubborn to move back here – what can I do?"

Cara took a deep breath. "I would say that's between

you and Jameson – it's not my business."

Verity looked up with a dazzling white smile. Too dazzling for the circumstances. "Precisely," she said. "I think . . . I rather presumed that there was more to your little friendship . . ."

Little friendship? Cara sucked in her breath, and willed herself to keep silent.

"How silly of me," Verity rattled on. "There are so many different types of friendships, even between grown men and women. And there are so many obvious, *fundamental* differences between you. Even at first meeting I can see that."

Cara raised her eyebrows, waiting.

"The age difference for a start," Verity stated. "Then of course the cultural differences. America must seem like another planet to someone like you . . . I believe Ireland is rather . . . how should I put it? *Different?*"

Then, before Cara could respond, Jameson arrived back at the table.

"Thank you, darling," Verity said, accepting the plain white cup. "I was just saying to your friend Cara how *different* our American ways must seem to her. You know, compared to life in Ireland."

"Yeah," Jameson said, rather distractedly. "There's bound to be a lot of differences."

The piece of croissant in Cara's mouth suddenly seemed to swell until she felt it might choke her. Then, as she eventually swallowed it, a dreadful feeling of being in the way – of not *belonging* – engulfed her.

"Do you think we should go up to the ward soon?" Verity asked. She turned sideways in her chair, blocking

Cara from the conversation.

Jameson checked his watch and shrugged. "We'll have our coffee, and by the time we head back up he might have started to come round."

There was silence for a few moments as all three drank the hot, strong coffee. Then, Verity looked at Jameson again, her eyes bright with enthusiasm.

"D'you know what I was just thinking? When Thomas comes through all this – why don't we take him on a trip to Disneyland? Christmas might be a good time."

Jameson put his coffee cup down and looked at his ex-wife. "*Disneyland*?" he repeated in a stunned voice. He rolled his eyes in despair.

Verity tossed her hair in a manner reminiscent of a teenage girl, oblivious to – or ignoring – his reaction. "Why not? It would be livelier and more suitable for him than spending it up at that lake . . . or spending it at your folks' place again." She took a delicate sip of her coffee. "Anyway," she said, "after what's happened to him while he was staying with your parents . . . we'll have to be more careful."

"*We*?" Jameson looked as though he was going to explode. "Did you actually use the word '*we*', Verity? Since when have you been interested in Thomas's welfare?"

"Oh, come on, Jameson." Verity narrowed her eyes. "We don't need to rake over old arguments . . . not at a time like this."

Jameson shrugged and gave a loud, annoyed sigh.

Cara wished she were anywhere now – anywhere rather than stuck in between Jameson and this awful woman he had once been married to.

Apart from worry about poor Thomas, lack of sleep was beginning to catch up on her. And she was annoyed at herself for looking such a mess and not being able to do anything about it.

Verity suddenly stood up. "I'm going on ahead to the ward." She took one last dainty sip of her black coffee. "I'll see you later." Then, without a glance in Cara's direction, she tapped her high-heeled shoes out of the canteen, as though she were a model on the catwalk.

"Christ!" Jameson's voice was a low moan. "Verity is all we need to make a bad situation worse!"

Cara stared at him without speaking, for she really did not know what to say. She was in very unfamiliar waters with this ex-wife who she had not bargained on meeting.

Jameson leaned across the table, his hand seeking hers. "I'm so sorry, Cara . . . what a hellish mess I've brought you into."

Cara shook her head. "It's nobody's fault . . . poor Thomas didn't ask to get knocked down."

Jameson's brow deepened. "I just feel everything is my fault . . ."

"But you weren't even there," Cara told him. "It's really silly blaming yourself."

"Maybe I shouldn't have left him with my folks . . ." He shook his head. "They're in their seventies . . . and maybe he was too much for them. But they always seemed so capable . . . and they love Thomas."

Cara squeezed his hand tightly. "It was an accident," she said firmly. "It could have happened when he was with you."

"Yeah," he sighed. But the tone of his voice did not

sound convinced. "You heard what Verity said – maybe other people will think the same thing."

"People only have to see you and Thomas together to know how much you care for him."

Jameson managed a shadow of a smile. "Thanks. You somehow make me feel okay about myself . . . even now." And then, in the middle of the sterile, almost-empty café, he leaned over the formica table and kissed her tenderly. Then he looked into her eyes and said: "Cara, I'm real sorry about Verity turning up. I should have realised, but with everything else – it never crossed my mind that we'd meet her. I should have known my parents would have given her name to the hospital."

"Don't worry about that," Cara said. "You have enough real problems."

"She's such a bitch . . . and it's more blatant when she's compared to someone like you." He took a gulp of his coffee then stood up. "Shall we go?"

"Are you okay?" Cara checked.

"I'm not looking forward to it," he said, his eyes misting over. "I'm not looking forward to seeing him again all strapped up with wires and everything."

Cara stood up and stretched a hand out to him, and then together they walked slowly out into the corridor to catch the elevator back to Thomas's ward.

Chapter 31

There was little change in the boy, although his breathing did not seem quite so laboured. Verity stood at one side of the bed, and Jameson and Cara at the other. Very little conversation passed between them. Everyone's attention focussed on the fragile figure in the bed.

After a while one of the nurses appeared at the door. "There are hospitality rooms downstairs," she told them. "I checked them out, and they're not taken tonight. They're basic, but it would give you a chance to have a rest and still be close to Thomas."

"Not for me, thank you," Verity said, giving the nurse a forced little smile. "I'm going back to my apartment for a few hours . . . I have to change and sort out some things." She looked at Jameson. "There's a spare room for you . . ."

"We'll be OK here," he replied curtly without even looking at her. Then, he turned to the nurse. "My parents will be back fairly early, I should think. Could you call me when they arrive at the hospital? I'm just a bit concerned about my father . . ."

"Of course," the nurse told him, "and I'll leave a message down at the reception desk just in case."

"Your father's sick, Jameson?" Verity's ears had pricked up. "It's not serious or anything?"

He shrugged, barely glancing at her. "No . . . but he's not a young man, and the stress of the accident won't be too good for him." He turned to Cara. "He takes medication at specific times, and with the accident and rushing to hospital – he had to go home to sort it all out."

"Well," Verity said, turning on her heel, "I shall see you later then, Jameson."

He sighed as the door closed behind her. "I thought she would never go. This situation is difficult enough without having her around constantly."

Whether Jameson had said anything to the nurses or not, Cara was surprised that they were given one room with two beds – albeit single, high, iron hospital beds. She couldn't imagine that happening anywhere in Ireland. Even in a hotel you could be asked to prove that you were married.

While Cara showered and shampooed her hair, Jameson went off to collect their stuff from the car. By the time he had showered too, she was already in one of the white-painted iron beds and dozing lightly, her hair still damp. She was vaguely aware of Jameson sitting on the side of her bed, stroking her hair and saying how sorry he was about everything. She smiled sleepily and kissed the back of his hand.

Several hours later, Cara woke with a start. It was the nurse knocking on the door, to inform them that Jameson's parents had arrived, and had gone upstairs to see Thomas.

As she watched Jameson rushing around getting ready, she suddenly said: "Maybe it would be best if you go on up to see Thomas on your own this time."

He shook his head. "No . . . we'll go together. I haven't brought you all the way down here just to abandon you."

Cara hesitated. "I'd rather you went on your own." She gestured to her clothes, some on the back of a chair and some in her bag. "I'm not ready yet . . . and it'll give you time to talk to your parents on your own." She could see the disappointment in his eyes. "I'll come up soon, I promise."

"Okay," he said, "if that's what you want." He finished dressing, kissed her and left.

Cara stayed sitting on the bed for a long time, thinking. She thought about Thomas lying upstairs, and her stomach and throat tightened in fear. Then she thought about Jameson's parents and wondered what they would think when they met her.

And how they would feel if they knew she was a married woman.

So much had happened recently that she was struggling to keep up with everything. Then her thoughts moved to the most trivial – but irritating – issue of all. *Verity*.

The cool, perfect Verity.

And she didn't need to wonder what Verity thought about her. First impressions were hard to forget – and Cara knew her creased travelling clothes and scruffy hair had not done her any favours.

Her thoughts came back full circle to Thomas again. And then she made herself move, because sitting around feeling sorry for herself was not going to help anyone. As she brushed her hair out in front of the mirror, she was grateful that she had been able to freshen up. She might not look as perfectly groomed as Verity – but she looked a whole lot better than she had earlier on.

The rain had finally eased off, so she looked through her clothes for something brighter to wear. Something to lift her self-conscious mood. She pulled on her new check Capri pants and a white shirt and left her freshly washed hair hanging loose. She put on the slightest touch of lipstick and mascara, and left it at that. This wasn't a day for vanity.

She made her way back up to the fourth floor, her heartbeat getting quicker with every step – wondering what she was going to have to face. Then, as she turned out of the lift and headed down towards Thomas's room, Jameson stepped out of an office and came striding towards her.

"He's going to make it!" he said, a grin from ear to ear.

The greatest surge of relief shot through her as Jameson's arms swept her up and pressed a warm, damp cheek against hers.

"He came round about an hour ago, and he's been able to say a few words! I know he's going to be all right now."

"Oh, thank God," Cara whispered into the hollow in his neck "Can I see him?"

Jameson gripped her hand and they walked down the corridor.

As she came into the room, Cara's eyes moved straight to the bed, where Thomas was in a deep sleep. But it was an easier sleep – not as laboured as it previously had been, and his face looked more relaxed.

"I can see a big difference," she whispered to Jameson.

And then, the worst over, Cara turned to the people on either side of the bed: the older couple who were obviously Thomas's grandparents, and at the opposite side – Verity, dressed in a more subdued navy summer coat and matching hat, with polka dot trim.

Jameson moved forward, still clasping Cara's hand, and made whispered introductions to his parents. When Cara lifted her eyes, she was hugely relieved to see the obvious warmth in the elderly couple's faces.

Jameson's father was an older version of his son without the beard, while his mother's coiled hair showed the obvious link to Thomas. Although toned down with threads of silver, there was an unmistakable reddish hue.

The older woman moved from the bed and gestured to Cara to go with her out into the corridor.

"My dear," she said in a clear, youthful tone, "how good of you to come all this way with Jameson. We really can't thank you enough."

"It was nothing – " Cara started to reply, but her protests were waved aside.

"Nothing!" the older woman said, her eyes shining. "You've given up the last few days of your holiday, and you call that nothing?"

"I'm very fond of Thomas," Cara said simply, "and I couldn't have gone back to Ireland without seeing that he was going to be okay."

"And Thomas is very fond of you," his grandmother said. "He talked about you all the time when he was with us, and . . ." she looked into Cara's eyes, "Jameson talked to us about you, too."

Cara felt herself blushing. She moved her hands

behind her back, afraid the wedding band might catch the older woman's eye.

Then Jameson stuck his head of the room. "He's awake!"

His mother joined her hands in prayer. "Thank God . . . thank God, our prayers have been answered." she whispered, Then, as they walked back into the room, she caught Cara's arm. "We'll have a little chat together later."

Cara smiled back shyly, and nodded her head.

Thomas awoke to a sea of smiles, and then there were some barely concealed tears as he attempted a rather lopsided grin back. His eyes moved around the group, taking in each and every one, and Cara could see the look of surprised pleasure on his face that his mother was there.

Jameson sat on a chair at the head of the bed, gently stroking Thomas's hand.

"Da-ad," Thomas whispered. "Da-ad . . . was it . . . the car?"

"Yes, buddy," Jameson said, "it sure was that bad old car." He lifted Thomas's hand and kissed it tenderly. Those few words had told him that his son's brain was functioning as it should. The relief in his eyes was enormous.

As Cara watched, her own eyes flooded with tears.

"Thomas . . ." Verity said softly, in a little-girl voice. "When you're better, your dad and I are going to take you on a lovely holiday. Can you guess where?"

Thomas gave a weak smile and shook his head very gingerly.

"*Disneyland!*" she said, her eyes wide.

Thomas's eyes lit up at the magical word.

"Yes," she said, nodding her head, "I promise you –
when you come out of hospital, and you're all better,
we're going to have a wonderful holiday in Disneyland."

"Swell!" Thomas whispered.

No one else reacted to what Verity had just said.
Everyone else took their turn speaking quietly to the sick
boy, being careful not to overwhelm him. The nurses kept
a constant check, and after about half an hour, suggested
that he really needed to rest for a while.

"Come back in a couple of hours," the nurse told the
group as they all stood in the corridor. "We should have
the doctor's report and some of the test results back by
then."

As they walked along the corridor, Jameson's father
suddenly came to an abrupt halt, almost falling in against
the wall. "I don't know how it happened," he said in a
choked voice. "One minute he was by my side – between
us. And the next minute – the car just appeared out of
nowhere . . ."

Jameson put his arm around his father's shoulder.
"Forget it, Dad. All that matters now is that Thomas gets
well. It could have happened at any time."

"But it happened when he was with us," his
mother said quietly. "And neither of us can forgive
ourselves . . . we'll always be asking ourselves what we
did wrong."

"Oh, Mom!" Jameson's voice was weary now, almost
on the edge. "I can't handle all this stuff." He put his other
arm around her now, and drew them both close to him.
"Once and for all – it was *nobody's* fault." He threw a
glance in Verity's direction. "If we're going to blame
everyone, we might as well blame Thomas, too. Even if

some people feel he's not as smart as other kids, he's been taught how to cross roads and keep safe. Up until yesterday everything had worked fine . . . but yesterday he got unlucky. It could have been you and me – it could have been *anyone*."

"OK, son – OK," his mother said, not sounding as if things were OK at all.

"Sorry to interrupt," Verity said, elbowing past Cara, "but I thought we might sort out some kind of visiting rota."

Jameson turned towards her, his brow creased in confusion. "A *rota*? Sorry, Verity – I think you've kinda lost me here."

"A *visiting* rota," Verity stressed. "You know – for visiting Thomas." There was an edge to her voice.

"Why on earth do we need a rota?" Jameson asked.

"Because," Verity explained, trying to be patient, "we are all going to be exhausted, if we spend our days going backwards and forwards to the hospital. And since Thomas is improving, it's just not necessary. We all have busy lives."

Jameson's face turned pale. He turned to the others. "Do you folks all mind waiting in the café downstairs for me, please? I'd like to speak to Verity alone."

When everyone was out of earshot, he turned to face his ex-wife. "Jesus, Verity!" he said, his eyes blazing. "Thomas is still dangerously ill . . . surely it's not too much to expect you to stay close by him for a few days?"

Verity drew herself up to her full height – just a few inches shorter than his. "You deliberately misunderstand me, Jameson – but then, you *always* did. There's no need to make such a drama of things. I was merely thinking of your elderly parents and your little friend from Ireland." Her voice dropped. "It's different for us . . . we are, of course, his parents. And maybe if you had been more understanding of me before, we could still have been together – and none of this would have happened."

Jameson rolled his eyes to the ceiling, his whole body rigid with anger. "Spit it out, Verity," he said wearily. "I'm going to hear what's on your mind anyway. I always do."

She stared at him for a few seconds. "I was just pointing out," she said in an even tone, "that if you had shared responsibility for Thomas with me, perhaps you needn't have had to rely on your parents to help out."

He shook his head. "Don't make me laugh. You don't know the meaning of the word *responsibility*. If you did, then you would still be living with your son – and not have been so mortified when he didn't live up to your idea of perfection."

"That's despicable of you!" she said in an injured tone. "Absolutely despicable! You know that I was ill after Thomas was born. Lots of women have depression after giving birth. How can you still hold that against me?"

"Because, Verity," he replied, "post-natal depression does not go on for years and years." He lowered his head, so his eyes were looking directly into hers. "And I was willing to keep on trying to understand you, and pay for all the help you needed. I was willing to do anything, until you stated that things would only get better, if we put Thomas into an institution for morons!"

"Boy!" Verity spat back. "you really do go for the jugular, don't you? That was all a long time ago. I've changed. I've changed a whole lot. I can see now that my fears were wrong about Thomas." She halted for a moment to compose herself and lower her voice. "He's turned out much better than either of us could ever have hoped. Better than any parents could ever have hoped for."

"Oh, yeah," he snorted angrily, "and funnily enough, so has the family business turned out better than you hoped for, too . . . and maybe even the sales of some of my paintings."

"What exactly do you mean?"

"What I mean, Verity," he said, "is that I'm aware that you've been snooping around, checking up on my finances. I was even told that you called the exhibition, checking up on what sort of money my paintings would make."

Verity's face flushed with indignation. "Any interest I have in your business, or your money in general, is from Thomas's point of view." She halted. "It's natural enough to want reassurances that he would be financially secure if anything happened to either of us."

"Oh, really?" There was a hint of bitter amusement in his voice. "Well, in my opinion, there sure is nothing very natural about you as a mother."

"How dare you!" she said, her eyes wide in shock.

"If it were left up to you," Jameson went on, "none of us would be secure financially. I've never seen anybody get through money the way you did." He folded his arms and put his head to the side, studying her carefully. "Tell me, Verity – how is your love life at the moment?"

"What the hell has my love life to do with you?" she shot back. "And what the hell has it to do with this conversation?"

"To my reckoning," he said, "quite a lot. It would appear that my money becomes of great interest to you when the latest love in your life doesn't earn enough to keep you in your accustomed style."

"How dare you!" she repeated, aghast at his nerve. "How dare you! I don't interfere with your private life – even if you choose to flaunt it at such an inappropriate time." Verity knew by the set of his jaw that she had struck a chord. "Of course a younger, impressionable woman who has a soft spot for Thomas would be very useful to you. Are you hoping that she won't go back to Ireland? That she might stay on and be a housekeeper to you both – up at that depressing lakeside house?"

"My relationship with Cara has nothing to do with you," he said in a low voice, "and I refuse to discuss it with you. The only one thing I will say – is that Thomas adores her."

"Well, yes," she said, giving a little condescending smile. "I can see how he would. She has that childish, naïve quality, which would appeal to him. And of course, she would fit into that little rural life you have up at the lake." She folded her arms. "But what about when this phase of your life is over? This fascination for the isolated life in the country – the bohemian artist image? What happens then? Do you really think she'll fit in with your business life – your *real* career?"

The amused smile on Jameson Carroll's face grew wider. "That is the big difference, Verity. The one thing you knew nothing about – was *me*. The life I'm leading now is the one I intend to go on living for the rest of my time. And if I decide to share it with anyone apart from Thomas – then it will be someone who wants the same things from life as I do."

Verity closed her eyes for a few moments, shaking her head in exaggerated disbelief. "Well," she said, now looking her ex-husband in the eye, "I reckon that you are deluding yourself – but – this is not the time or place to say any more."

"Swell!" His tone was final. "Now we have established where we both stand, I must go and join the others." He turned away from her.

"Jameson!" she said, coming after him. "Please . . . can't we try and be friends at least?"

He turned back, and gave her a long look. "For Thomas's sake," he said, "I'm willing to try anything that makes life easier for him."

She nodded. "Good." Then she checked her watch. "I've got to go now – I have to meet someone."

* * *

As he moved down in the lift, Jameson felt anxious about how things had gone between his parents and Cara, and he felt awful for throwing them together. *Bloody Verity!* When he reached the ground floor he rushed along to the café, and as he entered it, he caught sight of Cara's blonde head bobbing up and down in conversation with the older couple.

"Coffee?" his mother said, holding the pot out to him.

"Yeah, thanks," he smiled. He turned to Cara. "And sorry about the situation with Verity. I don't have to explain things to Mom and Dad . . . they know exactly what she's like."

"Oh, it gave us time to chat to Cara," his mother said airily. "She's been telling us all about Ireland and that sweet little school she teaches in."

His dad smiled thoughtfully. "I never got to Ireland. It's one of the places I had a hankering to visit, to look up the place my folks originally came from."

"There's places where you can look up names, and find out where they came from," Cara said. "If you like, I could send you some information about the Carroll family. It's quite a famous name in Offaly, so it shouldn't be too hard to find out."

"That would be real good," the older man said.

Cara took a pen and a little notebook from her bag. "I'll take down your address, and I'll send anything that I find out."

"When do you actually go back, Cara?" Jameson's mother asked.

"Late next week," she said, not looking at Jameson.

When they went back upstairs, Thomas seemed easier. He spoke to them for longer, although every so often he had to stop to take deep breaths that hurt his ribs.

When their visit was over, Jameson turned to the others. "I'll just have a look in at the office," he said, "and see if any of the test results have come through."

* * *

The doctor lifted a file from the drawer. "Everything," he said, "looks as though Thomas is healing well."

"The internal bleeding?" Jameson asked.

The doctor pushed his glasses high up on his nose. "The removal of the spleen and the other work we did seems to have stemmed it." He paused, looking over the notes. "Of course, it's early days . . . but all in all, he seems to be on the road to recovery."

"What difference will losing his spleen make?" Jameson asked anxiously.

"When he's all healed up, it shouldn't make any

obvious difference – but I'm sure someone will be happy to go over any technicalities with you later." He pursed his lips. "The ribs are causing him the most pain at the moment, but the medication will help that."

Jameson nodded. "So how long d'you reckon it will be until he's back to normal?"

"Woah, now," the doctor held his hands up. "Let's not rush things . . . but I reckon that there will be a huge difference in Thomas in around a month's time."

Jameson let out a low sigh of relief. "Thank you," he said quietly. "And if there's anything at all that will help my son get better quick – money is not an issue."

The doctor inclined his head. "Everything that can be done for Thomas," he said, "will be done."

Chapter 32

Verity reappeared on the scene later in yet another perfectly coordinated outfit. She wore fashionably short-cut beige trousers with a pale green twin-set and matching green-stoned bangle and earrings. Her attitude was much more subdued than earlier, and she directed most of her conversation at Thomas.

Around eight o'clock that night, the nurses advised Jameson that Thomas would be best left to rest until the morning. Verity was the first to stand up. She planted a frosted pink kiss on Thomas's forehead, then she bade everyone goodnight and hurried off.

Back downstairs, Frances Carroll turned to Jameson and Cara. "What are your plans for the night? You know you're both welcome back home with us."

Jameson looked at Cara. "I reckon we'll stay in the hospital rooms again tonight . . . just in case Thomas needs us."

"Do whatever you feel is best," his mother said agreeably.

"Tomorrow night," Jameson said, "we might take your offer up – if Thomas is continuing to mend."

"Oh, good!" she said, clasping her hands together in delight. "I'll have the rooms aired first thing in the morning."

* * *

After his parents had left, Cara turned towards to a payphone in the lobby. "I think I'll give Jean a ring," she said. "Everyone will be anxious to know how Thomas is."

"Sure," Jameson smiled, "it'll be good to give them the news. I'll go ask the staff in reception where would be good to eat in town."

She watched him as he walked across to the desk – so confident, so easy about organising things for them. A little knot came into her chest as she lifted the receiver. Everything about him was now so achingly familiar. His hair that she loved to run her fingers through, his tall, but solid frame – his strong back. Just every little thing about him.

"Oh, honey!" Jean exclaimed on hearing her voice. "How are things?"

"Improving – thanks be to God," Cara said. "He's very badly injured, and he's had a serious operation – but he's going to pull through!"

"Oh, honey!" Jean said again. There was a pause, and Cara could hear a conversation going on in the background. Then, Jean said. "Listen . . . your mom wants a word."

Cara's heart sank. She'd hoped to get away with just passing a message on. She wasn't up to arguing with her mother tonight.

"Thank God!" Maggie came on. "The poor lad – the poor, poor lad. As if he hasn't enough problems in life –"

"I was just giving a quick ring to let you know how things are," Cara said quickly. Then she added, "We've got to go back up to the ward now." It was a lie, but she had to get away from her mother.

"Where are you staying?" Maggie said quickly.

"In rooms in the hospital," Cara replied. "But tomorrow we're going out to . . ." she hesitated, picking the right words. "Tomorrow we're going out to Thomas's grandparents' place. Seemingly, they have a big house just half-an-hour's drive."

"Grand," Maggie said, not sounding grand at all. "And Jean says can you give us the name of the ward in the hospital, and we'll send get-well cards down to the poor lad."

Cara dictated the address to her, then said, "I'll ring again when there's any more news."

"Cara?" her mother said in a low voice. "We haven't much time left now . . . just over the week."

"I know that, Mammy," she said, desperate to get off the phone.

"Well . . . don't forget it." She halted. "We have everybody depending on us back home."

Then, seeing Jameson striding across to her, Cara said quickly. "I'll ring again soon," and hung up before Maggie could say any more.

"A guy on reception told me there's a nice Chinese restaurant a few blocks away," Jameson said. "A good meal might do us good, and we can let the hospital know where we are. What do you think?"

Cara looked slightly awkward. "I've never had

Chinese food," she told him. "The food back home is very plain in the local places. Do you think I'll like it?"

Jameson came over and put his arms around her neck. "You'll love it," he said with a smile."

The walk out to the restaurant in the warm night air, plus the good news about Thomas perked them both up, and Cara felt more relaxed than she had in days as she went over the exotic-sounding menu.

"Something easy for the first time," Jameson suggested, looking down the list of main meals, "with familiar ingredients. How about sweet and sour chicken with some egg-fried rice?"

Cara thought for a moment. "Okay," she said, grinning, "let's go for it." She didn't tell him that the only rice she had ever eaten was rice pudding with a spoonful of jam in the middle to sweeten it.

Cara loved the meal, and they finished off with some fruit she had never heard of and ice-cream. Later, as they chatted over coffee, Jameson suddenly reached across the table and took Cara's hand. "Are you OK about everything?" he asked, his face anxious.

"It was lovely," Cara reassured him. "I liked everything I tried—"

"Not the *food*," he said, giving a little smile. "I meant my parents . . . and Verity. All that shit about us going to Disneyland . . . it's so typical of her." He paused, shaking his head. "It's been difficult for you – being thrown in at the deep end like that."

"Your parents are lovely," Cara said. "They're really warm, genuine people." Then she paused. "And I wouldn't like to comment on Verity. The circumstances in which we've met can't be easy for anyone . . ."

"You're very kind," Jameson told her, "because Verity is not a very likeable woman." He shook his head. "God knows what I saw in her all those years ago. Although . . . she was different before Thomas was born . . ." He broke off now. "Let's not waste any time talking about things like that." He looked into her eyes, checking. "As long as you're OK . . ."

"I'm grand," Cara whispered. "Neither of us need to explain the choices we made in our earlier lives."

"I'm glad you feel that way," he said, grinning now. "And I'm real glad you enjoyed the Chinese food."

Back in the hospital room, Cara showered and padded around the room with one towel wrapped around her and another wrapped around her damp hair. She started sorting out clothes for the following day.

"Leave that until the morning," Jameson said, coming up behind her. He wrapped his arms tightly around her. "In all this awful business," he whispered, "we seem to have lost time for ourselves." He put a finger gently under her chin. "I'm real sorry about the way things have turned out . . . I would have loved your last days here to have been different."

"So would I," Cara sighed.

They looked at each other for a few moments, and then his head bent down towards her and he kissed her properly for what seemed a long time. His hand moved up to unravel her hair from the towel, and tousle it around her shoulders. Then they moved across the floor to one of the iron beds, where Jameson gently removed the other towel and gathered her up into his arms.

* * *

They woke early in the morning, still wrapped around each other in the cramped single bed. They whispered quietly for a few moments, then Jameson got up and quickly dressed, then went off to check how Thomas had fared during the night.

He came back as Cara was brushing her hair out in front of the mirror. The broad grin on his face told her all was well.

"Another good night!" he announced, pulling off his shirt, "and we can go up in an hour or so to see him."

He disappeared into the shower while Cara finished her hair and sorted out her clothes from the night before. She was just hooking her white lacey bra when the bathroom door opened, and Jameson came out with a towel around his waist, and his hair damp and tousled.

"I don't think you have time to put that on," he said, in a low voice.

"Why?" Cara said. "What's the rush?"

Then before she had a chance to say anything more, he eased her arms out of the bra, and bent down and pressed his mouth hard on hers. Then his lips moved downwards to cover the bud of one breast first, then slowly move across to the other. Cara caught her breath, and closed her eyes, savouring the lovely warm feeling that was now coursing through her body.

His lips came back up to hers again – this time harder and more urgent – and she could feel his hardness through the thick, white hospital towel. She took his hand and led him over to the bed. And this time – she unwrapped his towel.

The sight of his smooth, powerful body lifted something inside her, and as he kissed and caressed her,

Cara felt a sweet sensation invade every part of her body, and she knew that no other man would make her feel the way he did now.

The hour disappeared in a haze of warmth and pleasure – and all too soon they were up and moving to dress and rush back up to Thomas's bedside.

* * *

Cara's mood lightened further when they entered the room to see the teenager propped up in a sitting position. The bruises he had received in the accident were now at their colourful worst – dark blue and yellowy-red. But despite them, his eyes shone brightly and his whole manner was definitely returning back to normal

"Do you think," Cara asked Thomas, "that you could manage to hold a book or a comic? And maybe, with a bit of help, do a jigsaw?"

Thomas's eyes lit up. He stretched out his arms, miming the actions of reading, then held a thumb out to signal OK. Next, he reached forward as though putting pieces of a puzzle together. He winced slightly, not entirely comfortable.

"Okay, buddy," Jameson said, stroking his hair. "The books are good – but you will definitely need help with the jigsaw."

Shortly afterwards, Jameson's parents' arrived – the relief all too obvious at Thomas's improved condition. The atmosphere in the room was much more relaxed and easy, everyone chatting and taking their turn reading to Thomas from a *Superman* comic that him grandparents had brought.

Towards lunch-time, Cara looked across at Jameson when she heard the unmistakable sound of Verity's heels tapping along the corridor. Jameson rolled his eyes, but said nothing as his ex-wife swept into the room.

Verity's gaze circled around the room, a fashionably pearly-pink lipstick on her curved, smiling lips. "Hi, everyone," she said in a slightly breathless voice. She widened the smile for Thomas. "And how's my boy today?" she gushed, pushing past Cara to reach the top of the bed.

Jameson reached to the bottom of the bed and gently touched Thomas's foot. "While you have such a crowd here, Cara and I are going to head off into town to get those things for you – okay?"

Thomas held up a thumb and grinned, enjoying all the attention.

"That was perfect timing," Jameson said, squeezing Cara's hand as they stepped into the lift. "I couldn't bear another session of Verity this morning." He chuckled. "She's probably prattling on about Disneyland again as I speak."

"It must be difficult for her," Cara said diplomatically.

"Well," Jameson smiled, "it sure is difficult having to listen to her."

* * *

They headed for a children's toyshop. "I'd love to let the kids at school loose in here," Cara laughed. She wound up a brightly coloured butterfly mobile that played a tune, then she stroked the teddy bears sitting in toddler-size chairs, holding picture books in their laps. "It's like a wonderland for kids. I wish I'd brought my camera with me, to show them all back home."

She looked up, smiling, at Jameson, and was surprised to see a distracted, serious look on his face.

"Okay?" she asked, slipping her hand into his.

362

"Sure . . ." he said, but Cara felt he didn't look too sure at all.

They wandered around the shop, picking up bits and pieces for Thomas.

"I can't believe that we're actually buying books for a boy who I was convinced was going to die a couple of days ago," Jameson said, holding up a Batman book.

Cara touched his hand. "It's amazing the difference that two days can make to someone's life . . ."

Jameson put the book back down on a shelf. "Yes, they can," he said, taking her hand. "Meeting you has made an amazing difference to my life."

"Jameson . . ." she said quietly.

He touched his finger to her lips. "Don't say anything right now, Cara . . . please just listen. "I don't want you to leave me and go back to Ireland. I don't want you to leave me and Thomas." His voice dropped to little above a whisper. "I want you to stay here . . . and when Thomas is better, we can all go back to Lake Savannah together."

"There is nothing," she said, "that I would like more . . . but I *can't*."

"Don't say that," he told her, a desperate edge to his voice. "Don't say *that*."

"Jameson," Cara said, "you're not being fair. I need time. I need to go back home to sort things out. I need time to see how things are . . ." She stroked his arm. "I just need time."

"I nearly lost Thomas," he said, turning away from her, "and now I'm afraid I'm losing you, too . . ."

"It's not the same, Jameson." She didn't know what to say to make him feel better. "And when we sort things out . . . when we've had time to think – there's every chance that I will come back."

"Every chance . . ." he repeated in a flat tone. He shook his head. "You don't really believe that, Cara, do you?"

"Yes, Jameson," she said firmly, "I really do believe it."

His eyes darkened. "Well, I think you're gonna just walk away from this and forget it all happened. Forget all the times we've spent together . . . all the times we've spent with Thomas." His voice lowered, and there was a tone in it Cara didn't recognise. Or at least hadn't heard since she'd got to know him properly. "I reckon you're just gonna go back to little old Ireland," he said, "and think that what we had was some kind of holiday fling. Something you can look back on and think was a dangerous and exciting episode in your boring life – something that *might* have been. Something you can think about during the long winter nights, when you're in a cold bed wondering where your bastard of a husband is!"

Cara moved back, flinching at his words. "I can't believe you're saying all this!"

"And I can't believe you won't stay!" he said, oblivious to what was going on in the shop around him.

"I've told you," she argued, her own voice rising now, "that I've got to go back home to things to sort out! My family, my job –"

"Your goddamn family and job are all you think about!" he said. "What about *yourself*? What about *Cara Gayle*? Why does everyone and everything else have to come first?"

"That's not true," she said. "I wouldn't be here with you if it was true!"

"Waken up, Cara! This is *real* life – my life and yours. It's not the kind of stuff you read about in your romance books. You're letting other people and an outmoded Church lead your life for you."

She looked at him, and there was a long, painful silence between them, during which Cara's eyes filled up with tears.

"Aw, hell . . ." Jameson said, his anger deflating. "I didn't mean it to happen like this . . ." He put both his arms around her neck, suddenly back to his old caring self.

Just then, a shop assistant came towards them pushing a trolley full of books and nursery toys. She cast a wary glance in their direction, then started unloading the trolley onto a display table just a few feet away.

Cara quickly wiped her eyes with the back of her hand. "Come on," she said in a croaky voice, taking his hand, "we'll pay for these . . . and then we can talk about things over lunch." But as they walked to the pay-desk, Cara knew in her sinking heart that all the talking in the world was not going to change anything right now. Only time could do that.

* * *

Later, as they sat at the back of a small, Italian restaurant, Jameson tried to reason with her again. "What if I phoned your parents *and* your husband, and told them the situation? It's not fair that you should carry all this. I could lay it on the table for them, and in a while – when they've all got used to the idea – you could go back to Ireland for a holiday and sort things out face-to-face properly."

Cara looked down at the Roman-style lettering on the tablecloth, and said nothing. What was there to say?

"Cara?" he said, waiting.

She looked up at him. "I know we come from very

different backgrounds, Jameson – and it must be hard for you to understand how things work back in Ireland. But from the things I've told you about my family, surely you must know that I couldn't handle stuff like that?" Cara's voice sounded tired, on the verge of exasperation. "Even Verity pointed out the differences between us, and predicted this sort of thing happening."

Jameson's eyes blazed. "Verity is hardly an expert on other people's relationships. Christ! She didn't even look after her only child!" He shook his head. "The only good thing that happened between us was Thomas, and she couldn't even see that. Thank God we didn't have any more children."

"Would it have made any difference if you'd had?"

"Hell – no," he said, his brow furrowing. "At one time I thought it could have changed things . . . but I'm everlastingly grateful that we didn't. Thomas and I get along just fine on our own, and after this terrible accident, I know that he's going to need every bit of my attention for some time to come."

"You give him that already," Cara said, touching his hand.

"Having only one child allows me to do that – but I'd hoped at some point he would become more independent." He shrugged. "I guess he will become independent to a limited extent. But – I have to face the fact that he's reached his potential in most areas, and not expect more from him than he is capable of giving."

Cara reached over the table and took his hand. "And I'm so sorry for saying this, Jameson – but you must not expect more than I am capable of giving, either."

Chapter 33

"So we'll see you both back at the house later?" Jameson's mother smiled and wagged a finger at Cara. "And don't you *dare* forget – we don't want any more of those Irish formalities. No more *Mr and Mrs Carroll*. From now on it's Sam and Frances – OK?"

"OK," Cara said, giving an embarrassed smile. "We'll follow you up in a bit . . . *Frances*."

Everyone laughed, Thomas laughing the loudest of all.

"Careful with those damned ribs!" Jameson warned. "We don't want you in this place any longer than you have to be."

Thomas grinned and held his hands palm up. "But I like it – here! I like the nurses."

"I think it's swell that you like it here," his father told him, trying not to laugh, "but don't get too used to it. We want you fit and well, and running around back at Lake Savannah."

"And fit enough," came a familiar voice from the doorway, "to go to *Disneyland*, just as we promised."

Cara's throat tightened.

Everyone turned in surprise to see Verity, casually dressed in a light red sweater and jeans. Cara's gaze dropped to the ex-model's feet – flat, red leather loafers explained the lack of warning that Verity was approaching.

There was silence for a few seconds, then Frances Carroll stood up. "Hi, Verity," she said, "sorry about your timing – but I'm afraid Sam and I are just leaving." She tugged at her husband's sleeve. "C'mon, Sam, we'll head back home and get things organised for the others." She blew a kiss towards the bed. "See you tomorrow, Thomas." Then she and her husband headed for the door.

"Darling!" Verity said, moving up to take Sam's place at the side of the bed. She planted a scarlet kiss-mark on Thomas's cheek, then laughed and made a huge gesture of rubbing it off with a hanky. "You look so much better than yesterday." Then, she fussed around him, sorting pillows and asking questions about the hospital food and the treatment he was getting – and moving on to the next question before he had time to reply.

"How would you like," Jameson intervened, moving Thomas's tray-trolley towards him, "if we all help you with the jigsaw puzzle?"

Cara felt a wave of relief at Jameson's clever suggestion. It would just have been awful for her and Jameson and Verity to sit around the bed making polite conversation.

"Shall we go downstairs to have something to eat?" Verity later suggested when the nurses came to give Thomas his lunch. She gave them both a big friendly smile, and there was nothing else to do but agree.

Surprisingly, Cara found her much more pleasant company than on the previous occasions. She chattered away about the weather, and suggested places that Cara might like to visit in New York, before heading back upstate.

When Jameson went off to make some phone calls, Verity leaned her elbows on the table, moving closer to Cara. "You've been teaching a number of years," she suddenly said, "so I presume that would make you a dedicated career woman?"

Cara raised her eyebrows. "Well," she said cautiously, "I do enjoy my work – but I enjoy other things as well."

Verity nodded her head. "But you've obviously dedicated your whole working life to teaching so far?"

"Yes," Cara said, wondering where the conversation was leading.

"I presume," Verity said, smiling, "that you've forsaken both marriage and children to pursue your career?"

Cara suddenly realised the point she was making, for Verity's gaze was now firmly fixed on her wedding ring.

After a long, painful pause, Cara finally found the words she had dreaded having to say to anyone who knew about her and Jameson's relationship. "I am actually married . . . although – "

"And *children?*" Verity cut in, her eyebrows arched in interest. She was determined to waste no time in getting the information she needed in order to work out the relationship between Jameson and this young Irishwoman. How she had missed the wedding band before, she did not know. But she was determined that she would not miss anything else.

After another pause, Cara said, "I don't have any children." She looked around the coffee-shop, wishing that Jameson would appear and rescue her, but there was no sign of him. She took a sip of her coffee, hoping that the conversation had ended, now that Verity had got all the information she wanted.

"So," Verity said, fishing in her handbag for her lipstick and compact, "I presume this relationship with my husband is nothing more than a holiday fling?"

"We're very good friends," Cara answered carefully. "What the future will bring . . ."

A few deft strokes of lipstick left Verity's lips scarlet and perfect. She snapped the compact case shut, then leaned across the table, closely enough for Cara to smell her expensive floral perfume. "I should think," she said, staring straight into Cara's eyes, "that when you go back to Ireland, and have had time to think everything over – that you'll decide to forget all about Jameson."

"Why should I want to forget him?" Cara said.

Verity could see she had the Irish girl's attention now, and was not going to waste one second lest Jameson should return now and cut the conversation short. "I married Jameson when I was much younger . . ." She narrowed her eyes. "Much younger than you are now. And, it was the right thing to do – but rather unfortunately, it was the wrong time." She leaned closer. "Jameson wanted different things from me in those early days of our marriage." She paused. "And then of course, along came Thomas, with all the problems that a mentally-handicapped child brings . . ."

Cara reached across the table for her handbag. "I don't think you should be telling me all this . . ."

Verity clamped her hand down on top of the bag. "Make no mistake," she said, her eyes glinting, "being all *buddy-buddy* with a handicapped teenager is a very different ballgame to giving birth to a handicapped baby, and then struggling to bring him up."

Cara stood up and pulled her bag away from Verity's grasp. "What happened between you and Jameson and Thomas has nothing to do with me." Her eyes glinted with anger. "And what happens between Jameson and me has nothing to do with *you*."

"But it *has*, my dear," Verity said. "It *has*." She tilted her head to the side. "Am I correct in assuming that you are going to stay with Sam and Frances for a few days?"

Cara took a deep breath. "As I've just told you – it's none of your damned business."

"But won't you feel intimidated?" Verity continued in a low voice. "The grandeur – all the rooms – the tennis courts and swimming-pool?"

The look on Cara's face and the resulting silence was Verity's reward. She had correctly deduced from the little information that she had gleaned from Cara, that there was more than just a difference in nationality between her and Jameson.

Verity's eyes were well trained to detect clothes that were not expensively hand-stitched, and shoes and handbags which were not of the finest leather. Her first glance at Cara's perfectly adequate – but rather ordinary clothes – had told her all she needed to know about her lifestyle in Ireland. Her teaching salary would earn her no more than a bare subsistence-level standard of living.

And the fact that Cara had never travelled out of Ireland before, and was staying with relatives rather than at a plush hotel said it all. Verity was very good as working people out – and it was a talent which she had

371

found very useful.

"I don't feel intimidated in the slightest," Cara snapped. "Jameson's parents are very nice, and I'm looking forward to visiting them." Then she lowered herself back into the hard metal chair. All her instincts told her that she should walk out on this awful woman – but there was something compelling her to stay. Something that told her to wait and listen – and maybe learn something that would finally make her able to walk away from this dangerous affair.

"I'm sure they'll be very kind to you," Verity went on, taking her cigarettes and lighter from her handbag. She had more or less given them up, but at certain times she felt the need overwhelming. "I take it that Jameson hasn't told you about his folks' home – or about the change in his fortunes with the family business?"

"We've talked about lots of things," Cara said, "but Thomas is our main concern at the moment."

"Of course," Verity said, taking a deep drag on her cigarette, "and I know Jameson has been just wonderful during this awful hospital business. He can be a strange man at times. Very difficult to live with. He's so deep – at times almost unable to express himself And I am so afraid that there's going to be an aftermath to all this awful business with Thomas."

"In what way?" Cara said, hating herself for engaging in this kind of conversation, because she knew that Jameson was so intensely private and would be horrified to hear himself being discussed in such a way.

"I imagine that Jameson will need my help – as Thomas's mother, of course." She paused, then put the cigarette to her lips again. "It's obvious that his parents are too old to be of any support to him. In my opinion, they should never have been left in charge of the boy. He's too much for them to handle."

"I don't agree," Cara said. "He's a well-behaved, sensible boy. He doesn't need much handling."

Verity just smiled, as though she had never spoken. "I really want to thank you, Cara," she said now, reaching a hand out to cover Cara's. "I want to thank you for looking after the two men in my life. And for giving up your holiday to come all the way up to New York to visit Thomas in hospital."

Cara snatched her hand out of Verity's reach. "I don't need any thanks from you. I did it for Thomas and Jameson."

"*And,*" Verity continued, the smile growing sweeter, "I want to give you a piece of advice. *Go home*. Go home back to Ireland – and go home back to your husband. It's where you belong, and where you'll be happiest."

Cara felt a tight knot forming in her stomach.

"Jameson is not for you," Verity went on. "I'm sure you're a very nice girl – but I'm sorry to say that you're just a holiday fling. A novelty which will soon wear off – just like all the other girls he's had."

Cara got to her feet, unable to listen to any more. She placed both hands on the table squarely in front of Verity. "I don't need advice from a mother who deserted a helpless child when he needed her most!" She stared directly into Verity's eyes. "If I want to stay on in America – as Jameson has asked me to do – then that's exactly what I will damn well do!"

Verity ran a hand through her immaculate black bob. "When you think this over," she said, "you'll thank me for my plain speaking. Your naïve, optimistic outlook on life would not last long living with Jameson." She rolled her eyes. "His morose, so-called *artistic,* ways nearly drove me mad when I was younger."

"And you think you could cope with it better now?" Cara challenged.

"*Experience,* honey," Verity said, with a bitter little smile, "*experienc*e. I wouldn't let it get to me again. I would make sure that I had compensations." She raised her eyebrows. "It really would be much better all round, if you just head back home to your little husband in Ireland."

Without a further word, Cara swept her bag up, turned on her heel, and marched straight out of the coffee-shop – out through reception until she reached the front door of the hospital and the fresh air outside.

Verity crushed her cigarette in the ashtray, and then clicked her fingers to a waitress clearing a nearby table. "I'll settle up now," she said, without looking at the girl. And as she took a note from her purse, she reckoned that the time with Cara had been worth every cent.

* * *

"So you managed to get rid of Verity?" Jameson said, grinning. He pulled a chair out and sat down at the café table.

"I don't know where she went," Cara replied. "I just left for a bit . . . and when I came back, she was gone. The waitress told me that she paid the bill."

"Wonders will never cease," Jameson said, raising his eyebrows. "Do you want another coffee, or shall we go back up to Thomas?"

"Back to Thomas," Cara said in a flat tone.

"You OK?" Jameson said, looking worried. "You seem kind of . . ." He stopped. "Verity didn't upset you or anything? She's good at getting to people. She has it down to a fine art."

Cara hesitated. She didn't know how she felt. She could hardly take in all the things that Verity had said. Verity, whom Jameson *must* have loved at some time. Verity, who seemed to know a side of Jameson that she didn't.

"She has said something – hasn't she?" Jameson persisted. "Lies about me . . . or about my folks? Tell me, Cara – please. If you don't tell me I can't sort it out."

"Look," Cara said, "she just mentioned something about you and other girlfriends . . . and about how you get fed up of them when the novelty wears off –"

"That fucking, goddamned woman!" he hissed. "There is nothing she won't stoop to!" He stopped for a second. "You didn't believe her – did you? Please don't tell me she got to you – because that's all she wants." He suddenly looked almost frantic. "Don't let this put you off, Cara," he said, taking her hand in his. "We have enough problems with the Irish side of things without that bitch making things worse."

Cara suddenly felt lost, out of her depths with everything. At this point in time, she didn't know what she believed – and she couldn't face another scene with Jameson about their relationship. "I think I know exactly what Verity was trying to do," she told him. "And I really don't want to have another argument with you, Jameson – I'm tired and weary of all these problems." She took a deep breath. "I was just thinking that now Thomas is getting better . . . maybe I should be thinking of getting back up to Jean's . . ."

Jameson looked at her now, worry written all over his features. Worry that he was going to lose her sooner than he'd even dreaded. "There's no need to rush back yet," he said. "Why don't you give your folks a ring tonight if you feel you need to check on them."

"Yes," Cara said quietly, "I might do that."

* * *

Thomas was delighted to tell them that he was now able to eat proper food. He gave them a run-down on all the things he had eaten, and what the nurse had said about the menu later on that evening.

The afternoon passed with conversation being directed at – and through – Thomas, rather than to each other. Every time Jameson looked at Cara or spoke to her, she found herself thinking of all the things that Verity had said . . . or hinted at. About him having lots of different girlfriends, and about his parents' house.

Once or twice, she thought she should maybe tell him everything that Verity had said – so that he would reassure her – but she just couldn't find the words. Suddenly, this man with whom she had spent most of the last few weeks had become like a stranger she hardly knew.

A dark, deep stranger who was asking her to give up *everything* she knew for him.

* * *

They left Thomas for his afternoon rest and headed out to Jameson's parents' house. As before, the conversation centred around Thomas. Whenever she spoke, Cara felt as though she was listening to someone else speaking and not herself. She could feel a tight knot in her chest. A mixture of hurt that Jameson hadn't warned her about the grand house he was now driving her to, and a feeling of mounting anger because she was so completely dependent on him while they were here.

She looked out of the car window, noticing that the sun was properly shining for the first time in days.

"Cara?" Jameson said, his voice sounding hoarse. "There's something wrong . . . I know it." He paused. "Can we sort it out before we get to Mom and Dad's? *Please*?"

Cara kept staring out of the window, unable to find the words to describe her feelings.

"Cara?" he repeated. "Please tell me what's wrong."

She took a deep breath. "Verity told me things," she said, "about your family and about you and her . . . I just wish you'd told me yourself. I feel hurt that you didn't explain things . . . and that I'm all alone down here in a strange situation."

Jameson put his foot on the car brake, and skidded to a halt at the side of the highway. He turned in his seat and gently pulled Cara around until she was facing him. "What the hell did Verity say?"

"She told me about the house . . . how big and grand it is, and about your family business."

"What else?" he asked, waiting.

"She said . . . she said that you were difficult," Cara whispered, "that you could be very temperamental and awkward."

"My *artistic* temperament?" he asked. He gave a deep sigh, and then his face broke out into a relieved grin. "Is that *all*?" He shook his head. "I thought you were going to

377

say something shit-awful!"

"Jameson!" Cara hissed. "I don't find it at all funny. There have been times recently when you have been awkward and difficult . . . and it makes me feel very uncomfortable."

"Oh, Cara," he said, his face now serious. "I'm real sorry I've made you feel like that." He pushed his hand through his hair. "I guess at times I get a little hot-headed, but it doesn't mean anything. It's just frustration . . . a feeling of not having control over things. Important things like you and me." He turned towards her. "Most of the time I don't feel like that – *honestly*. Back at Lake Savannah before all this shit happened, I'd never felt happier and more content in the whole of my life. Just doing the simple, ordinary things with you – it's all I really want. It's just the pressure of things at the moment . . ." He stroked her hair now. "I'm real, real sorry for hurting you – I don't mean to. And I promise I will keep my stupid temper under control."

"OK," Cara said, "but there was another thing Verity went on about, and it's something that really concerns me – our financial differences."

"How many times," he said, gently tilting her head so that she was looking into his eyes, "do I have to tell you, that there is *no* difference between us? I haven't made a big deal about the business and my folks' place because those things are not important to you and me."

"I'm not too sure about that," Cara replied.

"Look," he said, "we haven't enough time to discuss the really *big* things, without wasting time on details that can wait. And the way things have turned out, we've spent most of the time talking about Thomas – and that's because he's one of the really big things."

Cara looked at him, tears welling up in her eyes.

"Everything else can wait, Cara," he said gently. "There's lots of things I don't know about your life. You haven't described your own home or your parents' home back in Ireland. And I don't know too much about your brother and sister . . . but I know that eventually we'll have the time for all of these things."

Cara looked at him from lowered eyelids and then, despite herself, a little smile started on her lips. "A very ordinary old farmhouse does not take a lot of describing, Jameson."

"Well," he said, laughing with relief, "there you are. That's another really important detail that I know about you now. I might just have changed my mind about you, if you said you lived in a very modern farmhouse."

"You are unbelievable!" Cara said, laughing along with him now, all her tension lifted. And as they drove along the last leg of their journey, she made a decision to put Verity's poisonous words out of her mind, and concentrate on enjoying their last few days together.

Jameson had pulled off the main highway, and headed on down a smaller, quieter road. The further he drove, the bigger the houses became and the larger the grounds surrounding them. He slowed down as they reached a corner and then, straight in front of them, Cara could see two high gates with a large wall on either side of them. It was like something from the American movies that Cara saw back in the cinema in Tullamore.

She held her breath as the car drove in through the gates and on up the winding driveway. Tall trees flanked either side of the drive like soldiers on guard, and the flower-beds were square and uniform. Where the garden back at Lake Savannah was a riot of random colour from trees, shrubs and flowers – there was nothing left to chance in the grounds of this house.

When they pulled up in front of the imposing stone house, Cara glimpsed the tennis courts at the side of the building, and behind them, a large wooden summerhouse. If possible, the house was actually bigger and grander than she had imagined it. Cara could feel her throat and chest tighten with nerves as she got out of the car.

Then, before the feelings of inadequacy completely enveloped her, she heard a voice calling from the front of the house.

"Welcome! Welcome!" Sam Carroll was coming down the front steps, as quickly as his no-longer sprightly legs and his breathing would allow. He came across to kiss Cara on the cheek, and then insisted on carrying her bag into the house.

"I'll do that, Dad," Jameson said, making to take the bag from him.

"Like hell you will," his father said, his eyes twinkling. "There's life in this old dog yet – and a light bag ain't gonna kill me."

Jameson's mother was waiting at the door to greet them, and her welcome was as warm as her husband's. "I see you've brought the sunshine with you on your first visit, Cara," she said, smiling warmly and hugging her. She hugged her son, then asked: "And how was dear Thomas this afternoon?"

"Much, much better," Jameson said, "and eating everything in sight. He was even planning what he would have to eat later this evening."

Sam put the bag down in the hallway, and threw his arms up in the air. "Thank God!" he said. "Our prayers have been answered." He looked at Cara. "I never prayed so hard for anything in my life as I prayed for that boy's recovery."

Jameson put a hand on each of his parents' shoulders. "Well, I guess your prayers were answered, and we can all stop worrying. Thomas is well on the road to getting back to his old self again."

"Good, good, good," Frances Carroll said, her voice quivery with emotion. She clapped her hands together. "Now, I'll show Cara up to her room." She turned to Jameson. "You come, too . . . I've given you adjoining rooms with a bathroom in between, so you don't have to come out into the corridor if you want to talk."

Cara lowered her head and avoided meeting Jameson's eyes. It was obvious that the situation was not causing embarrassment to anyone else, so that was at least one thing she could stop worrying about.

As she followed the older woman upstairs, Cara took in the ornate hallway with the Persian rug, the huge Chinese vases full of fresh flowers, and the countless paintings and sculptures that adorned the perfectly painted walls.

"When you've freshened up," Frances said, throwing open the door of a huge, airy bedroom, filled with creamy-coloured, very feminine furniture, "we'll all have a drink and then we'll eat." She opened the bathroom door, and showed Cara where the towels and toiletries were. "I'll leave you both now to get settled, and then we'll see you downstairs when you're ready."

"My mom would make a great diplomat," Jameson

said, when the door closed after her. "She's given us complete privacy without actually asking if we wanted to share a bedroom or not."

"She's a lovely person," Cara said, "and this house is just out of this world . . . I can't find the words to describe how beautiful it is." She paused. "Verity said that . . ."

But before she could utter another word, Jameson swept her in his arms and covered her mouth with his. When they came up for air, he looked into Cara's eyes. "I don't want to hear that damned woman's name mentioned for the rest of your stay in America."

"She knows I'm married, Jameson," Cara whispered. "Do you think your parents might know, too?"

"They already know the situation," Jameson said firmly, "and they won't ask you anything." He stroked her hair. "I'm a fully grown man, Cara, and what I decide to do with my life is my own business. Mom and Dad accepted that a long time ago. We respect each other's choices in life. It's as simple as that."

Cara looked up at him. "Have you – have you brought other women back to this house?"

"No." His reply was instant. "Apart from Verity, I haven't brought any other women here." He shrugged. "For God knows how many years it's been just me and Thomas. So," he said, touching a finger under her chin, "Mom and Dad will know how important *you* are to me. OK?"

Cara looked into his eyes. "OK."

When they went back downstairs, Cara was surprised to see lots of lacework on the walls of the sitting room – similar to the type that Jameson had framed in the house back at Lake Savannah. "This is beautiful," she said, gesturing to an intricate creamy piece in a black frame.

"That lacework is real old," Jameson told her. "My grandmother and my great-grandmother did a mountain of it. They used to make collars and cuffs for some of the big shops in New York."

"Your *grandmother?*" Cara said, suddenly smiling. "I thought it was Verity . . ."

Jameson rolled his eyes to the ceiling. "Are you kidding? Verity hasn't a creative bone in her body. She spends any talent she has matching up her lipsticks to her outfits." He looked at Cara, raising an eyebrow and nodding like he did when Thomas was in trouble. "I thought we weren't gonna mention *her* name again?"

"Sorry," Cara said, covering her mouth like a scolded child.

"When we moved upstate," Jameson explained now, "I had my mom come up and sort out drapes and that kind of thing." He shrugged. "I wasn't too sure about some things apart from the paintings and stuff like that, but I knew that I didn't want it looking like the place I lived in with . . ." he laughed, *"you-know-who."* He touched one of the picture frames. "I think all this lace stuff is beautiful, and I like having it around. It reminds me of my grandmother and when I was growing up."

Frances came into the room now, and came over to rest her arm on Jameson's shoulder. "Your grandmother would have loved to have seen her hard work decorating two beautiful homes." She smiled at Cara. "Sam's mother and grandmother made their living from the lace and the tatting." She pointed to the frames that held the smaller, circular pieces. "When Sam's grandfather died, his grandmother brought up the family on her own, and she supported them all on the little bit of money she got from the lacework. She taught all of them – even the boys – how to do this work."

Cara moved around the walls, studying each piece carefully. "They are lovely," she said, "and worked in such intricate patterns. My mother would love them – she crochets and knits, but I don't think she's ever tackled lace."

"I think it's one of these things that you have to learn early," Frances said. "My own family never learned any kind of handcrafts – but all I know is, Sam treasures those little old bits of lace more than anything else in this house." She moved across the room to a beautifully carved cabinet and opened the doors to reveal an array of drinks. "What are you having?"

Cara flushed, not quite sure what would be the right thing to ask for. "I really don't mind . . ."

"Dry Martinis?" Frances suggested. "Gin? Champagne?"

"How about some champagne?" Jameson said, smiling at Cara.

"Wonderful!" Frances said. "And perfect for celebrating Thomas's quick recovery!" Even as she spoke, tears started to glisten in the corner of her eyes. She cleared her throat, and gave an embarrassed little smile. "I'll go get a chilled bottle from the fridge."

"This is good," Jameson said, squeezing Cara's hand. "We can relax now . . . things are getting better."

Frances came back with the bottle of champagne, and Sam followed behind with four crystal champagne flutes. They all toasted Thomas's health and then Frances touched Jameson's hand. "Sam and I want to go back and spend the evening with Thomas, so that you two can have an evening on your own."

Jameson looked at Cara.

"Please, honey," Frances said in a gentle but firm tone. "We really want to go back in. I have a new game and two new books that my friend Alice bought for him, and I'd like to take them in to him."

"Besides," Sam chipped in, "when Thomas goes back home we won't see him for some time." He smiled. "You have him all to yourself the rest of the time – it'll give us a little while with him. Like we'd planned."

Jameson looked at Cara and smiled. "Hell, we're only thirty minutes drive away . . . we'll ring the hospital and speak to Thomas after dinner. If he's OK, then maybe Cara and I will go out and catch a movie – or maybe just watch TV here."

Frances looked serious for a few moments, her brow creased in thought. "When do you fly back to Ireland, Cara?"

Cara had to think hard – the days all seemed to have run in together. "Friday," she said, "this coming Friday."

"And have you anything planned – back up at your aunt's house?"

"Not really," Cara replied, "but all my clothes and presents and everything are there."

"I've just had a thought," Frances said brightly. "Why don't we get your parents to bring all your things down here? They could stay overnight on Thursday – we have plenty of room – and then you could all fly out on Friday from New York."

Cara's heart skipped a beat. She could just imagine her mother's face on the other end of the phone if she suggested them coming to stay in the Carrolls' house. And not just because of the size and style of the house. Regardless of what her aunt Jean had said, the fact that she was a married woman acting like a *single* one, would be more than enough to send her mother's blood pressure soaring through the ceiling.

"I'll have to think about that," Cara said quietly, not looking anywhere near Jameson, "but thank you so much for offering. It's really kind of you."

"You decide, honey," Frances said, "and the phone is out in the hallway if you want to call them."

* * *

Dinner was perfect. Well-done steaks served with dishes of roast potatoes and mashed potatoes and some colourful vegetables that Cara had never heard of, followed by apple and blackberry pie and thick cream.

"That was one of the most beautiful meals I've ever had," Cara said, helping Jameson's mother carry things back into the kitchen.

"I'm so glad you enjoyed it, honey," Frances laughed, "but I have to confess that although the pie was home-made, it wasn't home-made by me. I have a nice lady, Mrs Scott, who helps me out a couple of days a week, and she's famous for her baking." She beckoned Cara to close the kitchen door so that they wouldn't be overheard. "Mrs Scott's husband helps Sam with the garden and the grounds, and if Sam's having one of his off-days, then Bill Scott drives us around too."

As she and Frances tidied things away Cara's mind was only half on the chirpy conversation she was having with the older woman. She found herself wondering what her mother would find to say about everything. About the house, the couple who looked after them – the different kind of food they ate . . . everything. And then a cold shiver ran down her spine, as she wondered what her mother's reaction would be if she dared say she was not coming back up to Lake Savannah.

Cara turned towards the kitchen door, and then she suddenly caught sight of Jameson crossing the hallway. She took in his tall, well-defined frame in his casual jeans and shirt, his long hair swinging in a way that made her want to run out and bury her face in it. But it was the slight frown on his face that caught at her heart, as he passed on by into the large sitting-room to rejoin his father. The frown that she knew was caused by all the uncertainty that had suddenly exploded into his life. Meeting Cara, falling in love with her, Thomas's accident – and now *losing* Cara.

In that instant she knew that she would face anything to stay a few days longer with him. If she went back, there would only be polite conversations in Jean's kitchen while she and Jameson pretended that they were just friends – platonic friends.

She would tell her mother and father that she was staying on in New York. That she was staying there until it was time to go back to Ireland – and back to Oliver.

* * *

Jean answered the phone. "Oh, Cara," she said in a rush, "it's so good to hear from you. How is little Thomas?"

Cara told Jean all about Thomas's improvement, and how their plans had taken them out to Jameson's parents' house. Then, after checking that Maggie was not within earshot, she explained the situation to Jean.

There was a silence for a few moments, then Jean said: "I've already prepared your mom for this happening . . ."

Cara held her breath. "And what did she say?"

"Her biggest worry is that you might refuse to come home with them at all." Her voice dropped to a whisper. "She sat up talking to me for hours last night – telling me about Oliver and all the worries she's had with Pauline and little Bernadette. And then she broke down, saying that she was afraid you wouldn't come back home with them."

"I'd never do that," Cara said, "and Jameson understands that."

"I think she's come round to you staying in New York until you fly out," Jean said, "and I've a pretty packed schedule for them until then." Jean's voice suddenly lifted to a bubblier note. "We're going on a trip to Cooperstown tomorrow, the place famous for baseball – and where James Fenimore Cooper came from." She paused as though checking with someone. "Bruce says it's the guy who wrote *The Last of the Mohicans* or something like that."

"Oh, Jean," Cara said, a little sob coming into her voice, "how can I thank you? You've been so good to me . . . so understanding." She swallowed hard. "The only thing is . . ."

"What's that, honey?" Jean asked.

Cara hesitated. "It's just that . . . I won't be able to spend any more time with you and Bruce. And despite what's happened . . . I really did enjoy being with you in your lovely house. I feel awful – everything has happened so quickly."

"Don't worry about a thing," Jean told her. "We had some really nice times together. And anyway, Bruce and I will be down in New York with your parents, to see you all off."

A huge wave of relief washed over Cara. "Oh, that's good," she said, "that's really good."

There was a pause. "Well, Cara," her mother's low voice came on the line, "I hear everything has gone well with the poor lad."

"He's coming on," Cara said. "He should be out of hospital in a few days."

There was a long pause. "And I suppose it's too much to ask of his father to bring you back up here?"

"It's not just that," Cara said. "It's leaving Thomas. He's still not well enough to travel." This wasn't going the way Jean had described.

"Oh, well," Maggie said in a hollow voice, "I suppose you've made all your own plans? You've no intentions of making your way back up to the house you should be staying in?"

"It's not that," Cara argued. "It just makes more sense for me to stay here until it's time to go back to Ireland." There was a long, long silence. "Oh, Mammy," she suddenly remembered, "there's an ornament – a Christmas figure – and a little picture in the room I was in. Would you bring them down to the airport for me?"

"We'll have all your stuff with us," Maggie said stiffly. "Your father and I know the right thing to do . . . and it's very, very hard to take that none of our children do."

"Mammy," Cara said, "that's not fair." She found herself struggling now, trying to find words that would ease the situation. "Sometimes the thing that's right for one person isn't right for another."

"Well," her mother sighed, "it's lucky we have the Church and the priests to guide us. That's why they have rules and sacraments that aren't meant to be broken."

"I'll see you on Friday," Cara said.

"Cara," her mother said, quickly now, "you *will* be there, won't you?"

Cara took a deep breath. "Whatever you might think of me," she said, "I'd never do that to you and Daddy."

"I'm glad to hear it," her mother said. Another strained little pause. "We'll see you in the airport at the check-in desk on Friday so."

* * *

After Sam and Frances Carroll went off to the hospital, Cara and Jameson took a walk in the grounds.

"I'm real glad you're staying on until Friday," Jameson said as they walked through the trees hand in hand. He gripped her hand tighter. "Jeez . . . *glad* doesn't begin to describe it!"

"I'm glad too," Cara said quietly, "but the time is just disappearing now." She paused for a moment. "Although it seems such a long time ago since the day I met Thomas down by the lake . . . and then the day I met you both in the shop."

"And the day at the wedding," Jameson said, smiling at the memory. Then he suddenly stopped and pulled her close to him. "Do you regret all this, Cara? Will you look back on it and feel that you gave up your holiday for me? Do you think you'll wish you'd never met Thomas and me?"

Cara looked at him without saying anything for a few

seconds. "I don't regret a thing, Jameson. Whatever happens, I'll never regret meeting you and Thomas." She turned her head to the side. "I believe that some things are just meant to happen in life . . . and that's what's happened between us. We were meant to happen."

He touched her cheek lightly. "I never have – and I never will – love anyone the way I love you, Cara Gayle."

Later, as they made their way back up the front steps of the house, Cara turned to Jameson. "I'm sorry about the fuss I made about coming here. Your parents are lovely people, and I really like them. And the house is just beautiful – I love it."

Jameson's face lit up. "When you come back to America – when you've had time to sort things out – we could spend more time down in New York if you want." He opened the door. "Eventually this place will be mine, if I want to keep it on." He took both her hands in his. "I was never really interested in it before – I felt it was too big for me and Thomas. But if things turn out the way I hope, it would be a great New York base for us. We could go between this and Lake Savannah – whenever you choose."

Cara stood on her tiptoes and wrapped her arms around his neck. "I love both your houses and I'd happily live in either or both." Then, she put a hand on either side of his tanned face. "If that was the only decision I had to make – I'd be the happiest woman in the world."

Chapter 34

Tullamore, County Offaly

"So you're going off out for a run, Charles?" Pauline called from the kitchen, as she knelt rubbing Bernadette briskly with a large towel. She reached up to the table for the tin of Johnson's Baby Powder.

Charles held the car keys behind his back, as he came into the kitchen. He surveyed his sister closely for a moment before answering. She had sounded civil enough, and she didn't look cross – so he took a chance. "The engine," he said, pushing his shirt sleeves up, "I thought I might give it a bit of a run out . . ." He looked out of the window towards the field. "You know . . . with my father due back shortly."

"Grand," Pauline said, moving back on her heels to avoid the cloud of baby powder that Bernadette had risen by clapping her hands on her white body and legs.

"I'll see you . . . so," Charles said, backing out of the kitchen. "I shouldn't be too long . . . I might have to tinker about a bit with the engine or suchlike . . ."

"Grand," Pauline said, now holding Bernadette's

392

pyjama bottoms out for her to step into. "I'll see you later."

The kitchen door closed, and Pauline allowed the broad smile she had been holding back to appear on her face. Jack Byrne had rung half an hour ago, asking if she might like to take a run out since it was a nice evening. She told him that she didn't like to ask Charles to mind Bernadette again, since he'd been good enough to do it the other evening when they drove into the cinema. And in any case, she had her parents coming back the day after tomorrow and things to do before then – but she'd said if he'd like to take a run over for a cup of tea, then that would suit fine.

It would also, Pauline thought, give him a chance to meet Bernadette before she went to bed.

She'd had a good idea that Charles might be heading off out tonight. He always had that furtive, edgy way about him when he was planning something – plus, he had changed into a fresh shirt, and he didn't do that for nothing. Pauline wondered now if he did in fact have a girlfriend, as Peenie Walshe had been heavily hinting at recently. You never knew whether to take Peenie seriously or not – but there was definitely something about the way he had reacted whenever Pauline asked, that made her wonder.

* * *

Charles drove around the street Mrs Lynch lived in for the second time, unable to decide on a suitable parking place. This evening, he had made up his mind he was going to knock on Mrs Lynch's door and ask her if she would like to accompany him to the theatre in Dublin next week.

A Shakespearean group from London were putting on a production of *Othello*, which was right up Charles's street as far as entertainment was concerned. The thought of asking her to a dance or even to the cinema in Tullamore filled him with terror – but an evening in the Abbey Theatre sounded just perfect. Maybe even a nice meal beforehand and a glass of wine in the theatre – and a programme in hand which would give them a talking-point until the play started. Afterwards, they would have the actual play itself to discuss, which would keep them talking all the way back in the car to Tullamore. Charles smiled to himself at the thought of having a companion who would actually be interested in the same things as himself. Someone on the same wavelength – who would not think having interests outside work and drinking were peculiarities of nature.

Of course, he pondered, he had no *real* evidence that Mrs Lynch was a fan of Shakespeare but, given the heavy tomes of literature he had seen her carrying from the library, in all probability she would be inclined towards any area of culture.

He eventually decided on a parking spot a little further up the street from where the madman had pounced. And also a bit closer to the Garda station, should there be – God forbid – a repeat performance.

He sat for a short while, cleaning and polishing his glasses with his hanky, and then carefully adjusting them to the right position on his nose. He had put on a fresh white shirt, and was now wishing that he had followed his instincts about wearing a tie. He felt rather bare and exposed around the neck without his usual jumper or sleeveless pullover, but it was too late now for regrets.

The street was quiet as he emerged from his father's car. He looked up and down then stepped smartly across the street towards Mrs Lynch's house. As he walked along, he reminded himself to hold his shoulders back, and keep his chin up. He could almost hear his mother's voice reminding him of these things, as she did on a daily basis. Normally, he let all the instructions wash over his head – but on this occasion, he wanted to make the right impression on all fronts, which included having a straight back.

He stood for a few moments, negotiating the sliding bolt on the seamstress's low, wooden gate, then eventually decided to by-pass its awkwardness by stepping over it. He moved confidently towards the front door, and gave the knocker three good raps.

There was no answer.

Charles gave a further three raps – louder this time. But still no reply. He stood for a couple of minutes, hand stroking his chin, while he pondered the situation. Where was a widow woman with a child likely to be at eight o'clock on a midweek evening? The obvious answer was the library, but Charles knew well that this was not one of the evenings that it opened this late.

The next obvious deduction was the church. A funeral immediately sprang to mind. Not the actual funeral – which would take place in the morning – but the removal of the remains from home to church. *Of course*, Charles thought to himself, *she would be at the church*. He looked at his watch now, deducing that Mrs Lynch would be due back at the house in the next quarter of an hour or so – giving her time for the odd few words here and there with neighbours and acquaintances. He would amble back to the car and wait for her there – because he was determined not to go home tonight until he had a firm date secured for the theatre. He wanted everything arranged and watertight before his parents returned – and before his mother found something wrong with Mrs Lynch to put him off the whole business.

On that positive note, he made his way down the path and actually leapt back over the gate without tripping or catching his trousers on any treacherous rosebushes. He then headed back to the car, rehearsing his opening gambit about how delighted he would be if such a cultured person like Mrs Lynch would agree to accompanying him to an acclaimed performance of *Othello*.

Charles was seated in the driver's seat of the car only a couple of minutes when an awful thought suddenly struck him. A thought that Peenie Walshe had put into his mind earlier in the evening. What if Mrs Lynch was actually out for the evening with a male friend? Perhaps at this very moment, she could be taking a slow walk along the Grand Canal towpath? And what if that male friend was indeed the madman who had leapt on the bonnet of his father's car?

A hot, flushing feeling came up over Charles's chest and neck. Surely, he wouldn't have got things so terribly wrong? The seamstress had come across as a nice, gentle sort of woman. Not at all the sort to take up with a rough individual. But maybe it wasn't wise to presume such things. Maybe he should head off home now, rather than risk meeting up with the widow and a male friend.

Then, just as he went to turn the key in the ignition,

the door from the house next to Mrs Lynch's opened, and a young, black-haired woman came out with a pair of garden shears in her hand. She came across the little square of grass in front of her house, then set about trimming the straggly bush that grew between her house and Mrs Lynch's.

It suddenly struck Charles that the woman might have seen the seamstress going off earlier on, and could enlighten him as to whether she had gone off on her own or with the child – and whether there was a male companion.

Depending on how the conversation went, Charles thought he might be able to get a description of the man-friend to see if it tallied with the lunatic's description. Then, he would soon know whether pursuing the affections of Mrs Lynch was indeed appropriate or not.

Oh, Peenie Walshe need have no worries about Charles Kearney. Women weren't the big mystery Peenie made them out to be. A little bit of logic was all that was required to work them out. No mystery at all – according to psychology books he had studied on the subject of human relations.

He eased himself out of the car once again and, as he headed back towards the house, he pondered over the exact nature of his interest in Mrs Lynch. The physical side was the least – although Charles had to admit that there was an element of curiosity regarding the courting ritual. Even from a scientific point of view, he was interested to see how things would progress if Mrs Lynch took him up on his offer of an evening at the theatre.

He wondered if the physical stirrings he had read about might manifest themselves when they were in closer proximity than standing on the doorstep.

So far, he had never felt anything that resembled physical desire in his life. According to Peenie's graphic descriptions, Charles knew he was definitely a late starter – but it didn't bother him in the slightest. There was more to life than basic physical urges.

Far more important to him was the idea of suitable company for excursions out, excursions that nobody else he knew was interested in, excursions to places like the theatre, museums, art exhibitions and the like. Maybe even some day in the future an excursion to Jodrell Bank over in England to see the space observatory – that kind of thing.

And then further down the line, the relationship might develop into the sort where they could eventually think of marriage and a home together. It was time after all. Charles was over thirty years of age, and still living in the family home. He knew it was time to spread his wings, and think of a place of his own. A place he could share with a like-minded individual, where they could read their own books and listen to their own music – and enjoy the rest of the time discussing these things in great depth.

And of course if that like-minded individual could also take over the domestic side of things, then that would really be the icing on the cake. And it was a fair assumption to make in the case of the seamstress, for someone who was handy with a needle would likely be a dab hand at baking and washing and the like – all the routine chores that made life very complicated for a person like himself.

And it wouldn't be all one-way traffic, for Charles had a nice little nest-egg in the bank that would give them a good start on buying a house. It would all depend now on Mrs Lynch's reaction to his offer of a night at the theatre.

As he ambled along to the house now, he reminded himself about the seamstress's son. He might well be a fly in the ointment – if he was the kind that demanded a lot of attention. Some children were inclined that way. Still – that was a problem for the future. A day at a time, Charles thought. A day at a time – as they say.

"Good evening, ma'am," Charles called to Mrs Lynch's neighbour. He came to a halt at the gate, giving a friendly smile and jangling his father's car keys in an attempt at a casual manner.

The attractive, dark-haired woman stared at him for a moment, then she started moving backwards over the little square of grass, glancing anxiously over her shoulder towards the house.

"I was just wondering if you'd know the whereabouts of –"

"Get away!" the woman hissed, waving the garden-shears. "He'll murder you if he comes out!"

Charles stood for a moment, wondering if he'd just imagined her telling him to 'get away' and mentioning the word 'murder'. "I'm looking for Mrs Lynch . . ." he continued hesitantly, pushing his glasses up to the bridge of his nose.

The woman suddenly rushed forward and brought the shears down heavily on the hedge. "Feck off, will you – ya *amadán*!" she said in an urgent, almost hysterical voice. "Feck off!"

Charles stepped back, straightening up an imaginary tie on his neck. "I think," he said, clearing his throat, "we're at cross-purposes here . . ."

The front door opened now, and the woman's head jerked backwards as she checked to see who was emerging from the house. "Oh, Christ!" she moaned to Charles, her eyes glazed as though she were in agony. "If you don't move now – you're going to get it!"

Charles took a deep breath and turned towards the open door, his hand tightening on the car keys.

And there, standing on the doorstep – with a look of complete incredulity spreading on his face – was the man who had thrown himself on top of the car.

"*You* again, yeh bastard!" the man roared, stabbing a finger in Charles's direction. "I don't feckin' well believe it!"

"Hang on there, now . . ." said Charles, holding his hands up to halt the man. A bit of reason was needed to sort this nonsense out once and for all.

"I'll hang on to yer bloody neck!" shouted the man. Then, he started moving down the steps towards Mrs Lynch's house, all bulging eyes and arm-swinging gestures.

Something about the man's blazing eyes suddenly gave wings to Charles's feet. All thoughts of trying to reason things out were cast aside and he found himself taking off down the street, the lunatic in hot pursuit.

Charles made it to the car – the man only a few yards behind – and threw himself inside. He fumbled for a moment getting the key in, and then started up the engine. Thankfully, it roared into life straight away. Then, he yanked the gearstick into position and went to put a heavy boot down on the accelerator when the driver's door flew open.

In less than a second, a fist had caught him squarely on

the cheekbone just under his eye. Then, another box descended on his ear, as he struggled to fend off the man and lock the car door.

"That'll learn yeh!" the man roared as the car started to move away. "Comin' round here looking for other men's wives! I'll feckin' strangle yeh if I catch yeh near the house again!"

Charles moved away, his brain firmly fixed on trying to both manoeuvre the car and take in what the man was shouting, trying to glean any kind of meaning from all this violence and mayhem.

Then, as he pulled away along the road, he missed the two figures rushing towards the seamstress's house. It was Mrs Lynch and her young son. She stopped in her tracks, waving frantically into the car as Charles passed her by, blood trickling down the side of his face.

But her over-regular customer saw neither the seamstress or her waves. His gaze was firmly fixed on the road ahead, and he was concentrating on getting back home to the safety of the shop and home before his life's blood drained completely away.

Chapter 35

New York

The day before Cara was due to leave, Frances Carroll insisted that she have a trip up to New York city to see some of the more famous shops.

"Thomas is well enough now to not miss us for one afternoon," Frances said, "and we can't have you going back to Ireland without seeing something of our wonderful city. Besides," she went on, "Sam and Jameson can have a boys' afternoon with that blow football game they bought him, and Bill Scott will drop you and me into the shops."

Although she was hesitant about leaving Jameson, even for a few hours, Cara agreed to go, because there were still some presents she wanted to buy to take back and she wanted to buy a small gift for Jameson and Thomas before leaving.

Thomas had continued to improve, and everyone gave a cheer of relief when they visited after breakfast Thursday morning, and saw that all his main tubes had been disconnected. This meant that he could now walk about more freely, and move around as much as his tender wounds would allow.

Cara had explained to him that her holiday was coming to an end, and that she would be going back to Ireland in a day or two. The fact that he didn't quite understand helped Cara a little. Thomas just kept repeating that he would be strong again when she came back, and they would go out in the boat and swim in the lake. Cara smiled in agreement but kept her eyes lowered from Jameson's gaze.

The afternoon shopping was sunny and hot, and Cara was delighted as they wandered around Frances Carroll's favourite stores, which surprisingly were not the wildly expensive places Cara had imagined.

"I still find it hard to be extravagant," Frances confessed to Cara over a coffee and hot cinnamon cookies with vanilla sauce. "I much prefer to search for a bargain. I get a real kick when I feel I've got something at a knockdown price." She smiled now. "I remember when Sam and I first got married, and we had to count every penny. Everything we had went into the business in those days." There was a far away look in the older woman's eyes for a moment. "I was Sam's secretary, you know. The first secretary they could afford to hire." She touched Cara's hand and laughed. "It's funny how things turn out, isn't it?"

Cara smiled back, feeling totally relaxed with this lovely American woman, and now suddenly realising where Jameson Carroll got his down-to-earth attitudes about money.

"I think that it's a good thing to have to work for money at some point in your life," Cara said, "because it means you value it more. My own parents have always encouraged us to help out in the shop. When we were younger we all had jobs to do after school and on a Saturday, and I still help out if anyone's away or sick."

"I'm glad to hear that," Frances said, pouring the vanilla sauce from a little jug over the buns. "But you must tell me more about your life back in Ireland – there's so much that we haven't had time to talk about."

Cara's heart jumped, and it must have shown on her face because Frances said quickly, "I don't mean to pry into your *personal* life – just things like the school you work in, and what your part of Ireland is like."

Cara smiled and took one of the cookies, then she launched into a big description of school and the midlands of Ireland and all about her parents' shop – and everything else that wasn't connected to the husband waiting for her back in Tullamore.

Later, they left the restaurant and went back out into the shops. Cara found a lovely blue sweater for Thomas with a sailing-boat motif on the front, and a leather-bound collection of Irish poetry for Jameson. It was an anthology, with delicate illustrations that she knew he would like. Cara was delighted when she found it, because she had never seen anything like it back in the shops in Ireland.

When she came out of the bookshop, Frances presented her with a big bag of Hershey's chocolate bars to take back to the children in school. Cara was both grateful and touched at the gesture.

She was also grateful to this kind, elderly American woman for not quizzing her about her private life. She had carefully skirted around any conversation about home or where Cara lived – or anything that might just verge towards the personal.

Mr Scott picked the two women up at five o'clock as planned outside the largest department store. Cara had picked up more souvenirs, a winter outfit for little Bernadette and a smart golfing sweater for Charles. Maybe, she thought, it just might be the incentive he needed to take up some sort of outside interest. And if he didn't – it was a nice sweater in any case.

As Cara looked through an American fashion magazine that she had bought, Frances Carroll reflected over the afternoon they had spent together. She had watched Cara as she shopped and listened carefully to everything she said. And everything about Cara Gayle told her that this woman was perfect for her son. Her honesty and lack of pretentiousness was refreshing.

Of course she knew the poor girl had been terrified in case she asked about her marriage. But Frances Carroll knew that these traditional things – the things that *should* be the most important bits in life – did not always turn out the way people dreamed they would. She and Sam had had a long and happy marriage, and that was what she had hoped would happen to Jameson. But life didn't always give you what you hoped for.

She had enjoyed her afternoon immensely with Cara, and she knew there was something very special about the girl. And it wasn't just because of Jameson or even the way she just clicked with Thomas. It was a whole lot of things. Never, in the years her son and his wife had been together, had Frances relaxed in such a way with Verity.

Whatever it was about Cara Gayle, Frances Carroll knew one thing for definite. This blonde, Irish girl meant more to her son than any other woman ever had – and ever would in the future.

If there was anything she could do to help them be together, then Frances Carroll would do her damnedest to make it happen.

"Cara?" Frances suddenly found herself asking: "Do you really think you'll come back here – back to Jameson and Thomas?"

Almost immediately, she saw Cara's eyes fill with tears.

"Oh, I'm so sorry," the older woman said, "I had no business asking you such a thing."

Cara groped in her handbag for a hanky. "No . . . no," she said, shaking her head. She stopped for a moment, trying to compose herself. "Don't apologise, please. I'm the one who should be sorry. I've been trying to shut it out of my mind – the fact that I'm going home tomorrow." She swallowed hard to remove a lump in her throat which seemed as though it might choke her.

"Don't upset yourself, Cara," Frances said, tears now appearing in the corner of her own eyes.

"I don't want to go back," Cara said, shaking her blonde hair, "but I came with my parents . . . and I have to go back with them. I have to go back and sort out the situation with my husband . . ."

Frances's gaze dropped, and she just slowly nodded her head.

"I know Jameson explained it to you," Cara whispered, "and I hope you understand." She took a long, painful breath. "I never, *ever* thought I'd meet another man. But my husband – however bad he's been – deserves an explanation. I can't just stay on here and never go back."

"Of course, of course," Frances agreed.

Cara shrugged, dabbing at her eyes. "I don't even know if I'd be allowed to stay on legally like this." She looked up now at Jameson's mother. "I honestly, honestly . . . in my wildest dreams never expected to fall in love. I've never felt like this before – I couldn't even have imagined it."

"I understand, dear," Frances said quietly. "I really do."

"I've just got to be sensible," Cara said, "for Jameson's sake, too. He's got to have time to think it all over – from a distance. After I've gone back, he might forget me . . . he might decide that it was only a holiday romance." She swallowed hard again. "However hard it is for me to go back home now . . . I think it's the right thing for everyone's sake."

Frances Carroll took Cara's hand and nodded in agreement – but she felt a complete hypocrite for doing so. She knew that Cara's departure would not be a good thing for Jameson even in the short term. It would not be a good thing for Jameson *at all*.

In fact, she couldn't imagine anything worse happening to him. She had watched him this past week – as the days grew nearer to Cara's departure – and she could see the haunted, defensive look returning to his eyes. But, however protective she felt towards him, she knew that Cara was only being sensible.

She only hoped with all her heart that being sensible was the right thing to do.

Chapter 36

Cara's last day flew past in a whirlwind of activity, trying to fit things in before the late evening flight back to Ireland. The early part of the morning was spent re-packing her bags, to accommodate all the extra things she hadn't really meant to buy. Then, she phoned Oliver to remind him of the plane arrival times. The line had not been good, and she used it as an excuse to keep the conversation brief.

Then, she decided to give Jean a last ring before leaving.

"How have things gone, honey?" Jean asked in a low voice, explaining that she didn't want to be overheard by Cara's parents who were also in the last throes of packing.

"Really well," Cara said. "Thomas is making a good recovery, thank God . . . and Jameson's parents are as nice people as you would ever meet. They made me so welcome . . ."

"And Jameson? Is everything okay with you both?" There was a pause on the line for a few moments. "Has it been worth all the heartache with your mom . . . or are you having regrets?"

"No regrets at all," Cara answered immediately, "but there are complications . . . I'll write to you when I get back, and I'll explain everything. And once again – thanks for everything. Especially for your understanding."

They chatted for a few more minutes, then Cara asked her aunt to reassure her parents that she would see them at the airport later that evening.

"I'm real glad I got to know you before you left," Jean said, "and I've missed our relaxed chats over our cocktails in the evening." She gave a little tinkly laugh. "It was tea morning, noon and night after you left. And no doubt, we'll all have a cup of terrible American tea at the airport!"

Cara laughed too, then her voice dropped a little. "Jean . . . is my mother okay? I've been worried . . . I hope I didn't ruin the rest of her holiday . . ."

"No, you did *not*," Jean whispered. "We had some lovely trips out, and your mom and I did some serious talking. The thing is, Cara – your mom is only doing what she thinks is best for you, and what she's been brought up to think is right. And in her case, a bad marriage   is better than broken marriage vows." She paused again. "Any mother from Ireland would see things the way she does. She really loves you all, you know – but it's hard for her."

"I know that, Jean," Cara replied, "and I feel awful for hurting her."

"I understand what you're going through, honey," Jean said, "but it's better to risk hurting her now than to end up blaming her for the rest of your life."

* * *

Jameson followed Cara about, trying to help – but basically just not wanting to be away from her even as she packed. It was difficult, because it was as though time was not theirs any more, and now belonged to the trivial practicalities of preparing for the dreaded journey back to Ireland.

A final visit to the hospital filled in another part of the day, and left Cara feeling much happier, because Thomas looked almost like his old self. She gave him his sailing-boat sweater, which he loved, then they played some games together, and finished off the tiny-piece jigsaw puzzle with the boating scenes.

"You – take this home," Thomas said, crushing the finished jigsaw back into the box. Bits of it spilled on the bed and the floor and Cara and Jameson moved around, picking the pieces up.

"That's really nice of you, Thomas," Cara said, "but it's yours. You can do it again back at Lake Savannah. You could even glue it together and make it into a picture for your bedroom wall."

Thomas held his thumbs up. "Swell! A swell idea!" he said. He winked at Cara. "Better than – old paintings – *he* makes!"

"Wow!" Jameson said, laughing. "You really are getting better, buddy! You didn't have the energy for that kinda brave talk before!"

Cara laughed and looked at Jameson. Then she noticed that his face was laughing – but the laughter had not reached the darkness in his eyes.

Eventually, the time came for her to say goodbye to the boy, the boy who had brought Cara and his father together, the boy who had unwittingly brought a deep, passionate love into her life.

Thomas gave her a big hug. "See you . . . *real* soon," he told her, with a big grin.

Cara nodded and managed to keep a smile pinned on her face until she was out of the ward. She kept her gaze straight ahead as she and Jameson came down silently in the lift together, and walked silently back out to the car.

* * *

The trip to the airport was fraught with difficulty, with heavy traffic all heading in the same direction as themselves. Conversation was stilted, as Jameson had to keep his concentration on the weaving vehicles as they jostled for spaces in the packed lanes.

They had left Jameson's parents' house early to allow for traffic, and to give them a little time on their own in the airport before they met up with the others.

Once they were in the airport and the car safely parked, they headed for a restaurant in the airport, and found a table in a quiet corner.

"I'm sorry there's nowhere a little fancier," Jameson said, spreading his hands out on the formica table, "but I reckon we're better here in the airport than looking for somewhere else outside with all the traffic."

"It's grand," Cara said quickly, "and you've been so good driving me here and waiting with me . . . under the circumstances with Thomas and everything."

Jameson lifted his head so that his eyes looked directly into hers. "I wish I could say I was happy to bring you here," he said in a flat voice, "but I reckon it would be the most untruthful thing I've ever said."

Cara looked back at him, unable to find anything suitable to say. What was there to say?

They ordered sandwiches they didn't really want, a cold glass of beer for Jameson and a Martini for Cara. Apart from helping to ease the tension between them, Cara felt the drink just might relax her a little for the meeting with her parents.

Jameson got up several times to check the plane schedules on the board, whilst Cara sat staring into the large chunky glass and idly playing with a mixing-stick and a slice of lime.

The feeling of depression that had started on the car journey had really crept over her. Watching Jameson, she was sharply reminded of the stranger she had met that first day in the shop with Thomas. He had that same frowning, defensive look . . . and Cara knew that while she had quickly changed that look, today *she* was the cause of the return of it.

He came back to sit down beside her, and then he lifted a carrier bag from under the table. "Hell!" he said, his eyes brightening a little. "I nearly forgot." He lifted a large, thin square package out from the bag. "I got this for you . . . I know you liked it."

"You shouldn't have . . ." Cara said, now feeling even more awkward. Her throat tightened with emotion as she took the gift from him. It was wrapped in paper decorated with silver stars and moons and tied with gold thread – the sort of details he knew she would like. "It's so beautifully wrapped that I don't want to open it."

"Well," he said, shrugging, "you can wait till you get back . . . back to Ireland."

Then, just to fill the dark, empty silence, Cara found

herself carefully untying the gold thread and unwrapping the decorative paper to reveal a long-playing album. When she examined it, she recognised it as the Bob Dylan album they had listened to on the long, warm evenings back at Lake Savannah.

"Oh, Jameson . . ." she whispered, putting the record flat down on the table. And, when she looked up at him, and found his eyes upon her, the stranger from the shop had vanished. She was once again looking at the man she knew so well and loved so much.

He gripped both her hands across the worn table – a serviceable, formica-topped table that had undoubtedly witnessed countless emotional goodbyes.

"I wanted to buy you something real special," he said, a hint of self-consciousness in his voice. "Jewellery or something feminine like that – the kind of thing you could keep. But I knew it might cause you a problem, having to explain where it came from." He lowered his gaze. "I reckoned that the album would let you take a few memories back without anyone else knowing what it meant."

"The memories the music will bring back," she said, "are worth much more than jewellery to me." Then, she reached into her bag and gave Jameson the gift-wrapped, leather-bound poetry book.

He opened the package and looked at the cover, then opened the pages, halting to read a line here, and to examine an illustration there. Then, he closed the book and just held it in his hands. After a few minutes he lifted his head, and his eyes were shining with tears. "It's not too late," was all he said.

"Please," Cara said in a quivery voice, "don't say it . . .

please."

He slowly nodded his head. "OK," he said quietly, "I've made a deal with myself that I won't cause any big scenes here, although I really want to just pick you up in my arms and take you back home with me." Then he took a small blue card from his shirt pocket and laid it out on the table in front of her. It had his address and phone number in Lake Savannah, and on the other side he had handwritten his parents' address in New York.

"If – or when – you get things sorted out," he told her, "contact me any time." He gave a wry smile. "Don't worry about the time difference, just call when it suits you. The same invitation as before – middle of the night, breakfast time – *any time*. I'll be waiting."

"Thank you," Cara whispered, "thank you." She dropped her head, her blonde hair closing over her face like two pale wings.

"We could have a good life together, the three of us," he went on, "and if you got homesick for your family, Jean is just a few minutes' walk away."

Cara reached across the table and very gently pressed her finger to his lips. He caught her hand and held it – kissing it for a final time.

Then, it was time to go.

Cara led the way, head down and heart aching, with Jameson following silently behind with her bags. They walked out of the restaurant and into the concourse, and then out into the departure area. And there – sitting on the first bench inside – were Maggie and Declan.

"Cara!" Maggie was on her feet, running towards her daughter and hugging her as though she hadn't seen her for years. "Thank God you've come! Thanks be to God and his Blessed Mother, you've come!"

Surprisingly, both her parents managed a civilised and fairly warm welcome to Jameson, immediately asking for Thomas. He told them that he was making a good recovery, but that it would be several more weeks before he was ready to come out of hospital.

Then, he faced them both squarely. "Thank you for loaning us your daughter for the last week," he said in a polite, almost formal tone. "She was a wonderful support to Thomas and to my family. I know it was difficult for you letting her go off with strangers – and I'm mighty grateful to you both."

Maggie's eyes darted from Cara to Declan. "She's a married woman, you see . . . that was the difficulty. How it looks to people . . . and how it would sound back home. And of course there's the Church's views on these things . . ."

"Maggie – " Declan hissed, pulling at her sleeve.

"As long as it helped the poor lad," she said, smiling all round, "then it was all worthwhile."

They made small talk for a few minutes, then, unable to bear the awkwardness that would inevitably descend on them, Jameson made his goodbyes. He shook Declan's hand, and kissed Maggie's cool paper-dry cheek. Then, he gave Cara the lightest kiss on her cheek. So light, she missed the familiar feeling of his beard and moustache.

And then, without a backward glance, he was gone.

A tall, confident figure, striding off into the crowds of strangers.

Chapter 37

Tullamore, County Offaly

The flight to Dublin passed in a blur. The plane was not as busy as their trip out, and Cara managed to get a row of three seats to herself, giving her parents the excuse that she was tired and wanted space to stretch out to sleep. For the first half of the flight, sleep was actually the last thing on her mind, as she went over her whole holiday in her mind – from the first moment she set eyes on Jameson, until the last glimpse she had of him heading off out of the airport.

After something to eat, accompanied by two glasses of wine, eventually her body and mind gave in to several hours of peaceful oblivion.

When she wakened, she freshened up as best she could in the tiny aircraft toilet, and then she joined her parents for the last lap of the journey. Maggie was not as anxious as she was coming out, as there was little or no turbulence, and her humour was much better now she had Cara winging her way back home to Ireland.

416

Winging her way back to the arms of her waiting husband.

No reference was made to Jameson or Thomas, and Maggie filled the time by giving Cara a blow-by-blow account of all the things herself and Declan had done while she was away. Apart from nodding when Maggie said, 'Isn't that right, Declan?" or 'You wouldn't have believed it, would you, Declan?" Cara's father said very little. He dozed on and off and in between had a couple of whiskeys which made him even quieter.

In what seemed no time at all, the air-hostess was coming along the aisle asking everyone to fasten their seat-belts and prepare for their landing in Dublin airport.

Prepare for Dublin, and prepare for Oliver, Cara thought to herself.

He was there as promised. Waving to them as they came in through the doors in the arrival area. Although it was little after seven in the morning, he was there looking bright and breezy, a beaming smile on his smooth, handsome face. He held a small coloured bunch of freesias in his hand, which he presented to her with a hug and a kiss.

There were few men in Tullamore who would have stood holding a bunch of flowers without feeling like the proverbial pansy. But Oliver Gayle was not one of them. And no one, on seeing him, would have made more than the odd lighthearted passing remark. He was the kind of man who made men wish they had the nerve and the charm to buy a bunch of flowers, and not care a damn what anyone said.

Oliver chatted away on the drive home, in turn giving them local news of who had died or given birth while they were away, and asking all the right questions about the flight, the wedding and America in general.

To which Maggie happily supplied all the answers.

"Oh, it was marvellous," she enthused to her son-in-law. "We had a grand holiday altogether, but the one thing I have to say is I won't miss their tea!"

"Is that right, Maggie?" Oliver asked on cue.

"Indeed it is. The Americans don't know how to make a decent cup of tea. It was lucky that the priest warned me to bring a few packets out with me, otherwise we would have been poisoned in the house as well as in the restaurants." She shook her head. "How Jean has got used to the food and drink over there, I'll never understand. What d'you say, Cara?"

Cara found something suitable to say, although she felt as though her brain was operating on two different levels. One part was back in New York with Jameson Carroll, reliving – over and over again – every minute she spent with him. The other part was like a robot. She was asked a question, and she automatically smiled or looked serious according to the subject – then she hopefully gave some kind of appropriate answer. Never – even at her lowest points with Oliver – had she experienced this weird kind of thing.

* * *

They pulled up at the shop first, and Maggie insisted that all four went through into the house for a decent cup of Irish tea and a bit of breakfast to revive them after the journey.

Charles was up and about to greet them, and stood in the middle of the kitchen smiling with embarrassment, one hand cupping the area under his eye.

"How was the flight and everything," he said, "and the weather out there in the States?"

"Grand, Charles," his father said, dropping a case on the kitchen table, "and everything's grand back here at home and in the shop?"

"Oh, grand – grand, the finest," Charles said, digging his hands deep in his pockets, and rocking back on his heels.

"Are Pauline and Bernadette still in bed?" Cara asked, putting her bag of presents down in a corner near the radio.

Charles crossed his arms, one hand still up to his eye. "Oh, they're moving . . . I heard Pauline only a few minutes ago." He looked up towards the ceiling. "I'd say they'll be downstairs shortly. Bernadette likes to have her breakfast as soon as she's up and moving." He smiled and nodded his head, the hand still hovering around his eye. "Cornflakes it is at the minute – cornflakes every morning."

"Well, make yourself useful and get them out of the press," Maggie said briskly, finding her son's latest mannerism more than a little irritating, "and don't be standing there in everyone's way. Get the cups and plates out, and then go and check that Pauline and the child are moving."

"Indeed . . . indeed," Charles said vaguely, turning towards the cupboard.

Maggie suddenly halted. "What's the plaster for? What's wrong with your eye?" she asked, her own eyes narrowed suspiciously. "And your ear is swollen too!"

Charles's hand moved up to cover the orangey-coloured sticking-plaster under his eye. "Ah – it's nothing," he said, darting a glance over in Oliver's direction. "I hit it . . . probably carrying in a sack of potatoes."

Maggie clucked her tongue and turned back to the whistling kettle. "It's more attention you need to pay to things," she said. "If you'd keep your mind on what you're doing, instead of all the other things you do be thinking of."

Charles moved to the press at the side of the fireplace where all the dry goods were stored. He lifted out the packet of cornflakes, and just as he was closing the door, reached back in for a packet of porridge oats.

"Anyone?" he said, holding them up.

"Oh, we've no time for making porridge now," she said. "Bread and butter will be fine. Have you a fresh loaf for us, Charles?"

"I have," he said, handing the box of cornflakes and a bowl to Cara, "I'll just go through to the shop and get it for you. I left it under the counter yesterday evening, knowing that the bread van probably won't appear until after ten this morning."

"Wouldn't you think," Maggie muttered to no one in particular, "that he would have brought it through into the house and had it out on the table for us?"

"Oh, leave the lad alone," Declan said. "Hasn't he kept things going for us while we've been away?"

"True," Maggie said, sounding surprisingly chastened, "true enough." She poured water from the boiling kettle into her beloved old brown china teapot. "Sure, I was only saying . . . I meant no harm."

"Granny!" a little voice called from the door, and in

came the curly-headed Bernadette in her pyjamas, followed by her mother in her pink, candlewick dressing-gown. The child ran across the floor and threw herself squarely at her grandmother.

"Hello, my little chicken!" Maggie said, scooping the child up into her arms. "Did you miss your oul' granny and granda? Did you think we were never coming back?"

"My mammy said you were coming back this morning," Bernadette said in a clear voice, "and she said you had presents for me."

"Bernadette!" Pauline warned. "Now, don't be bold . . ."

"Oh, she's fine," Maggie said, coming to sit down with the child on her knee. "Pour those cornflakes out into the little bowl there for her, will you, Cara? And put a drop of milk in it for her and a good spoonful of sugar." Then she turned to Pauline. "Everything all right while we were away?"

Pauline got a cup for herself from the hook on the dresser. "Fine . . ." she said quietly. "Everything was fine." She reached for the teapot. "Charles was up at the crack of dawn every morning – he saw to the bread deliveries and everything."

"I'm delighted to hear it," Maggie said, taking the bowl of cornflakes from Cara. "Now," she said to the child, "let me see how big you've got while we've been away. Let me see how you can eat all the cereal up on your own."

The little girl beamed up at her, and proceeded to spoon the cornflakes very carefully into her mouth.

"Good girl, yourself," Oliver told her, "and when you've finished, you can see what your Auntie Cara has brought you back from America. She was telling me all about it on her way down from Dublin."

Cara pointed to the big bag in the corner. "You'll never guess what I have in there," she said smiling warmly, "and neither will your mammy."

There followed a half an hour of oohing and ahhing over the gifts, and the trying on of some of the outfits over nightwear by Bernadette and Pauline. "I'll try on the other things later," Pauline said, her eyes shining with delight at the array of fashionable things that Cara had picked out for her.

Charles demurred about trying on his golfing sweater in front of an audience, and after thanking Cara profusely for the books, headed off to examine them in the silence and privacy of his bedroom.

When he was out of earshot, Pauline recounted the story about the Virgin Mary's nose, lest Maggie should come upon the nose-less statue and wonder what had happened. Thankfully, her mother saw the funny side of it, and was more concerned about any ill-effects it might have had on Bernadette's digestion, than any religious feelings about the statue.

"It was awful good of you to drive all the way to Dublin before going into work, Oliver," Maggie said when they were all sitting around the table with cups of strong tea and slices of brown bread and the good Irish butter that Maggie had missed, "but I suppose you were desperate to see Cara after her being away for so long."

"No problem, no problem at all," Oliver beamed. "Sure, amn't I only delighted to see you all back safe and sound. And you're all looking grand. Fair play to you all, there's few people around here who've been on planes, never mind on a plane all the way to America."

More pleasant chat followed, then Maggie looked up at the clock.

"You'd better watch your time, Oliver," she said. "I wouldn't like you to be late for opening the shop on account of us."

Oliver sighed and stood up. "I suppose we should make a move," he said, stretching his arms up as though he'd just got out of bed. "I've young Fergal opening up for me this morning. I never said what time I'd be in – it keeps them all on their toes." He put a hand on Cara's shoulder. "I'd say this one will be ready for the bed shortly."

"Oh, we'll all have a few hours," Maggie said, suddenly sounding tired. "Then we'll be as good as new."

* * *

"You look great," Oliver said when they were in the car on their own heading home. "That's the best tan you've had for years – and it really lifts you." His eyes were shining with admiration. "And the sun has brought out the blonde in your hair." Oliver always noticed things like that with women.

He kept his cheery conversation up all the way back to the house and if he thought Cara was quiet, he didn't comment on it.

"I could cook you some rashers and sausages," he offered, when they'd unloaded the car and carried all the bags upstairs to the bedroom. "I'm an expert with the old frying-pan since you've been gone."

"That's good of you," Cara said, giving a weary smile, "but I think my stomach's a bit mixed-up with the travelling and everything. I'll leave it until I've had a sleep."

"Fine, fine," Oliver said. "What about another cup of tea – or maybe some hot milk to settle your stomach?"

"No, I won't have anything, thanks," she told him. She ran her fingers through her hair, then fiddled about with it in a distracted sort of way. "I'll just bring a glass of water upstairs with me, and go off to bed." She paused. "I have some things for you in one of the cases . . . a couple of presents."

He came over and put his hands on her shoulders. "Don't be worrying yourself about presents," he said. "It's bed you need just now."

Cara turned away from him. "I'll just get the water."

He patted her affectionately on the behind, and Cara had to steel herself from flinching from his touch. She could feel his eyes on her as she went over to fill a glass at the sink, and then she moved quickly out of the kitchen and upstairs to the bedroom, while he followed behind.

She opened her wardrobe door and took a fresh pair of pyamas from one of the shelves.

"I'm just going into the bathroom for a quick wash," she said.

"The water's good and hot for you," he told her. "I made sure the fire was roaring when I left this morning."

After a short while, Cara came back into the bedroom dressed in pink-striped, cotton pyjamas. Oliver was standing by the window, and he turned towards her as she came into the bedroom. He came over to her and caught her by the hand.

"I really missed you," he said in a low voice. "If you like, I could go into work a bit late . . . they can manage on their own for a few hours." His hand moved to encircle her waist, and he bent his head down to kiss her.

Cara felt herself flinching from his touch again. "I'm sorry, Oliver," she said quickly, "but I'm absolutely wrecked. I feel as though I'm falling asleep on my feet . . . as if I'm not really here."

"No problem," he said good-naturedly. "It'll be the oul' jet-lag. I've heard it's very bad." He ran a finger down her arm. "We'll have plenty of time together later."

Cara nodded without saying anything.

He leaned over and gave her a light, harmless kiss on the cheek. "See you tonight," he said. Then added, "It's nice to have you back home."

* * *

Cara lay awake for a long time after Oliver had left for work, staring at the watery sun as it peeped through the curtains, and thinking of Jameson Carroll back in New York. She looked at the clock on the bedside cabinet. It was just after eleven o'clock, which would make it around six o'clock in the morning there. She stared back at the window, then lay staring up at the ceiling, her mind full of him. Then, at some point towards midday, her eyelids grew heavy and she drifted into sleep.

When she awoke later in the afternoon, she padded about in pyjamas, making tea and glancing at the American magazines she had brought back with her. She flicked from page to page, seeing the words and pictures but taking nothing in.

Then, she had a long hot bath, dressed, and started on the task of unpacking her luggage.

She sorted everything out into piles on her bed. Some for washing and some for hanging back in the wardrobe or putting into her chest of drawers.

As she picked up a pile of nightwear and underwear – washed and ironed by Mrs Scott – Cara's eye caught sight of a silk, lace-trimmed bra she had bought in the lingerie shop, the first day she met Jameson.

She gathered the silky garments into her arms, and hugged them towards her, as though the material which he had run his hands over would somehow bring him closer to her. Somehow close the distance of thousands of miles.

When she had unpacked all the bags containing her clothes, she started on a smaller one, which contained some of the presents that she had brought back. She was hesitant as she opened each package, carefully feeling the shape and weight. Her heart sank further and further as she reached deeper into the bag. And then she realised that she had come back home without the two gifts Jameson had given her at Lake Savannah. The small painting and the Christmas figure.

She closed her eyes and could picture them at the back of one of the lower shelves in the wardrobe she had used. She had placed them on that shelf for safety. So safe, that presumably her mother had not seen them. She remembered asking Maggie to be sure to bring them to New York but then, in the midst of all the farewells and everything, she had forgotten to check about them.

An empty ache crawled all over her, for she had looked forward to touching and feeling both things. Remembering the white house by the lake where the painting had hung and the magical Christmas shop where the porcelain figures had stood in their red and green cloaks. And reliving – minute by minute – the days that Jameson had given them to her. The long, lovely days around Lake Savannah and all the other days doing whatever they did – and especially the nights and early mornings they had spent together.

But the fact was that she was back in Ireland – back with her husband – and without those mementoes. All she had left to remind her now was the album of Bob Dylan's soulful songs.

And Cara Gayle wasn't quite brave enough to listen to that just yet.

Chapter 38

"Mr Kearney got a cigarette-end on the floor among the mineral bottles this morning," Maggie said, coming across the shop to where Charles and Peenie stood by the bacon slicer. "I hope there was no smoking going on here, while we were away." She glanced at Charles's swollen, red ear, that he'd brushed off her questions about, as he had with the cut eye. "Or anything else going on, for that matter."

"Ah, true as God, Mrs Kearney," Peenie said, lifting a great lump of bacon onto the machine, then rubbing his hands down over his brown overalls to remove the watery grease from the meat, "there was nothing going on that doesn't go on as a rule. It must be a fag-end that was tramped in on the sole of a shoe. Or maybe one of the delivery men, comin' in with a fag in his mouth, and droppin' it down on the floor. Yeh couldn't be up to them lads."

"Indeed," said Charles, folding his arms and looking closer at the butcher's stamp on the rind of the bacon.

"True for yeh, Charles," Peenie went on. "Sure, it's fierce hard to be tellin' those fellas anythin'. They have their own way of workin' and their very own rules."

"Exactly," Mrs Kearney said, "just as we have our very own way of working around the shop here, and the rules that keep things in check." She looked at the cold-meat cabinet now. "You're running low on the sliced bacon there, Charles," she observed. "See that Peenie cuts a good bit now, and have it wrapped in the greaseproof in half pounds and whole pounds, so's we're not keeping people waiting."

Peenie started the blade whirring. "Five minutes, Mrs Kearney," he said, winking at her, "five minutes an' we'll have yards of bacon cut an' wrapped up."

Maggie smiled in spite of herself. "Less of the talking," she told him, "and more of the slicing." For all his crafty ways, she was fond enough of Peenie Walshe, and when he was in the humour he was an excellent worker. He beat Charles hands down – but then that wasn't saying much. Charles's mind was often elsewhere when he should be working.

"My father said to tell you that he'll be back from the bank around three o'clock," Charles suddenly remembered.

"Grand," Maggie said, checking her watch. It was around half-past two now. "Did Pauline mention where she was going?"

"Not to me," Charles said, racking his memory just in case she had, and he wasn't listening.

"Oh, well," his mother said, "maybe she's gone out for a walk, or cycled over to Cara's. She definitely didn't say?"

"Not," said Charles, in his hedging manner, "to the

best of my knowledge."

"So, ye all had a grand time in America?" Peenie asked, over the whirring noise of the bacon slicer. "Did ye see any cowboys at all when ye were out there?"

Maggie folded her arms and thought for a moment. "Not exactly *cowboys*," she told him, "but we saw plenty of fellows with big, cowboy-style hats."

"There yeh go, Charles," Peenie said, nudging his workmate. "See what yeh missed? Yeh'll have to make sure that you go with them the next time. Cowboys an' everythin'." He looked at the bacon slices that were piling up on the machine. "Yeh could cut me a few sheets of greaseproof, Charles, an' we'll get this lot weighed an' wrapped like yer mother said."

"I'll leave you to it, lads," Maggie said wearily, heading back to the house end of the shop. "I might have another hour's lie-down, because I never slept a wink this morning, and I've been up the whole night travelling. You can let your father know, Charles."

"Certainly," Charles said, looking around vaguely for the scissors to cut the greaseproof paper. "You can rely on me to pass on the message."

"Begod," said Peenie, as Maggie disappeared through the connecting house door, "the head-woman's back and make no mistake about it! It's all hands on deck this afternoon."

"Indeed," said Charles, suddenly locating the scissors on the hook where they were always kept. "The captain of the ship, and all that kind of thing."

Peenie brought the bacon slicer to an abrupt halt midslice. "I've been thinkin' about this neighbour business, Charles," he said in a low voice, "and it doesn't make a bit of sense to me, at all, at all."

Charles gave a mighty sigh that lifted his rounded shoulders up for a few moments. "Nor to me," he said. "I'm mystified about the whole thing." His hand came up to rest his chin. "What business is it of a neighbour's, *who* visits the house next door? It makes no sense at all." He fingers gently touched the sticking plaster under his eyes.

"He's a lunatic, that lad," Peenie said, "an' make no mistake about it. A born lunatic by the sounds of it. I've never heard the likes of it in me life."

"Well," Charles said, "he's made my mind up for me anyway. I wouldn't chance going near Mrs Lynch's house ever again."

Peenie took off his cap, and juggled it between both hands. "I'm sorry to say it, Charles," he said, shaking his head, "but I'd knock that one on the head if I were you. I would take no more chances with that quarter in Tullamore."

"I'm taking it as an omen," Charles announced solemnly, "an omen that our relationship wasn't ever meant to be."

Chapter 39

Oliver returned from work later in the evening, in the same attentive mood.

"Do you fancy eating out?" he asked. "We could drive out to Mullingar to that new restaurant we haven't tried yet. It would save you cooking, and you just back home."

Cara thought for a moment. "Yes . . . that's a good idea. I'll go and get ready."

It was between the devil and deep blue sea: sitting with him all evening in the same room, watching television or listening to the radio – maybe sipping a glass of the bourbon she had brought him back from America – or sitting opposite him in a restaurant. The choice was not too difficult. There was a big difference between public intimacy and private, inescapable intimacy.

As they sat in the packed restaurant checking the menu an hour and a half later, Cara wondered how long she would be able to keep up her avoidance of any closeness with Oliver. Then, she noticed a young, attractive woman at table opposite staring at him – as young women often did – and she sighed inwardly at the irony of it. Most women would be thrilled to sit opposite him – gazing openly at Oliver's smooth, dark good looks. As she once did herself.

"I've something to tell you," Oliver said brightly, as the waiter left with their order. "Something that will delight you."

Cara raised her eyebrows. "What is it?"

"I've finished with the drama," he said, "completely washed my hands of it."

Cara had no idea what he was going to say – but this was the last thing she expected. "But why?" she asked. "What's happened?"

"Oh, nothing very dramatic," he said, laughing lightly at his little joke. "I've just had enough of it. You get fed up with the whingeing and moaning about who's got what part – and then when they don't turn up for rehearsals. I've just decided that I could spend my evenings more productively at home with you, than wasting them in freezing church halls." He leaned forward, and took her hands in his. "I think that I'd prefer to devote the time to yourself and myself for a change. Get our priorities in order, so to speak."

Cara looked back at him, speechless. Then she looked down at their hands on the white tablecloth, and she was suddenly reminded of her hands being held across a formica table in a New York airport.

She withdrew her hands, using the excuse of reaching for a jug of water and a glass. "Oh, give yourself time to think about it, Oliver," she said. "Once the plays get going, you're the best of friends with everyone in them."

He shrugged. "It's different this time. And anyway . . .

I told them all at the AGM last night."

Cara looked at him closely over the rim of her glass. "I think you'll miss it," she told him, "but it's up to you." She took a sip of the water. "I know I've often complained about you being out over the winter evenings, but I suppose I've got used to it. And I know you've always enjoyed it."

His hand stretched out towards hers again, and held it tightly. "Just because people have got used to things, doesn't mean that they can't be changed or made better."

Cara stared at him, wondering what had caused this huge change of heart.

"We'll enjoy this meal," Oliver said, smiling. He touched his glass to hers. "To us . . . and to a lot more time together."

Cara wondered if her trip to America had *really* made all this difference to him? Was it possible that he had missed her so much that he had finally come to realise what he really felt for her?

Two waiters appeared with steaming dishes heaped with vegetables and potatoes – and stopped Cara from wondering for the moment.

* * *

The phone was ringing as they walked up the garden path. Cara was first in the door, so she answered it.

It was one of the men from the drama group. "How are you, Joe?" she said. Then, "He is . . . yes."

Oliver gestured back to her to say that he wasn't in – but it was too late. Cara handed the phone to him, and went into the kitchen to put the kettle on before going to bed.

Bed. She was dreading it. She knew only too well what would be in Oliver's mind and somehow, she had to put him off.

She couldn't bear the thought of him making love to her. Not *now*. Not ever again. Not after finding out what making love with someone you *really* loved meant. And then a feeling of hopelessness came over her.

She spooned two large heaps of tea leaves from the caddy into the teapot, and left it by the side of the kettle until the water was boiled. She could hear Oliver's voice in the distance, low, and with an argumentative tone in it. It was probably one of the committee who had just found out about him resigning, and were trying to get him to change his mind. Cara wished with all her heart that he would change his mind, because she couldn't imagine how they would fill every evening at home together. He had been involved with the drama since she had known him, and although there had been a time when she had resented it for taking him away so much, that time was long gone.

A weary sigh sounded in the kitchen before Oliver appeared. "Oh, feck it," he said, "I'm going to have to go to the hospital."

"Why?" Cara asked, her brow furrowed. "What's happened – who is it?"

"Oh, it's one of the group," he said, running a hand through his hair. "I didn't get any great details – some kind of accident. I think it's one of the girls from Limerick . . . she doesn't have any family round here. Joe was saying that some of us should go in and see how she is."

"In that case," Cara said, "you'd better go."

"It's not just me." he said. "A few of the lads are there

already. They've been trying to get me on the phone all night." He shook his head. "It's the last thing I feel like – having to go out at this hour. Especially with it being your first night back."

"Don't worry about me," Cara told him. "Take your key. I'll be going off to bed anyway . . . I'm very tired now."

"Sure," he said, nodding his head vaguely. "You probably still have jet-lag." He stepped backwards to the door. "They say – they say that jet-lag can be a nasty oul' thing. A good night's sleep is the only way to beat it."

She turned back to the kettle. "I'll see you later then."

As she heard the front door close, Cara wondered if there was something going on other than a hospital visit. Oliver usually preferred *something* to be going on, than nothing. A call late at night was a welcome alternative to sitting quietly listening to the radio or doing any of the chores around the house that he thought so boring.

Whatever it was tonight, Cara could tell by Oliver's manner that he was irritated or concerned about something – more than she would expect in the circumstances. But she didn't have the energy – or the interest – to care much.

She poured the boiling water into the teapot. Maybe it was genuine enough. Maybe she was misjudging him. Especially after the announcement he'd made about leaving the drama group. She stirred the tea leaves around in the boiling water in the teapot. Round and round in little circles.

Maybe Oliver was right. Apart from all the other things she was feeling, maybe she was suffering from jet-lag, and bed was the best place to be.

* * *

It was dark when she woke up with a start – drenched in perspiration and her heart thumping fast. She sat bolt upright in bed, trying to shake off the awful feelings of the nightmare she had just escaped from. The bedroom was almost black, and it was only when her eyes began to focus that she could make out familiar shapes. And then she realised that she was back in Ireland.

She stretched out a shaky hand to switch on the bedside lamp. The intense light blinded her for a few moments. When she could bear to look, she saw that it was just after four o'clock. She stared straight ahead, her brow creased in concentration, trying to recall what it was that had frightened her so much.

Gradually, it started to come back to her.

She had been back in America. Back at Lake Savannah. She'd been down at the bottom of Jean and Bruce's garden, where she'd sat so often, reading in the sun. A boat had appeared in the distance. A speedboat. It got nearer and nearer, until she could see Oliver steering the boat.

Then, two figures reclining on rocking chairs on the deck and drinking out of champagne glasses had come into view. Cara's mother and father. She had stood up and ran to the edge of the water, waving and calling out to them. But they didn't notice her. The boat went on to speed around the lake in circles – getting faster and faster.

Then, a tiny raft appeared on the edge of the lake at the opposite side from Cara. Seated in the middle were Jameson Carroll and Thomas. Thomas, still heavily bandaged like his first day in hospital, and clutching his father's hand. Cara had called out to them to watch out for the speedboat, but they didn't hear or notice her either.

Then, Oliver had turned the boat and headed straight for the raft. Cara had tried to scream to warn them – but although her mouth had opened, no sound had come out.

She started to run around the path on the lake, getting caught in the branches of trees and huge windchimes that seemed to appear from nowhere. She struggled on, freeing herself from one lot, only to be tangled up in the next.

Eventually, she managed to free herself completely and then ran on, until she came to a clearing in the trees, where she could see the speedboat and the raft – only yards apart.

Thomas and Jameson were faced in the opposite direction to the speedboat. Cara gave one final scream which at last they heard, and turned towards her. They stood up on the raft and waved, Jameson keeping a fatherly arm around his son, and at that moment the speedboat hit the raft at a side-angle, toppling them into the water, before speeding off and disappearing into the distance.

Cara ran and ran towards them – but the harder she ran, the further away she seemed to get. And then she decided that she would reach them more quickly by swimming across the lake. She dived into the water and she swam and swam. When she reached the part where the crash had happened, all that remained was the raft with the two champagne glasses sitting neatly in the middle of it. And floating in the water was a white strip of bandage with a picture of Mickey Mouse on it.

She had dived and swam deep into the water looking for Thomas and Jameson. She had come up and then dived again until she was so tired that she could not dive or swim any more. And then she dragged herself up onto the little raft and lay down.

And that – she remembered now – was where the dream had ended.

Cara covered her face now, and sat there in the bed, tears streaming down between her fingers. She cried and cried, her heart aching with the huge loss she had just relived in the dream. After a while, when the tears subsided, she switched off the light and lay back in bed going over the dream again.

It had been a very obvious dream. The kind of dream that did not need an expert in the psychology of dreams to analyse. It was a classic case of the parting in America being repeated in a weird, dreamy way.

But still it disturbed her.

And this time, sleep would not come as her mind flitted from one memory to another. She lay for nearly an hour, and then she decided to get up and have a bath. A short time later, she was downstairs, dressed in slacks and a warm sweater and comfortable walking shoes.

She raked out the fire and filled it up with wood and small pieces of turf, then she put the kettle on. After that, she moved around the kitchen and darkened sitting-room, opening curtains to allow the first rays of morning into the house, hoping that some of the light might just seep into her own dark mood and brighten it up. She paused at the sitting-room window to stare out to the garden.

It hadn't been touched since she left for America. Cara wondered now if she would ever find the energy and interest to tend it, as she had done so contentedly before.

Then, a strange noise suddenly drew her attention

away from the window, and when she turned around and saw a figure lying on the sofa she screamed in fright.

"Jesus!" Oliver was startled out of his sleep by her scream. "What's wrong?" he yelled. "What's wrong?"

"You frightened the life out of me!" Cara rounded on him angrily. "What the hell are you doing down here?"

Oliver sat up now, his hands rubbing at his tousled hair. "You were asleep when I came in," he said defensively, " and I didn't want to wake you up. I thought I'd sleep down here and give you peace."

"It's a heart attack you nearly gave me! What time did you get back?" she asked, wondering if he had been in the house when she was crying earlier.

He looked vague for a few moments. "I suppose it must have been around two o'clock . . . or thereabouts."

So he *was* in the house. He must have been fast asleep, because there was nothing in his manner to suggest that he had heard her.

"How is she?" Cara asked. "The girl from your drama group."

"She's not too good," he said, lying back down on the sofa with his arms behind his head, "but they reckon she's over the worst."

"So – what was wrong with her?" Cara queried.

There was a pause. "I think they said some kind of allergy . . ."

"An *allergy*?" Cara repeated. "An allergy to what?"

"Medication or some such thing," Oliver replied, in the same vague way.

Cara looked at her husband with narrowed eyes. "That's very unusual," she said quietly. "To be so ill with an allergy that you have to be hospitalised. Was it penicillin?"

"To tell you the truth," Oliver said, sounding weary, "I haven't a clue." He yawned. "You'd never know what people could have wrong with them these days." He looked towards the kitchen. "Were you making tea?"

"Yes, do you want some?"

He thought for a moment. "No . . . I won't bother."

"Maybe you should go to bed and have a few more hours' sleep, Oliver," Cara suggested. "You look washed out."

He got to his feet, checking his appearance in the mirror above the fireplace. Then he ran his fingers through his hair to flatten it, and patted his cheeks to put some colour in them. "Yeah," he said, turning to the side to check how he looked from a different angle. "A couple of hours mightn't do me any harm."

After an hour or so of pottering about in the rooms downstairs, Cara threw a jacket on and went outside into the garden. She walked slowly around it, stopping here and there to pick a dead head off a rose, or to check for any signs of greenfly. But every bush she looked at and every flower she stopped to admire only took her back to another, bigger and brighter garden in America. Jameson Carroll's beautiful, rambling garden at Lake Savannah. The garden where she had left her heart behind.

What am I going to do, she asked herself as she distractedly picked off the dead leaves and flowers. *What am I going to do?*

She had been determined to come back to Ireland to *sort things out*. She had been determined against all her heart's true feelings and totally against Jameson's feelings of what was the right thing to do. She had persisted in doing things her own way. The way she had always done things. The way that pleased everyone else back home.

But what about all the things she said she was going to do? All this sorting out of her parents and family, and all this sorting out of the business of school? Now she was back in Ireland – *what* was she actually going to sort out? And more importantly – *when* was she going to do it?

An awful feeling swept over her, and as soon as she recognised it she was ashamed of herself, for she knew instantly that it was *fear* that was holding her back. Fear of hurting her mother and father. Fear of walking away from her home and her sad – but familiar – marriage. Fear of leaving everything that was familiar to her.

And the biggest fear of all – that she wouldn't live up to the expectations that Jameson Carroll had of her.

Deep down she knew she wasn't the wonderful, beautiful woman he thought she was – and how was she going to deal with that? What could a small-town Irish teacher offer a wealthy, talented man like him?

She moved away now from the flowers and shrubs and walked down the little path towards the gate. She stood leaning over the gate for a while, and was surprised to see a number of bicycles and the few cars that were in the area, all heading down towards the town. *God!* she suddenly thought. *It's Sunday!* Cara shook her head, unable to believe that she's forgotten about nine o'clock Mass. America was different – she was on holiday then. But this was Ireland, and she had *never* forgotten about Sunday Mass. It was what Sundays were centred around as far back as she could remember.

She ran back up the path and into the house, and up into the spare bedroom where she kept some of her school clothes in a big, old wardrobe. After rummaging through the racks, Cara quickly fastened on suspenders and thirty-denier stockings that were too thick for summer, and put on an autumn suit and a blouse that didn't quite match. The outfit looked a bit odd, but it was the best she could do without going into the wardrobe in her own bedroom. Thankfully, she kept her mantilla with her scarves in the spare bedroom too, so she grabbed it and stuffed it in her jacket pocket.

She ran downstairs and out of the house to the shed where she kept her bicycle, and within minutes she was cycling down the road towards the church. She pedalled as quickly as she could, feeling the muscles pulling on her thighs – unused to the exertion after a month away from her bicycle.

Five minutes or so later, Cara arrived at the church, much too late to take her usual seat up near the front. She stood outside for a moment to catch her breath and cool down, then she walked quietly into the church and squeezed into a space in a pew three rows from the back. The pew was full of men, and it was unlikely that they would pay any attention to what she was wearing.

She knelt down and blessed herself, still catching her breath. At least she would be nearer the door for sneaking out quickly, and hopefully would make it home without having to stop and chat to anyone.

The priest appeared on the altar – Father O'Neill, the popular, understanding curate – and Mass began. The service went through its usual routine, with Cara standing up and kneeling down with the rest of the congregation, her mind a million miles away from the rituals that she had taken part in every Sunday for many years.

Then, she was startled back to consciousness,

suddenly aware of the silence that had descended upon the crowd of worshippers. The priest had started off on his Sunday sermon, and the theme of it had obviously caught everyone's attention. Most weeks, people left the church unable to remember a word of the monotonously delivered sermon.

"Ignore what is happening at your peril," was the priest's dire warning, "and we could become as bad as the English and the Americans."

Cara felt a tightness creeping into her throat and chest.

"If we don't cherish our family life above everything else, Irish Catholic values could be lost. Marital separation and divorce is a disease," he warned, "and it spreads – tainting all whose lives it touches. Not just the husband and wife and children – but the whole of the extended families."

Cara suddenly felt her face flush and her breathing shallow and uncomfortable. This was the last thing she wanted to hear – and church was the last place she wanted to be sitting listening to it. Even worse, that it should be the youngish priest she really liked, the one she might have considered approaching if she ever needed any personal kind of advice.

"It is far, far better," the priest went on, "for a child to have *two* parents who are at least *trying* to make things work – than to have a single parent struggling on his or her own." He paused, looking around the congregation. "You mightn't think it appropriate to be talking about these matters in our church – but times are changing, and we have to be on our guard."

A picture of Thomas and Jameson, and then one of Pauline and little Bernadette crept into her mind, as she listened to the priest going on for another ten minutes, every word he was saying cutting deeper into her heart.

Her feet seemed as though they had blocks of lead on them as she cycled slowly back to the house. She let herself in quietly so as not to disturb Oliver, and went into the sitting-room to sink into the big, soft armchair beside the fire.

For some time, she sat there, staring down at the fading, flowery rug. Then, for the second time that morning, an awful feeling of loss engulfed her. She stood up, determined not to give in to it. She went over and switched on the radio to distract her thoughts, only to hear the presenter enthusiastically introduce a track he was going to play from the 'The *Freewheelin'* Bob Dylan album'. Seconds later the room was flooded with the familiar voice singing, 'Don't Think Twice, It's All Right'.

As if she needed reminding about the distance between herself and Jameson Carroll

* * *

Maggie and Declan arrived for a visit that evening. "Well," Declan said, greeting her with a big smile, "have you recovered yet? Glad to be back to normal again?"

Her mother's smile was more pinched and didn't reach her eyes.

Cara led them into the sitting-room.

"Is Oliver not at home?" Maggie asked, loosening the flowery, silk scarf from around her chin.

"No," Cara replied, "he's gone to visit someone in the hospital."

"Oh?" Maggie said, her brows raised in question. "Anybody we know?"

"One of the drama group . . . I don't know her myself."

"*Her?*" Maggie said. "A woman, is it?"

Cara nodded. "So he said." Then she automatically added, "He's not the only one – there's a crowd of them gone into the hospital."

They sat chatting over tea and toast, Cara gritting her teeth every time her mother commented how nice it was to have a decent cup of tea again.

"Has Charles or Pauline said anything to you, at all?" Maggie asked at one point during the conversation.

"What about?" Cara said.

"Well," Maggie gestured with her hands, "nothing in particular as such. Just how things went on while we were away."

Cara shrugged. "I haven't had a chance to talk to them . . . and you know Charles isn't one for chatting much anyway."

"It's his eye and ear," Declan said. "We're just a bit worried that he's had a run-in with somebody and doesn't want to say. Maybe an awkward or a drunken customer – or some such thing."

Maggie nodded her head. "Pauline says she knows nothing about it either. She said he just appeared with the sticking-plaster and said he'd hit his head carrying a sack in from the door. And when she asked about the ear, he said he didn't remember what happened, and that maybe it was a bite from a horsefly or something like that."

Cara frowned. *God, all this going on and I haven't even noticed.* "It sounds strange, right enough," she said. "If I get the chance, I'll mention it to him quietly."

"And Pauline," Maggie said, "thankfully, she seems to have brightened up a lot. The little bit of responsibility running the shop might have given her a bit of a lift."

"All in all," Declan said, "they managed the running of the shop well. I've no complaints there – just so long as Charles is all grand in himself."

By the time they made moves to leave, there was still no sign of Oliver.

"Is everything all right?" Maggie asked in a low voice, while Declan revved up the car. "You know . . . between yourself and Oliver."

Cara took a deep breath. "Everything's fine, Mammy – everything is the same as normal."

Maggie nodded her head, like a bird pecking at a piece of bread. "It's just that you're not looking too bright . . . and I thought that maybe yourself and Oliver might have had words."

Cara folded her arms, waiting.

"It's just with him being out tonight . . . and you being just back home from America."

"Honestly, Mammy," Cara said snappily, "there's nothing wrong." Then, the car horn sounded impatiently. "Daddy's waiting for you – you'd better go."

Maggie went to the door and gestured to Declan to have patience. "Cara," she said, coming back to her, "you didn't say anything to Oliver about America , did you?"

There was silence for a few moments. Then, Cara said in a low, weary voice, "No, I didn't say anything about America."

"If you take my advice," her mother warned, "you never *will* say anything."

* * *

Cara was in bed for the second night in a row when Oliver returned from the hospital. He tiptoed into the bedroom, undressed in the dark, and then slipped into bed beside her. He lay still for a few moments, then he turned towards her, gathering her into his arms.

"Cara?" he murmured into her hair. "Are you awake, darling?"

"Mmm," she answered sleepily, hoping he would turn away to his own side of the bed.

There was a short pause. "Are you annoyed with me for being late again?"

Cara gave a short sigh. "No, Oliver. You told me you were going to the hospital." She wriggled out of his arms and moved further away from him. Anyway," she said, looking at the bedside clock, "you're earlier than last night."

"Well," he said, "I think we've all done our bit. She's a lot better – they're letting her out tomorrow."

"Did they find out what was wrong?" Cara said.

"Oh," he said, "you were right – it seems it was the penicillin."

There was a longer silence, while Cara wondered how she could muster up the interest to ask him any more questions – and she knew by his awkward manner that Oliver felt the same.

Then, he reached across the bed for the second time. His hands gripping her shoulder and turning her towards him. "Cara," he said in a low voice, "is there something wrong?"

Her body became rigid at his touch, and she was grateful she was wearing cotton pyjamas rather than a lighter nightdress. "No, Oliver . . . there's nothing wrong. I'm just tired . . . very tired."

"I can understand you being tired," he said, "the travelling and everything. But you still don't seem yourself . . . and we've not had a chance to have a good chat about America and everything." He rubbed his hand over her shoulder and back. "As long as you're OK in yourself . . . I wouldn't like to think there was something wrong – making us distant with each other like."

She sighed. "We've been distant before, Oliver," she said, "and it never bothered you to any great extent." She moved away again.

Oliver sat up and switched on his bedside lamp. "I'm sorry, Cara . . . but I really wanted to talk to you tonight . . . it's important."

Cara suddenly felt wide-awake, and worried. Did Oliver know something about what happened in America? No – he couldn't possibly. She hadn't talked to anyone. She hadn't made up her mind if she would even broach the subject with Pauline or Carmel. She hadn't seen Pauline on her own yet since coming back, and she hadn't seen Carmel at all. Whatever Oliver had to say, it had nothing to do with America.

She desperately hoped it wasn't anything to do with America – for she wasn't prepared for that yet. She knew she would have to be soon – but not just yet.

She turned back towards him now and sat up, shielding her eyes against the sudden light. "Well," she said, "you might as well go on then, since I'm now well and truly awake."

"I got these today," he said, lifting an envelope from the bedside table. "I thought they might be worth taking a look at." He placed it in her lap.

Cara looked down at the large, brown envelope. "What is it?" she said quietly – all sorts of things running through her mind.

"Open it," he said in a warm tone, "open it and see."

Cara suddenly felt uneasy as she slid the folded papers out from the envelope. She had no idea what to expect, and although Oliver liked to surprise her now and again with presents, the way he was acting now was not his usual style. He had never wakened her late at night before to give her a present.

Then, as she scanned the documents – page by page – she realised that nothing could have prepared her for this. Of all the possibilities that had flitted through her mind, this was the last thing she expected.

"Well?" Oliver had a smile from ear to ear. "What do you think?" There was not the smiling, excited reaction from Cara that he had hoped for.

"I don't know what to think," she said in a low voice. "To be honest, I'm totally confused. What's it all about?"

"Application forms for us to adopt a child," he said. "I thought you'd be delighted."

"But we've never discussed adopting a child before, Oliver."

"Not as *such*," he said, "but maybe we should have. Maybe things would have been different between us if we'd had a child." He looked at her now. "You've always wanted a child. The first few years when we were married you talked about nothing else."

Cara looked down at the papers, and then she took a deep breath. "Perhaps things would have been different if we'd adopted a child then."

He put a hand on her shoulder. "It's not too late now, Cara . . . we're still young. We could adopt two or three if we were accepted."

"No, Oliver." She shook her head slowly. "It's much too late . . . the way things are – and have been – between us for a long time, make it a silly thing to even consider."

He leaned across the bed, and put his arm around her shoulders. "Cara . . . I'm the first to admit that I haven't been a perfect husband – but I want to change all that." His hand came under her chin, and he looked into her dark, troubled eyes. "I can't tell you how sorry I am about all the nonsense I got up to before. But I promise you solemnly, that it's all over. We have a whole future ahead of us, if only you want it."

Cara looked at him, wordlessly. Then, the tears fell. Gently first – building up into torrents. She sobbed and sobbed, still in his arms and rocking backwards and forwards. And he held her, giving her time to get all the sadness out of her system. And for once it was Oliver who waited.

After a while, the crying and the tears gradually eased. And it was only then, in a quiet and fearful tone, that Oliver asked: "Has something happened that I don't know about, Cara?"

Cara looked up at him, and with the barest nod of her head risked her marriage and the life she'd known for years.

Oliver's arms fell from her shoulders and rested on the bed-cover. "Is it . . ." he ventured, his brows deepening in disbelief, "is there another man?"

There was a brief moment's hesitation before she took the final step. "Yes, Oliver," she heard herself say quietly, "there is another man."

"Holy Jesus!" There was no disguising the blow that

her confession had just dealt him. "*How*? Who is it?"

And when there was no immediate reply, he answered his own question. "*America*. It was in America, wasn't it? You met someone when you were over in America?"

She looked up at him now, surprised that the roof wasn't falling in. Surprised that all the paralysing fear had vanished. "Yes. I did meet him in America." Her look was direct and honest and her voice was strong. "I'm sorry having to tell you all this, Oliver – but I'm not sorry that it happened."

"*How*," he croaked, "can you just say that to me?"

"I can say it," Cara told him, "because you have spent *years* stupidly messing about with other women – right under my nose. And I've been even more stupid – pretending that I didn't know – when we were the talk of the town."

"That's not true," Oliver blustered now, his face reddening with denial. "People respect us, Cara. They just see me as a bit of a *Jack-the-lad* . . . a ladies' man or whatever. But they know there's no real harm in it."

Cara's eyes were wide, amazed at his perception of the situation. "But there *is* real harm in it, Oliver – *very* real harm." Her voice was icy now and determined. "Anyway," she snapped, "there's no point arguing all this now – we've gone far beyond arguing about it."

He took a deep breath. "Look, Cara," he said, calmer now. "Just how serious was the business in America? I mean, it couldn't have been much more than a holiday fling – now, could it?"

Cara's eyebrows shot up as the suggestion. "Yes, Oliver – it could have been more than a holiday fling. And it *was* more than a holiday fling – much more."

He moved back from her. "What are you saying?"

452

Cara had never seen her husband like this before. Completely deflated – the wind taken out of his sails. "I'm saying," she said quietly, "that I fell in love with another man in America – and that I'm still in love with him now. He's a man who loves and respects me – and who I know would never betray me in the way that *you* have all through our marriage."

He shook his head. "Let me get this straight," he said, his voice incredulous. "Are you telling me . . . that our marriage is over – *finished*?"

Cara looked up at the ceiling. "I suppose I am."

"But, Cara," he said quietly, "we live in *Ireland*. We're Catholics . . . and there's no divorce."

There was a pause. Long enough for Oliver to detect the slight uncertainty.

"I know all that," Cara said in a low voice, "and I know what it all means."

"What about your mother?" he asked now. "And the rest of your family? Have you stopped to consider the effect all this will have on them?"

Cara flinched, and he knew he had hit the most vulnerable spot. "You forced all this tonight, Oliver," she said. "All this business with the adoption forms – you forced all this out of me."

"Maybe," he said, "it's a good thing I did, before you went ahead and did something stupid. Something that could wreck more than *our* lives." Oliver's voice had returned to being calm and reasonable. "Look, Cara," he said, seeking her hand, "I understand how all this has happened. Sure, I take a good part of the blame myself . . ."

"No!" Cara said, pulling her hand away. "You don't understand anything about it at all, Oliver. I love Jameson

Carroll in a way that I never, ever loved you!" She turned to look at him full on. "It wasn't just a cheap holiday affair – don't kid yourself. I really, really love him."

Oliver took a deep breath. "And is he a married man?"

"No," she answered defiantly. "He's been divorced for years."

"*Divorced?*" Oliver's brows were deep again, contemplating this new information. "Sure, that's no help to you, Cara. No help at all. There's no future here for either of you. As far as the Catholic Church is concerned, you're both still married to other people." He shook his head. "It would kill your mother, Cara. No two ways around it – it would kill her. Bad enough with what Pauline got up to – how will she face people in the shop every day, if it gets out about you?"

Cara's mouth gaped open in shock. "How dare you?" she gasped. "*How dare you?*"

"OK – OK!" he said, his hands raised defensively. "But I'm only saying what others will say to you." Then, his shoulders suddenly slumped. "I suppose I've only myself to blame. I've brought it all on myself."

There was a long silence. Then, Cara said quietly: "I suppose it's better that it's all come out. It would have had to come out eventually. At least we both know where we stand now."

"I can't believe it, Cara," Oliver said, his voice low and wounded. "When I was driving back tonight, all I could think of was us having a child of our own at long last. I thought it would make us really happy."

"At one time, Oliver," she told him, "it would have made us happy. But that time has long gone."

Chapter 40

The following morning, Cara pretended she was still asleep when Oliver was up and moving around, getting ready for work. She also pretended she was asleep when he bent down to kiss her, and whisper 'I love you,' in her ear.

Shortly afterwards she came downstairs and phoned her mother.

"You're surely moving around bright and early this morning," Maggie said approvingly.

"I thought I might cycle over," Cara said, "and see how the rest of the things we brought back fitted Pauline and Bernadette."

"Do then," Maggie said. "We're quiet enough this morning, your father has Charles and Peenie to keep things going in the shop."

When she arrived, there was some activity going on outside the shop with the men, regarding some burst sacks of flour. After greeting her flustered father and brother, and the ever-amiable, smiling Peenie, Cara picked her way through the clouds of white dust, and headed through the back of the shop to the house.

Maggie, Pauline and Bernadette were just starting breakfast.

"I kept you some French toast and bacon," Maggie said cheerfully. "It's in the oven."

Cara joined them at the table, and both she and her mother recounted some of the places they'd seen in America, and the things they had done.

When they were washing up, Maggie turned to Pauline. "Would you go out to the shed and bring in a bucket of turf?"

Pauline looked at her mother. "We have plenty in the basket," she said, "but I'll get you more when Cara has told me all about the wedding."

"Go now, I want a bucket of small, dry pieces," Maggie said, "to heat the oven up quick to make some bread. And anyway," she added, "I want a word with Cara on my own."

Cara's heart suddenly leapt. Had Oliver rung her mother this morning?

When Pauline closed the door behind her, Maggie turned to Cara. "What's going on?" she said in a serious voice. "Don't try to tell me any different – because I know there's something wrong."

Cara took a deep breath. "It's Oliver and me . . . we're not getting on."

Maggie closed her eyes and sunk down into the big chair beside the fire, the dishtowel clutched in her hands. "You haven't told him about the American, have you? I warned you – I warned you not to tell him!"

"It's got nothing to do with that," Cara said quietly. "Things weren't right long before I went to America."

"*Cara,*" her mother said, "don't try to change the

subject! Just answer my question. Have you told him about your carry-on in America?"

Cara felt a stab of anger at her mother describing it as *carry-on*. "Yes!" she snapped. "Yes, I have told him. But none of that would have happened if we'd been getting on before I even thought of going to America. And you knew that." She looked her mother in the eye now. "Tell me, did you advise Oliver to enquire about us adopting a child?"

Maggie sat up in the chair and folded her arms defensively. "I'm not going to deny it. I did suggest that you should adopt a child, Cara – and I still think you should." She got up from the armchair, and stood close to her daughter. "All this American nonsense has got to stop. Do you hear me?" Her voice now had a steely note in it. "It's got to stop *right now*. There's no future in it for you. You're a married woman – and nothing can change that. Even your Auntie Jean thinks it's for the best that you and Oliver make a go of things . . ."

Cara's heart skipped a beat. "Auntie Jean?" she said. "When were you talking to her?"

"Oh – one evening last week," Maggie said with a wave of her hand. "And the impression I got from Jean was that the big American fella was getting on just fine there without you. She agreed with me that it would be the best solution all round if you just settled back in Ireland – if everyone just went back to the way it was before all this nonsense started."

"But Mammy," Cara said pleadingly, "I don't love Oliver any more. How can I stay for the rest of my life with a man that I don't love?"

"*Love?*" Maggie snorted. "Love indeed!" She prodded

Cara's shoulder. "It's about time you grew up, Cara. You're living in a dream world. You need to face up to facts. You're a *Catholic* – and being a Catholic means certain things. It means sticking to your marriage vows for better or worse. It means putting up with the bad – and making the best of it. There's a lot worse husbands out there than Oliver Gayle."

"But Mammy . . ." Cara said, tears springing to her eyes.

Maggie held her hand up. "My advice to you is to go home and sort things out with Oliver as quick as you can." Her voice dropped. *"If* he'll have you back after your disgraceful carry-on. There's many a man would have shown you the door as soon as he found out."

"And what about *his* carry-on?" Cara said. "I know you're quite happy to pretend that he's the perfect husband, just because he's always got a smile on his face and a quick joke. If you want to know what kind of a reputation he has, you ask Pauline or Carmel!"

Maggie's chest puffed out with indignation. "Pauline has never had a bad word to say for Oliver. In fact, I'm sure she used to have a bit of a *grá* for him when she was younger. I've often heard her say how lucky you are to have married Oliver Gayle."

There was a sudden silence. Then, Cara took a deep breath. "Look, Mammy . . . I don't want this to cause a falling out between us."

Maggie nodded her head slowly. "But it *will*, Cara – if you don't listen to reason, it most certainly will." She halted. "The long school holidays don't suit you, Cara. I've seen you the same every summer, brooding there on your own, feeling sorry for yourself, when you should be thankful for your lovely home and all you've got." More than a hint of bitterness was evident in her tone. "You're well off and you don't even know it."

Just then, the door opened and Pauline came in with the basketful of turf. She banged it down on the hearth and with a loud sigh started to throw some sods on the fire.

"And there's no point in you signalling your disapproval," Maggie rounded on her younger daughter now. "Don't think I didn't see you listening there at the back door."

"Oh, Mammy, for God's sake give it a rest, will you?" Pauline snapped back. "Cara's a grown woman, and what she does is her own business."

"Is that right?" Maggie was up on her feet now, her voice high with indignation. "And I suppose what you did was your business, too? I suppose that you coming back here with an illegitimate child has nothing to do with the rest of us?"

Cara stood up. "Don't start on Pauline now, or I'm going home. I'm not feeling too bright, and I don't need all these arguments."

Pauline grabbed her jacket from the back of a chair. "Come on, Cara," she said. "I'll get Bernadette and the bike, and we'll come back to the house with you for a while. I could do with getting out of here." Both girls started towards the door.

Maggie's face dropped. "Now, there's no need for all of this," she said in a watery voice. "I'm only trying to advise Cara . . . there's the Church and the school and everything to think of, and I'm only trying to do my duty as any good Catholic mother would."

Cara turned back. "It's really not my fault, Mammy. If Oliver had done what he should have over the years, I wouldn't be in this situation now."

"Men are different," Maggie stated. "Some of them are made that way, and it's up to us women to keep them on the straight and narrow – not to be outdoing them."

Cara looked back at her mother, and then without another word, she followed her sister out of the house.

* * *

Back at her own house, with little Bernadette sleeping on the sofa, Cara poured the whole story about Jameson Carroll to Pauline. She missed nothing out, and was so exhausted re-living the whole situation, that she finished up cradled in her sister's arms.

"I can't believe it!" Pauline said at the end of it, rubbing Cara's shoulders to comfort her. "I could never in my wildest dreams have imagined you going with another man."

Cara sighed, searching in her pocket for a hanky.

"Before I went to America, I would have never imagined it myself. Maybe it would have been better if I'd never   gone . . . I can see it definitely would have been better for everyone else. And yet . . ."

"What?' Pauline asked.

"And yet," Cara whispered, "I don't regret a minute of it. It was the best thing that I've ever felt in my entire life . . . I would never have believed I could feel so happy with a man." She looked at her sister now. "I can't even begin to describe how he made me feel. The way I felt about Oliver at our very best . . . doesn't even come close to this."

Pauline bit her lip. "I really don't know what to say . . . Mammy was right about what I think of Oliver. I've always felt you were really lucky being married to him."

"But you must *know* the name he has around town for going with women," Cara said quietly.

Pauline gave a little shrug. "I'm sure most of it was harmless . . . a bit of flirting."

"If you were married to him," Cara said, "then you would find out that none of it was harmless." Her voice dropped. "Sure, he left me with hardly an ounce of confidence in myself. And I know well what you think of him, Pauline – I was head over heels about him when we met. I thought I could change him – but I couldn't."

Pauline turned away, embarrassed. "What can I say, Cara? I'm the last one to offer any advice. Look at the hames I've made of my own life already."

"I'm not asking for advice," Cara said. "It's too late for that now'"

"What do you *really* want to do, Cara?" Pauline asked.

"I want to go back to America," she said. "I want to go back to live at Lake Savannah with Jameson and Thomas. I know in my heart that it's the right thing to do."

Pauline bit her lip again. "*America?*" she said, with trepidation in her voice. She paused. "I suppose it would have to be America . . . there's no way you could be with him over here."

Cara nodded slowly. "I know all that . . . that's why it's so difficult."

"Have you heard from him since you came back?" Pauline asked.

Cara shook her head. "I said I would wait until I sorted things out with Oliver. There's no point in writing or phoning until I have something to tell him." She rubbed under both her eyes with her hanky, then tucked a blonde wing behind her ear. "Anyway, I'm not even sure where he is at the moment . . . he's probably still at his parents' house in New York."

"Oh, Cara," Pauline whispered. "I can't believe it . . . you were always the one that everything went right for. I always thought you were so lucky, with your handsome husband, your lovely house and your nice teaching job."

Cara smiled weakly at her sister. "You sound exactly like Mammy."

Pauline laughed now. "For God's sake, don't say that! I really don't mean it like Mammy. It's just that I'm frightened in case you make a mistake." She took a deep breath. "What if Oliver really has changed? What if you went ahead and adopted a baby and everything turned out fine?" Pauline realised now that that's what she hoped with all her heart would happen. If things worked out fine with her and Jack Byrne, sure they could all be one big happy family, with her and Cara out for Sunday walks with children running around and babies being pushed in their prams.

"I don't believe he can change," Cara said. "I'm sure it would all be a big novelty for a while . . . but like everything else, it would become too ordinary and boring for him. He would be like a caged bird, hopping about to see what he could move on to next." She looked at Pauline, tears starting again. "He'll never change, and what chance would I have then – tied to him and a house with a baby?"

"You could be worse off," Pauline said with a wry smile. She touched the sleeping child's leg. "You could be in my shoes . . . stuck at home with Mammy and Daddy forever. As Mammy never fails to tell me, there's no decent man will ever look at me again." She still hadn't told Cara or her parents about Jack Byrne. The time wasn't right. And anyway, what was there to tell at this stage? Just a few trips to the cinema, and a couple of walks out by the Mullingar lakes. There was enough going on at home with all Cara's problems, and Charles's increasingly odd behaviour – coming in with cut eyes and boxed ears and refusing to say where they came from. There was enough going on, without Pauline throwing yet another spanner in the Kearneys' works.

Telling them about Jack Byrne could wait. It was going too well to spoil it all by announcing their friendship at the wrong time.

Chapter 41

Charles slid down the bolts on one half of the shop door, and then went outside to check that there were no boxes or sacks left by mistake. There was nothing, Peenie had cleared the lot and swept up outside before heading home a few minutes ago. He stood for a while, his arms folded, looking up the street and then down. All was quiet. And indeed all was quiet in the house at the moment as well.

His parents had gone off to Tullamore earlier on with Pauline and Bernadette. They could be gone a while yet, as they said they might call in on Cara on the way back.

This was all a very bad business, Charles thought, the carry-on between Cara and Oliver. A very bad business indeed.

He pushed his glasses up on his nose. Things were more than a little fraught at home as a result of it all, and he was glad of the bit of peace and quiet for a change. His mother was like a cat on a griddle, watching and waiting for any bit of news that might indicate that things were settling back down to normal.

Charles stood for a few moments, watching the world go by, and then he turned back towards the shop. He would go in now, and make himself a cup of tea, and put his feet up with *Nostradamus*. *What a fellow*, Charles thought, *and what a brain!* He had just started a chapter about Napoleon at his tea-break this afternoon, and was anxious to continue reading Nostradamus's theory on the emperor being the first Antichrist.

Just then, he heard the familiar sound of Oliver Gayle's car coming up the street. The engine had a very particular sound that Charles recognised immediately. He turned, wondering what had brought Oliver out here straight from work. Not more marital problems, Charles hoped.

The car pulled up and Oliver hopped out smartly. He held a hand up to Charles, and then went to open the back passenger door. Out stepped a sturdy female figure dressed formally in a hat and coat, followed by smartly dressed young boy. The sight of them almost brought a pain to Charles's chest.

It was Mrs Lynch and her son.

One hand flew up to his chin and the other to his glasses. "Well, now . . ." he said, taking a step towards Oliver and then changing his mind and moving towards Mrs Lynch. "Well, now . . ." he said again.

"Mr Kearney," Mrs Lynch said, coming towards him, taking off her gloves. "I had to come to explain about the Mulligans –"

"The Mulligans?" Charles said, stepping back into the closed door and banging the back of his head against the padlock.

Oliver stepped forward, and took young Dominic by the hand. "I'll just find this fellow a packet of sweets or something in the shop," he said, and moved discreetly in past Charles and Mrs Lynch.

"My neighbours," Mrs Lynch explained solemnly. "I saw what went on that evening outside the house."

Charles raised his eyebrows in surprise. "You were in the house, then?"

Mrs Lynch shook her head. "No, I was coming back from a removal at the church, and I saw Johnny Mulligan and all his carry-on at your car."

"Well," said Charles, pleased that his deduction about the church had been correct, "in actual fact it's not my car. It's my father's."

"Yes," said Mrs Lynch, "your *father's* car." She paused for a moment, her hands tightly clutching her gloves. "They're terrible people, those Mulligans. The husband is a heavy drinker and fierce jealous . . . and he'd noticed your car parked out in the street a few times, and got the wrong idea."

"Oh?" said Charles. "And what idea did he have?"

"Well," said Mrs Lynch, "he thought you were . . . he thought you were a fancy-man of his wife's. All in his drunken imagination, of course – she's a poor soul who's terrified of him."

"Indeed!" said Charles, his brows moving in agitation. "So that explains the mystery."

Mrs Lynch's head bobbed up and down. "And I'm so, so sorry about it all. What a terrible thing to happen to one of my customers. I couldn't think where I could see you to explain . . . and I didn't like to phone the house. Then I remembered you saying that Mr Gayle was your brother-in-law. So I looked in at his shop this morning, and he offered to bring me out here himself. It was very decent of him." She looked at the plaster on his cheek. "Did he hurt you very bad?"

"Not at all," Charles said, his hand now moving to his swollen ear, "not at all."

"Well, I can tell you," the seamstress said in a high, indignant voice, "that I let Johnny Mulligan know just how wrong he'd got his facts. He was pulling his wife into the house by the hair of the head when I reached the gate."

"Dreadful," Charles muttered, "dreadful business altogether."

"I threatened him with the guards," she said. "I told him that he'd attacked an innocent man. A highly regarded businessman, who'd only come to see me about a harmless bit of sewing."

"Indeed," said Charles, quite flattered by the description of him being a *highly regarded businessman.*

Oliver appeared at the shop door now, with young Dominic sporting an orange-drink-coloured moustache and a bar of chocolate, which had left brown dribbles down the front of his hand-knitted jersey, clutched in his hand. The sight of it made Charles's stomach heave a little. He had a strong distaste for messy children, and had enough to contend with at home with Bernadette. Oliver took the child by the hand, and walked up the road out of the couple's earshot.

"Anyway," Mrs Lynch continued, "Johnny Mulligan has been back to the house to apologise to me on several occasions, and I told him he was a lucky man. If my friend, Mr Flynn, had been around when it happened, the guards would have been called on the spot –"

"Mr Flynn?" Charles said. "And would that be another of your customers?"

"Well, as a matter of fact," Mrs Lynch said, "he's just become my fiancé. He's the man I look after – the man I get the library books for. He's a great reader . . . I don't know how we get on, because I'm not much of a reader myself. He has books piled everywhere in the house, and I'm forever trying to tidy the blessed things up. If you ask me, they're only dust-gatherers."

Charles stared at her, his mind trying to digest this latest information.

"He's a good bit older than me," the seamstress went on quickly, "and a small bit of an invalid . . . but he's a fine man, and will look after me and Dominic well. It's not been easy being on our own."

Charles nodded his head. "Well," he said, "I'm delighted for you, Mrs Lynch – and I hope all three of you will be very happy."

"You are?" she said, sounding slightly disappointed. There was a little pause. "It's just that I thought you . . . " She took a deep breath. "With you calling round so much, I thought you might have thought there could be something between you and – and me."

Charles's eyebrows shot up. "Not at all," he said, catching sight of Dominic rubbing his chocolaty hands down the front of his jumper now. "As you say, it was only a bit of business. I was just getting my house in order, as they say. Sorting out my clothes, what needed mending and suchlike. Getting things in order for the winter coming in."

Mrs Lynch's head moved up and down slowly. "I see,"

she said quietly. "It was just with you calling so late in the evening . . . I thought it might have been personal, because, I have to say, Mr Kearney – I think you're a very fine man."

Charles put his hands behind his back now and smiled. "Well, thank you, Mrs Lynch," he said. "That's kind of you to say so."

They both stood for a few moments in silence. Then, when the silence became awkward, Mrs Lynch put her gloves back on. "I'll thank you for being so understanding, Mr Kearney," she said, moving back towards the car. Oliver and the boy were now coming back down the street.

"Think nothing of it," Charles said, rocking back on his heels and smiling. "All water under the bridge as they say, Mrs Lynch. All water under the bridge."

Then, another familiar car engine sounded as it came up towards the shop, and Charles unwittingly gave a loud groan. It was his mother and father. Why on earth could they not have waited a few more minutes, and avoided bumping into the seamstress?

Maggie was first out of the car. "We've just left your house," she told Oliver brightly. "We thought we might have seen you." She turned expectantly to Mrs Lynch, and Oliver quickly introduced them.

Mrs Lynch blushed red now, unsure of whether Charles had explained how he got his wounds, and wary of saying the wrong thing. "I called over with Mr Kearney's blazer," she said in a high tone. She gestured now to the car. "I've left it in the back seat . . ."

Maggie looked from Mrs Lynch to Charles, knowing instinctively that there was more to the situation. But both remained tight-lipped.

A few moments later, Charles waved Oliver's car off with Mrs Lynch and the dribbly Dominic safely in the back seat. What a narrow escape he'd just had, he thought. Almost betrothing himself to a woman who didn't read, and a child who dribbled all down himself.

Charles shuddered at the thought.

Wasn't it far, far better to be on his own, than tied for life to an unsuitable partner? A partner who had no time for books – and had referred to them as *dust-gatherers* in much the same manner as his mother would have done. A dire warning if ever there was one.

And anyway, what harm was there in going to the theatre on his own? If Mrs Lynch didn't read, it was highly unlikely she'd ever heard of William Shakespeare or *Othello*. Or Charles Dickens or Oscar Wilde. It would be a completely wasted exercise.

And then Charles suddenly remembered *Nostradamus*, and grinned to himself. He would take that cup of tea upstairs to his bedroom now, and continue where he left off.

Back to his own safe, solitary little world.

Chapter 42

For the next week, Cara and Oliver lived like strangers in the same house, maintaining only a polite silence between them. The only real conversation they had was when Cara moved into the spare bedroom.

"I'm sorry, Oliver," she told him, "but I need to be on my own. I've not slept properly since I came back . . . and I don't feel very bright in myself. If I wake up, I can put the light on without disturbing you."

"Is that the real reason?" he asked in an injured tone.

"I honestly don't feel too good," she said, "and if it doesn't improve, I'm going to have to go to the doctor. I might need a tonic or something to give me the energy for going back to school next week."

Oliver's eyes suddenly brightened. "Maybe going back to school will do you a power of good," he said now. "Getting back into a routine and everything."

"Maybe it will," Cara said quietly, turning towards the spare-room door.

"Cara?" Oliver suddenly said, catching her gently by

the arm. "What would you say . . . to us attending Catholic Marriage Guidance?" He waited, and when there was no reaction said: "We could go up to Dublin where nobody would know us. I could ring for an appointment tomorrow . . . if you're agreeable."

Cara stared at him with hollow-looking eyes. "I asked you to do that last year . . . and you refused."

"I know, I know," he admitted, "but I was too pig-headed to listen then." He took her hands in his. "Cara, please – give me a chance. If I could turn the clock back, I would."

Then, as she noticed tears glistening at the corner of his eyes, something rose up inside her. She didn't know if it was guilt, pity or the vestiges of the feelings she once had for him. Whatever it was, she suddenly said: "Give me a bit of time, Oliver – I need to think."

"Take all the time you need," he said gently. He squeezed her hands. "I'll be there waiting for you."

Cara eased her hands out of his grip. Then, she went in one bedroom door, and Oliver went in the other.

* * *

Cara visited the doctor the following Friday morning. There was a fair-sized queue in the waiting-room. Not in the mood for polite conversation, or to be interrogated about her family by nosey neighbours, Cara kept her head buried in a book until it was her turn.

"Well, Cara," the kindly doctor enquired over his little spectacles, "what brings you here?"

"To be honest, doctor," she started, "I don't really know. Basically, I've been feeling run-down for the last few weeks. I'm not sleeping great, and I'm absolutely exhausted. I wondered if maybe I'd picked up something while I was in America?"

"A possibility, I suppose," he said, his head tilted to the side in thought. "On the other hand, it could be a touch of anaemia or anything." He turned back to his desk and opened her file, then after a few seconds he made a small noise as though clearing his throat. "Are you still having the same trouble with your monthly – "

"Yes," Cara answered quickly. "It's over eight months since the last one."

The doctor stood up and went over to his instrument trolley. "We'll take a drop of blood from you," he told her, "and see if anything shows up. I'll give you a prescription to start you on some iron tables in the meantime." He gave her a beaming smile. "I can't tell whether you're pale or not, with that lovely tan you got in America."

Standing outside the surgery, Cara pondered whether to cycle down to the shop or go straight home. She had been avoiding her mother as much as possible, and the last time she had spoken to her briefly Maggie had come up with the suggestion of the Catholic Marriage Advisory. It had crossed Cara's mind that Oliver had been discussing things with her mother again. But maybe, she thought, she was being too touchy. Maybe it was the obvious thing for someone to suggest.

She mounted the bicycle and headed for home, deciding that she wasn't in the mood for a heavy discussion with her mother. What she needed was a rest, because apart from being tired, she now felt slightly queasy since she'd given the sample of blood.

Back at the house, she dozed fitfully for almost two hours, curled up in the armchair in the sitting-room. She woke when the sound of the postman's bicycle crunching on the stones outside startled her. She sat still for a few moments, her head still fuzzy with sleep. In normal circumstances she would have gone to the door and invited the cheery Kevin O'Reilly in for a cup of tea and a slice of cake, but this afternoon she was in no mood to make small-talk with the postman.

Instead, she just waited until she heard the bicycle heading off down the drive, and then she moved into the kitchen to fill the range up with wood and some small pieces of turf. When she got it going well enough, she put the kettle on top to boil for tea, and then started to make herself a ham sandwich.

While she waited for the kettle to boil, she sat back down in the armchair just gazing into space. *What,* she asked herself, over and over again, *has happened to my life? What have I done?* And then, eventually, *What am I going to do? Should I have been brave enough – or selfish enough – to stay in America with Jameson Carroll? Would it have been any harder in the long run than all of this?*

The kettle was whistling long before any answers seemed to be appearing, so Cara got up and made the tea. She brought her ham sandwich and mug of tea on a tray, and sat back down in the chair. She ate and drank mechanically, asking herself the same questions, over and over again.

Later, as she moved to wash up, she suddenly remembered the postman. There was one long airmail letter lying on the mat, and the nearer she got to it, the quicker her heart started to beat. She could see American stamps on it and unfamiliar handwriting. And as she picked it up, she racked her brains to remember if she had ever seen Jameson write anything in her presence.

She almost ran back into the sitting-room, clutching the letter to her breast. And then, she pored over every inch of the front of the envelope, before turning it over to check for a sender's name on the back.

And there – just as she hoped – was the Lake Savannah address. Printed neatly, but with no name on it. It didn't matter. The address was enough. It had to be from Jameson.

Cara reached up to the mantelpiece and lifted down a small paper-knife – a present from one of her uncles when she graduated from teacher-training college. It had a gold-coloured blade and a creamy-coloured porcelain handle, decorated with small pink flowers. She could hardly stop her hand from shaking as she carefully sliced the top of the envelope open, and then slid the single, flimsy sheet of airmail paper out.

Her heart was racing now, and her eyes moved excitedly down the page. Then, her eyes narrowed in confusion as she turned the paper over to read the signature on the other side.

"Oh, God!" she suddenly cried out loud, her hand coming to cover her mouth. The letter wasn't from Jameson – it was from *Verity!*

She turned the letter over to the beginning again, and forced herself to read every word of the flowery, dramatic handwriting.

Dear Cara,
I thought you might like to know that Thomas has made tremendous progress since you went back home to Ireland. He is now back in our house in Lake Savannah with a nurse in

attendance.

As you will no doubt have realised from the address, I, too, am back at the house looking after both Thomas and Jameson. I know that this may come as a shock to you, but I am sure that when you have had time to think about it, you will accept that things have turned out for the best.

I took the liberty of writing to you myself, because although Jameson promised me that he would write and explain everything – he would probably never get around to it. With Jameson, I'm afraid it's 'out of sight, out of mind'.

By the time you receive this, you may well be in a happier situation with your own husband in Ireland. I sincerely hope that that is the case.

Thank you for your kindness to my son when he was so ill, and for helping Jameson out at that most difficult time. We both wish you all the best for the future,

> *Yours,*
> *Verity Carroll*

Cara's eyes once again froze on the flamboyant signature at the back of the letter. *It was all lies!* It couldn't be true! It just couldn't be true – he would never do this to her! Not the Jameson Carroll she had spent all those weeks with. Not the man she had come to know and love.

All the weeks of pushing thoughts of Jameson to the back of her mind. Telling herself that it would all work out, and eventually they would be together. All her hopes and dreams – her escape from her lie of a marriage. It was only a short time ago that he had agreed to wait for her until she had sorted things out – surely he hadn't changed his mind? Surely Jameson hadn't given up on her that easily?

And yet, as she lifted up the envelope again and examined the postmark, a little worm of doubt crept into her mind, because the stamp confirmed Verity's statement about her being back in Lake Savannah. The postmark was clearly marked *Binghampton*, their nearest town. But what if Verity had driven up to Binghampton to post the letter? What if she had made the whole story up, in order to destroy the bond between Cara and Jameson?

Cara considered this for a few minutes – then eventually shook her head. *No one* would drive five hours to post a letter. No one who was in their right mind. Verity must have gone up to see Thomas and written and posted the letter while she was there.

But the nagging little doubt persisted, and started to conjure up all sorts of pictures in her mind. Pictures of Jameson and Thomas and Verity planning a trip to Disneyland. Pictures of them as a happy family by the lake. Just as it should be – and maybe just as it had become since she had left.

People could change. Look at the difference in Oliver since her return. Cara certainly hadn't expected all that. And, just as the time had come for her to face the truth about her marriage to Oliver – maybe the time had come to also face the truth about her relationship with Jameson Carroll. Maybe it was no more than a foolish, romantic fling – heightened by the beautiful surroundings and then intensified by the drama surrounding Thomas's accident. Was it possible that that's all it had been?

Maybe, after she'd gone, Jameson saw it for what it was. Just a pleasant – but short-lived – holiday fling. One that could easily be replaced if the woman he married – and the mother of his son – had now become the dedicated wife and mother he had always wanted.

And yet, as she considered all these options, a small ray of hope rose at the back of her mind, a small ray of hope that clung to the belief in all the days and nights they had spent together. There must be a way of finding out – of checking. She wasn't going to just take the words of a conniving, jealous woman like Verity.

Far, far too much depended on it. Maybe even the rest of her life.

Cara took a deep breath. She would phone Jameson and sort this all out.

* * *

Working out the time difference between the countries was automatic, as every time she looked at the clock in the kitchen or the sitting-room, she immediately transferred it into American time to work out what Jameson was likely to be doing. It was now around ten o'clock, and according to his regular routine he would be at home, probably downstairs working in his studio. It was unlikely that he would be anywhere else, as Thomas would still not be fit enough to go very far.

Cara's heart was in her mouth as she waited for the operator to dial the number for her, and then she seemed to wait an awful long time until she was eventually connected. Making phone calls to America was no everyday thing, and as she waited she wondered how good the line would be when they eventually spoke.

But the phone rang and rang until the operator came back onto the line. "I'm sorry, ma'am, but there's no reply. It might be best to try later. Have you checked the time difference, because it's still fairly early in New York?"

"Yes, I have," Cara said, sorely disappointed. "I'll ring again later, thanks." Then a thought suddenly struck her. "Sorry!" she said quickly. "Could you hold the line for me to try another number in America?"

"No problem," the cheery operator said. "Have you the number handy, or do you want me to check it out for you?"

"If you give me one minute," Cara said, slightly breathless, "I have it just beside me." She pulled a drawer in the hall table out and quickly located the address book and Jean's number. She read it out to the operator. Within a minute or so, the phone was ringing at the other end. Like Jameson's phone, it rang and rang.

And then, her aunt's voice sounded across the surprisingly clear line. "Harpers' – this is Jean speaking."

"Hello, Jean . . . it's Cara here – "

There was a pause as it took a second or two for their voices to travel over the line. "Cara!" her aunt's voice rose high with delight. "How wonderful to hear from you? How are things back in Ireland?"

"Well . . ." Cara started, her voice dropping, "it's a bit difficult . . . I wanted to ask you something . . . to see if you could help me out with some information "

"Well, honey," Jean said, "you know I'll always do anything I can do to help you. I'm just so happy to hear your voice. You just shoot now with the questions."

"It's about Jameson," Cara said, "or to be more specific – about his wife."

"His *wife?*" Jean repeated, her voice suddenly serious. "I'm not too sure I can help you there, honey . . . I've only spoken to her a couple of times."

Cara's heart lurched. Jean had never met Verity. At least she had never met her up until Cara had left

America. She made herself go on and ask the questions, although she was dreading the answer she felt now was going to come. "I just wanted to check if Verity is back up at the house – Jameson's house in Lake Savannah."

There was a silence, longer than was necessary for the line distance. "I'm not too sure on that one," Jean said, "I know she was around the last couple of weeks . . . she brought Thomas over to visit me and Bruce."

Cara suddenly felt weak. "Is she back . . . is she back living with Jameson and Thomas?" she made herself ask. "It's just that I need to know . . ."

"I'm a little confused here, honey," Jean said. "I thought that this was all sorted out . . . I thought that you guys – you and Oliver – had made things up, and were hoping to go ahead and adopt a child? I thought you'd put that thing with Jameson Carroll out of your mind."

Cara groped for the chair by the phone table and sank down into it. "Where," she gasped, "*where* did you hear that from?" And even as she said it, she knew she didn't have to ask.

"Your mom." Jean's voice was starting to sound strained. "I spoke to her just the other week . . . and she was so relieved that everything had worked out with you and Oliver."

Cara shook her head, and struggled to keep the tears from spilling out. "Jean," she said urgently, "It's really important – I need to know if Jameson and Verity are back together. Back together as man and wife . . . "

"I'm gonna be straight with you now, Cara," Jean said. "And I have to say that she's sure been spending a lot of time recently across the lake."

Cara felt nauseous at her aunt's words. She didn't

want to hear any more – but she had asked for the information, and now she had to listen.

"How long she plans on staying, and whether she's still there or not, " Jean continued, "I don't rightly know. All I do know is that she and Thomas called here last week with flowers and a 'thank you' card for the support we'd given Jameson – as if we wanted *thanking*! That poor boy, and all he went through."

"Did Verity mention me?" Cara asked in a low, strained voice.

"She did," Jean stated, "and asked for your address for her or Thomas to send a note to you, to thank you for all your help. To be honest, I was a little wary of giving it to her, but I couldn't do anything else with Thomas there and all . . ."

"And Jameson?" Cara dared to finally ask. "Have you seen him or spoken to him? Did he mention me?"

"Yes, he came across once since you left, on his own. He asked if I knew anything about what was happening with you back in Ireland. I said I didn't know, and it wouldn't be usual for me to phone up and find out. Truth to be   told . . . I didn't want to get too involved. It's not my business . . . but I thought about it and I did ring your mom."

Cara groaned inwardly. "And that's when she told you about the adoption and everything?"

"Yes," her aunt confirmed, "and I'm getting this real awful feeling that I shouldn't have meddled – because I had to make the call back to Jameson and tell him that news. He said very little – just listened. He said that deep down he probably knew you wouldn't come back. He said that once you'd gone back to Ireland, he reckoned that you would make it up with your husband. It was shortly after that conversation that Verity appeared up at Lake Savannah."

Cara took a big, deep breath. "I think," she said now, "that it's all beginning to make sense . . . I think I know what's happened."

"Cara," Jean said, her voice full of concern. "Do you really still have feelings for him?"

Cara hesitated for a moment. "I don't know what to think any more, Jean. I'm just very confused." She halted. "I'm not feeling too good, so maybe I just need time to work it all out."

"You look after yourself now, Cara," her aunt said kindly. "Look after yourself real good."

Tears sprung into Cara's eyes. "Thanks, Jean," she said quietly. "Thanks for everything."

* * *

After hanging up, Cara sat by the phone for a long time. She ran over the news that Jean had told her, trying to come to terms with it all. She moved into the sitting-room, clutching Verity's letter in her hands, and once again sat there, going over and over everything.

Then, as the awfulness of the situation became clearer, a sudden rage rose up inside her and she ripped both letter and envelope in two. Then she tore it again into smaller pieces, letting it fall to the floor like confetti.

"What a fool I've been," she whispered to herself. "What a silly, bloody fool!"

And then, in the absence of any other human contact, she wrapped her arms tightly around her body, in a small, pathetic attempt to bring some comfort to herself. And then she rocked back and forth in the chair, the motion keeping time with her sobs.

She cried for the comfort and passion that she had found in Jameson Carroll's arms – and for the love she thought she had found. She cried with regret for the marriage vows she had broken with him – and for the knowledge that he was unworthy of her sacrifice.

Whatever happened between her and Oliver now, she wished with all her heart that it had not been coloured by her affair in America.

But it was too late for regret now. Much too late.

* * *

Later, she forced herself to go out into the garden, to walk round and round it – as though looking to the flowers and shrubs for an answer. But she found none. Eventually, the sound of the phone ringing forced her back into the house.

"Hello," a female voice sounded on the other end of the line. "Is that you, Oliver?"

"No . . . no, it's not," Cara said, her voice hoarse from crying. "He's not in from work yet." She stepped back a bit to look through to the kitchen clock. "He's not usually in until around six o'clock."

"Is that . . ." the girl said, "is that Oliver's wife?"

"Yes," Cara replied dully. "Can I take a message?"

There was a silence on the line for a few moments, then the voice came back. Almost a whisper this time. "I was hoping that Oliver or some of the others . . . from the drama group would drop by the hospital this evening. There's a few things I need."

Cara thought for a moment. "Oh, you're Jacinta," she said, amazed at how normal her voice sounded. Amazed

483

that she could carry on any kind of a conversation at all. "You're the girl from the drama group. I'm glad to hear that you're feeling better."

"Yes," the girl said, "it's Jacinta." Another pause. "Could I ask you a favour, please?"

Cara frowned. "What is it?"

"It's just," the girl hesitated, "that I need some personal toiletries . . . and I hate to ask any of the men to buy them for me. You're not too far out from the hospital, are you?"

"About a ten-minute cycle," Cara said.

"I wonder," the girl said, "I know it's a real cheek . . . but I'm desperate. You wouldn't be able to cycle in with them for me, before the chemist shuts?"

"Do you need them immediately?" Cara said, sounding surprised.

"I'm sorry to be such a nuisance," the girl went on quickly. "I wouldn't ask normally . . . but I'm desperate. There's nobody else to ask until this evening, and by that time the chemist will be closed."

Cara thought for a moment, and then she checked the time on the clock again. "Okay," she agreed, "what ward are you on?"

The girl gave her directions to the ward and the list of things that she needed, and then she rang off.

Cara moved quickly, one half of her annoyed at having to go to Tullamore and the other half grateful for something to take her mind off the horrendous news she had received earlier. She scribbled a note for Oliver before leaving, explaining about Jacinta, and saying that there was stew and potatoes over a pan of water that just needed heating up.

She cycled into Tullamore, and headed up the High Street to the chemist shop and collected the items that the girl had asked for. She secured the brown-paper bag in her basket on the front of the bike, then she cycled on up to the hospital, her mind full of Jameson and all the things he'd said. All the lies he'd told her.

Jameson, who was now back in Lake Savannah with Thomas and his ex-wife.

* * *

Cara found the ward fairly easily, but had to hang around for a few minutes until she found a member of staff to direct her to the room that the girl was in. She checked her watch as she followed the nurse along the corridor. Oliver would be back home by now, and would have got her message. She wondered if he had managed to heat up the meal over the pan of boiling water.

Then, as she followed the nurse along the corridor, she wondered if she were going mad. Wondering about pots of *stew and potatoes* – when her life was falling apart. What did these things matter any more? What did anything matter any more?

As they came up to the room, the nurse said in a low voice, "It's nice she has a visitor . . . she's been very low all day."

Guilt now tore through all Cara's other thoughts, and she knew that she would have to go into the room and face the girl. "To be honest," Cara said, "I don't really know her . . . I'm just bringing her in a few things."

When she turned in the door of the ward, Cara recognised Jacinta immediately. She had seen her on stage in the last play that Oliver produced. A petite, attractive, dark-haired girl, with an almost oriental look about her. The girl was sitting up on top of the bed in a matching blue satin dressing-gown and nightdress, reading a magazine. There were three other beds in the room, but there was no one else around.

"Jacinta?" Cara said, and for some reason another knot started to tie itself in her stomach.

"Is it Cara?" the girl asked, swinging her legs off to sit on the edge of the bed. When Cara nodded, she said: "I thought it was you." She gestured to a chair by the side of the bed. "Come in and sit down."

"I haven't really got time." Cara explained. "I have to get back home."

"Sit down for a few minutes," Jacinta said in a friendly tone, pulling the chair closer to the bed. As she did so, Cara suddenly noticed that her arm was heavily bandaged from the wrist up.

Cara placed the chemist's bag on the bottom of the bed, and sat down. "I hope that's everything you need."

Jacinta smiled. "It was very good of you to get them for me." She reached inside the bag for the receipt, then lifted money from her bedside cabinet and put it down on the bed beside Cara. "That should cover it all." She folded her arms and then turned her gaze on Cara. "I could have really waited until tomorrow for them . . . but I needed an excuse to see you."

Cara's eyebrows lifted in surprise. "To see *me*?" she asked.

"I wanted, " Jacinta said, "to talk to you about me and Oliver."

"Oh?" Cara said, tilting her head to the side and waiting. The knot in her stomach had tightened considerably, and the queasy feeling had returned.

"Oliver and I . . ." Jacinta started haltingly, but then moved on more confidently. "I'm sure you already know that Oliver and I have been having an affair." She looked at Cara, waiting for her reaction.

Cara folded her arms and sat back in the chair, waiting.

Jacinta suddenly coloured up. "He told me he was leaving you . . . that we would both go over to England to start a new life." She brushed her dark hair back off her face, and Cara suddenly thought that she had been attacked by two women today. Two dark-haired women. First Verity and now this Jacinta girl.

Cara raised her eyebrows. "You might as well go on."

"Well," Jacinta said, getting out of the bed to stand in front of Cara, "I think I have some news that might shock you. I'm going to have Oliver's baby – and that means that he'll have to take responsibility for us both."

There was a little pause. "And how," Cara asked in a calm voice, "does Oliver feel about all this?"

"Actually," Jacinta said, "Oliver doesn't know yet . . . but he soon will."

Then a male voice came from the ward doorway. "What will I soon know, Jacinta?"

And there, framed in the doorway, stood Oliver himself. He came in the room to stand facing the two women – his face chalk-white and with a thunderous look on it.

"I've just been telling your wife all about us, Oliver," Jacinta said, as though she were discussing the weather, "about our affair."

Two little pulses on either side of Oliver's forehead began to visibly throb. "Have you now?" he said quietly.

"Well, I hope you told her that it finished some time ago, and that you've been trying to blackmail me since with all this attempted suicide crap?"

Cara caught her breath. *Attempted suicides? Pregnancy? What else was to come today? What more could possibly happen?*

Jacinta's face crumpled and tears started to spill down her pretty cheeks. "How can you say that to me?" she said in a choked voice. "You told me that you would leave her, when she came back from America – and now you've chickened out! You fucking coward!"

Oliver shook his head, unperturbed by her outburst. "I only said that to pacify you, because of your threatening suicide!"

Jacinta's eyes darted from Oliver to Cara. "Did he tell you about this?" she said, holding up her wrists "I nearly *died!* I could have bled to death – and all because of him" She tapped the side of her head. "He's got me so mixed up in here, I can't think straight any more." Her voice took on a higher pitch. "And what about my nursing career? It could be all over after this . . . and it's all your fault!"

"Look, Jacinta," Oliver hissed, "Cara and I have had our problems . . . but we're sorting them out." He turned to Cara. "Aren't we, Cara?" When she didn't respond, he kept on talking. "We're going to Marriage Guidance, and this time next year we could be adopting a child."

"There's no need to do that, Oliver," Jacinta said quietly, "because you're going to have one of your own." Then, as his eyes were wide with shock, she said, "I was just telling Cara all about it when you came in. I found out today that I'm pregnant."

Oliver rolled his eyes to the ceiling. "Don't mind a

word of what she says, Cara . . . she's mad! She's making up every word of this, just to split us up."

Cara looked at him now. "After what I've just heard – I think that might be the one sensible thing left to do." She stood up now, and made towards the door.

"No, Cara," Oliver said, grabbing at her arm. He followed her out into the corridor. "You don't understand – we can work it out. I'm sorry about all this – but I promise you sincerely that it won't happen again. Things will be the best they've ever been, if you'll just give me another chance." He glanced back over his shoulder. "I can prove she's lying – so don't mind what that eedjit says."

"I think," Cara said, attempting a smile, "that you've had quite enough chances. Don't you?" Her voice was steady and cool.

He stepped back, and looked at her now. "But where will you go?" he asked, a note of confidence in his tone. "You can't go to the American fellow now – his wife is back living with him."

"What do you mean?" Cara's words were slow and measured.

"The letter," he said, "the one you tore up in the sitting-room. I read it." His hand came up to touch the side of her cheek. "Please, Cara," he pleaded, "we've both made stupid mistakes, but we can learn from them."

Cara looked at him. Somewhere at the back of her mind she knew she should feel embarrassment, shock – *something* about Oliver finding Verity's letter. But she felt nothing. Apart from a numbness and a vague empty feeling.

All these things that had happened in one day. Things

that should be shaking her to the core, and still she was standing. Standing facing Oliver now.

"Please, Cara," Oliver repeated. "I've been doing so much thinking about everything recently, and I know that all I want is us to stay together – forever. It's what your mother – your whole family – would want. And it's what the Church tells us that we should do. Maybe if we both started all over again . . . following the right things, then we would get it right ourselves."

"If you had been faithful to me, Oliver," Cara whispered, "then none of this would have happened. I would never have gone to America without you if things had been fine between us."

Oliver's face dropped. "I've said how sorry I am . . . what more can I do?"

There was a silence. Then, hearing Jacinta's furry mules tapping across the ward floor they turned towards her.

"What about *our* baby, Oliver?" she asked, coming to stand in front of them, hand on hips.

Oliver sighed loudly and threw her a contemptuous look. "Ignore her, Cara. There's no way she can be pregnant – I know it for a fact."

"I am!" Jacinta screeched. "I'm a whole week late – and that's never happened before."

Oliver lowered his head so that he was looking directly into the girl's face. "Shut up! You stupid, stupid girl," he hissed. "Stop all this silly nonsense! There's not a chance in a million that you're expecting – not unless it's the Immaculate Conception all over again!"

"What d'you mean?" Jacinta whined.

"I mean that it's not possible for me to get *anyone* in

the family way," Oliver said angrily. "I had a little operation done a few years ago – to make sure this sort of thing couldn't happen."

Cara looked at him in bewilderment. "What did you just say, Oliver?"

"I had a sterilisation operation – a vasectomy – done over in England a couple of years ago – when I was going back and forward on business," he told her. Then, when he saw the horror spread on her face, he rushed on. "It was when things were desperate between us – and I had *this situation*," He threw a dismissive hand in Jacinta's direction, "happen before. Another silly girl trying to pin something on me – so I decided to sort it out. It was something I did on the spur of the moment –"

"How could you?" Cara gasped. "You let me think it was all my fault . . ."

"I don't know what made me do it . . ." Oliver's voice trailed off weakly. "It was this fellow I knew who'd just had it done . . . and it seemed like a good idea at the time. Later, I realised what an eedjit I was . . ." Then, Oliver suddenly saw something in Cara's eyes that made him take a step backwards. "I'm sorry, Cara . . . honest to God, I am. If we get accepted for adopting, maybe it would make up for all this . . ."

"The only thing that you're sorry about," Cara said quietly, "is that you've been found out once again." She inched closer to him. "Or are you sorry that I've found out that our whole marriage has been a sham? A lie? All those years believing that we couldn't have children because of me. Feeling that I was a failure . . ." Her unspoken words hung in the air.

Oliver just stood there, totally bereft of a soothing

word for once.

And as Cara looked at him, she saw for the very first time what a shallow, weak man he was. And she knew now that she was finished with him. Whatever happened now, and whatever her mother or anyone else had to say – she was finished with him.

"I want you to know now, Oliver, that I'll never forgive you. Never! Our marriage is dead and gone." She managed a smile. A small, bitter smile. "It doesn't matter about having someone else to go to. I'd be much better on my own, or even back at my parents' house than living a lie with you."

She threw a glance over at Jacinta, who was sitting on her bed, snivelling into a hanky. "If you still want him – you're welcome to him. I'd say you both deserve each other. A pair of liars like you two belong together. And you'd be so busy thinking of yourselves, that you wouldn't have time for a child in any case."

And then, without a backward glance, Cara Gayle marched straight down the hospital corridor. Out of the hospital. And out of Oliver Gayle's life.

Chapter 43

"Phone for you, Pauline," Charles called from the hallway into the kitchen.

Pauline dropped the roasting pan she was washing into the soapy water in the sink, and quickly dried her hands. Jack was calling earlier than she expected. He'd said he'd give a ring after seven, and it wasn't even six o'clock yet. "Go on through into the shop, Bernadette," she told her daughter, who was making a bed up for her doll on Declan's rocking-chair, "and ask Peenie for a sweetie. Say your mammy said you could have one."

She smiled as the little girl trotted off down the hallway towards the connecting shop door, and then she went to pick the receiver up.

"Pauline? It's me . . . is there anyone else around that might be listening?" her sister's voice said.

"Cara?" Pauline said, her voice high with surprise. "No, there's no one else around. Charles and Peenie are through in the shop and Mammy and Daddy have gone off shopping to Tullamore. Is there something wrong?"

There was a little pause. "Well . . . I suppose you could say that." She halted. "I don't know where to start . . . but I had to talk to somebody."

"What is it?" Pauline said, feeling a cold shiver coming over her. "What's happened?"

"It's Oliver," Cara said, her voice trembling. "I've just discovered . . . that he's been sterilised and didn't tell me."

Pauline groped to feel for the wall behind her, and leaned up against it. "I don't believe it . . . surely Oliver wouldn't do such a terrible thing?"

"That's exactly what he did," Cara said. "And he kept it a secret until now."

"How did you find out?" Pauline asked in a low voice.

"He told me this evening," Cara said, "when a girl accused him of being the father of her baby."

Pauline's hand flew to her mouth, and she shook her head silently.

Cara halted for a moment, trying to piece all the events in the right order. "This girl from his drama group – Jacinta – rang the house and got me to go into the hospital with some things from the chemist. It was all an excuse just to get me there to tell me about her and Oliver and their supposed baby."

Pauline's legs suddenly went all weak. "What happened then?"

"Oliver turned up," Cara said, "and the whole thing came out when Jacinta accused him of making her pregnant."

"Oh, my God, Cara!" Pauline said. "You know I've always thought a lot of him – but Oliver's a rotten bastard for doing this to you! There's no other way of saying it – he's an absolute rotten, lying *bastard*!" Pauline felt really weak now, and wished there was a chair by the phone. Maggie wouldn't have one beside it, as she said it only encouraged people to waste more time and money talking nonsense. "What did you say when he told you?" Pauline whispered, utterly shocked. "And what did you do?"

Cara sighed. "What was there to say? Didn't it only confirm what I knew all along? How many times have I told you and Carmel about his carrying on?"

"I know, I know," Pauline said, "but finding it out like this must be terrible . . ."

"Yes," Cara said, her voice falling flat now. "I'd be a liar if I denied it. The sterilisation thing was the worst – and him letting me go back and forward to the doctor for tests and everything, and then being told that it looked as though I had fertility problems." She gave a weary sigh. "Between the two of us, there wasn't a hope in hell of me ever becoming pregnant."

"Are you OK?" Pauline said gently. "Do you want me to come over? I could ring Carmel if you like, and we could both come over . . ."

Cara thought for a few moments. "I'll leave it for tonight if you don't mind," she said. "I'm completely washed out . . . and anyway, Oliver will probably land back any minute, and I'd say there will be a bit of carry-on because he's still trying to persuade me that we could make a go of it."

"Have you definitely made up your mind?" Pauline asked quietly.

"Definitely," Cara confirmed. "There's nothing would make me take him back after this – *nothing*. If I'd had any kind of guts, I should be gone long, long ago."

"What about the American?" Pauline asked. "If you're

sure about Oliver, maybe you could go back to America. There's nothing to stop you now."

"That's another story," Cara said, her throat suddenly tightening. "Another disaster I just found out about today. I got a letter today from Jameson's wife . . . and it would seem she's back up at the house. It would seem they're all back living together quite happily."

"Oh, my God!" Pauline said again. Then, after a moment's thought, she said, "I wouldn't be inclined to believe her, Cara. Maybe she's made it all up – she could easily have written that letter to put you off, and he mightn't know a thing about it. The whole thing could be a pack of lies."

"I thought that, too," Cara said quietly, "but I checked it out with Jean this afternoon . . . and it's true. Verity called over to see Jean and she more or less told her what had happened. She said how Thomas's accident had brought everyone closer."

"I still wouldn't be so quick to believe that one – she sounds a right bitch."

"She is," Cara replied dully. "A first-class bitch."

"Why don't you phone Jameson, and find out for yourself?" Pauline suggested.

"There's no point," Cara said. "It's all too late. I should have stayed in America when I had the chance. I've no one to blame but myself. It's all my own fault."

* * *

There were a few of the usual last-minute customers in the shop when Pauline went through to collect Bernadette, so she stopped to give the two lads a hand. Weighing out cooking apples and carrots and wrapping them up in newspaper was a whole lot easier than dealing with the terrible thoughts that were racing around in her head.

"Thanks, Pauline," Peenie said, giving her a wink as she passed the fruit and vegetables over to him. He turned to his elderly customer. "Doesn't she brighten the place up no end, Mr Murphy? Wouldn't you pay just to stand and look at her?"

"Go away with you!" Pauline said, giving him a friendly push. She turned to the customer. "And don't mind a word that fella says – I know well the minute I turn my back he'll be calling me."

"I wouldn't say so," Mr Murphy said. "I wouldn't say so at all. Peenie Walshe would be only too delighted at yeh turnin' yer back on him. He'd be delighted at the lovely view he'd get with you in them nice, tight trousers."

"Now, now," Peenie said to the man, in a serious tone. "That's a bit too near the bone, so it is." He gave Pauline another of his famed winks. "If Mrs Kearney was to appear and hear that kind of talk, we'd all be in a heap of trouble. A whole heap of trouble"

"Ah, sure, we're only codding the girl," said Mr Murphy, putting his purchases into his battered old shopping-bag. "And doesn't Pauline know that well? An' all the years we've been comin' in and out of the shop. She knows well that we're only coddin'."

"True for yeh, Mr Murphy," Peenie said, grinning. "Sure it's only a bit of coddology. It's a bad day when yeh can't have a bit of the oul' banter without somebody takin' offence."

"Well," said Pauline, wrapping up a block of cheese in muslin, "if there was more work being done around here,

497

there would be less time for all the codding. There's them that are customers and entitled to be messing around, and there's them that should be doing a fair day's work for a fair day's pay. Isn't that right, Mr Murphy?"

The old man roared with laughter and then, just as Peenie went to come back with an even better line, the shop door opened and in walked Oliver Gayle.

* * *

"I hope you don't mind me coming out like this, Pauline," Oliver said, as they pulled away from the shop in the car, "but I had no one else to turn to. I'm almost demented. I don't know how all this has come about . . . I feel as though the roof has fallen in on top of me."

Pauline turned to check that Bernadette was all right in the back of the car. The curly-headed child was kneeling up, quite happily looking out of the back window, oblivious to the tension between the two adults as they drove through the town of Tullamore, and then out the Charleville Road towards Birr.

"I know about *everything*, Oliver," Pauline said in a low, voice. "Cara phoned me a short while ago . . ."

Oliver sucked his breath in hard. "The carry-on with the girl from the drama group meant nothing – it was just a bit of harmless nonsense. I'd no idea she was one of those hysterical types – bad with her nerves."

"And the sterilisation business?" Pauline asked. "Was that just a bit of harmless nonsense, too?"

Oliver groaned. "No," he said, staring straight at the road ahead. "That was one of the biggest mistakes I've made in my life. I got that one completely wrong."

Pauline swept her long, dark hair back from her face.

"You're very good at making mistakes, Oliver. And the worst thing is – you don't seem to learn from them."

"Pauline," Oliver said, "please give me a break." He swallowed hard a few times, his Adam's apple visibly bobbing up and down over the neck of his shirt. "I thought you at least would understand . . . that you would know that at times life was difficult with Cara. That at times we weren't the most suited couple in the world." He paused. "She's not like you – she can be very deep and serious – and you know I need a bit of a laugh and a joke. It's in my nature, it's just the way I'm made – but deep down I do love her, and I wanted us to make a go of things again."

"You've a funny way of showing it," Pauline told him. "And you know Cara would never have done anything to hurt you."

"Well," Oliver said, "up until recently I might have agreed with you, but of course there's been all the business with the American fellow. Don't tell me you don't know about that?"

"I do," Pauline said brusquely, "and I don't blame her one little bit."

Oliver moved the car down the gears now, and then turned off the road down a bumpy little lane. A few moments later they came to a halt beside a small lake.

Without a word, Pauline got out of the car, and then went to the back passenger door and let Bernadette out.

"It's the water!" the little girl said, jumping up and down clapping her hands. "It's where all the – fishes live!"

Pauline pointed to a make-shift stone bench a little way off down towards the lake. "You can sit there for a few minutes like a good girl," she told the child, "but don't move unless I'm with you."

When the child was scrambling over the rough grass and out of earshot, Pauline turned to her brother-in-law, her arms folded defensively. "I think it's too late, Oliver," she said. "I think you've burned your boats with Cara this time. What you did to her was terrible – unforgivable – and you're going to have to pay the price."

"Christ Almighty!" Oliver hissed between clenched teeth. He walked a few feet ahead of Pauline, his hands jingling keys or loose coins in his pocket, and stared down towards the lake. "If that Jacinta hadn't turned up and caused all this fucking trouble, we might have just sorted things out once and for all. I'm sure Cara was coming round to the adoption thing – and the business with the American was more or less over." He turned to Pauline. "Did she tell you he's back with his wife? That the wife sent her a letter?"

"She told me *everything*," Pauline said flatly, "but I wouldn't be too quick to believe that one – the wife. She sounds capable of saying anything."

Oliver whirled around. "Do you think she might go back to him?"

"I hope with all my heart she does, Oliver."

Oliver's hands came up to cover his face. "What a mess . . . what a fucking, fucking mess!"

Pauline looked down at the stony ground. "You've brought it all on yourself – you pushed her too far." She scuffed a small stone with the toe of her shoe. "She never deserved anything that happened to her, and it's time she had a bit of happiness. She's a good-looking girl, and she's never looked better than since she came back from America."

Oliver ran his hands through his tidy black hair,

making little tufts stand on end. "What am I going to do now? We'll have to sell up the house and everything – and can you imagine your mother and father's faces when they find out? Your mother will have a heart attack. She won't be able to handle us separating – she had pinned all her hopes on the adoption business."

Pauline shrugged. "She'll just have to get used to it . . . the same as the rest of us."

Then Bernadette jumped off the bench and came running up the path towards them. "A swing!" she said to Oliver. "Give me a big swing, Uncle Oliver!"

Oliver did as the child asked, and spent a few moments swinging her around and playing with her. After a while, when she went back running to the bench, he turned to Pauline with agonised eyes. "How have I managed to make such an arse of everything? How have I managed to ruin so many good people's lives?"

* * *

A short while later, they set out again, Bernadette settling down in the back seat for a little sleep, tired out from all the activity in the fresh air.

"Are you still seeing that fellow from Mullingar?" Oliver asked.

"I am," Pauline said quietly, amazed at him being able to talk about ordinary things at such a terrible time.

"And how's it all going?" he said. "Is it serious?"

"I suppose it's more serious than it's ever been," she replied.

There was a silence. And then, just as the silence was becoming too uncomfortable for Pauline, Oliver said, "Do you really mean that, Pauline?"

"Yes," she said quickly, "I do mean it."

Oliver threw a glance over his shoulder at the sleeping child. "And what about her? Weren't you serious about her father? Surely you must have been. Surely, you didn't sleep with a man you didn't have deep feelings for?"

Pauline's face suddenly reddened with awkwardness and anger. "Leave it, Oliver! Just leave it!"

"What if he was suddenly free to marry you?" Oliver persisted. "What if he was suddenly free to be a proper father to Bernadette?"

"Don't you dare!" Pauline said, her jaw clenching with rage. "Stop all this shite right now! I'm warning you, Oliver Gayle!"

Oliver put his foot down on the brake and pulled in to the side of the road. Again, he turned to check on the sleeping child. "Maybe it's the best option for the both of us," he said, reaching for Pauline's hand. "Maybe it's the chance for us both to make right the wrong we did. To make something good of all this mess . . . Maybe we could go to England together – make a fresh start, just the three of us."

Tears sprang into Pauline's eyes, and she dragged her hand out of his grasp. "How can you even think of it? How can you?" Her voice sounded ragged, as though it was torturing her having to keep it low enough not to disturb the child. "What we did was *terrible*! And to my own sister!" She moved now to find a hanky in her trouser pocket, and then dabbed her eyes. "I'll never, *ever* forgive myself – and neither should you!"

"But nobody needs to know," he argued. "There's not a living soul knows that I'm Bernadette's father. Haven't we kept it a total secret since the child was born?"

"We have!" Pauline said. "We have kept it a secret – and it's the only decent thing we've ever done!"

"I'm genuinely fond of Bernadette," he whispered, "and surely it would be good for her? And when all's said and done – she's the only child I'm ever going to have." When Pauline said nothing, he took it as a good sign. A sign that she might be considering his suggestion. "And you know I've always had feelings for you, Pauline, and you told me yourself that you had feelings for me. What happened between us was meant to be – there was always something there between us."

Pauline turned very slowly to look at him, her eyes rimmed with tears. "Listen to me very carefully, Oliver – there has always been *something* between us. And that *something* happens to be my sister!"

"But – "

Pauline held her hand up to silence his protests.

"Anything I ever felt for you is long gone." She shook her head. "Long, long gone. And there's nothing that will ever make me change my mind. I have much stronger feelings for Jack than I ever had for you, and he knows *everything* he needs to know about me."

Oliver raised his eyebrows in question.

"Oh, if I have to tell him about you, Oliver – I will! Believe me, I will." Her eyes narrowed. "If I have to tell anyone else to stop you pestering me – or to make sure you give Cara a fair deal with everything – then make no mistake, I'll tell them."

"You might not come out of it too well, if you decide to speak out, you know," Oliver warned her. "It wouldn't look too good for you, at all, at all – when you think of your poor sister who was never able to have children."

"Ah, well," she said, in a resigned but strong voice, "it'll depend on the story they hear from me. If they hear that my sister's husband turned up in England unannounced and fed me drink and then took advantage of an innocent virgin girl –"

"You wouldn't! You wouldn't do that to me, Pauline – would you?" Oliver said, his face turning pale with shock.

"Make no mistake, Oliver, I *would*," she said solemnly. "If you force me – I would. If you break the promise we both made. That secret must go to the grave with both of us."

There was a little silence. "And in any case," she added, "even if you weren't Cara's husband – or any other woman's husband – I'd never have anything to do with you after this last episode with both the girl and the sterilisation. I could never, ever trust you again. And I don't blame poor Cara one little bit."

Oliver nodded, the sag of his face and shoulders telling his feelings.

"If you can get yourself sorted out," Pauline told him, "and do the decent thing by Cara, then I might consider you seeing Bernadette now and again. Everyone knows you are fond of her, and that she's fond of you – so it wouldn't look too odd if you were to take her to a pantomime at Christmas or some such thing." She looked him square in the face. "But that's *all*. Don't go hoping for any more – because it's never going to happen."

Chapter 44

Cara took a deep breath as she pushed open the door of Kearney's shop. The delighted grin of Peenie Walshe and the anxious smile of Charles that greeted her did nothing to alleviate the feeling of dread that she had carried all morning – from the dark early hours, when she had woken up in the spare bedroom and decided to get the visit to her parents over and done with. The visit to impart to them the news about her marriage breakdown.

The news that would break her mother's heart.

But there was nothing else for it – it had to be done.

She passed a few light-hearted comments to the boys, and then she went on through the back of the shop and into the house. Both her father and mother were in the kitchen, her mother just setting the table for the breakfast she had half-cooked in the frying-pan.

"How's my girl?" Declan greeted her cheerily.

"Not too good," Cara said in a low, serious voice. She took her coat off and put it over the back of one of the chairs, then sat down in another.

Maggie went over to the big old range and moved the frying-pan to a cooler area on the top to slow down the cooking. "Well," she said, in a flat, resigned voice, "what's happened now?"

Cara suddenly felt tears coming into her eyes. She had been determined not to get upset – to get this business over and done with as quickly as possible – but the tears were choking her nonetheless. "Oliver and I . . ." she started in a croaky voice. "It's all over . . . we're finished for good."

Maggie's back and shoulders stiffened, but she said nothing. She kept her back to Cara, her gaze focussed on the sizzling bacon and sausages.

"He got sterilised without telling me," Cara blurted out in a hoarse voice. "He had it done a few years ago over in England. That's why we never had any children."

"Jesus, Mary and Joseph!" her mother said, slowly turning around. "What in God's name has he done?" Her face suddenly looking very old and very pale. "If it's the truth – that's a mortal sin, you know! A mortal sin . . ."

"I'll leave you to it," Declan said quietly, picking up his brown shop overall. "I think the lads might need a hand through in the shop."

When the door closed behind him, Maggie came over to the table and sat down beside her daughter. "What are you going to do?" she asked. "How are you going to get over this?"

"There's nothing to get over any more – he's gone . . ." Cara said, a tremor in her voice. "It's all finished for good."

Maggie suddenly leaned forward. "This is what you've been hoping for, isn't it?" she demanded. "This is the excuse you've been looking for!"

"What do you mean?" Cara said, a choking feeling gripping her throat.

"The American!" Maggie said. Her tight little fist pounded on the kitchen table, making the cutlery jangle and the milk spill from the full jug. "That fecking American! He's the cause of all this trouble."

Cara swallowed hard to get rid of the tight feeling in her throat, and to keep back the flood of tears. "How can you say that?" she said. "How can you use Jameson Carroll as a scapegoat for all this? He had nothing whatsoever to do with me and Oliver. This trouble has been going on between us since the day we got married." Cara took a deep breath. "I've only put up with it because of all the upset it would cause in the family – and what a separation would mean in the eyes of the Church."

"Well, I'm relieved to hear you have some kind of a conscience," her mother said, her voice ragged. "I'm relieved to hear that you have some regard for the Church – because your disgraceful carry-on over the summer made me think you had none!" She halted for a moment, the situation whirring around in her mind. "I think we might need to look to the Church for some kind of advice on this . . . but I'm sure they'll manage to talk some sense into Oliver, and get him to go to Confession – or to go for some kind of help." She reached a hand out to touch Cara's arm. "I'm sure you'll get help – they might even be able to speed the adoption business up when they hear the circumstances."

Cara gasped in shock. "You don't honestly expect me to have him back after what he's done?"

"You've no other choice," Maggie said, her voice

determined and steely. "He's your husband."

Cara suddenly realised that the rest of the sad, sordid story would have to come out. "I spent yesterday evening in at the hospital in Tullamore with a girlfriend of Oliver's . . . a girl from his drama group."

Maggie's eyes narrowed into two little slits.

"She phoned to ask me to bring her in some things," Cara went on, "and when I arrived, she announced that she was expecting Oliver's baby."

"Well," Maggie said, "from what you've just said – that couldn't be the case at all."

"Exactly," Cara said. "And when Oliver walked in on us talking, the girl went hysterical and accused him of making her pregnant. Then she showed me her bandaged wrists – the real reason she was in hospital . It seems she had made a fairly serious attempt at suicide . . . and all because of Oliver."

Maggie got up and went back over to the frying-pan on the cooker. She lifted a wooden spoon and started moving the bacon and sausages around. "I never would have believed such a thing would happen in my family . . . never, never, *never*." Her eyes were now brimming with tears. "And *you* of all people, Cara – you were the one I thought I could depend on! The only decent one out of the three. The only one with a professional job and a nice house to give a bit of dignity to the family."

"That's a terrible thing to say!" Cara said, her voice suddenly rising. "Pauline's a decent girl who made *one* mistake in her life – a mistake you've made her pay dearly for! And there's nothing wrong with Charles – he's highly intelligent and hard-working and he does everything you ask him to do."

"With all this nonsense now," Maggie said, "there's not one of you I could hold my head up about – not one of you!"

The kitchen door opened and Pauline came in. "What's going on?" she asked. "Daddy said there was some kind of trouble – "

"It's the business with Oliver," Cara said, standing up. She lifted her coat from the back of the chair. "I just came to tell Mammy and Daddy that we're finished – that Oliver's moving out, and we're separating for good."

Maggie suddenly slammed the frying-pan against the back panel of the cooker, sending splashes of bacon grease hissing over the hot surface. "No doubt you'll go running back to the American and the simple son!" she said venomously. "Now you have your excuse, there will be nothing to stop you. I can just see you all cosy there with Jean and Bruce Harper. Oh, you'll get on grand with them and their godless ways!"

"My Auntie Jean," Cara said, "is the nicest, kindest woman I've ever met – and it would do you good to think as much of your family as she thinks of hers!"

Maggie's hand suddenly shot out and caught Cara on the side of her face. "Don't you dare quote Jean Harper to me! Don't you dare quote that woman and her blasphemous family to me!"

"For God's sake!" Pauline shouted, moving between her mother and sister. Cara stood rooted to the spot – unable to believe that her mother had actually slapped her. Neither her mother nor her father had laid a hand on her since she was a child. And now this.

"Come on," Pauline said, helping Cara into her coat. "There's no reasoning with her when she's like this. I've had a few slaps myself off her since I came back to the house, but I'm not going to stand and watch it happening to you. Not when I know what Oliver Gayle has done to you."

"Hang on, Pauline," Cara said quietly. "I'm not finished –" She turned to her mother. "For your information, I've no intention of going back to America to Jameson Carroll." She felt a stab in her heart even as she said his name. "But it's not because I don't want to – it's because I've left it too late." Her voice was higher and stronger now. "I should never have come back here – I should have taken my chance when I had it – because I truly loved him."

"*Love!*" Maggie mouthed, her eyes looking up to the ceiling.

"Jameson is a far better, far more decent man that Oliver Gayle will ever be." She moved her hand up to touch the red, tender mark on her cheekbone. "I only came back from America because I was a coward – because I hadn't the guts to stay! I was too afraid to go against *you*. I was afraid of my own mother! A mother who would have me suffer a lying, cheating husband who has no respect for me."

Maggie lifted the end of her apron up and rubbed her eyes. "Don't talk about suffering to me! There's nobody knows more about – every day that I have to go into that shop and face all the tittle-tattling customers is a penance to me." She gave another sob and then stabbed her finger in Pauline's direction. "And that's the one that's brought us all down into the gutter – and that's where we may stay when word of this business gets around!"

Cara buttoned her coat up. "I'm sorry I have to leave

you here, Pauline," she said quietly. "You shouldn't have to take this kind of treatment. Maybe when Oliver has his stuff all gone, you and Bernadette might want to come over and stay until we've sold the house. It would do Bernadette no harm to get out of this bitter atmosphere."

Pauline felt a hot rush of guilt sweep over her. How could she have done such a terrible, terrible thing to her sister, who had always looked out for her? "You have enough to think of, looking after yourself," she said quietly.

Cara walked over to the door. "You won't need to worry about me causing you any embarrassment," she said to her mother, "because I'll keep well out of your way. I can manage just grand on my own."

Maggie looked back at her – her eyes puffy and her face chalk-white. "All I ever prayed for was a normal family life – the way most people around here live. For everybody to get on, and for everybody to live by the Church's rules. Surely that wasn't too much to ask for?"

Cara held her mother's gaze for a moment. "All I ever prayed for was love and respect in my marriage – and that was obviously far too much for me to ask for."

Then, without a backward glance, Cara Gayle walked out of the kitchen – and out of her mother's house without knowing whether she would ever return.

Chapter 45

Cara stood looking out of her bedroom window at the white garden – the grass and shrubs covered in an early November snow. Her gaze shifted to take in the *For Sale* sign in the middle of the white lawn. The man from the auctioneers' office would be out later in the afternoon to take the sign away.

And that would be it. The end of her life in this house.

Cara sighed and, as she did so, a tiny fluttering feeling made her hand move to the slight bulge in her stomach. It was so ironic. All the carry-on when she and Oliver had split up a couple of months ago. Only for her to find out that it was she who was pregnant – as opposed to the scheming Jacinta.

And pregnant with Jameson Carroll's child.

After that awful day when her world collapsed, she had decided that it was up to her to take the reins of her life. And she did so immediately.

Oliver had moved out – eventually accepting that there was no hope for their marriage – and any

512

communications were now through solicitors and auctioneers. Oliver had also put the shop up for sale, and had engaged a manager in the interim to allow him to move back to Dublin while he decided what he was going to do in the long run.

The house was now more or less sold, with the people hoping to move into it in late January. Shortly after Christmas, Cara planned to move to Mullingar or maybe Naas – she had seen suitable houses in both places, and was still looking around. Wherever it was, it would be close to a town centre that would allow her to walk around easily with a pram. Depending on how things went, Pauline and Bernadette would join her. She knew Mullingar would suit Pauline as it was the area where Jack lived and she could see him and his little girl more regularly – but it would all depend on finding the right house.

No doubt it would give the local people something to talk about – two sisters with children and no husbands – but she would deal with that as it arose. The same as she would deal with the school.

It was sad but inevitable that her teaching career would have to go for the foreseeable future. She would tell her head-teacher coming up to Christmas, explaining about her marriage break-up and her pregnancy, omitting the fact that Oliver was not the father. That was something no one would even *think* to question.

As yet, no one apart from Pauline knew about Cara's pregnancy, and Cara planned to keep it that way as long as possible. Relations had not been repaired with her mother yet – and Cara had no idea if they ever would be. Maggie still blamed Cara for the way things had turned out, and could not come to terms with the marital break-up. No matter what had happened, her mother believed that Cara should have kept on trying. And strangely enough, after years of being terrified of crossing her mother – it actually upset her far less than she had imagined.

In fact, there was a sense of freedom about the whole thing. A feeling of no longer having to gauge how her mother or other people would react. A feeling of at long last living her own life – and not having to live the life other people thought she should.

Her father had been out to visit her on a number of occasions, and had told her not to worry, that Maggie would eventually come round. "She loves you all," Declan had said, giving a weary sigh, "in her own way. It's just that she finds it hard to go against the Church's views on anything."

Of course, there would be more upset and accusations when Maggie learned of Cara's pregnancy, but it would be have to be dealt with. She couldn't pull the wool over Maggie's eyes regarding the child's father, because Oliver had well and truly given her no option there.

And anyway – after the initial shock – Cara was delighted that she had gained something wonderful from her love affair in America. What she had felt for Jameson Carroll was something she knew she would never, ever, experience again in her whole life. She knew it was a once-in-a-lifetime love she was lucky to have known. And whatever happened – and however hard it was bringing up a child on her own – she would never regret it.

She looked out of the window again, and then she saw a little bird land on top of the *For Sale* sign.

She quietly opened the window to see better and, when she recognised the bird, she smiled to herself. It was the same type of small bird – a goldcrest – that she had watched in the summer. Just before her trip to America. She stood for a while, watching it flit about from the post to a small pine tree and back again, then she eventually made herself shift to get on with sorting out things for the move.

* * *

Some time later Cara heard the gate banging and then the sound of footsteps coming up the path. *The Auctioneer*, she thought grimly – a good few hours later than he had said. She sighed to herself, and rose up from the sofa and moved quickly to the front door to let him in.

Her hand was on the latch when she realised there was not only one auctioneer, but two. She could see the two figures through the frosted panel on the front door. She straightened her woollen pinafore over her stomach and smoothed down her hair. Not that anyone would notice her little bump, but already she was becoming more conscious of it.

Then, she opened the door. And suddenly – she was rooted to the spot.

Her eyes travelled upwards as she looked at the taller of the pair standing on the snowy step. When she recognised him, she felt her whole body start to shake.

"Ash – leen!" an excited voice said, and then there was the clapping of hands. "We've – we've found you . . ."

She turned and there, beaming back at her, was a healthy, fully recovered Thomas. Her hand flew to cover her mouth, from which not one word would come.

"Hello, Ash-leen," the boy said, a grin from ear to ear. "Me and Dad – we flew to Ire-land on the – on the plane." He came towards her now and gave her a delighted bear hug.

Then Jameson Carroll moved forward – a cautious look on his face – the tanned, handsome face that Cara had touched every inch of. "Can we come in, Cara . . . please? I'll explain all this to you when we get inside."

But Cara couldn't move. Her feet were glued to the spot. And although her body had come to a standstill, her mind was racing. *No, no, no!* she thought. *This can't be happening . . . I can't go through this all again!*

"Please, Cara," Jameson said, "you need to hear what I have to say . . ." He gently guided her into the hallway, out of the worst of the cold.

"What." she finally croaked, "what about Verity? The terrible letter she sent me . . ."

"It was all lies," he explained in a low voice. "You know how devious she is. She followed us back up to the lake and somehow must have wheedled your address out of Jean. I got rid of her as quickly as I could." He glanced towards Thomas, afraid of hurting his feelings by talking badly about his mother – but the boy was now occupied looking around the garden. "Verity only stayed a couple of days. I had to let her for Thomas's sake – but I knew nothing about her writing to you and I'm so goddamn sorry she did."

He looked at Cara now, waiting for some kind of reaction. When there was none, he carried on with the explanations. "Shortly after you left I called over to Jean, and she told me that you were working things out with your husband . . . then she told me about the plans you were making to adopt a child."

Cara closed her eyes and shook her head.

"So," Jameson shrugged, "I reckoned that I was out of the picture . . ."

"That was never the case," Cara whispered. "I never stopped thinking about you."

"And I," he said, looking deep into her eyes – the way he had looked at her so many times back in Lake Savannah – "have never stopped loving you."

"What happened," Cara asked. "What made you change your mind and come looking for me?"

"The Christmas figure," he said, grinning.

"Jean found it in the bedroom, and rang your folks to ask whether you would like it posted to have it for Christmas. She spoke to your sister, and I guess she told her all that had happened to you."

"Did Pauline tell her *everything?*" Cara whispered, glancing down at her stomach. "Did she mention about the baby?"

"*Our* baby . . ." Jameson said, a sudden catch in his voice. "I just can't believe it . . . I reckon it's something I wouldn't have dared dream about."

"There's no mistake," Cara told him firmly, lest there be even the slightest hint of doubt. "You're the only person I've slept with since we met, and anyway, it's turned out that there's no way Oliver could have fathered a child with any woman . . . "

"We can talk about all that stuff later," Jameson told her gently, running a finger down the side of her face. "Whatever your sister told her, it was enough to make Jean come straight across to our house. She reckoned that I needed to know just how things stood. She told me all about Verity's letter and about how you were now living on your own." He looked down at the bump now, and smiled broadly. "Apart from this little crittur here!"

Cara smiled and nodded, things now falling into place.

"So," Jameson said, "after the whole goddamn mix-up – here we are! Thomas and I reckoned that we'd best come and see you and straighten a few things out – see if we could get us all four of us back out and settled in Lake Savannah for Christmas ."

Hearing the word *Christmas*, Thomas came back rushing back over to Cara. "And – Mother and Father – Christmas – they're back home!" he said beaming. "They're waiting – for you!" He held his thumb up excitedly.

"I can't believe it!" Cara said, covering her face. "I feel as if this is all a dream!"

Jameson smiled at her. "This cold sure isn't a dream," he said wrapping his arms around her, "and I think we'd better come inside properly or we'll freeze." He put a hand on Thomas's shoulder. "What d'you say, buddy? Should we stay outside here until you're covered in snow like the Christmas figures?"

Thomas's head bobbed up and down in laughter at the joke.

Then, as Cara finally ushered them inside and went to close the door behind them – she spotted the goldcrest again and she gave a little smile to herself.

She had finally found her own wings. It was now time for Cara Gayle to fly away.

THE END